To our fathers
Patrick Joseph Wynne
and
Aurèle Vanacker

Sherlock Holmes and Conan Doyle

Also by Catherine Wynne

THE COLONIAL CONAN DOYLE: BRITISH IMPERIALISM, IRISH NATIONALISM, AND THE GOTHIC VICTORIAN LITERARY MESMERISM (*co-edited with Martin Willis*)

Also by Sabine Vanacker

REFLECTING ON MISS MARPLE (*with* Marion Shaw)

Sherlock Holmes and Conan Doyle

Multi-Media Afterlives

Edited by

Sabine Vanacker and Catherine Wynne
University of Hull, UK

palgrave
macmillan

First published 2013 by
PALGRAVE MACMILLAN

Palgrave Macmillan in the UK is an imprint of Macmillan Publishers Limited,
registered in England, company number 785998, of Houndmills, Basingstoke,
Hampshire RG21 6XS.

Palgrave Macmillan in the US is a division of St Martin's Press LLC,
175 Fifth Avenue, New York, NY 10010.

Palgrave Macmillan is the global academic imprint of the above companies
and has companies and representatives throughout the world.

Palgrave® and Macmillan® are registered trademarks in the United States,
the United Kingdom, Europe and other countries

ISBN: 978–0–230–30050–7

This book is printed on paper suitable for recycling and made from fully
managed and sustained forest sources. Logging, pulping and manufacturing
processes are expected to conform to the environmental regulations of the
country of origin.

A catalogue record for this book is available from the British Library.

A catalog record for this book is available from the Library of Congress.

10 9 8 7 6 5 4 3 2 1
22 21 20 19 18 17 16 15 14 13

Contents

Illustrations

Acknowledgements

In presenting this collection of critical essays we would like to acknowledge the generous support of the University of Hull, and also the University's support in the organisation of our conference (*Arthur Conan Doyle and Sherlock Holmes: Their Cultural Afterlives*) which was held in July 2009, the year which marked the 150th anniversary of Doyle's birth. George Talbot, then Dean of the Faculty of Arts and Social Sciences, backed the conference. We were fortunate in being awarded study leave from the University during that period, which helped in our preparations for the conference and for this collection. We are very grateful to Ian Calvert of the Derwent Centre, University of Hull, for helping us with conference accommodation, and to Carl Schofield, who designed the conference poster. This collection, like Doyle and Holmes themselves, has lived through a number of transformations and re-imaginings, small deaths and reappearances. Throughout, however, we would like to acknowledge the support and advice of our colleagues in the Department of English and the Faculty of Arts and Social Sciences at the University of Hull, most particularly to those who gave their support in the run up to and during the conference, including James Booth, Janet Clare, Katharine Cockin, Lesley Coote, Ann Heilmann, Bethan Jones, David Kennedy, Veronica O'Mara, Jane Thomas and Valerie Sanders. We would also like to thank David Beck, Matthew Crofts, Sara Williams and our wonderful students on our Crime Fiction and Gothic modules over the years. We would like to express our gratitude to our other colleagues and friends in the Department of English, to Martin Willis from the University of Glamorgan, and to the contributors to the conference too. Special thanks to David Kelly, Keith Spence, Lawrence Wynne-Spence and David Wynne. We would also like to warmly thank our mothers, Odette Vercaigne and Rose Wynne. Finally, we would like to thank our editors at Palgrave Macmillan, Felicity Plester and Catherine Mitchell, for their patience and advice.

Contributors

Clive Bloom is Emeritus Professor of English and American Studies at Middlesex University, a best-selling author and publisher. When Bloom isn't writing and researching he divides his time between New York University and the University of Notre Dame. In 2011, he was the historical consultant to the BBC and a number of national and international newspapers on the summer riots in Britain. He is an occasional feature writer for *The Financial Times, The Times, The Guardian, The Independent, The Irish Times* and the *London Evening Standard*. He regularly appears on television and radio, and is quoted in the *Columbia Book of World Quotations*. He recently featured on the Australian version of 'Desert Island Discs'. His numerous books include *Violent London: 2000 Years of Riots, Rebels and Revolts* (2003) and *Riot City* (2012).

Claudia Capancioni is Lecturer in English at Bishop Grosseteste University College Lincoln, UK. Her research is on nineteenth- and twentieth-century literature, with a focus on women's writing. Her most recent publications include chapters in *Translating Gender* (2011) and *Il viaggio e I viaggiatori in età moderna: gli inglesi in Italia e le avventure dei viaggiatori italiani* (2009).

Amanda J. Field was an advertising and promotions manager at IBM UK until she left to pursue academic study, gaining an MA and a PhD in Film Studies from the University of Southampton. Her book, *England's Secret Weapon – The Wartime Films of Sherlock Holmes* was published in 2009 and drew extensively (as does her chapter in this volume) on material in the Arthur Conan Doyle Collection at Portsmouth Museum, where she worked for five years as a volunteer.

Andrew Lycett is the biographer of Sir Arthur Conan Doyle. He has also written lives of Ian Fleming, Dylan Thomas and Rudyard Kipling. He is currently working on a book about Wilkie Collins. He is a fellow of the Royal Society of Literature.

Neil McCaw is Reader in Literature and Culture at the University of Winchester, where he teaches Victorian Fiction and Detective and Crime Narratives. His publications include *George Eliot and Victorian Historiography* (2000), *Writing Irishness in Nineteenth-Century British*

Culture (2004), *How to Read Texts* (2008) and *Adapting Detective Fiction: Crime, Englishness and the TV Detectives* (2010), in addition to numerous articles and chapters on aspects of the nineteenth and twentieth centuries.

Souvik Mukherjee has been researching videogames as an emerging storytelling medium since 2002 and completed a PhD on this subject from Nottingham Trent University (2009). His research also examines how videogames inform and challenge current conceptions of technicity, identity and culture. Souvik is a long-time Sherlock Holmes enthusiast.

Bran Nicol is Reader in Modern and Contemporary Literature at the University of Portsmouth, UK, where he is also Director of the Centre for Studies in Literature. His publications include *Stalking* (2006), *The Cambridge Introduction to Postmodern Fiction* (2009) and the co-edited volume *Crime Culture: Figuring Criminality in Fiction and Film* (2010).

Harvey O'Brien lectures in Film Studies at University College Dublin and is former editor of the journal *Film and Film Culture*. He is the author of *Action Movies: The Cinema of Striking Back* (2012) and *The Real Ireland: The Evolution of Ireland in Documentary Film* (2004).

Jennifer S. Palmer is a retired teacher and an independent scholar. She gained her PhD at Delaware University, USA. Her interest in crime fiction has been lifelong: she lectures to adults on 'Famous Historical Mysteries' and reviews crime fiction.

Patricia Pulham is Reader in Victorian Literature at the University of Portsmouth, and the author of *Art and the Transitional Object in Vernon Lee's Supernatural Tales* (2008). Recent publications include two co-edited collections: *Haunting and Spectrality in Neo-Victorian Fiction: Possessing the Past* (2010) and *Crime Culture: Figuring Criminality in Fiction and Film* (2011).

Terry Scarborough is Professor in the Department of English at Okanagan College, Kelowna Canada, where he has taught literature and composition since 2006. His research interests include Gothic fiction, the ghost story, Dickens studies and narratives of urban exploration. He has presented and published articles and chapters on Dickens, Doyle, the Victorian city, Sherlock Holmes and M. R. James. He has twice been keynote speaker at Okanagan College's *Dracula* symposium. Currently, he teaches composition, popular narrative and surveys of British literature and is a fellow of the Institute for Learning and Teaching.

Sabine Vanacker lectures at the University of Hull. Her research and teaching interests centre on twentieth-century literature, focusing on crime fiction, women's writing and migrant writing. With Professor Marion Shaw, she has published *Reflecting on Miss Marple* (1991) and has written about Sara Paretsky, Patricia Cornwall, John le Carré and Janwillem van de Wetering. She is currently preparing *The Crime Fiction of P.D. James: Death and the Melancholic Detective.*

Catherine Wynne is Senior Lecturer in Victorian Literature at the University of Hull. Her publications include *The Colonial Conan Doyle: British Imperialism, Irish Nationalism, and the Gothic* (2002); an edition of Doyle's *The Parasite* and Stoker's *The Watter's Mou* (2009); and a collection of essays (co-edited with Martin Willis), *Victorian Literary Mesmerism* (2006). She received the Derrick Murdoch Award from the Sherlock Holmes Society of Canada for the best essay published in *Canadian Holmes* in 2011.

Introduction: From Baker Street to Undershaw and Beyond

Catherine Wynne

A tale of two homes: from 221b to Undershaw

The Sherlock Holmes Museum at 221b Baker Street in London is well worth a visit. Alighting from the tube on a cold winter's evening, imaginatively inclined Holmesians can transport themselves to a world of yellow fogs and hansom cabs, and during a visit to the house – its sitting-room is considerably smaller than the ones presented in numerous film adaptations – can immerse themselves in cosy Victoriana.[1] The museum website invitingly notes that visitors 'can sit by Holmes's fireside' but 'must bring' their own 'pipe[s] to smoke'. The enthusiast can even try on Sherlock Holmes's deerstalker, perched on a nearby table.

But this hat is, as we know, a creation not of the Arthur Conan Doyle stories but of the Sidney Paget illustrations for *The Strand Magazine*. The deerstalker made its first appearance in 'The Boscombe Valley Mystery' (October 1891).[2] Subsequent incarnations of Holmes on stage and screen commonly, as Amanda J. Field argues in *England's Secret Weapon*, 'adopted the look and style of the illustrations' and 'each new interpretation of Holmes was therefore both the Victorian creation of Doyle and the "man of the moment"' (2009: 3, 4). Indeed, Holmes was neo-Victorian long before the term attained academic and popular vogue.[3] Christine L. Krueger reminds us that we are 'in many respects post-Victorians' (2002: xi). Indeed, our obsession with Holmes confirms this. The detective has always been at the forefront of popular consciousness, and the early twenty-first century's accelerated attention to him can, at least in part, be attributed to the rise of neo-Victorianism over the last two and a half decades.[4]

Holmes, however, also challenges neo-Victorian categorisation (ironically Doyle's Holmes is a figure obsessed with classification) with claims, almost since his inception, to both lived reality and cultural immortality. The Baker Street museum promulgates the notion of Holmes as a person who actually existed, with the promotional material recording that, 'Sherlock Holmes and Doctor Watson lived at 221b Baker Street between 1881–1904, according to the stories written by Sir Arthur Conan Doyle. The famous 1st floor study overlooking Baker Street is still faithfully maintained as it was kept in Victorian Times.' While attributing the stories to Doyle, the website simultaneously cultivates a response to Holmes as both real person and as fictional character. It questions: 'What are the attributes which combine to make a *person* [emphasis mine] a world-famous legend? His achievements must surely be unforgettable and remarkable. He must be a brilliant and credible *character* [emphasis mine] whom people can believe in. He must be ageless in so far as dates of birth and death become irrelevant. He must enjoy everlasting fame.'[5]

This tendency to see Holmes and Watson as real people is long established, and is supported by the publications of the various Sherlock Holmes societies. 'Was Watson an Uncle?' ponders Dana Martin Batory, for instance, in *The Baker Street Journal* in 1988. Founded in 1946, *The Baker Street Journal*, like its counterpart *Canadian Holmes*, combines serious, scholarly essays with playful imaginings that Holmes, Watson and Mrs Hudson exist.[6] And what of Dr Watson? Was his first name James or John? And where exactly did he receive that bullet wound: in the shoulder or in the leg? (Steven Moffat and Mark Gatiss's *Sherlock* (2010) has opted for 'John' and the leg, respectively). In 1985 Richard Lancelyn Green published *Letters to Sherlock Holmes*, a compilation of the global 'correspondence' to the great detective which had arrived at the Abbey National Bank which, at that time, occupied the building at 221 Baker Street,[7] and the detective has been the subject of spoof biographies; William S. Baring-Gould's *Sherlock Holmes of Baker Street* (1962) 'take[s] to its extreme the Sherlockian game of treating Holmes as an historical figure' (Redmond, 2009: 45).[8] Holmes's world exerts a powerful and enduring cachet.

This 'embodiment' of Sherlock Holmes has its *fin-de-siècle* precedents. The first serialised Holmes story, 'A Scandal in Bohemia' (July 1891), appeared in George Newnes's *The Strand Magazine*. This was not the first published Holmes story; *A Study in Scarlet* appeared in *Beeton's Christmas Annual* in November 1887 and *The Sign of Four* was published in *Lippincott's Monthly Magazine* in February 1890. However, it was through the serialisation of the stories in *The Strand* that Holmes achieved immense popularity. The cultivation of the myth of the detective as a real person was allegedly derived from the notion that Paget modelled Holmes on his brother Walter, thus endowing the character with, as Doyle describes in his autobiography *Memories and Adventures* (1924), a 'handsome' physicality which 'took the place of the powerful but uglier Sherlock' which had been Doyle's initial 'conception' of the character.[9] Holmes's further embodiment rapidly followed in William Gillette's stage adaptations, with *Sherlock Holmes* opening in New York in 1899. In *Memories and Adventures*, Doyle remarks that 'the impression that Holmes was a real person of flesh and blood may have been intensified by his frequent appearance on the stage' (1989: 101).

Early twentieth-century screen representations, such as those of Eille Norwood and Basil Rathbone, compounded Holmes's popularity. Doyle comments on Norwood's conception of the character in the films made by the Stoll Film Company between 1921 and 1923: '[Norwood] has that rare quality which can only be described as glamour, which compels you to watch an actor eagerly even when he is doing nothing. He has the brooding eye which excites expectation and he has also a quite unrivalled power of disguise. My only criticism of the films is that they introduce telephones, motor cars and other luxuries of which the Victorian Holmes never dreamed' (1989: 106).

Other factors contributed to Holmes's iconicity. Uniquely, the Victorian *fin-de-siècle* produced a panoply of sensational fictional creations: Dr Jekyll and Mr Hyde, She, Dorian Gray and Dracula, to name but a few. Less well-known, perhaps, are the figures of contemporaneous detective stories, which Hugh Greene depicts as the 'rivals of Sherlock Holmes' (1971: 9).[10] Emerging from the recesses of a late-Victorian psyche infused with social theories of scientific progress and moral degeneration, such literary figures were unleashed in a period of rapid expansion in both the publishing industry and the reading public. Lippincott's, for instance, commissioned both *Dorian Gray* (1890) and *The Sign of Four* and invited Wilde and Doyle to lunch, an event recorded by Doyle in *Memories and Adventures* (1989: 78–80).

In the late twentieth century the titillating possibility of conjoining two of the period's most iconic fictional characters, Holmes and Dracula, emerged in the pastiche *Sherlock Holmes vs. Dracula: or, the Adventure of the Sanguinary Count* (1978), narrated by John H. Watson.[11] More recently, a muscular and square-jawed Holmes, far removed from Paget's fine-featured figure, appears in the graphic novel, *Sherlock Holmes vs. Dracula*. Set in a post-Apocalyptic city (a preoccupation of twenty-first century literary and visual production)[12], here a Victorian London ravaged by revenants, Holmes defeats Dr Jekyll, a 'cognitive cadaver' (2011: 30), before doing battle with the Transylvanian Count in an encounter that requires more Holmesian brawn than brains.

Holmes policed the Victorian psyche: 'no ghosts need apply' ('The Adventure of the Sussex Vampire', January 1924); allowed the reader to traverse the London underworld of opium dens ('The Man with the Twisted Lip', December 1891); absorbed the criminal 'other' ('The Final Problem', December 1893), both indigenous and foreign; and safeguarded the bourgeois home and nation by expunging it of its threats ('The Adventure of the Copper Beeches', June 1892 and 'The Adventure of the Bruce-Partington Plans', December 1908). The detective, as Slavoj Žižek argues, demonstrates how '"everything is possible" including the impossible': 'The very presence of the detective guarantees in advance the transformation of the lawless sequence [of events] into a lawful sequence; in other words the reestablishment of "normality"' (1992: 58).

Holmes abides by the same moral code as the conventional law enforcers, Inspectors Lestrade and Athelney Jones but he is not defined by it. He breaks and enters ('The Adventure of the Naval Treaty', October–November 1893) and allows the perpetrators of murder to go free if their cause is justified ('The Adventure of the Devil's Foot', December 1910). Each case is weighed on its own merits and Holmes becomes the final arbiter of justice ('The Five Orange Pips', November 1891). Some variation is allowed in his character: the drug-taking Holmes of the early stories dissipates and the later published adventures show an increased sympathy with human foibles ('The Adventure of the Veiled Lodger', February 1927). Holmes – fixed and flexible (where the law is concerned), stable and eccentric, English and foreign (of French descent), celibate protector of women and homosocial – restored domestic sureties threatened by rogue stepfathers ('The Adventure of the Speckled Band', February 1892), English and continental spies ('His Last Bow', September 1917), secret societies, and wayward colonials ('The Adventure of the Dancing Men', December 1903; 'The Adventure of the Solitary Cyclist', January 1904) from the intellectual powerhouse of 221b Baker Street. That he continues to do so throughout the twentieth and twenty-first centuries in literary and visual pastiches and adaptations is the principal subject of this collection of critical essays, with chapters ranging from the use of Holmes in advertising (Amanda J. Field) to video games (Souvik Mukherjee).

Doyle even anticipated the Baker Street museum: in 'The Empty House', in which Holmes is resurrected after his apparent demise at the Reichenbach Falls, the sleuth places a wax dummy of himself in his sitting-room window to lure a Moriarty acolyte, Colonel Sebastian

Moran, to the empty house opposite, and when Moran pops a bullet at the figure he is trapped by Holmes and Watson. Indeed, the wax dummy represents an immortality of sorts as the detective, Watson and the reader observe Holmes's simulation lure a criminal to justice. Further prefiguring the stories' filmic afterlife, one of Paget's illustrations depicts Holmes and Watson, like spectators at a movie, looking out of the window of the empty house at the detective's fake silhouette, framed by the Baker Street casement.

Holmes's house, furthermore, reminds us of another: Doyle's former residence, Undershaw, at Hindhead in Sussex. In 1890, Doyle's first wife Louise was diagnosed with tuberculosis, for which, at that time, there was no medical cure. Recuperative stays in Egypt and Switzerland helped to alleviate Louise's symptoms. However, Grant Allen, who also suffered from the disease, told Doyle that 'he had found his salvation in the soil and air of Hindhead in Surrey' (*Memories and Adventures*: 126). Doyle immediately purchased a plot of land, and the house was completed in 1897. It was here that Doyle wrote, amongst other works, the most famous of all the Holmes's stories, *The Hound of the Baskervilles* (1901–2).

Undershaw was described by Bram Stoker, who interviewed Doyle at the house in 1907, as an 'almost fairy pleasure' filled with 'things got together for their interesting association with the author's life and adventures'. It imparted a 'sense of "home" which is so delightful to occupant and stranger alike' (Stoker 2009: 154), and Stoker noted that the drawing-room and adjacent rooms were filled with Charles Doyle's (Arthur's father) fairy pictures, described as 'delicate fancies and weird flights of imagination' (155).[13] For Stoker, the house and its verdant setting was one of 'idyllic beauty' (154).

Ironically, in light of the celebration of the 'home' of the great sleuth, the literary home of his creator is under threat and a campaign by Doylean scholars is presently attempting to save Undershaw for cultural posterity.[14] Indeed, the 'home' of the fictional detective is supporting the campaign to save the writer's residence as the Baker Street museum's website provides a link to the 'Save Undershaw' campaign. Doyle's fame as an author still remains in inverse proportion to that of his creation, and this is underscored by the status of the two homes: Undershaw and 221b Baker Street.

Arthur Conan Holmes

The Hound of the Baskervilles, written during Doyle's Undershaw years and serialised from August 1901 in *The Strand Magazine*, six months after the death of Queen Victoria on 22 January 1901, provides an interesting point of departure for an examination of both Doyle and Holmes in their post- and neo-Victorian contexts. *The Hound of the Baskervilles*, set in the 1880s, is published after the supposed death of Holmes at the Reichenbach Falls and presented as an early Holmesian exploit by Watson. For the Edwardian reader Holmes is dead but resurrected from the past, before his proper emergence from the Reichenbach Falls in 'The Adventure of the Empty House'. Like the hound, an entity from an earlier time that terrifies the Victorian Baskervilles, Holmes's ghostly Victorian form haunted *The Strand's* readers in 1901. Doyle, the spiritualist, would spend the latter part of his life attempting to bring ghostly forms into materiality. Of course, the hound turns out to be real in the detective fiction, but in the legend that shapes the narrative its ghostly form cannot be laid to rest. Holmes and Doyle variously embrace the ghostly, the fictional, the real and the immortal.

Doyle attempted to produce an account of his own life for posterity with his autobiography, published six years before his death in 1930. *Memories and Adventures* (the title, consciously or unconsciously, embracing his collected volumes of Holmes stories, *The Adventures of Sherlock Holmes* and *The Memoirs of Sherlock Holmes*) follows a conventional, chronological path from family history, education, adventures as a ship's doctor to a whaler and passenger ship respectively, early medical practice in Southsea, literary endeavours and successes (with a chapter dedicated to Holmes), the Anglo-Boer War, political and legal campaigns (his Liberal Unionist candidature, George Edalji, Oscar Slater, the Congo Reform Association, Roger Casement), sporting interests, and a lengthy discussion of the First World War (Doyle visited the frontlines to inspire troop morale). The autobiography ends with a chapter on the spiritualism which would preoccupy the final years of his life. Doyle's autobiography adheres to the conventional Victorian 'telling' of 'great lives' as it begins with the decline of family fortunes and details the triumph over personal adversity to success and fame.

As a Victorian 'Renaissance' man, Doyle provides an apparently endless source of interest for biographers, and increasingly for neo-Victorian novelists. In *The Observer* on 14 November 2010, Vanessa Thorpe explored how Doyle occupies a position alongside Hitler, Churchill, Dickens and the Brontës as the most desired subjects for publishers of biographies.[15] Indeed, the apparent disjunction in Doyle's life as both the creator of *the* ratiocinative detective and a convert to spiritualism and fairy belief is a continuing source of fascination to both biographers and novelists, as we see in the chapter by Doyle's leading biographer

Andrew Lycett, in Patricia Pulham's chapter on Julian Barnes's *Arthur & George*, and in Jennifer S. Palmer's critical survey of Doyle in contemporary neo-Victorian detective novels. Our cultural preoccupation with the Victorians, reborn and reframed in the neo-Victorian novel, is multifaceted, as Cora Kaplan argues, ranging from nostalgia to the reimagining of history (2007: 3). In Britain the Victorian past is omnipresent: physically through the remnants of its cities' architecture, artwork, and literature, and psychologically through its representation of loss (Empire, global significance, industry). The Victorians continue to haunt the contemporary psyche, and Doyle and Holmes are fitting figures for such a role: the detective writer who pursued ghostly forms and spirits, and the detective who never died. In his Victorian 'life' Sherlock Holmes was a colossus, and in his afterlife he continues to dominate cultural forms; long after his death, his creator continues to inspire biographies and is reshaped in fiction.[16]

The biographical form, of course, engages in acts of interpretation. Interpretations of Doyle's life commenced shortly after his death with John Lamond's 1931 spiritualist biography, *Arthur Conan Doyle: A Memoir*, authorised by the Doyle family and with an epilogue by Doyle's second wife, Jean (Leckie) Conan Doyle. A selection of subsequent biographies is worth considering. Pierre Nordon's biography, first published in French in 1965, demonstrates Doyle's appeal beyond the Anglophone world. Translated into English in 1966, Nordon's *Conan Doyle* separates Doyle into the man and the writer. Doyle, the man, is presented as a patriot, lover of justice and prophet, and Holmes occupies half of the section devoted to Doyle the writer. Like Dickson Carr's biography (1949), Nordon benefited from access to archival materials closed to biographers in the late twentieth century. He presents Doyle the man as a 'knight-errant' (1966: 342): 'Conan Doyle was essentially a fighter, a man of action, stimulated and even enriched by opposition. And spiritualism gave him an adventurous view of the next world, as well as the feeling of fulfilment and pride in the face of death that prompted his very last words: "The Lord is on my side. I will not fear what man doeth unto me"' (1966: 167). In 1983, Sherlock Holmes preoccupied Owen Dudley Edwards as he pursued the creation of the detective through an examination of Doyle's early life. *The Quest for Sherlock Holmes: A Biographical Study of Arthur Conan Doyle* is coterminous with the Granada *Sherlock Holmes* starring Jeremy Brett, the definitive screen depiction of Holmes in the late twentieth century and the subject of Neil McCaw's chapter in this collection. Meanwhile, within the broader field of Doyle scholarship, Richard Lancelyn Green and John Michael Gibson recovered the 'unknown' Doyle by publishing his forgotten short stories (*Uncollected Stories*, 1982), his *Essays on Photography* (1982) and *Letters to the Press* (1986).[17]

Two more significant biographies of Doyle emerged in the 1990s and, although they take different paths in their approaches to him, both Martin Booth and Daniel Stashower acknowledge in their respective prefaces the established perception of Doyle in the late twentieth century. Booth recalls that 'all I really knew of him was his creation of Sherlock Holmes and his conversion to spiritualism' (ix) and *The Doctor, the Detective and Arthur Conan Doyle* (1997) presents Doyle within his medical context.[18] In the preface to his 1999 biography, Stashower recalls that when he admitted an interest in Doyle the response was invariably '"Sherlock Holmes was brilliant, but Doyle went a bit potty at the end, didn't he? Fairies, ghosts, and that"' (1999: xii). Stashower acknowledges that '"Fairies, ghosts, and that" have been the millstone of Doyle's reputation for the better part of a century' (xii), but he presents a sympathetic and humane 'teller of tales'. In 1997 Doyle's interest in fairies received the Hollywood treatment with *FairyTale: A True Story* (dir. Charles Sturridge), a children's film – and, indeed, a decidedly juvenile one – drawing inspiration from the notorious Cottingley fairy incident which had embroiled Doyle in 1920. This otherworldly Doyle occupied popular consciousness in the 1990s.[19]

In the twentieth-first century biographical interest in Doyle shows no sign of abating. In 2007 Stashower, Jon Lellenberg and Charles Foley published Doyle's previously unpublished letters, which considerably enhance an understanding of Doyle's family relations, the arduous path of his early medical practice, his incipient writing career and his preoccupation with income. For instance, in September 1897 he writes to his mother that he has 'serious thoughts of a Sherlock Holmes play' and if it 'came off' he could pay for Undershaw 'at one stroke' (2007: 389). Indeed, he describes Undershaw in this letter: 'Everyone falls in love with it who approaches it' (389). In 2007 Lycett produced the definitive biography of Doyle. Benefiting from extensive archival research, Lycett presents Doyle as a figure who crossed lines: an 'Irishman, born in Scotland' with 'English values' (2007: 434), deeply imbued by a sense of justice, and a public figure and campaigner, deeply immersed in and shaped by the scientific thinking of his age, 'straddling the fault line in the British psyche between rationality and superstition' (2007: 434).

Doyle exists as the penumbral figure behind Sherlock Holmes whom biographers seek to explore. Meanwhile the acclaimed BBC's *Murder Rooms* (2000–1) foregrounds a fictional Doyle – though based in some respects on his early career as a medical student in Edinburgh and doctor at Southsea – behind whom exists a shadowy Sherlock Holmes. The five-part series commences with *The Dark Beginnings of Sherlock Holmes*, focusing on Doyle's training at Edinburgh where he becomes Professor Joseph Bell's clerk (based on biographical fact). What this Doyle also becomes is Bell's sidekick as he investigates a series of Edinburgh murders that take them from lecture theatre to brothel. Although Bell solves the case, the murderer escapes after committing his final crime, the murder of Doyle's fiancée Elspeth. This sense of loss pervades the remaining episodes. Cleverly, the second episode, *The Patient's Eyes*, based in Southsea, involves Bell investigating a mystery surrounding one of Doyle's patients, a cyclist who is followed by a mysterious figure. Like 'The Adventure of the Solitary Cyclist' in the Holmes canon, the crime has its South African associations, but unlike Violet Smith of the Holmes story, this cyclist is revealed as the murderer of both of her parents. The third and arguably most interesting episode in the series, *The Photographer's Chair*, involves murders committed by a photographer. Against a backdrop of mesmeric performances by Milo De Meyer in Southsea, Bell and Doyle investigate a series of killings that draws Doyle to séances where he encounters Madame Petchey. Her credentials as a medium are substantiated, not only by the ghosts who appear to her, but by her message to Doyle from Elspeth. While the murderer is a spiritualist investigator who photographs his victims before killing them in order to attempt to capture their souls leaving their bodies, Madame Petchey is vindicated as a genuine medium when she tells Doyle to return to the studio and, as he develops a photograph taken when the murderer was attempting to use Doyle as his final victim, a fleeting image of Elspeth appears. This Doyle, then, is attracted to spiritualism as a consequence of a tragic lost love, a fictional explanation that is more understandable for contemporary audiences than the historical Doyle's public conversion to spiritualism in 1916.[20] In the episode the sceptic Bell warns Doyle that he has seen too many good minds destroyed by the supernatural quest – a comment perhaps on the twenty-first century interpretation of the historical Doyle.

Sherlock Doyle

At the close of the first decade of the twenty-first century Sherlock Holmes has re-emerged on screen in *Sherlock Holmes* (dir. Guy Ritchie, 2009) and on television in *Sherlock* (Moffat and Gatiss, 2010). The former, a pastiche (with Robert Downey Jr. as Sherlock), and the latter, an adaptation (with Benedict Cumberbatch as Sherlock), form the subject of Bran Nicol's chapter in this book. Ritchie's sequel, *Sherlock Holmes: A Game of Shadows*, was released in December 2011, and the second series of *Sherlock* commenced at the beginning of 2012. In the last quarter of 2011 two new literary texts have also emerged, which demonstrates a continuing interest in Doyle and Holmes: one is an afterlife, a Sherlock Holmes pastiche, and the other can be defined as a 'resurrection', an unfinished Doyle manuscript, written when he was twenty-three and resident at Southsea. *The Narrative of John Smith* (2011) relays the thoughts and conversations of a middle-aged John Smith as he recuperates from gout on his sitting-room couch. Presided over by a landlady, Mrs Rundle (a prototype for Mrs Hudson), Smith reflects on literature, medicine, contemporary politics and his neighbours. The text exhibits another Holmesian flourish as Smith studies his neighbours opposite his sitting-room window, a father (the former principal of a private school) and daughter who live in reduced circumstances. Smith's detailed attention to, and sympathy for, the economically constrained middle-class woman frequently appears in the Holmesian canon.[21] Furthermore in an observation later made famous by Holmes in *A Study in Scarlet*, Smith argues that 'brain-attics' have limited capacity and, as any new knowledge replaces the old, 'It becomes of the highest importance therefore that we should take nothing unnecessary into our brains and that we should docket and arrange all that we have so as to be able to use it to the best advantage at a moment's notice' (74) – a sentiment shared by Benedict Cumberbatch's Sherlock.

Anthony Horowitz's pastiche, *The House of Silk* (2011), was commissioned by the Doyle estate. Here Holmes and Watson are drawn into a case which initially involves them investigating a mysterious stranger who stalks the English country home of an art dealer, Edmund Carstairs. Carstairs reveals to Holmes that he had become involved in pursuing the theft of paintings by an Irish–American gang from a train bound to Boston for a rich art collector, Cornelius Stillman, and believes that this might be the reason for the stranger's appearance. For this part of the mystery, Horowitz cleverly and seamlessly draws on Doyle's American settings in the Holmes canon and, more directly, on 'The Adventure of the Dancing Men' (1903). However, the Elsie Patrick of the Holmes story, who has escaped her criminal family, is replaced by Mrs Catherine Carstairs (aka Keelan O'Donoghue) who is in fact a member of the Irish–American gang hunted down by Stillman and Carstairs; she takes revenge on the gang's destruction by assassinating Stillman, and then assumes a false identity in order to marry Carstairs, infiltrate his home, and begin the murder of his family. The mysterious stranger who stalks the Carstairs' home at the beginning of the story is a Pinkerton detective determined to blackmail Catherine Carstairs/ Keelan O'Donoghue by threatening to reveal her real identity. With its duplicitous Pinkerton detective there are echoes here of the Holmes story *The Valley of Fear* (Sept. 1914–May 1915).

The second, more appalling, but parallel, crime draws Holmes into the investigation of Chorley Grange School for orphaned boys, set up by the Society for the Improvement of London's Children (SILC, pronounced 'silk'). The school is a cover for a paedophilia ring (House of Silk) which provides young boys for abuse by the upper classes. The crimes lead to the brutal murder of a Baker Street Irregular, a former inmate of the school, who recognises Carstairs as one of the men who frequent the House of Silk and unwisely seeks to blackmail him. Due to the horrendous nature of this crime, Watson, so he states, has withheld publication of it until decades after its occurrence.

This neo-Victorian text, set as it is amongst the familiar Holmesian terrain of English country homes, London opium dens, and Baker Street, is both Victorian and, with its focus on paedophilia – a crime which is very much a preoccupation of the twenty-first century – neo-Victorian. Recalling Field's observation at the beginning of this introduction on the updating of Holmes, Horowitz's detective embraces Doyle's Victorian creation and, at the same time, he produces a reassuring figure who investigates crimes of the moment. The abhorrent activities of the House of Silk compel Moriarty to assist Holmes through Watson as an intermediary.

In the afterword which accompanies the ebook, Horowitz ascribes the enduring appeal of the Holmes stories to 'the character, the friendship of Holmes and Watson, the extraordinary and very rich world they inhabit and the genuine and often under-rated excellence of Conan Doyle's writing, a touch melodramatic at times but still very much in the tradition of gothic romance (ebook)'. He notes Doyle's spiritualist beliefs, and further relates how he went out and bought an old edition of Holmes signed by Doyle: the 'tiny, neat signature became something of a talisman' and he 'even felt occasionally (or was tempted to feel) that Conan Doyle was in some way watching over me, guiding my hand' (ebook). Horowitz also sets out the ten rules that guided him in writing the novel. Rule number ten, 'the most important rule of all', was 'when publicizing the book, never, ever be seen wearing a deerstalker hat or smoking a pipe' (ebook).

The deerstalker, one of the most iconic symbols of Holmes's after-life, recurs, like the detective himself, in the same form to serve many purposes. In the second episode of the *Sherlock* series, *The Hounds of Baskerville* (written by Mark Gatiss, co-creator Stephen Moffat), for instance, Watson points to a photo in a newspaper of Holmes wearing a deerstalker and says, 'another photo of you with the ...' – the word 'deer-stalker' is unspoken (perhaps unspeakable). Sherlock merely groans.

Chapters

The chapters which follow in this book interpret the cultural afterlives of Holmes and Doyle as they are remodelled and repackaged for new global audiences and new historical contexts. However, the point of departure – the Holmes stories and Doyle's life in context – provides the point of origin for these chapters. As Holmes thrives in the popular imagination, the bulk of this collection is dedicated to Holmesian adap-tations (advertising, TV series, film and videogames). With the advent of neo-Victorianism, Doyle, however, is increasingly appearing as a fictionalised figure and the final four chapters in this collection frame Doyle biographically (Lycett), and contextually (Bloom) as the histor-ical figure slips increasingly into the neo-historical fictional world of 'high' literature (Pulham) and popular crime narratives (Palmer).

In the opening chapter Amanda J. Field uses the rich resources of the Richard Lancelyn Green Collection at Portsmouth City Library to examine the use of Holmes in advertising. Quoting Somerset Maugham's contention that Holmes's longevity as a character was attributable to the way Doyle fixed the detective's idiosyncrasies into readers' minds with 'the same pertinacity as the great advertisers use to proclaim the merits of their soap, beer or cigarettes', Field explores what happens to Brand Holmes after it escapes *The Strand Magazine*. She explores numerous advertisements, identifying the aspects of their products that adver-tisers align with their Holmes. Holmes's advertising afterlife ties him to his Victorian period with 'deerstalker and Inverness', but Field demon-strates how the figure 'moves through time' to sell products from later periods.

The three chapters which follow explore late twentieth-century TV series and films. The first of these, Neil McCaw's chapter, provides a detailed examination of Granada TV's iconic series, *The Adventures of Sherlock Holmes*, which ran during the 1980s and 1990s. McCaw reads the series in the context of Thatcherite ideology. Initially, he argues, it attempted to produce a faithful interpretation of Doyle's stories, and here McCaw identifies the Thatcherite celebration of notions of the Victorians rooted in conservative values. As Thatcherism declined in the 1990s, McCaw observes how the series' obsession with fidelity to Doyle's text dissolved as values and ideologies were reappraised. Just as the Holmesian canon functions as a barometer of its times, McCaw demonstrates how the Granada adaptations are rooted in the changing socio-cultural values of Thatcherite and post-Thatcherite Britain.

Doyle's *Hound of the Baskervilles* (1901–02) is probably the most famous of all his Holmes stories, and Terry Scarborough's chapter focuses on a particular adaptation of the story, the 1988 film by Brian Mills. Here Holmes's appeal derives in part from the Gothic qualities of the original story. Scarborough examines how the Gothic elements of Doyle's narrative – specifically those based in architecture and landscape – are presented in Mills's film. The chapter focuses on the characters' gaze in order to examine the revision of Gothic sensationalism and to analyse how nineteenth-century discourses are reworked in the late twentieth century as the contemporary viewer 'observes' Victorian culture.

Harvey O'Brien's chapter focuses on films that have not emerged directly from the canon, but have re-imagined Holmes in different contexts from Doyle's original stories. O'Brien engages in an extensive examination of films from the 1960s to the 1980s in which Holmes is the 'point of origin' but in which 'variances' on the 'classical' Holmes 'revise and complement' the original. Deploying Maxim Gorky's contention that cinema is a 'kingdom of shadows' O'Brien argues that just as cinema is an 'illusion that transmogrifies recognisable matter into an imagining', Holmes too has 'endless possibilities for reconstitution and revision', rooted, O'Brien demonstrates, in their specific cultural contexts.

The next two chapters signal a return to the literary origins of Holmes. Claudia Capancioni explores how the fictional detective's appeal extends beyond the Anglophone world by analysing how Holmes is re-imagined by the Italian writer Joyce Lussu (1912–98). Doyle's stories, she notes, are replete with continental cases, and Italian writers have provided numerous pastiches and adaptations. Lussu, a writer not yet translated into English, produces a postmodern pastiche, *Sherlock Holmes: anarchici e siluri* ('Sherlock Holmes: Anarchists and Torpedoes', 1982), which takes Holmes to Italy on a case of espionage in 1908. In Doyle's stories published in the first decade of the twentieth century Holmes becomes involved in continental intrigues ('The Adventure of the Second Stain', 1904; 'The Bruce-Partington Plans', 1908), but Capancioni demonstrates how, to use O'Brien's term, the canon as 'point of origin' is re-visioned and, in Lussu's case, transported to another language, location and audience.

Sabine Vanacker's chapter continues the literary exploration by focusing on a specific subgenre of Sherlock Holmes pastiches: the feminist revision. Both Laurie R. King and Carole Nelson Douglas independently re-engage with the series format of the original Holmes stories by producing their own, feminist series. In *The Beekeeper's Apprentice* (1994), King marries a 'retired' Holmes off to Mary Russell, Jewish, half-American, and a scholar of Rabbinic Judaism. Carole Nelson Douglas interweaves her Irene Adler series with the Doyle canon, situating the first novel, *Good Night, Mr. Holmes* (1990), around the events described in 'A Scandal in Bohemia' and featuring both John Watson, the Watson-like Nell Huxleigh, and an academic editor, 'Fiona Witherspoon, Ph.D., F.I.A.' in a complex narrative framework. In different ways, King and Douglas engage explicitly with history by involving real historical characters and events in their plots. Vanacker's chapter uses a comparison with fan fiction writing to examine the ways in which these writers embed Holmes in a chronological framework and exploit the narrative gaps in the Holmesian canon, to consider the fictionalization of history.

The final two chapters in this section return to the visual medium, updating Holmes for the twenty-first century. Souvik Mukherjee examines Holmes in the context of videogames by pursuing the notion that just as Holmes re-emerged from the Reichenbach Falls after Doyle apparently 'killed him off' in 'The Final Problem', Holmes returns in a multiplicity of narratives, notably the videogame. After 'dying' in an attempt to 'complete' the multitelic narrative, the videogame player performs a Sherlockian 'resurrection' and replays his existence. Deploying theories of new media and engaging with Gilles Deleuze's concept of multiplicity, Mukherjee examines videogames and argues that the Holmes stories function as proto-videogames.

'Work and occasional indiscretions' are key to Holmes's 'enduring appeal', argues Bran Nicol in his chapter on Guy Ritchie's 2009 film and the first series of the BBC's *Sherlock*. Both adaptations, he argues, can be seen as 'crime thrillers', but in Ritchie's film intense action sequences take precedence over puzzle-solving; in the BBC *Sherlock*, which Nicol regards as the superior adaptation, the suspense is bound up with what he presents as Holmes's 'sociopathology', a 'disregard' for the emotions of others. Nicol explores how the pleasures of the crime thriller are also curiously 'sociopathological' with regard to viewers' responses to characters on screen. Nicol presents the BBC's Sherlock Holmes as a 'character for our times', arguing that the 'unassailable dominance' of the crime thriller, is not merely the 'capacity to incorporate "the other"', but that it 'parallels the depiction of the volatile "intensities" of our age' as the reader is 'invited to enjoy the text'.

Andrew Lycett introduces the final series of chapters, which are dedicated to Doyle and his fictional adaptations. Here Lycett presents his biographical position from *Conan Doyle: The Man Who Created Sherlock Holmes* (2007). Biography is an act of interpretation, but it becomes an increasingly important means of seeing an historical figure who is increasingly becoming subjected to fictionalised representation. Lycett's Doyle is deeply immersed in the scientific climate of his age which, coupled with the loss of his Catholic faith, leads him to an early exploration of spiritualism. Lycett's biographical case explores how the 'medically trained creator of the supposedly super-rationalist detective Sherlock Holmes could become an apostle for spiritualism' – a facet of Doyle's make-up that has dogged Doylean biographers like the hound of the Baskervilles, just at it intrigues neo-historical novelists.

Patricia Pulham provides a detailed exploration of Julian Barnes's *Arthur & George* (2005), a 'neo-historical biofiction' in which Barnes blends fact with fiction to re-present Doyle's real-life investigation into the case of George Edalji, wrongly accused of mutilating cattle in 1907. Pulham examines how Barnes blends the 'facts' of Doyle's and Edalji's lives with a 'fictional interiority'. Through her focus on the novel's 'hybridity' and Barnes's interest in the Freudian uncanny, and the exploration of issues of sight, seeing and observation, crucial both to criminal detection and spiritualist investigation, Pulham considers the issue of what 'do we see' when we read the novel. Invoking notions of the séance where the medium sits behind a curtain, Pulham questions whether the 'blinds' of the past and 'our own blind-spots' will continually affect our ability to resurrect it?' As such, Pulham probes the broader issues which surround the contemporary dominance of the neo-Victorian and neo-historical novel.

Jennifer S. Palmer's chapter explores the emergence and use of Doyle in historical crime fiction. Palmer identifies how Doyle is one of the Victorian period's most popular figures to appear as a fictionalised detective in this genre and is often paired with other historical figures such as his former professor, Joseph Bell (the prototype for Sherlock Holmes) and the escapologist Harry Houdini. In these fictions, Palmer demonstrates that that this fictionalised Doyle rarely solves the crime and functions more as a Watson figure.

Finally, Clive Bloom draws creator and creation together by opening his chapter with the problem that has hounded Doyle research in the twentieth century and beyond: 'There is a conundrum inside Arthur Conan Doyle and inside Sherlock Holmes. Why did the creator of the master of deduction turn to a belief in fairies and all things invisible: Sherlock Holmes contra his creator.' However, Bloom posits that Doyle was more in harmony with his creation that we might have supposed. Here he focuses on the late-Victorian 'isms' and, through reading Doyle in relation to the period's socialist thinkers, proposes a new way of understanding the historical figure not only in his own time but in ours as well.

Bernard Partridge's famous cartoon in *Punch* (12 May 1926) portrays a miniature Holmes in dressing gown and pipe, eyes fixed firmly on the ground, chained to an elderly and buffoonish Doyle with his eyes closed and his head in the clouds. The contributors to this collection variously examine Doyle and Holmes as iconic figures in their own right. Contemporary audiences, just as much as readers of Doyle's own period, are inevitably drawn to the paradox and enigma inherent in the fact that the inventor of the rational detective embraced the irrationality of a spirituality that twinned creator and creation and enchained them in perpetuity. In the doggerel accompanying Partidge's image it is the figure of Holmes, Doyle is informed, that 'holds you foot-cuffed when you're fain/ To navigate the vast inane' (*Punch*, 12 May 1926: 517). Both figures engage the dominant questions of their time as well as ours – of order and chaos, stability and instability, materialism and spirituality. As such, and as demonstrated by the reimagining of Holmes by each successive generation and the more recent fictionalisation of Doyle, they continue to simultaneously shape and disturb our culture and consciousness.

Notes

1. Cora Kaplan broadens the definition of Victorian, which in the 1960s might only have meant artefacts, stating that the term 'has widened to embrace a complementary miscellany of evocations and recycling of the nineteenth century, a constellation of images which became markers for particular moments of contemporary style and culture' (2007: 3).
2. Paget drew Holmes in a deerstalker for 'The Adventure of Silver Blaze' which Michael Pointer describes as 'one of the finest illustrations of the whole canon' (1976: 11). For a discussion of the various illustrators of the Holmes stories in *The Strand*, see Pointer (8–25).
3. The twenty-first century has seen a rise in interest in 'revisioning' the Victorians, and critical interest in neo-Victorianism and the neo-Victorian novel has gathered pace. See Christine L. Krueger (2002); Cora Kaplan (2007); Simon Joyce (2007); Penny Gay, Judith Johnston and Catherine Waters (2008); Rosario Arias and Patricia Pulham (2009); Ann Heilmann and Mark Llewellyn (2010).

4. See Marie-Luise Kohlke's important introduction to the inaugural issue of *Neo-Victorian Studies* in 2008. Kohlke writes of the proliferation of 'Neo-Victorian artefacts, fictions and fantasies' (1) for which the journal is providing a platform for exploration and discussion. Kohlke's article also plays on the investigative language of nineteenth-century scientific discourse and colonialism. See 'Introduction: Speculations in and on the Neo-Victorian Encounter', *Neo-Victorian Studies* 1(1): 1–18. [Online] Available at www.neovictorianstudies.com (Accessed 1 December 2011).

5. The Sherlock Holmes Museum. [Online] Available at www.sherlock-holmes. co.uk. (Accessed 1 November 2011).

6. *Canadian Holmes* is the publication of the Bootmakers of Toronto: The Sherlock Holmes Society of Canada.

7. Christopher Redmond notes that more recent correspondence is delivered to the Sherlock Holmes Museum at 239 Baker Street. *Sherlock Holmes Handbook*, 2nd edn (2009: 45).

8. See also, Nick Rennison's 'unauthorised' biography published in 2005.

9. In a celebration of the 150th anniversary of Sidney Paget's death, Peggy Purdue, curator of the Arthur Conan Doyle Collection at Toronto Public Library, assembled a selection of Paget's illustrations online. Purdue demonstrates that 'whether or not Holmes' famous profile did in fact originally belong to Walter Paget, it can't be denied it was a face Paget used often' in his non-Holmesian work.[Online] Available at http://ve.torontopubliclibrary. ca/sidney_paget/holmes.html (Accessed 25 November 2011).

10. Greene collected a number of detective stories in which the detectives have 'identifiable, or nearly identifiable addresses in the London of the day' (1971: 11) and included the work of Max Pemberton, Arthur Morrison, Guy Boothby, Clifford Ashdown (R. Austin Freeman), L. T. Meade, William Le Queux, Baroness Orczy, William Hope Hodgson and Ernest Bramah Smith. All are remarkably inferior to Conan Doyle's work.

11. Loren D. Estleman's pastiche was dramatised on BBC Radio 4 Extra on 30 October 2011 with John Moffatt and Timothy West.

12. See, for instance, *28 Days Later* (dir. Danny Boyle, 2001), which opens in a post-Apocalyptic London, and Cormac McCarthy's *The Road* (2006).

13. On the eve of his second marriage to Jean Leckie, Bram Stoker interviewed Conan Doyle at Undershaw. The interview was published in the *New York World* on 28 July 1907 and republished in the *Daily Chronicle* on 14 February 1908. In this interview Stoker provides a detailed description of the house and its surroundings.

14. Save Undershaw. [Online] http://www.saveundershaw.com/ (Accessed 15 December 2012).

15. The article quotes Jeremy Lewis, who argues that publishers 'seem obsessed by Hitler, Churchill and Conan Doyle'. 'Biographers fear that publishers have lost their appetite for serious subjects'. *Observer* [Online]. Available at http://www.guardian.co.uk/books/2010/nov/14/victoria-glendinning-biogr aphies-publishers (Accessed 1 November 2011).

16. Heilmann and Lewellyn describe contemporary culture's 'ongoing obsession' with that 'prolonged and continuous historical moment' that began in 1837 with Victoria's accession to the throne and ended 'alongside the chronological cessation of Victoria's own life on 22 January 1901' (2010: 9). Holmes

dies in the last decade of Victoria's reign in 'The Final Problem', published in 1893, and was resurrected two years after her death in 'The Adventure of the Empty House', published in 1903. With the death of an historical icon, a literary one is reborn as a Victorian, as the case of the 'Empty House' is set in spring 1894.

17. See also Green and Gibson's *A Bibliography of A. Conan Doyle* (1983).
18. Booth was unable to access family papers and in a note to his Preface he records: 'For several decades access to Sir Arthur Conan Doyle's private papers has been refused to biographers, due to an ongoing and complicated legal dispute' (Booth, 1997: xii).
19. In the same year another film drew inspiration from the Cottingley fairy incident. In Nick Willing's weak film *Photographing Fairies* a young photographer, a bereaved widower, is drawn into fairy investigations. The film features a cameo from Edward Hardwicke (Watson of the Granada TV series) as Conan Doyle.
20. Doyle's spiritualist conversion continues to be a source of argument. It can be seen as a response to World War I, the quest for the numinous after the rejection of his Catholic upbringing, and a middle-aged rapprochement with a misunderstood father, a fairy painter. Spiritualism was a religion that promised proof of an afterlife and deployed photography in its quest to prove the existence of ghostly forms at séances.
21. See Helen Stoner ('The Adventure of the Speckled Band'), Violet Hunter ('The Adventure of the Copper Beeches') and Violet Smith ('The Adventure of the Solitary Cyclist'). See Morley, *The Penguin Complete Sherlock Holmes*.

1

The Case of the Multiplying Millions: Sherlock Holmes in Advertising

Amanda J. Field

> ... *in the case of* The Multiplying Millions, *Sherlock Holmes investigates saving schemes. ... This investigation, chronicled by his great friend Doctor Watson, is now dramatically revealed to the people of Nottingham by the famous sleuth in person*
> National Savings advertisement (ACD1/F/15/102)

Somerset Maugham believed Sherlock Holmes's longevity as a character was attributable to the way Arthur Conan Doyle hammered the detective's idiosyncrasies into readers' minds with 'the same pertinacity as the great advertisers use to proclaim the merits of their soap, beer or cigarettes' (1967: 160). Likening Holmes to consumer products in this way raises two interesting issues, firstly because it implies that the detective was becoming a 'brand' or 'product' in his own right with his own distinct set of widely recognised values, and secondly because Holmes was indeed appropriated by manufacturers of those very products – and many more – as a lucrative aid to their sales campaigns.

This essay examines how business and industry have used Holmes in their advertising, which elements of his visual iconography and characteristics they have exploited, and how they have attempted to make the link between Holmes and their products in consumers' minds. It also considers why they might have chosen him in the first place – and whether his fictionality makes a difference to the way he is used or the way consumers might respond. It draws on primary source material from the Arthur Conan Doyle Collection, Richard Lancelyn Green Bequest, at Portsmouth City Museum.[1] Among the documents in the collection is an archive of 340 advertisements from over

170 different companies and organisations, all featuring Holmes, and spanning the period 1900 to 2000.[2] None of these advertisements are direct promotions for Holmes books, pastiches, films, or memorabilia, nor are they promoting places related to Holmes. Instead, they draw upon the Holmes 'brand' to promote products or services that appear to have no pre-existing connection with him. Whereas Peggy Perdue, in her survey of Holmes in advertising, offers a global perspective, this study looks specifically at the British market. Holmes is the quintessential Englishman, though his every utterance, and as C. A. Lejeune notes, is 'a household word in ... Tamil, Talugu, Urdu and Pitman's Shorthand'. Examining how he is promoted in his own country highlights the place he occupies in British popular consciousness (Lejeune, 1991 : 155).

David Ogilvy, founder of the Ogilvy & Mather advertising agency, defines a brand as being:

> a complex symbol. It is the intangible sum of a product's attributes, its name, packaging, and price, its history, reputation and the way it is advertised. A brand is also defined by consumers' impressions of the people who use it, as well as their own experience. (Roman, 2004)

If Holmes can be said to be a brand, then – just like a product – it is made up of a combination of all these elements. Brands are much more than logos, and although Holmes's 'logo' might consist of his deerstalker, pipe, and magnifying glass, these are not empty symbols: the deerstalker implies someone who will patiently 'hunt down' their quarry; the pipe indicates a man given to thoughtful contemplation; the magnifying glass represents someone for whom close observation is a key skill. Together, they also suggest a nineteenth-century man. Holmes's 'attributes', 'history', and 'reputation' might include his rooms at 221b Baker Street, his friendship with Dr Watson, his violin, reputation for 'cracking the case', use of deduction, rationality, imperviousness to women, ability to move with ease through social strata, talent for disguise, and cocaine use when bored. Thus there is a link between what is denoted by the image of Holmes and what is connoted, a connection which Roland Barthes calls a 'code'. This is, as Sut Jhally explains, 'the store of experience upon which both the advertiser and audience draw in their participation in the construction of commodity meaning' (1990 : 3). In Holmes's case, this 'store of experience' may come from multiple sources, given the character's transmedia presence: the consumer may know him through Doyle's stories, radio, TV, cinema or stage productions, pastiche novels, comic-strips, or through any of the other media which have appropriated the detective since his first appearance. In a sense, therefore, everyone brings their own notion of Holmes to bear when they see each new representation, weighing it against the Holmes of their imagination.

Due to the commercial value of consumer brands they are tightly controlled by their owners, and although today similar rigour is often applied to fictional characters in terms of licensing and copyright, Doyle arguably ceased to have complete control over Holmes from the moment the manuscripts left his desk en route to *The Strand Magazine*. His detective changed; indeed, a number of what are now thought to be Holmes's most essential characteristics – his curved-stem pipe and deerstalker, and his tendency to say 'elementary, my dear Watson' – are examples of this evolution. Doyle seemed unconcerned, telling William Gillette that he may 'marry or murder or do what you like with him' in his play *Sherlock Holmes*, first performed in 1899 (Starrett, 1974: x), yet he protested at the depiction of Holmes as looking 'about five feet high, badly dressed, and with no brains or character' in an unnamed proposed advertisement at around the same time.[3]

Doyle seemed fairly relaxed about the appropriation and exploitation of Holmes – it was not until 1920 that he authorised the Stoll company to make a series of Holmes films starring Eille Norwood, after a number of unauthorised films, including *Sherlock Holmes Baffled* (1900) and *The Adventures of Sherlock Holmes* (1905), had been released. After Doyle's death, his sons Denis and Adrian Conan Doyle, realising Holmes's financial potential, exercised assiduous control of every aspect of the brand. Their focus, however, was more about extracting the maximum possible revenue rather than protecting the use of Holmes; the 1942 agreement with Universal studios for a series of films permitted 'the fullest latitude' in changing, modernising and adapting Holmes and Watson, as long as they were 'characterised in the same general way' as in Doyle's stories. The only restriction imposed was that the film company must not 'kill off' the characters, presumably with an eye to future revenue streams.[4] In terms of advertising, the Doyle Estate did not seize the initiative quickly enough and was often surprised by seeing Holmes feature in unauthorised promotions. In 1941, Denis was incensed to see a billboard on which Holmes was endorsing New Golden Glow Beer, which he deemed to be a 'monstrous misuse of our property'; in 1942 he had much the same reaction to a campaign by the International Shoe Company, and in that same year he forced Angostura Bitters to pay $1,350 retrospectively for their use of a cartoon Holmes figure in nine advertisements.[5] Fitelson and Mayers, the Estate's lawyers, threatened legal action in every case, often on shaky grounds. The owners of New Golden Glow Beer said, with some justification, that they 'had noticed many uses of Sherlock Holmes for advertising purposes and ... were certain that they were not licensed or paid for'. Even as late as 1949, Fitelson and Mayers were advising Denis that 'the mere use of the hat and magnifying glass' were not enough to constitute an infringement of Doyle's rights: an advertisement would need also to 'employ ... the dialogue or names of Sherlock Holmes and Dr Watson'.[6] Denis wrote to licensing specialists Abbot Kimbell in New York in order to seek help in exploiting the Holmes name and symbol, and suggested that 'his violin, pipe, deerstalker hat etc as well as the world-famous phrase "elementary my dear Watson" could be used' in advertisements for pipes, tobacco, musical instruments – and even honey.[7] There is no evidence to show whether this was successful. After Adrian, the remaining brother, died in 1970 the rights to the Holmes and Watson characters were bought by Denis's widow, Nina Mdivani, who set up a company, Baskervilles Investments, in order to administer them. Chaotic finances meant that the company quickly went into receivership – which probably partially explains the surge of 'unregulated' advertising featuring Holmes in the 1970s.[8]

Holmes advertised a wide range of goods in Britain, and whereas it might be expected that he would be used to promote products that had some connection with his character, such as pipes and tobacco, he has also been employed to sell biscuits, liqueurs, tea, tyres, toffee, jam, car manuals, finance, shirts, mouthwash, bread, computers, pharmaceuticals, moth-proofing, packaging, double glazing, and many more consumer and industrial products. Rather than discussing the advertisements by product-group, however, the aim here is to explore advertisements that convey the same brand message: in other words, to examine which qualities in their product or service the advertiser is seeking to align with Holmes.

Advertisers frequently use celebrity endorsement: such a technique is, according to Matthew Healey, 'the quickest way to attach a personality to a brand' (Healey, 2008: 82). Thus Judith Williamson, in her analysis of how this transfer of personality from celebrity to product is achieved, says that the mere juxtaposition of the two enables an exchange of meaning to take place: she uses an advertisement which features Catherine Deneuve's face alongside a bottle of Chanel No 5 perfume. The advertiser seeks to appropriate the link between what Deneuve signifies (glamour, beauty) 'so that the perfume can be substituted for Catherine Deneuve's face and can also be made to signify glamour and beauty'

(Williamson, 2000: 25). In using Holmes for endorsement, however, such an exchange of meaning is more complex, firstly because Holmes is a fictional character with accrued layers of meaning, and secondly because he has not been aligned with one particular product or service, but with hundreds of disparate ones.

Usually, celebrity endorsement comes from actors, sportsmen, or TV personalities: indeed, Hamish Pringle, in his book *Celebrity Sells*, does not even acknowledge that a fictional celebrity, with a life outside the brand, might be used to sell it (*passim*).

The advertisements analysed here share one common denominator: all use elements of Holmes's visual iconography to create an instant identification for the consumer. The most common visual symbols used are the deerstalker, Inverness cape, pipe, and magnifying glass. In terms of indicating that the person illustrated is indeed Holmes, often the deerstalker and magnifying glass suffice. Out of all of the advertisements examined, only five portray him without a deerstalker, and these show him in his rooms at 221b Baker Street where he is identified by his dressing gown and violin. So well-known are all these elements that Holmes does not even need to be portrayed as a man, or even as a human. In one advertisement (Tootal fabrics ACD1/F/15/20) he is shown as a woman, in one he is a moth (BMK ACD1/F/15/126), in another a child (Sharps Toffee ACD1/F/15/2), a bottle (Teachers' whisky ACD1/F/15/300), and a phone directory (Yellow Pages ACD/1/F/15/193). Any portrayal seems possible as long as the iconography links the consumer's mind to Holmes. In many advertisements he is not even named.

In terms of illustration style, most advertisements use drawings to portray Holmes, ranging from simple schematic outlines, silhouettes, or cartoons, through to sophisticated colour illustrations. Where photography is used it tends to avoid showing too 'distinct' an image of Holmes, instead using one element – such as a single eye enlarged by a magnifying glass – to signify the whole; showing just enough of the figure to identify it as Holmes without revealing the face, or positioning the deerstalker and pipe on an inanimate object which substitutes for Holmes's head. In this way, Holmes is 'suggested' rather than depicted too literally, allowing the advertisement's viewer to project their own idea of Holmes. Ogilvy notes that this mediation by the consumer can be an important part of brand formation (Roman, 2004). Only four advertisements show a clear photograph (that is, one showing the face) of a model dressed as Holmes, and only one uses the image of an actor well-known for playing Holmes on the contemporary stage and/or screen: Eille Norwood endorsing Phosferine in a *Girls' Cinema* advertisement of 1923 (Perdue, 2009: cover). Despite the large number of British actors who have played Holmes in the last eighty years, including Clive Brook, Arthur Wontner, Basil Rathbone, Peter Cushing, Douglas Wilmer, Jeremy Brett and many more, they have not been used to endorse products in Britain, probably due to the introduction of more complex and more expensive licensing regimes.[9] Basil Rathbone and Nigel Bruce have occasionally been used retrospectively to depict Holmes and Watson in advertisements, such as the promotion for Alphaderm's eczema treatment (undated but c. 1980 s), which indicates that their definitive portrayal of Holmes and Watson could be used to reach a new consumer generation (ACD1/F/15/153).

Because of the deerstalker and Inverness cape, Holmes is tied visually to the nineteenth century and never appears in contemporary clothing, even though he clearly moves through time to endorse products that did not exist in his 'true' period. In advertisements for Weaver to Wearer suits, for example (ACD1/F/15/259), he is observing the fashions in a 1950s street scene; in a promotion for Honeyrose Nicotine-Free Tobacco (ACD1/F/15/ 98) he is taking part in a 1960s 'ban the bomb' type protest march; and in an advertisement for Canon (ACD1/F/15/296) he carries an electronic typewriter tucked under his arm.

Dr Watson appears in only fifteen per cent of the advertisements, never without Holmes, and has a less structured iconography, usually being portrayed as elderly, portly, and with Victorian-style whiskers, wearing a bowler hat and carrying a walking stick. Occasionally he is illustrated with his medical bag. Watson, therefore, is recognisable only when he is teamed with Holmes. Surprisingly, a sense of place is absent from the advertising. Whereas on screen Holmes is often introduced by an 'establishing shot' of London's Houses of Parliament, such as in *The Hound of the Baskervilles* (1939), thus suggesting Holmes to be a symbol of, or a metonym for, London, in advertisements he is usually shown in a non-specific location. The Houses of Parliament do not appear, and other key identifiers of Victorian London such as hansom cabs, cobbled streets, gaslights, and fog are rare. Holmes's rooms are depicted in a small number of instances, usually with great attention to Victorian detail, and Baker Street is referenced in cases where either the advertiser has a connection with the street (Power Gas and Abbey National had Baker Street addresses), or because a pun is being made on the word 'baker' (such as in the 1986 Sherlock Holmes and 'Mr Baker' advertisements for Rank Hovis granary loaves; ACD1/F/15/188). If it were only the British advertisements which do not site Holmes visually in London, this might be understandable on the grounds that the British audience takes for granted that Holmes and London are synonymous, but this is also the case with US advertising too. Perhaps Holmes needs to be 'stripped' from his surroundings if the consumer is to focus on the brand message that the company is trying to communicate?[10]

Analysis of all of the advertisements reveals a number of selling propositions which Holmes is being used to convey: principal among these are expertise, observation, common sense, the clever consumer (a way of flattering the audience that they are as brilliant as Holmes), and elegance and distinction. The use of Holmes establishes a link between these qualities and the product. Judith Williamson argues that all advertising uses this technique of correlating 'feelings, moods or attributes to tangible objects, linking possible *un*attainable things with those that *are* attainable, and thus reassuring us that the former are within reach' (Williamson, 2000: 31). A third of the advertisements use Holmesian iconography but make no clear connection between the detective and their product or service, other than using his image to signify 'looking' or 'examining'. In these advertisements, the vital link between signifier and signified is broken and the transfer of meaning is therefore only partial. As Healey observes, 'the brand has enormous power to enhance the thing it represents, so long as it never loses its connection with the reality of that thing' (Healey, 2008: 11). Adding a Holmes image arbitrarily to an advertisement may draw the reader's eye (and perhaps that is the only intention) but offers no consumer 'promise' in terms creating an analogy between Holmes's attributes and the product.

Advertisements that emphasise expertise draw a parallel between the way Holmes deployed his expertise in difficult cases, and the knowledge and skills the company offers. If the consumer relies on the advertiser, they can be just as successful as Holmes – without the need to go through a lengthy process of deduction or investigation to find the solution. For example, Hogg Robinson used this technique in 1967 in an advertisement for its Estate Duty service (ACD1/F/15/130): alongside a graphic of deerstalker and pipe, the copy reads: 'Simple, as the late Mr Sherlock Holmes so often said...*after* he had solved his problems'. The topic is, of course, a highly complex one and Hogg Robinson are positioning themselves as making it look 'simple' because of their expertise. The reference to 'the late Mr Sherlock Holmes's is interesting: this is the only advertisement in the whole survey to suggest that he is no longer alive.

The source of the expertise is not always articulated. For instance, in an advertisement for AB Velox Tyres for cars in *Romance* magazine from the early 1900s, next to an illustration of Holmes wearing a dressing gown, is the copy: 'Sherlock Holmes says these tyres are the best. You wouldn't contradict him, would you?' (ACD1/F/15/1). The expectation is that the consumer, though not told how Holmes came to this conclusion (unlike the reader of the Doyle stories who would, of course, have had Holmes's deductions explained at the end of the narrative), would respect his judgement because of Holmes's expertise in many esoteric areas.[11] Similarly, an advertisement from the 1950s for Weaver to Wearer suits (ACD1/F/15/259) features a mock case which Holmes solves without explanation (see Figure 1). At the top is a monochrome illustration of Holmes and Watson seated in a modern taxi, gazing out of the side window at the pavement. Holmes wears a deerstalker and smokes a pipe, and both men have side-whiskers, positioning them in the Victorian period. The scene they observe, however, is a contemporary one, with a young fashionably dressed couple walking by. Underneath the illustration are the details of the case: the young man's fiancée had issued an ultimatum telling him to get a new suit or else she would return his engagement ring. Holmes found a source of quality suits from Weaver to Wearer at an affordable price, and the couple is reconciled. Though the source of Holmes's expertise is not clear, interestingly he and Watson have time-travelled in order to help the couple. Thus, good quality and taste is associated here with the Victorians.

A similar number of advertisements emphasise Holmes's success at solving mysteries through close observation, with the advertiser conveying that if the consumer looks closely at the product or service, they will note its superiority. Usually Watson figures in the role of Holmes's foil, the 'ordinary man' who cannot see the solution until it is explained to him.[12] Because of Watson's inclusion, many of the advertisements are in the form of a mock case, often in dialogue between the two men. A 1950s advertisement for Rexine leather cloth (see Figure 2) has the headline 'Watson is deceived' over a black and white illustration of Holmes reclining on a chaise playing his violin (ACD1/F/15/161). Both wear Victorian costume, but the chaise's covering and the style of furniture in the background is decidedly contemporary. The story hinges on Watson thinking that Holmes has bought new furniture, whereas he has actually had his old furniture recovered in Rexine. Holmes chides Watson: 'you really must cultivate your powers of observation' and the sign-off line is that 'it takes a pair of keen eyes' to distinguish Rexine from real leather. The implication here is that the average person who sees your newly-covered furniture will, like Watson, not be able to tell it from leather – only someone exceptional, like Holmes, would be able to tell the difference.

Figure 1 'Weaver to Wearer' (Courtesy of the Richard Lancelyn Green Collection, Portsmouth Museum)

Figure 2 'Rexine Leather Cloth' (Courtesy of the Richard Lancelyn Green Collection, Portsmouth Museum)

Watson is sometimes used in a humorous way to demonstrate points about observation. In a 1980s advertisement for Kellogg's Crunchy Nut Cornflakes he is depicted in a colour photograph at the breakfast table at 221b Baker Street with Holmes standing alongside wearing a dressing gown and holding a pipe (ACD1/F/15/214). The headline reads: 'Sherlock Holmes and the mystery of the vanishing Crunchy Nut Cornflakes'. Watson complains that the box is half-empty and Holmes, spotting the flake of cereal on Watson's lapel, observes that there has been no other thief but Watson. These powers of observation are actually irrelevant to the sales pitch of the product, the only point they convey being that Watson finds the cereal irresistible: good taste, therefore, is here ascribed to Watson rather than to Holmes, as is more usual. In a Teachers's whisky advertisement from the *Daily Telegraph* in 1971 Holmes's head is substituted for a bottle of whisky surmounted by a deerstalker (ACD1/F/15/300). This also takes the form of a mock case, though this time Watson is being teased by Holmes. Using his powers of observation, Holmes identifies the precise distillery from which the whisky originated, and then declares that the whisky was delivered to their premises by 'an ex-sergeant major with a wooden leg wearing a gold signet ring on the third finger of his right hand'. When Watson gasps in amazement, Holmes confesses he knows because 'I answered the door'. Although Watson here is being teased, their witty exchange draws on the persona established for Holmes in the Doyle stories, namely the way he was able to deduce an extraordinary amount of information about a client from one brief glance at them, or by examining one of their possessions: in 'The Adventure of the Blue Carbuncle' (1892), for example, he dazzles Watson with his analysis of a man's hat, deducing the owner's declining fortunes, intellectual ability, sedentary existence, and even the fact that his wife no longer loves him (Doyle, 1892: 147). Thus the Teachers's advertisement makes light of Holmes's powers of observation while still conveying the point that the taste of their whisky is distinctive enough to allow Holmes, with his excellent palate, to recognise the distillery, just as customers with discerning palates may do the same.

Why would anyone need Sherlock Holmes, when with a little application of common sense, the problem can be solved? This is the proposition in advertisements which appeared from the 1940s onwards, with most instances occurring in the 1970s and 1980s. Their debunking of Holmes correlates to the spoof Holmes films that were released during that period, such as *Sherlock Holmes' Smarter Brother* (1975), *The Hound of the Baskervilles* (1978) starring Peter Cook and Dudley Moore, and *Without a Clue* (1988). An early example of this common-sense technique is the BMK advertisement from the 1940s for carpet moth-proofing (ACD1/F/15/126). A cartoon moth, clad in deerstalker and Inverness cape, and accompanied by other moths in police helmets, is examining a BMK label through a magnifying glass: 'It doesn't call for much detection to discover whether a carpet's really deadly to moths', says the copy. The common-sense proposition also often implies that a straightforward examination of the facts will inevitably lead to a particular conclusion, even though these 'facts' may be contentious. For example, in 1984 the London Borough of Bromley issued a flyer arguing for the abolition of the Greater London Council (ACD1/F/15/30). On the cover is a cartoon of Holmes and Watson, with speech bubbles. Holmes says: 'It's elementary, my dear Watson. All the facts show that the GLC just isn't necessary.' Watson replies: 'But what about all these scare stories, Holmes? By Jove, I'd better read on'. The theme is then abandoned in the rest of the flyer, but has done its work: it has made the issue seem a matter of common sense rather than debate, particularly by using the word 'facts' which are associated with Holmes, and by having the more gullible Watson mention 'scare stories'. Even Watson's use of the phrase 'by Jove' is not there by accident, as it establishes him as an old-fashioned figure. Consumers will therefore align themselves with Holmes's argument.

Another major category of advertising is consumer flattery: a product or service aligned with Holmes suggests cleverness, and therefore by implication the product's consumer is also clever. Such advertisements range from 1900 onwards, mostly in the consumer press, but achieve prominence from the 1950s to the 1970s. Some are overt: a 1961 advertisement in *The Observer* for Sandeman's Armada Cream Sherry invites readers to identify with one of three characters, who are photographed alongside a giant bottle of sherry (ACD1/F/15/159). The figures are a fashionably dressed young woman, an older academic-looking man in tweed suit and bow tie, and a man dressed as Holmes, wearing deerstalker and Inverness, holding a pipe in one hand and a glass of sherry in the other. The copy-line reads: 'professors drink it, it sharpens their wits...young things drink it, it thrills them to bits...private eyes drink it, then everything fits'. Whereas the academic might represent the sherry market's traditional consumer, and the 'young thing' a new market sector, the man depicted as a 'private eye' is not, despite the American term, Philip Marlowe or Sam Spade, but Holmes. This combines a glamorous profession with the consumer's prior knowledge of Holmes's cleverness – qualities that the consumer can now buy for themselves. A 1950s advertisement in *Good Housekeeping* magazine for Tootal non-iron fabrics shows glamorous women wearing the latest fashions (ACD1/F/15/20). Each woman also wears a deerstalker and holds a giant magnifying glass. The copy makes clear that these are savvy high-fashion consumers, but without the washing and ironing problems this usually entails. The use of women subverts the traditional Holmes iconography. In the Conan Doyle stories, Holmes was synonymous with masculinity through his links to 'science, practical application, exact knowledge, logic and system', all of which were gendered as masculine in the nineteenth century (Kestner, 1997 : 29) and, though he is not mentioned in the advertisement, the imagery flatters the consumer by comparing her to Holmes. The trade press have also used the 'clever consumer' technique: an advertisement from 1979 for Kodak Microfilm shows a black and white illustration of Holmes and Watson, in Victorian costume, leaning over a modern microfilm desk at which a fashionably dressed young woman is sitting in front of the latest technology (ACD1/F/15/196). 'With one or two clues, you can locate a long lost document in seconds', reads the headline. The copy mentions Holmes by name and describes the Kodak automatic retrieval system as searching through the microfilm files 'like a detective'. The juxtaposition of the Victorian detective with his magnifying glass, and the 1970s technology, isolates these two eras as symbolising the pinnacle of achievement in detection and thus allies the Kodak product with greatness. A business, therefore, that chooses the Kodak product is not only as clever as Holmes but can surpass him: after all, the machine performs in seconds what would have taken Holmes time to achieve.

Another form of consumer flattery is for the advertiser to suggest that Holmes is synonymous with elegance and distinction, and that by buying a particular product, the consumer can acquire such qualities. Crawfords biscuits and Drambuie have both stressed the elegance and distinction message in their advertisements. A series of Drambuie advertisements in 1989 took the form of an elaborate mock case. In each instance, Holmes provides the solution, which resides in the brand qualities of Drambuie. In one, headlined 'A Singular Case of Duplicity', he uncovers an imposter, a thief who took the place of his twin brother but was found out because he did not have a Drambuie after dinner. 'Looks can be deceptive', says Holmes, 'but good taste is always unmistakable'. In another, 'The Adventure of the Disappearing Diplomat', Holmes realises a man has been abducted because he has not drunk his glass of Drambuie: 'no man of discernment ... would leave a glass of that fine liqueur untouched unless it was against his will', he says. Holmes is thus positioned as a man who is not only observant, but who understands exactly what good taste and discernment are. Each advertisement is accompanied by a colour photograph of a scene from the drama, where the setting is clearly Victorian, and within the copy there is a small line-drawing of a glass of Drambuie in a style that gives it an old-fashioned look, revealing of the importance of tradition to the age-group and class at which the advertisement is aimed (ACD1/F/15/57–59).

It was noted earlier that a sense of place, in terms of visual reference, is missing from almost all of the advertisements. Only Typhoo Tea makes Britishness a key message in their use of Holmes, despite the fact that his nationality is a key component of his character. London icons were used in the Typhoo Tea campaign (undated, but possibly the 1970s or 1980s) which featured locations such as Piccadilly and Green Park on a series of postcards. The 'Baker Street' postcard has a colour photograph of a deerstalker and pipe, with a cup of Typhoo revealed through a magnifying glass (ACD1/F/15/185). No other London location in the series is identified with a character, real or fictional, in this way.

Only one advertiser capitalised on the Holmes–Watson partnership, implying that the product or service on offer is also the fruit of a great partnership. The (undated) Alphaderm advertisement is in the form of a mailshot to UK doctors on the theme of 'classic combinations' and the envelope, letter, and accompanying brochure feature photographs of Basil Rathbone and Nigel Bruce in stills from their 1939 film *The Hound of the Baskervilles* (ACD1/F/15/153). The theme of the copy is that Holmes would have been nothing without Watson, a parallel being made with Alphaderm's eczema treatment which has a particular combination of ingredients which ensure success.

Despite the strong 'brand values' associated with Holmes, not every advertiser interpreted these correctly: one wonders about the effectiveness of the 1960s advertisement for Erinmore tobacco in which a woman in a low-cut Victorian dress stands under a gas-lamp in the street (ACD1/F/15/228). Standing with his back to her is a Holmes in deerstalker and Inverness cape, smoking his pipe and taking no notice. The headline reads 'nothing can tempt you away' and the implication is that the taste of Erinmore tobacco is finer than any other experience that might be on offer. Holmes is frequently used in tobacco advertising, alluding to his pipe-smoking and monograph on the different kinds of tobacco ash, but his well-known imperviousness to women means that the brand value on which Erinmore is attempting to draw has been turned upside-down. In 'The Adventure of the Copper Beeches' (1892), Watson notes: 'as to Miss Violet Hunter...Holmes...manifested no further interest in her when once she had ceased to be the centre of one of his problems' (Doyle, 1892 : 285). Had the advertiser used an illustration of a murder taking place behind his back, it might have drawn more sure-footedly on Holmes's established persona.

The largest category of advertisements examined makes no successful connection with Holmesian qualities. Some use Holmes's iconography but do not link it to the product: for example, a point-of-sale dispenser for Honeyrose Nicotine-free Tobacco from the 1960s has a cartoon of a number of figures on a 'ban the bomb' type march, carrying banners reading 'save a bomb with Honeyrose' (ACD1/F/15/98). Holmes is present in this line-up, as is a traffic warden, a Cuban guerrilla, a burglar carrying a bag of swag, and a Scot in Highland dress. None are smoking and no reference is made to any of these characters in the subsequent copy: the use of Holmes therefore seems arbitrary. Myer's Beds' advertisement in *Ideal Home* in 1961 tries to evoke a mystery but does not follow it through. It features a photograph of a double bed with a Holmes-figure wearing a deerstalker and Inverness cape, with a pipe clamped in his mouth, bending over it, examining the surface of the 'buttonless' mattress with his magnifying glass (ACD1/F/15/89). Despite words like 'investigating' and 'elementary' in the copy, it is unclear what contribution Holmes is making.

Even though the campaigns discussed here vary in terms of how successfully they link the product with Holmes' attributes, these advertisers, by tapping into his widespread recognition to generate profit, were signalling Holmes's value. For Perdue, the clarity of Holmes's public image makes him such a powerful icon, which recalls Maugham's point about the way Doyle hammered Holmes's idiosyncrasies into the minds of the reader (Perdue, 2009: 19). There is a danger, of course, that such a universally recognised character, who has become a transmedia brand in his own right, might often overshadow the advertised product, particularly as no advertiser seems to have undertaken a sustained campaign using Holmes whereby he might have become synonymous with one particular product and its brand qualities. Holmes continues to be 'his own man', a floating signifier that can be applied at will to different advertising campaigns in different historical situations.

Holmes's omnipresence in advertising is due to something more fundamental than his widely recognised attributes of appearance or character. What Holmes offers is a neutral and almost classless authority figure, whose judgement is utterly reliable. He represents, as Stephen Knight defines it, 'a bridge between the disorderly experience of life and a dream of order' (1976: 105) and that is why advertisers have returned to him again and again to endorse their products.

Advertising aims to create, and tap into, consumer aspirations, so selecting a figure who already represents an aspirational model for a wide cross-section of consumers provides a short-cut to the alignment between the product and its perceived qualities. Even in the 'common sense' advertisements of the 1970s and 1980s, though the copy might imply that good judgements can be made by the consumer without recourse to Holmes, his very presence indicates that he is still a necessary 'yardstick' by which to make decisions. Not one advertisement in my survey of the Doyle archive mentions that Holmes is a fictional character: indeed his 'unreality' has helped to prolong his use in advertising, as generations of consumers project their preconceptions of the character onto each new incarnation. Holmes is so embedded in British popular consciousness that most of these preconceptions do not stem from the Doyle stories themselves, but from plays, films, TV series, or cartoons – or indeed from other advertisements. In his definition of cultural icons, Douglas Holt argues that they are 'exemplary symbols that people accept as a shorthand to represent important ideas'. They serve as 'foundational compass points – anchors of meaning continually referenced in entertainment, journalism, politics and advertising' and as a result of this continuous referencing they are transportable across time, performing 'the particular myth society especially needs at a given historical moment' (Holt, 2004 : 2). All of the Holmes's advertisements are not only drawing on the many historical layers of meaning which make up his established persona, they are also adding new layers of their own, and thus Holmes continues to evolve as a cultural reference. This constant evolution means that Holmes is always relevant and his presence in the public imagination allows audiences to suspend their disbelief even when, in the 'case of the multiplying millions' campaign, Holmes himself appears 'in person' to convince the people of Nottingham to put their money into National Savings.

Notes

1. Richard Lancelyn Green amassed one of the world's largest and most comprehensive collections of material on Doyle. When he died in 2004, he left his collection to Portsmouth: in addition to 16,000 books and hundreds of objects, there are around 40,000 documents ranging from film stills, scripts, and theatre programmes, to original Doyle manuscripts and family correspondence, Spiritualist photographs and pamphlets, booklets and mailings from over 200 Sherlockian societies, and a wide range of material on the continuing phenomenon that is Sherlock Holmes (including stamps, greetings cards, menus, calendars, newspaper cuttings, and games). The collection of advertisements forms just one small part of this archive.

2. Advertisements in the Doyle Collection consist mostly of tear-sheets from magazines and newspapers, so in some cases estimates have had to be used for dates and media. All ads are from this collection unless otherwise noted. The reference numbers used when referring to specific advertisements are the Portsmouth Museum catalogue numbers for these items.
3. Gillette's play opened in 1899, and Perdue speculates on the date of Doyle's letter to the publisher of *The Strand Magazine*, H. G. Smith, as being around 1897 (Perdue, 2009: 3).
4. Universal agreement with Doyle Estate, 24 Feb. 1942, Arthur Conan Doyle Collection.
5. Letters between Denis Conan Doyle and Fitelson & Mayers: 18 June, 24 June and 26 June 1941; 6 Feb. 1942; memorandum relating to International Shoe Co Sept. 1942 (all from ACD Collection, uncatalogued).
6. Letters from Fitelson and Mayers to Denis Conan Doyle 18 Oct 1941 and 26 May 1949 (ACD Collection, uncatalogued). Honey was suggested as a suitable product because Holmes was said, on his retirement, to have moved to Sussex to keep bees: in the Conan Doyle story 'His Last Bow', Holmes describes the 'magnum opus' of his later years as being his 'Practical Handbook of Bee Culture' (Doyle, 1997: 193–4).
7. Letter from Denis Conan Doyle to Abbot Kimbell 16 Aug 1951 (ACD Collection, uncatalogued).
8. Dave Itzkoff, in the *New York Times*, has attempted to unpick the complexities of how the rights to the characters changed hands.
9. Actor endorsement was more widespread in the US, with Basil Rathbone appearing in promotions in the 1940s and 1950s for Booth's House of Lords Gin, Walker's Bourbon, Chesterfield cigarettes, Petri Wines, and Stratford Pens, and Clive Brook endorsing Otis elevators in 1934.
10. Interestingly, this absence of place does not apply to greetings cards featuring a Holmes figure, where the Houses of Parliament, London skylines, fog, and cobbled streets are much more common (ACD1/F/11).
11. Clearly *Romance* magazine, despite its title, had male readers.
12. This convention is turned on its head in the 2009 television commercial for Red Bull, where Watson proves himself to be more observant and quick-witted than Holmes, thanks to his intake of Red Bull.

2
Sherlock Holmes and a Politics of Adaptation

Neil McCaw

The history of the adaptation of Arthur Conan Doyle's Sherlock Holmes stories is unrivalled in terms of the sheer number and diversity of adaptive works. Holmes has been part of (to give just a few examples) the evolution of silent cinema, World War II propaganda, and, most recently, the information technology explosion of the twenty-first century.[1] As such, Brian McFarlane's (albeit slightly anodyne) statement that '[the] conditions within the film [and television] industry and the prevailing cultural and social climate...are two major determinants' (1996: 21) of adaptations has been borne out time and again. And because Holmes adaptations are perhaps the most palimpsestuous[2] of all popular-cultural reworkings, the interaction with socio-cultural contexts is often multi-textured, with adapted texts appearing to both reinforce and challenge the prevailing status quo in a host of ways, sometimes within the same text. This is certainly the case with the focus of this chapter, the televisual imagining of Sherlock Holmes during the 1980s and 1990s in the UK, which has a complex relationship with the 'Thatcherite'[3] political rhetoric and ideology of the period. As shall become clear, the adaptations function as arenas within which traditional Tory[4] and more fluid free-market impulses compete with each other over the vexed status and significance of the national past within the context of the present. Television, in this case, does not 'inoculate' the audience against the implications of social change; rather, it is an active feature of this change.[5]

During the final decades of the twentieth century the political, governmental rhetoric of 'Thatcherism' was predominant. It was an ideology that was, on one level, fundamentally concerned with themes such as 'authority, law and order, patriotism, national unity, [and] the family' (Jacques, 1983: 53), with an accompanying nostalgic rhetoric conjuring up an esteemed national past: 'we ... are certain that we belong to a "happy breed," as Shakespeare put it in the mouth of John of Gaunt' (Thatcher, 16 July 1979). Crucially, for this study of contemporaneous versions of Sherlock Holmes, this nostalgia celebrated *in particular* the supposed moral, political and economic order of the Victorian era as a historical model. This was a time when (so the story went) the 'country became great' (Thatcher, 16 Jan. 1983). The nineteenth century, therefore, was to be imitated, an idealised paradigm of harmonious, commerce-focused, respectful social interaction amidst a mythologising quasi-hagiography of the Victorians themselves. This mythology urged the similarities between past and present as the basis for a regeneration of contemporary British/Englishness at a time of perceived collective debilitation following years of turbulence (the 1970s) and a decline in national self-esteem. A return to the values of the nineteenth century was thus viewed as a return to a national *essence*, a Tory vision of the UK in which *tradition* underpinned the present.

The accompanying ideological reading of the nineteenth century as stable and composed implied a romanticised, ultimately ordered, *detectable* Victorian world that was (like that of the Granada series) a 'pleasurable fantasy' (Tulloch, 2000: 37). The carefully-realised staging of and implied reverence for the nineteenth century in the Holmes episodes accorded with this selective national-historical discourse, offering what Martin Kayman has called 'genuine narrative satisfactions' (1992: 5). The earlier Granada stories in particular work to soothe the anxieties of the national present with narratives in which England is ultimately manageable and comprehensible; it was not until the ninth episode broadcast that anyone is actually murdered, for instance. Viewers, therein, are transported back to an imagined past where social and political tension is smoothed over and (eventually, by the time of the narrative closure) replaced by an atmosphere of harmony and quietude: 'the restoration of the law' offered by the 'archetypal detective story's structural foundation' (Plain, 2001: 4).

A significant part of the comfort provided by the initial adaptations and their images of the past comes from the way they draw on the Doyle stories in great detail, going 'back to Holmes's roots, so to speak, with a series which faithfully recreates the Victorian milieu' (Harris, 1984: 2) All of the episodes in the first series show a clear reliance on Doyle, with *The Dancing Men, The Solitary Cyclist, The Crooked Man, The Speckled Band, The Blue Carbuncle, The Copper Beeches, The Norwood Builder, The Resident Patient,* and *The Red-Headed League* maintaining their original plotlines and settings and fulfilling their familiar function as detective narratives: 'ritual acts of expiation which isolate and project cultural guilt upon some scapegoat rather than offer any social analysis or critique' (Thomas, 1999: 42). In so doing they took their place in the minds of contemporary viewers as 'amazingly faithful adaptations of the original stories [with] ... respectful and atmospheric performances ... and settings' (Nollen, 1996: 234).

This 'literal' quality marked out these adaptations from other examples of the wider cultural recycling of the great detective across a multiplicity of forms during the twentieth century. Because Granada's incarnation of Holmes so clearly rejected the ethos of pastiche it had more in common with the British television versions of Holmes of the 1950s and 1960s starring Douglas Wilmer and Peter Cushing than it did many of the others. And, if anything, Granada's producer Michael Cox was striving for an even greater sense of textual fidelity than was apparent in the Wilmer/Cushing vehicles. There was an almost dogmatic sense of the Holmesian 'canon' of original stories being the definitive guide to the series, with fidelity to this canon seen as an indicator of cultural value and (seemingly) moral righteousness; there was a perceived *duty* to be loyal to the originating sources. This commitment to *authenticity* underpinned the development of the series and its diligent focus on the Doylean texts, a feature recognised by viewers and critics alike: 'the 32 Sherlock Holmes films which Michael Cox produced for Granada Television maintain the integrity of Doyle's texts in ways which other adaptations, including the famous series of films featuring Basil Rathbone and Nigel Bruce, do not' (Trembley, 1994: 11). This authenticity was embodied in Cox's Holmesian reference manual, *The Baker Street File*,[6] which all of the crew working on the series were expected to follow to the letter.

The producer's commitment to an idealised authenticity manifested itself very clearly in the first episode broadcast, *A Scandal in Bohemia*. There is a concerted attempt to secure the veracity of the Holmesian *product* through the title credits, which conjure up a Victorian world of carriages, glistening cobbled streets, newspaper vendors advertising salacious headlines of crime and deceit, inquisitive beggars, and all the while Holmes looking down on this Victorian maelstrom with a knowing air of calm and superiority. The casting of Gayle Hunnicutt as Irene Adler is particularly well observed, for although the image she presents is that of a refined Englishwoman rather than the worldly American of the Doyle story, the reality is that Hunnicutt is in fact American, and so the deference shown to Doyle is particularly subtle. The narrative itself contains almost all of the key elements of the originating tale:

the thwarted attempts to recover the incriminating photograph, Holmes's worship of 'the woman', the vulgarity and dim-wittedness of the foreign King, and the uncanny methods of detection. There are *some* changes of emphasis in relation to the original short story, however. Watson is not married (this does not fit the revised chronology of the TV series), Holmes's drug-use is profiled (with Watson interrogating him, 'morphine or cocaine?'), and Adler is rather more of 'an adventuress' than before. Much of the late-Victorian chauvinism towards women is also gone – whereas in the Doyle story Holmes reads Adler's behaviour based upon a stereotypical view of women in their maternal and wifely roles, the Granada episode is silent on exactly *how* he predicts her behaviour. Yet, despite these *refinements*, what is most apparent in the episode is the sustained attempt to be faithful to the implied essence of the original short story, culminating in Cox's 'homage to Sidney Paget' (1997: 42), wherein sketches by the original illustrator of the Holmes stories in *The Strand Magazine* move centre stage; the closing shot sees Brett bent into a pose which then morphs into a Paget illustration, before closing credits which feature a range of other Paget sketches.

As such, the commitment to bringing the Doyle stories to life in an authentic fashion (i.e. in keeping with what the producers *believed to be* their original style, setting and tone) was diligently apparent. Indeed, both of the early series of the Granada Holmes adaptations, *The Adventures of Sherlock Holmes* and *The Return of Sherlock Holmes*, demonstrate a sustained engagement with the originating texts, a quest for the holy grail of authenticity supported by Jeremy Brett as Holmes and his own form of textual Puritanism.[7] Even when the Doyle short stories are, at times, amended (extra contextual history in *The Empty House*, the recasting of Anglo-Italian identity in *The Six Napoleons*, the twisting of criminal culpability in *The Priory School* and *The Abbey Grange*, and so forth), an overarching dedication to conjuring up what was seen as the spirit of Doyle – Holmes in his Victorian context – was apparent in each of the episodes, with the primacy of the original writings respected to the *nth* degree.

One consequence of this is that the image of 'the Victorian' conveyed in the series is idealised, with the English nation of the past represented as a desirably attractive escape from the present. Social problems and dilemmas can be overcome (the audience could infer) if the society of the later-twentieth century became more like that of the nineteenth century, drawing on a prevailing sense of the inherent continuities between the selectively-imagined past and the unstable present.

The Granada television productions thus seem to be complicit (albeit perhaps unwittingly) in the ongoing political validation of seductive, romanticised 'Victorian Values', the popularity of the series illustrating a broader cultural *ache* for what Raphael Samuel has called 'lost stabilities' (1992: 9) in its articulation of 'the mythology of a [past] unified national self' (1992: 18). The Victorian period becomes all that the present is not, the desired Other of Thatcherite policy-making which claimed that the result of men and women being 'encouraged, and helped, to accept responsibility for themselves and their families' (Thatcher 'The Healthy Society', 1977: 81) was an apotheosis of coherence, and order, and triumph over both external and internal threat. Therein, the Holmes adaptations serve as an 'area of safety, of confirmation of identity, of power ... "outside" that of risk, of challenge to identity, of helplessness' (Ellis, 1992: 166).

For Andrew Higson, this celebration of, and longing for, the Victorian past manifested itself in what he calls 'visually spectacular pastiche' (2006: 91), a description Granada would have contested. Nevertheless, it is true that within these Holmes episodes there is a calming, critique-free corrective to the troubled political context of 1980s Britain. Central to this is the way in which the narratives of detection ensure that (in Auden's terms), 'the guilty other has been expelled, a cure effected' (Auden, 1988: 24). Images of an age of fundamental order, characterised by the unifying processes of criminal detection, stood in stark contrast to the political backdrop of the UK, with neat and tidy detective tales encouraging viewers to (at least partly) forget the harsher external social realities[8] and the only too apparent fact that contemporaneous crime was not a matter of such socially-detached televisual play. Instead, it had 'a material base. The dispossessed in our society are not only more likely to be involved in crime, but they are also more likely to be victims of crime' (Brown & Sparks, 1989: 151).

This side-stepping of the troubles of 1980s Britain through reassuring tales of crimes honourably solved was particularly important at a time when the British police force was, as Robert Reiner has indicated, almost continually 'subject to a storm of political conflict and controversy' (2000: ix). Contentious police actions during the social unrest of the miners' strike (1984–5) and the urban riots in Liverpool, Brixton and Handsworth (1985) cast the police as villains as much as heroes. The characterisation of the great detective and his partner (despite the tendency to lampoon the *official* police) in Granada's *Sherlock Holmes* overlays this negative perception of law enforcement with an enduring myth of beneficence and compassion in the operation of the wider criminal justice system. The result is crime experienced as little more than what Anita Biressi has called 'a leisure pursuit' (2001: 1), within narrative configurations that ameliorate the position of the socially-situated viewer.

The Holmes series thus offers a riposte to the more dramatic – even hysterical – media representation of crime on television, wherein the 'post-modern maelstrom of perpetual disintegration and renewal, of fragmentation and fear, of struggle and contradiction and of seemingly random violence and criminality' (Osborne, 1995: 27) is replaced by a re-establishment of moral order and the seduction of 'high production values, strong supporting casts, atmospheric scores and so on' (Jackson, 1993: 26). For many viewers this escapism is to be *celebrated*: 'compared with the BBC's current run of gloomy pointless plays, the adventures of Granada's *Return of Sherlock Holmes* are little pools of period fun in the dramatic desert. They are beautifully acted, lovingly dressed up and exciting' (Kingsley, 1986: 19). The series took on the status of a period heritage classic, one that entertained and distracted the audience by conjuring up images of the nineteenth century that (if the contemporaneous reception is to be believed) stopped short of the sort of clichéd pastiche of 'over-furnished parlours, horse-drawn carriages on cobbled streets and a lot of arch acting by persons in sidewhiskers or bustles' (Kingsley, 1984: 19) that audiences had come to expect from other Victorian adaptations of the period.

Nevertheless, despite the fact that the early series of Granada adaptations sat well with the Thatcherite sense of a rehabilitating modern nation defined by an ongoing acknowledgement of its heritage, this ideology was, in truth, Janus-faced. The major paradox is that Thatcherism simultaneously lauded a less explicitly Tory strand of Victorian-ness, one originally articulated by the prominent nineteenth-century celebrant of seemingly unbounded ideas of social mobility and economic self-determination, the populist Samuel Smiles: 'the spirit of self-help ... [is] the root of all genuine growth in the individual; and, exhibited in the lives of many ... the true source of national vigour and strength' (1866: 1) The inherent energy of this Smilesian philosophy suggested a challenge to, rather than a reinforcement of, existing social structures, and as a result Thatcher's modern incarnation of his 'wisdom' (alongside her traditionalism) makes clear both the 'selectivity of ... [her] Victorian vision' and 'its innate ambiguities' (Evans, 1997: 601).

Thus, although the Conservative government seemed to zealously worship at the altar of (pseudo-Victorian) tradition, it was also aspiring and iconoclastic and rooted in the necessity for change. An envisioned compatibility between the imagined, more fossilised sense of the nineteenth century and the lived twentieth century might have been an important aspect of the Thatcherite popular mythology, wherein self-determination, individual responsibility, and careful economic stewardship were deemed central, but the implications of a coterminous individualised self-determination offered threat as well as succour to 'the way of things'. The dynamic energy of Thatcherism was its 'politics of aspiration' (Shankardass, 1989: 2857), an energy that was far less protective of the status quo than its more unambiguously Tory foundation. The thrust of its economic underpinning was the worm in the bud of Tory order and convention, an impetus towards individual people achieving individual aims for individual (almost always economic) motivations, as Margaret Thatcher's personal self-promotion as the grocer's daughter who had risen up from humble stock to achieve high political office made manifest: 'my father was a grocer, but he employed some people in the shop and in another small shop at the other end of the town, so he, having left school at thirteen, provided employment for other people' (Thatcher 'TV Interview for Channel 4'). The relentless Smilesian logic of 'self-help' was at odds with the image of a nostalgic, socially static Victorianism, illustrating the wider ideological shift from 'an essentially collectivist climate of opinion ... [to] an essentially individualistic' one (Douglas, 1989: 404), implicitly validating fundamental changes to the nature of British society.

Thus, for the British government during the 1980s, 'being British' came to be identified not only with a sanctioned national past, but also with a dynamic, changing present. Britain was to be 'restored' on the basis of 'competition and profitability; with tight money and sound finance ("You can't pay yourself more than you earn !!")' – the national economy based upon 'the model of the household budget' (Hall, 1983: 29). Consequently, Thatcher's worldview looked beyond exclusively Tory values such as 'nation, family, duty, authority, standards, [and] traditionalism' and towards 'the aggressive themes of a revived neo-liberalism – self-interest, competitive individualism, anti-statism' (Hall, 1983: 29), which opened up an underlying fissure in contemporaneous rhetoric about the security and fixity of the nineteenth-century past as a political/rhetorical paradigm.

By the time of *The Case-Book of Sherlock Holmes* series (1990), this fissure was writ large on the landscape of the Granada project. Since the end of 1984, the production company had experienced massive commercial success with its internationally-exported Holmes adaptations;

almost immediately, company pre-tax profits had risen sharply to £53.7 million.[9] And by 1990 the series had been exported all over the world and successfully merchandised, even generating revenue through marketed tours of the set as part of the Granada Studios visitor experience in Manchester. Yet, paradoxically, at the same time Granada's commitment to the loyal translation of Doyle's source texts was on the wane. The apparent confidence the producers had that these worldwide audiences were buying into their Holmesian *brand* notwithstanding any reverence for Doyle's works, combined with the impact of the free-market influenced Peacock Report of 1986 and the consequent *Broadcasting Act* of 1990 (which facilitated an expanding role for the private sector in UK broadcasting),[10] led to budgets for programmes being slashed and episodes filmed more cheaply than before in an attempt to maximise commercial yield so as to meet the running costs of the entire production company and turn a healthy profit. This was vital because the economies of scale that had existed previously, whereby cameramen and behind-the-scenes staff were employed by the broadcasters and shared across a variety of programmes, were lost in an environment where in-house staff eventually became a thing of the past:

> nothing would ever be the same again, the old certainties were dead and the harsh realities of capitalism arrived at Wood Lane and Portland Place. Whole departments were razed and working practices abolished, and something called an internal market was put in place. *Radio Times* was outsourced, the permanent make-up staff went, engineers, editors and set-designers were suddenly out of a job. (Fry, 7 May 2008)

The Sherlock Holmes episodes thus came to embody a momentous shift in the culture of UK TV production, with profit (rather than quality or esteem) becoming the inescapable measure of value for independent broadcasters, and with the marketing of a series (especially overseas) deemed exponentially important. This change was so wide-ranging that its victims even included the Chairman of Granada TV himself, a man with a long-standing reputation for *quality* rather than economic profitability: 'Now David Plowright, highly respected boss of Granada TV, has been axed – and throughout the world of independent television alarm bells must be ringing' (Bonner, 1992: 6). As if to signal the new way of things the Chief Executive of the company, Gerry Robinson, immediately announced an agenda 'for both redundancies and cuts in programming costs' (Benzikie, 1992: 39).

It was inevitable that these momentous Thatcherite changes would have particular consequences for expensive, logistically-challenging historical TV dramas such as the Holmes series. Despite an ongoing wider cultural rhetoric about the need for 'quality' television, which led to the establishment of the 'welcome and necessary'[11] 'Campaign for Quality Television', the Holmes adaptations began to feel the pinch in their quest for the *authentic* Holmes. The grand ambitions of Granada were scaled down, undermining the attempt to offer 'literal' inter- pretations of Doyle's stories. Adaptations such as *The Disappearance of Lady Carfax* (the first episode of the *Case-Book* series), had their settings rewritten, in this case from the Lausanne of the original story (which was judged as being too expensive to film) to 'Cumberland', fundamen- tally changing the tenor of the episode and the tone and focus of the narrative.

This relaxation of the ties between originating tales and adapted scripts was furthered when the profit-conscious TV schedulers in the UK became transfixed by the commercial success of the two-hour *Inspector Morse* films produced by Zenith Productions for Central Television (which had begun in 1987), thus encouraging Granada to develop a series of two-hour Holmes episodes. The problem was that this market-conscious decision took no cognizance of the fact that feature-length episodes adapted from short stories would require significant 'padding out' if they were to fit this TV format (whereas the initial Morse films were drawn from full-length novels). Consequently, the original commitment to the Doyle works became increasingly compromised as additional (non-canonical, contemporary-influenced) material was added. *The Master Blackmailer*, for instance, the first of these feature-length episodes and based upon the story 'Charles Augustus Milverton', is radically different from the Doyle tale, with the extent of the rewriting summed up by the TV critic Susan Young: 'Granada's scriptwriters added most of the interesting bits, including a soldier blackmailed for flirting with a transvestite dancer, and even the identity of the murderer' (1992: 33). The next film, *The Last Vampyre*, is little more than a Holmesian pastiche, what Jeremy Brett later called 'pretend Doyle' (Stuart Davies, 2007: 164), an adapta- tion 'trolloping about with shrieks and gibbering and sexual innuendo' (Banks-Smith, 1993: 10). And its successor, *The Eligible Bachelor*, bears almost no resemblance to the originating story.

In truth, throughout the feature-length series of adaptations and the subsequent *The Memoirs of Sherlock Holmes* (even though this returned to the shorter format), fidelity to Doyle's work seemed at times little more than a coincidence, as episodes such as *The Three Gables*, *The Dying*

Detective, The Golden Pince-Nez, The Red Circle and *The Cardboard Box* illustrate. By the end, the Granada producers had become almost limitlessly flexible in terms of the specification provided by the originating Holmes stories: 'any fool can ascertain that it's the work of Jeremy Paul, who used to adapt Doyle's stories but now writes his own' (Bailey, 1994: 9). It was clear that Granada were now 'taking liberties with its characters' with screenplays only 'loosely based' on Doyle's work (Miller, 1994: 47), and that the vision of the Victorian world that the series had originally perpetrated had been usurped by one of stereotypes and exaggerations: 'Granada's handsomely-upholstered series revels in the flamboyant flourish of Victorian melodrama. The first flaring of Jeremy Brett's nostrils is the equivalent of firing a starting gun in the race to go over the top' (Paton, 1994: 29). For one critic, Holmes had, by this stage, lapsed into the 'operatic' (Bailey, 1994: 9), signalling what was widely seen as a relentless decline into cliché and caricature.

The Cardboard Box was the final story to be broadcast, and this poignantly captures the extent of the 'liberties' being taken. Many of the defining elements of the Doyle story have been changed, and the narrative is embellished with numerous extraneous elements. It begins with the marriage of Mary and Jim Browner, amidst a new storyline about bodysnatchers in London that Holmes is helping Inspector Hawkins investigate. There is a running joke about Holmes's supposed unease at Christmas (with the episode moved from the baking hot summer to a season of picture-postcard, snow-laden festivities), and Holmes is seen throughout as being uncharacteristically preoccupied with Christmas trees and decorations and a desire to buy Watson an ideal Christmas present. Additional characters are created for the occasion, such as the Belgian lodger and lover of Sarah Cushing, and personalities are reworked, most notably in the case of Sarah's own flagrant promiscuity: 'you drive me mad Sarah, sometimes I think I'm possessed'. There is also a much more explicit focus on English sexual double standards: 'you English are such hypocrites'. The script improvises on the theme of the original rather than taking any particular notice of Doyle's story, adding in elements that conjure up a broader, stereotypical conception of the Victorian nineteenth century, including a fascination with secretive sexual machinations and commercial, Christmas-card images of the past.

As Brian McFarlane suggests, the tumultuousness of a period such as the Thatcherite years inevitably imprints itself upon the cultural texts of the time. Indeed, in terms of the Granada Sherlock Holmes adaptations, changes in British cultural life between 1984 (the year of the first episode) and 1994 (the year of the last) were inextricably interwoven into the series. And because of the profound nature of these changes, especially within British television broadcasting, an examination of the Granada series offers a particularly graphic illustration of the inter-action between context and adapted texts. The broadcasting world into which the first series emerged was radically different from that of the later episodes, wherein the consequences of a free-market ethos in inde-pendent television production fundamentally reshaped the British tele-vision industry. Ultimately, the 1990 *Broadcasting Act*, a symptom of a wider process of socio-cultural transition and an embodiment of the prevailing Thatcherite ideology, worked against Granada's originating aspirations for an *authentic* reconstruction of the Victorian world of Sherlock Holmes as defined by the work of Arthur Conan Doyle. The meticulous methodology of the earlier series was first hindered and then ultimately abandoned as commercial income generation and financial viability became ever-greater concerns. Rehearsal schedules were cut back, filming took place more quickly, narratives were relocated, and episodes were padded out with stereotypes and the accoutrements of un-Conan-Doylean melodrama in order to more profitably exploit the hungry market for Holmes which was, by that point, firmly established. By the end of the series the ailing Brett was phoning his performances in, reliant not on Doyle but on the goodwill of the viewer to carry the whole thing off: 'there is something approaching a *tradition* [emphasis added] ... in Jeremy Brett's assumption of the role' (Paterson, 1994: 29). His Holmes had become a montage of known, understood and expected conventions of delivery and mannerisms that he had defined for himself and which (through reputation as much as anything) papered over the cracks of the later pastiche scripts.

Thus 'getting it right' in terms of adapting the original stories became an increasingly forlorn task, one which was then abandoned completely. The Thatcherite worship of a particular version of the world of the Victorians, suitably embodied in the earlier lavish Granada episodes, was ultimately undermined by its own free-market reforms, rooted in an inherent, ideological avariciousness for a form of success measured in exclusively economic terms. Consequently, the series makes manifest the internal contradictions of this ideology, wherein Tory traditionalism and Thatcherite laisser-faire capitalism co-exist in uneasy (and ultim-ately incongruous) relation. 'The Victorian' was no longer realised in the same way it had been at the beginning of the series, namely as a template for an idealised nation state, and the idealised, 'faithful' adap-tation of Holmes was incrementally compromised. The market-obsessed post-1990 Granada production company grew much more interested in cashing in on one of its most successful international brands.

Maybe (at least part of) the truth is that by the 1990s Britain did not need the same degree of consolation and reassurance from the Holmes series. What is certainly true is that by the conclusion of the series the viewer was too often confronted with little more than what Nancy Banks-Smith has called 'melodrama with knobs on' (1992: 28). It was a major departure from the earlier Holmes, a nineteenth century minus its lustre and its illusion of manageable coherence. The extent and nature of Granada's *commitment* to what they imagined to be the spirit of Doyle's work thus dimmed dramatically, to the point where, as Jeremy Brett acknowledged, in the last episodes only 'bits' of the Doyle canon were being utilised. Doyle's canon had become something to be negotiated, rather than followed to the letter; always hauntingly present but, over time, sidestepped with ever-greater frequency.

Notes

1. For further details see (respectively) Stuart Davies (2007), Amanda J. Field (2009) *England's Secret Weapon*, and the most recent BBC *Sherlock* series (2010), featuring Benedict Cumberbatch as Holmes, in which the modern incarnation of the great detective is shown to be an obsessive user of smartphone technologies.
2. This sense of 'palimpsestuousness' was first conceptualised in this way by Gérard Genette in *Palimpsests: Literature in the Second Degree* (1982).
3. This is the term commonly used to summarise the political philosophy (and resultant government policies) of the British Prime Minister Margaret Thatcher during her term in office (1979–90), although its origins lie before 1979 and its impact extends beyond 1990.
4. The term 'Tory' has a long history, and in UK politics was originally associated with the political group supporting first the Stuarts and later royal authority more generally, as well as the established church. It is used generically in this chapter to denote a supporter of traditional political and social institutions against the forces of democratisation or reform, i.e. a political conservative.
5. In *Television Culture* (2003 edn) John Fiske identifies this 'inoculation' as a crucial element of the relationship between television and viewer, evolving Roland Barthes' own concept of the same name (first develop in his *Mythologies*) Fiske argues that television is ultimately conservative in the ways it focuses on how 'disease' [the radical, disruptive] is contained, even within 'progressive' (47) programming.
6. Later published as Michael Cox, *The Baker Street File: A Guide to the Appearance and Habits of Sherlock Holmes and Dr Watson, specially prepared for the Granada Television Series* (1997), this volume was based on Cox's own detailed readings of Doyle's original stories.

7. Brett was notorious for carrying around his own copy of Doyle's stories and referring back to them at particular moments of filming to check if the scripts were 'correct'.

8. For example, the UK rate of homicide between the years 1980–90 was the highest it had ever been since records began. See *A Century of Change: Trends in UK Statistics Since 1900*, House of Commons Research Paper 99/111. 21 December 1999 (14), http://www.parliament.uk/commons/lib/research/rp99/rp99–111.pdf. Accessed 09 Dec. 2010.

9. See 'Company Briefing: Jewels in Granada's Crown', *The Guardian*, 6 December 1984.

10. See the Broadcasting Act 1990, at http://www.opsi.gov.uk/acts/acts1990/Ukpga_19900042_en_1. Accessed 17 July 2009.

11. Charlotte Brunsdon, 'Problems with Quality', (1990: 67). Brunsdon also notes the work of the Broadcasting Research Unit, including their pamphlet *Quality in Television* (1989). The BRU operated from 1981–91.

3

'Open the Window, Then!': Filmic Interpretation of Gothic Conventions in Brian Mills's *The Hound of the Baskervilles*[1]

Terry Scarborough

When Arthur Conan Doyle introduced Sherlock Holmes in 1887, he began one of the most diverse, resilient and adaptable narrative traditions in modern literature. From Sidney Paget's alteration of Holmes's physical appearance in *The Strand* to Jeremy Brett's dramatic emphasis on his aesthetic sensibilities, Holmes has undergone constant adaptation in multiple contexts, mediums and genres. As Doyle and his contemporaries appropriated elements of the Gothic tale and other popular genres to suit a late-Victorian readership, Sherlock Holmes emerges today as a champion of popular narrative whose diversity is often based in Gothic conventions and tropes. One of the most popular of Doyle's works and by far his best-known novel, *The Hound of the Baskervilles* (1901–2), openly employs such traditional Gothic tropes as the locked-room situation, the ancestral portrait and the found manuscript, but although recent criticism has focused on Doyle's application of such elements in *The Hound*, little has been said of their appropriation in Brian Mills's 1988 Granada adaptation and their effect upon contemporary reception of this constantly evolving narrative.

This chapter examines Mills's emphasis on Gothic elements – specifically those based in landscape and architecture – with attention to the narrative function of windows and the concept of urban exploration. I compare the characters' gaze from within structures in Doyle's novel and Mills's adaptation to discuss how the contemporary *viewer* observes Victorian culture and thought from a masterly, panoptic perspective, which remains rooted in the Gothic. Emphasis is placed upon the geographical locations and architectural functions of 221b Baker Street and Baskerville Hall, positing that the Devon moor and its surroundings present an allegory of urban exploration of late-Victorian London. The analysis further compares representations of Gothicised Victorian landscapes to demonstrate the shift from the alignment of the sensory perspectives of Watson and the reader to that of Holmes and the viewer in order to fix a contemporary, masterly gaze on to Victorian culture through which landscape becomes viewing screen and epoch artefact.

London, Dartmoor and the urban Gothic

Although not classified as a Gothic novel, *The Hound* clearly employs Gothic conventions and underpinnings. The found manuscript relating the origin of the Baskerville Curse, the gloom of the enclosed, primeval moor and the ominous presence of Baskerville Hall work to create what Sir Henry Baskerville refers to in the adaptation as 'an old melodrama'. This general atmosphere of dread and gloom stands in opposition to the bustling shops and diurnal life of Baker Street earlier in the film, as it does in the novel, but unlike the original, the adaptation begins not with the traditional Baker Street prologue, but with the ominous atmosphere of Baskerville Hall, complete with gargoyles and sinister musical score. This juxtaposition of Baker Street and Dartmoor emphasises the narrative function of windows, whereby a transparent boundary – one which may expel or admit certain atmospheres or threaten physical intrusion – triggers and maintains a connection to a Gothic landscape and accompanies the eventual return to the daily routines of Victorian London. However, in the adaptation the omission and augmentation of key scenes shifts the narrative perspective from an immediate and threatening reflection of Victorian social and imperial anxieties, as conveyed through Watson's retrospective narration in the novel, to a contemporary, masterly gaze through which the viewer experiences late-Victorian London as a cultural artefact.

As in the novel, Mills introduces his protagonists with the traditional display of deductive acumen common throughout the canon, which culminates in Holmes's gaze from his window at Baker Street. Here, through the gaze both Doyle and Mills firmly establish the foundations of what Lynda Nead identifies as 'two modes of vision in the modern city: the panoptic view from above, in which all is visible and immediately comprehensible; and the unfolding vista of the pedestrian at ground level' (qtd. Pittard, 2007: 3). In the adaptation, Holmes's panoptic view onto Baker Street, by which he identifies Dr. Mortimer and his spaniel, establishes a masterly gaze which provides the base from which to structure an altered narrative transition from Baker Street to Dartmoor. The viewer immediately experiences this alteration through the omission of the epistolary evidence of the manuscript relating the Baskerville curse and its replacement by exterior and interior analepsis.

Of critical importance to these scenes is the semiotic function of the window. Sebeok and Margolis examine the window as a conduit and 'perhaps *the* key figure used by Conan Doyle' (1982: 114). They assert that 'Watson is the person most often associated with windows, for he is Doyle's normal point-of-view character through whose sense organs the reader's perceptions are channeled' (1982: 121). This observation highlights the significance of the window as a means of sensory experience through which the reader or viewer experiences the narrative from perspectives which are affected by architectural, geographical and social constructs. Following Judith Walkowitz's assertion that London became 'envisioned as two distinct cities' (1992: 20),[2] Mills's application of Gothic conventions and tropes reveals Baskerville Hall and the moor as an allegory of the other and alien within London. The late-Victorian 'literary construct of the metropolis as a dark, powerful, and seductive labyrinth' (Walkowitz, 1992: 17) then suggests the moor as a type of Gothic double for the urban environment of the late-nineteenth century metropolis.

Christopher Pittard views *The Strand* as a 'particularly urban text' (2007: 4), which privileges the second of Nead's modes of vision. Pittard contends that its contents reveal 'a palpable bias towards the urban, most obviously in the title of the magazine itself' (2007: 3). He continues, citing George Newnes's comment that 'it is through the [London] Strand itself that the tide of life flows fullest and strongest and deepest' (2007: 3). In following Pittard's observation, we then recognise the initial serialisation of *The Hound* as providing a spatial model by which the Victorian fascination with the tension between 'ordered design and untidy contingency' (Pittard, 2007: 4) may be examined. The window in the prologue sets the scene for Holmes's – and thereby the reader's – anticipation of disorder, and the eventual return to an ordered, controlled urban landscape through Holmes's mastery of the situation.

Although the adaptation follows Doyle's basic narrative structure, a salient difference augments the narration and strengthens the emphasis on the urban environment: the viewer often assumes Holmes's panoptic gaze, rather than experiencing Watson's retrospective narration. Here, the sensory experience, which is traditionally established via Watson's memory and epistolary evidence, is established through Holmes. Omission of Watson's narration, then, aligns with Nead's conception of the panoptic, masterly gaze – one which resembles that of Holmes's methodical observation of the moor and its inhabitants, and which is firmly established in his 'hover[ing]' (Doyle, 2002: 27) over an Ordnance map of Devonshire. At times the viewer directly assumes Holmes's panoptic perspective, as when a mysterious gloved hand directs the viewer's gaze as he observes Watson and the Stapletons at Merripit House, or when a scene focuses on Watson writing to Holmes from without an open window at Baskerville Hall. As the latter correspondence with Holmes takes the form of voiceovers, the viewer's perspective, like that of Holmes, is privileged through an oblique and controlled position in relation to the characters' experience.

Mills's depiction of the transition from London to Devonshire is imbued with the theme of regression, as is the original, but as Watson and Mortimer travel to Dartmoor the train windows overtly achieve the effect of 'rewinding' or inverting linear time as the landscape passes from behind Watson. This effect is later answered as Holmes returns to London from the moor. The theme of social transgression so common to late-Victorian narratives of urban exploration indicates, on an allegorical level, the common bifurcation of London into East and West. Here, the windows reveal that Holmes travels forward as he *progresses* toward his intellectually and socially superior Baker Street view, and locates the social binary within the city itself. As Watson and Sir Henry continue to a highly Gothicised environment not uncommon to late-Victorian representations of the metropolis, this unstable landscape harbours both the destitute and organised criminal classes (Selden and Stapleton, respectively) and an impotent policing force within the disordered, unpredictable and dangerous geography of the moor. This environment and military presence also elicits the theme of urban exploration, which, as Walkowitz contends, '[a]s early as the 1840s...adapted the language of imperialism to evoke features of...[Victorian] cities...[and] transformed the unexplored territory of the London poor into an alien place, both exciting and dangerous' (1992: 18). Quoting Peter Keating, Walkowitz continues: 'urban explorers "penetrate[d]" inaccessible places where the poor lived, in..."foul-smelling swamps", and the black abyss' (in Walkowitz, 1992: 19). Holmes's and the viewer's penetration of the locked-room situation of the moor, then, accords with a basic convention of the urban Gothic and the Sherlockian tradition: the detective's disguised venture into the realm of the criminal classes and his participation in and experience of a social landscape other than his own, while rarely leaving London.

Perhaps the most salient of alterations relating to windows is the scene in which Holmes visits the moor in 'spirit' (Doyle, 2002: 26). A distinct parallel is drawn between London and the moor through both the noxious environment created by Holmes's tobacco smoke in his rooms and the gloomy fog and cloud cover of the moor; however, Mills curtails the ritualistic and mystic elements of Holmes's methods and emphasises the visual effects of windows. Rather than Watson's 'vague vision of Holmes in his dressing-gown coiled up in his armchair with his black clay pipe between his lips' (Doyle, 2002: 26), an image which Jesse Oak Taylor-Ide reads as Holmes's 'ritual transformation' through which he 'pass[es] into a dark, liminal world outside the societal structure' (2005: 59), Mills de-emphasises the ritualistic, exotic connotations of this scene and draws the viewer's gaze to the window at which Holmes identified Dr. Mortimer and which is now a thematic backdrop for Holmes's and the reader's panoptic perspective. This association of Holmes with the window indicates a shift from the liminal, both methodologically and geographically, to a central position within the metropolis as he firmly establishes his omniscient situation above the cityscape.

Mills furthers the significance of the window as Holmes directs Watson to the Ordnance map of Devonshire. The original scene depicts Holmes 'unroll[ing] one section and [holding] it over his knee' (Doyle, 2002: 27), whereas the adaptation presents a draped, mounted and, most significantly, *framed* map. Through semiotic similarity to the window, this alteration symbolically fixes the gaze of both the characters and the viewers from a panoptic, ordered and omniscient perspective and reinforces Mills's employment of the window trope to connect the perspectives of Holmes and the viewer. This emphasis on mapping again conjures, to use Nead's terms, 'the opposition between the controlling, aerial viewpoint of the city planner and the point of view of the walker at street level' (2000: 74). Through connecting window and map in this manner, Mills underscores Nead's theory of the 'panoptic towers of coercive power' by which the city is rendered 'legible and comprehensible' (Nead, 2000: 75), and further strengthens the emphasis on the urban centre. But the significance of the Ordnance map extends further in its historical contexts as it connects the unstable and changing condition of the moor to that of London. In her examination of the history of the Ordnance map, Nead states that in the map 'London was to be represented as potential process, as a geography of flow and movement... [and reflected] the transition from an older, static view of the city to its conception as changing and progressive' (2000: 21), which further connects the city and the moor through images of instability and danger. Furthermore, the Ordnance map represents a movement toward 'pragmatism and accuracy' (Nead, 2000: 22), both of which accord with Holmes's typical projection of reason over the urban landscape.

Having established in the map a geographic connection between the urban landscape and the moor, it must be mentioned that the Ordnance map falls under the category of the geometric, rather than the panoptic, view of the city (Nead, 2000: 22). However, as Nead points out, in the Ordnance map unfolds a 'narrative of progress and improvement', which connects, importantly, to sewerage (2000: 22). During the mid-century, in response to the severely unsanitary conditions of the city, the Metropolitan Board of Works assumed 'sole responsibility for constructing the London sewer system... [which required] a technically measured plan showing land and watershed levels' (Nead, 2000: 19), and which was to represent London as process (Nead, 2000: 21). The unstable and threatening connotations connected to images of the moor and the Gothic nature of a labyrinthine, underground sewer system elicit on a social level the problematic attempts to bifurcate London into criminal and law abiding, East and West, as the question of above and below street level furthers the Gothic nature of the city. In 1862, journalist John Hollingshead journeyed into the sewerage system and recounted his experience in a chapter from his *Underground London* entitled 'A Day Below' (Nead, 2000: 24). Nead explains his journey:

> [H]e might have called this piece 'A Saunter Through the West End.' But this saunter is below the West End, and Hollingshead guides his readers down into the sewer as he embarks on his subterranean trip. The noise in the tunnel and unfamiliar sources of light disorientate his sense of time and place. Shafts of light through ventilator gratings look like rays of moonlight, and the sound of a boy whistling in the street above makes the journalist feel like an *escaped convict*. (25; emphasis added)

The Gothic inversion apparent in Hollingshead's experience reveals a subterranean reality which Nead refers to as 'a disturbing, alternative route through the city' (2000: 26), and which affords an uncanny similarity to Doyle's narrative construction of Dartmoor. Holmes's fixation on the framed Ordnance map in the adaptation therefore reveals a distinct connection between London and the moor through the Gothic rendering of an unstable environment, which threatens duality, crime, degeneration and death.

Transition, regression and narrative alteration

An examination of Mills's presentation of the moor as a Gothic reflection and, at times, an inversion of upper-class London, requires specific attention to the transition between the metropolis and Dartmoor. As the novel foregrounds regression through the journey of Watson, Sir Henry and Mortimer, first by train and then by horse and cart to Baskerville Hall, Mills initiates this theme in London. The breakfast meeting at the Northumberland Hotel opens through an interior window and pans over what the viewer experiences as a type of Victorian cabinet of curiosities. In this scene, the viewer's masterly gaze is reinforced as Victorian artefacts are displayed – it must be noted, in a bourgeois context – as the camera pans the room. Moreover, Holmes is positioned in front of an illuminated window as he presents his theories concerning the mysterious letter. Also, at this point Mills presents a significant narrative alteration as Holmes spots the mysterious stranger. Rather than recognising the bearded suspect through a reflection in a shop window at street level, Holmes directly observes him in an upper level of the Northumberland Hotel. As Holmes exclaims 'Come Watson!!' the viewer observes the protagonists giving chase and descending the staircase through a rotating lens positioned beneath them. Viewed in light of the impending transition to Dartmoor, this downward spiralling effect achieves a theme of regression to street level, at which point the suspect escapes by horse and carriage.

This narrative alteration achieves a significant change in the viewer's perspective and the narrative structure: the theme of regression is highlighted in a first-class London hotel through the descent from an enclosed space above the winding streets of London to the streets themselves, creating a thematic shift which repeats when Watson and Sir Henry encounter Selden on the moor. London and Dartmoor are connected through images of windows as Watson gazes on to the moor through an open window and Holmes simultaneously ponders a letter while staring into a mirror – an image which itself enforces the notion of the double – thus drawing a parallel between the bourgeois curios associated with the interior window at the Northumberland Hotel and Stapleton's cabinets of entomological specimens. As the locations of the Hall and 221b dissolve, these objects of curiosity align with the viewer's gaze through the screen on which they are viewed.

The theme of urban exploration continues as Watson examines the moor and its inhabitants. As he explores the winding paths and recesses of this criminal landscape, he passes between views from above the moor to street level. Paralleling the spiral descent at the Northumberland Hotel, Watson ascends a spiral staircase at Lafter Hall and scans the landscape through a telescope. More significantly, the climax of Mills's urban allegory occurs through a window at Baskerville Hall. In the chapter 'The Light on the Moor', in which Selden's relation to Mrs. Barrymore is revealed, the augmentation and omission of key elements associated with the window alter the narrative perspective and reception. Having firmly established the parallel between 221b and the Hall, Mills amplifies the ominous atmosphere and locked-room situation of Dartmoor with effects of thunder and a typically Gothic dinner party. But the scene in which Watson and Sir Henry pursue Selden is unambiguously altered to reinforce the opposition of panoptic versus street level perspectives by the viewing of Barrymore's communication with the criminal through a second window in a separate wing of the Hall.

The novel twice depicts Watson observing Barrymore at the window: the first time alone, the second with Sir Henry. Mills omits the first occasion and alters the second to situate Watson, Sir Henry and the viewer in an oblique position from which they view Barrymore and Selden communicating. As Mills highlights the similarity between window and map at Baker Street, Doyle's emphasis on framing directs the reader's perspective, through Watson's limited gaze, to see 'a tiny pin-point of yellow light...[which] suddenly transfixe[s] the dark veil, and glow[s] steadily in the centre of the black square *framed by the window*' (Doyle, 2002: 92; emphasis added). Mills shifts this perspective to the panoptic as Watson and Sir Henry descend from the second floor of the Hall and set out on to the moor to confront the criminal. Through this gesture Mills highlights the moral category of the 'sympathetic resident' associated with urban exploration (Walkowitz, 1992: 18). Doyle and Mills provide commentary on the practice of night-walking and the moral duty of the urban observer to actively 'explain and resolve social problems' (18). Doyle's reference to this practice is overt as Watson relates that 'Any night...[the] neighbors...might be attacked by [Selden], and it may have been the thought of this which made Sir Henry so *keen upon the adventure'* (Doyle, 2002: 95; emphasis added).

Mills alters the confrontation between urban explorer and criminal as Watson and Sir Henry enter the Gothic landscape of fog and skeletal branches and encounter a lobotomised Selden who lacks the evil and hateful features attributed to him by Doyle. Having descended to street level, the characters retain a high moral status in relation to the criminal as the viewer retains the panoptic view of Holmes. At this point both texts present Holmes in a distinct parallel to the window at 221b as he gazes down upon Watson and Sir Henry as they achieve their climax in Holmes's pre-eminent appearance as the Man on the Tor overlooking the feral and grotesque criminal and the morally and socially elevated adventurers at street level. Mills's addition of a lobotomised (indeed, mutilated) Selden indicates a shift from a Victorian perspective of immediate fear to that of contemporary intrigue. As Pittard notes, 'the later nineteenth century saw a fall in recorded crime, particularly in theft, between 1880 and 1914' (2007: 4), a fact which highlights the disjuncture between Victorian and contemporary perspectives on the urban environment. In a dramatic shift from the novel's sensationalised anxiety, Mills adapts Doyle's Gothic reflection of the destitute criminal class into parody, a gesture which itself suggests a masterly gaze through melodramatic representation – in a self-reflexive allusion to Sir Henry's earlier comment – of the Victorian misinterpretation of a metropolis spiralling into criminal chaos, which again alludes to the earlier spiral descent at the Northumberland Hotel.

A significant shift in Henry's and Watson's moral status also occurs in the adaptation of the scene in which the urban explorers confront Selden. A significant alteration in the morality of justice occurs as the figure of the upstanding citizen of the novel assumes the role of the sympathetic subject. As Mills shifts the decision of whether to shoot the unarmed Selden from Watson to Sir Henry, the confrontation is accompanied by a shift from ominous to pitiful, indeed melodramatic, musical score. Selden, who assumes a pathetic, childish expression of confusion and fear, elicits a pitiful response in Sir Henry as he lowers his revolver and states, 'I thought to shoot him, but I couldn't'. Upon Watson's and Sir Henry's return to the Hall, Selden's pitiful representation continues as the latter angrily questions the Barrymores about their communication with the criminal. Similar to his reaction to the destitute Selden on the moor, a sobbing Mrs. Barrymore pleads, 'The poor creature came to me for help, sir. How could I refuse after what they have done to him?' which produces a sympathetic response from Sir Henry. Mills's characterisation of Selden, as Mr. Barrymore describes him, is of a 'broken man' who is 'like a child', which is in stark contrast to Doyle's Selden, whose

> evil yellow face, a terrible animal face, all seamed and scored with vile passions... [is] Foul with mire, with a bristling beard, and hung with matted hair [;] it might well have belonged to one of those old savages who dwelt in the burrows on the hillsides. (Doyle, 2002: 97)

Such significant alteration from the Lombrosian image of the violent criminal to the pitiful, mutilated subject in relation to the moor suggests a significant shift in Victorian interpretations of urban geographies and contemporary perspectives on lower-class crime in Mills's interpretation and revision of Doyle's use of Gothic conventions.

Crime and urban geography

In 'The Victorian Slum: An Enduring Myth?', David Ward identifies some common geographical perspectives from which Victorian slum life is viewed as 'distinctive enough to be described as a separate culture', one which 'has long been associated with the "uprooting" experience of the cityward movement upon the traditional patterns of life of rural people' (1976: 323). Emphasising the mid-century introduction of 'slum' and the deviant connotations associated with such geographies, Ward identifies the Victorian belief that the 'worthy poor would rapidly be degraded by the contaminating influences of the most depraved and discontented among them' (323). Following Ward's reference to the segregation of the original 'rural migrants' and their 'social superiors' within 'distinct territories' (323), the ominous and haunting presence of the Neolithic huts and cairns for both texts represent on an allegorical level the formation of distinct nations divided between privileged and destitute classes. Ward addresses the role which narratives of urban exploration played in the formation and maintenance of the 'unknown, foreign, threatening and *exciting* world of the slums' (323; emphasis added). Furthermore, he notes what he calls 'the most basic of Victorian assumptions about slums: the poor or slum residents are defined as a distinctive social group which, once established in social and spatial isolation from the rest of society, persists as a culture or subculture' (326). Like Doyle, Mills highlights such segregation through the transition between night and day, as the 'beauty of the moor' returns with the daylight. Whereas in the novel, after the encounter with Selden Watson reports 'a foggy day, with a drizzle of rain … It is melancholy *outside and in'* (Doyle, 2002: 100); emphasis added), Mills employs the recurring motif of an ancient stone bridge and maintains the juxtaposition necessary to reinforce the viewer's masterly gaze over Victorian anxieties surrounding the unstable geography of the urban environment, which threaten 'ever-present danger, which is the more terrible because [Watson is] unable to define it' (Doyle, 2002: 100). Here, Mills maintains the notion of geographical bifurcation, and the haunting presence of the Neolithic (urban) villagers and their claim to a haunting, pre-urban past through which the Baskerville curse survives.

Selden's altered presence on the moor and the characters' reactions to him in the adaptation, then, align with Ward's contemporary re-examination of the slum, through which he questions 'persisting Victorian ideas in a contemporary context' (Ward, 1976: 326). Maintaining that contemporary 'definitions of poverty and slums' tend to retain the 'Victorian notion that a different way of life is nurtured under circumstances of social and spatial isolation from the rest of the city' (1976 : 326) – an image upheld in both texts – he identifies adaptations in such views through which deviance attributed to slum conditions are 'increasingly identified as extreme levels of social isolation created by the stressful and uncertain environment of the slum rather than as immoral and illegal activities' (1976: 326). Although Doyle's urban explorers do not to report Selden's location on the moor to Princetown, their motivation clearly differs from that of Mills. Doyle's Watson reports that, 'it is hard lines that we have not actually had the triumph of bringing [Selden] back as our own prisoner' (Doyle, 2002: 99), while Mills creates a victimised subject through which all sense of triumph is negated by Mrs. Barrymore's plea for her brother. This significant shift in and emphasis on the image of the destitute criminal class thus affords critical reflection upon conflicting interpretations of the connections between geography and crime, one through which the contemporary, masterly gaze is further juxtaposed to that of the Victorian perspective.

Just as this juxtaposition reveals distinct parallels and differences between Victorian and contemporary perspectives on crime and urban exploration, so too does the image of the *flâneur* in Holmes. As Nead explains, 'The *flâneur* is a stroller and a looker whose environment is the city crowd, and who is able to perceive the truth and aesthetic significance in the transient and fleeting experiences of the city' (2000: 68). In this image resides a salient difference in the formation and maintenance of the adaptation of the viewer's gaze as Holmes embodies, as Ana Vadillo notes the mechanisation of the city which displaced the *flâneur's* fascination with walking and, by extension, the street level gaze (Vadillo, 2003: 247). Addressing in cinematic analogy the correlation between the late-nineteenth century shift from an interest in strolling to mechanised travel, Vadillo contends that 'If *flâneurs / euses* strolled in the city as if they were observing pictures in a museum, passengers sat in the omnibus, train or tram as if they were sitting in a cinema while the spectacle of the city passed in front of their eyes' (247). In light of this significant development in the nature of urban observation which, as Vadillo notes, corresponds to the 'origins of the cinema' (247), Mills's recurring association of Holmes with the steam engine (Holmes recurrently passes through, travels on and is shot in relation to the train) points to his, and again the viewer's, omniscient perspective in relation to that of Sir Henry and Watson, who return to the Hall and approach the Barrymores after passing through a static window-paned wall. As Holmes and the viewer ponder the case in relation to the moving landscape presented through a train window, the urban explorers of the moor observe an archaic urban environment through a fixed perspective, which juxtaposes the view of a late-Victorian readership immersed in the anxiety of the immediate threat of street level with the masterly, panoptic gaze of filmic adaptation.

Citing Charles Baudelaire's essay 'The Painter of Modern Life' (1863) Nead presents an important image of the *flâneur*: 'For the perfect *flâneur*, for the passionate spectator, it is an immense joy to *set up house in the heart of the multitude, amid the ebb and flow of movement, in the midst of the fugitive*' (qtd. Nead, 2000: 68). The concept of permeating urban spaces, distinctly those of difference and segregation as reflected in the idea of the urban village, takes shape in Mills's addition of an overtly domestic scene in which Holmes offers Watson to partake of a home-cooked meal in his residence upon the moor. Although the novel presents Holmes as comfortably housed and unnoticed within the haunting multitude of the Gothicised urban space, clean shaven 'and his linen as perfect as if he were in Baker Street' (Doyle, 2002: 123), Mills extends the image of Holmes's adaptability to the urban – a trait typical of his methods of detection within London – and highlights his willingness and even enjoyment in his participation within the urban village. The image of the *flâneur* then arises in relation to both the concept of the urban explorer and the criminal; as such, the shift from Watson's retrospective account of events fortifies the filmic rendering of Holmes's and, by extension, the viewer's gaze to the panoptic perspective.

But for the analyst, the true climax resides in Mills's addition of Mortimer's archeological excavation before Watson discovers Holmes on the moor. Here, the addition of a *necropolis* where Holmes resides in a stone hut distinctly parallels the *metropolis* and 221b. Mortimer's view of the former environment as artefact and object of study coincides with the viewer's gaze onto a Victorian past which passes through the window of filmic adaptation. Through this structural juxtaposition of Neolithic and Victorian urban space, the viewer is presented with an analogy for their relation to the Victorian past through which they afford a privileged gaze. Mortimer's archeological interest – one which, it may be noted, seems out of place during a murder investigation involving the possibility of further foul play – marks a significant gesture toward a stabilised, controlled and masterful gaze onto the historical past. Mills further highlights this theme in Mortimer's extreme annoyance with rabbits entering his excavation and threatening to interrupt the 'chronology of [his] dig'. Mortimer brings into focus the viewer's retrospective (indeed, panoptic) perspective over the archaic urban space and demonstrates mastery of its inner workings upon learning that Watson is going to the necropolis. Faced with multiple 'beautiful' Neolithic artefacts and remains, Mortimer states: 'I can show you around, if you like'. Mills further elevates Mortimer's quasi-scientific alignment with the viewer's gaze by stating that 'Most people think [the necropolis] a Neolithic village, but I have reason to believe it a burial ground'. Mortimer's archeological approach to unearthing the urban village brings to light the distinct separation of past and present modes of viewing urban culture and, not unlike Stapleton's insect collection, markedly categorises the urban within definite chronological confines in order to preserve the Victorian cultural predecessor within the strictures of scientific enquiry.

In a final gesture toward the viewer's masterly gaze over the Victorian past, Mills shifts the ambiguous conclusion of Doyle's novel to a closed ending in which the culprit meets his ironic demise in the mire, the significance of which suggests not only a closed end to the narrative, but also the literal verification of Mortimer's theory of the mire as a burial ground. As Stapleton is revealed as the culprit, Holmes enters Merripit House and strikes the window pane of the door before forcing his way in. This window, and Holmes's and Watson's transgression of its boundary, marks the final and conclusive gesture aligning Holmes's perspective with that of the viewer. After freeing the restrained and abused Beryl Stapleton (an image which in itself recalls the maiden of the Gothic novel and the Baskerville Curse), Holmes, rather than giving chase as in the novel, leaves Stapleton to his demise within the unstable environment of the mire. Fleeing Merripit House, Stapleton, donning dinner dress, enters the unlit, foggy and unpredictable landscape, and again highlights the social juxtapositions inherent within the bifurcated urban environment of London. In a crucial deviation from the novel's ambiguous disappearance of the culprit, of which Watson reports 'we were never destined to know' (Doyle, 2002: 157), Mills presents Stapleton faltering into the morass – in the novel it is Holmes who falters and experiences 'a mud bath' (156) – and sinking to his death. As the culprit meets his ironic end within the mire, Mills employs what may be viewed as the most significant Gothic motif in the form of a dissolve to Baskerville Hall, which frames a gargoyle resembling a bat. The ominous imagery and music contribute to an atmosphere of dread connecting directly to the urban allegory of the moor and maintains Doyle's end, which Stapleton suggests is 'Somewhere in the heart of the great Grimpen Mire, down in the foul slime of the huge morass which had sucked him in' (157); however, through the viewer's perspective, Mills removes any ambiguity as to Stapleton's demise and the 'Many traces... [found] of him in the bog-girt island where he had hid his savage ally' (157). This alteration again aligns the viewer's perspective with that of Holmes, as in the Baker Street epilogue Holmes explains to Watson the details of the case without having explored or investigated the Grimpen Mire immediately after Stapleton's flight. Having thus aligned Holmes and viewer, novel and film, and past and present, Mills enacts the process by which Gothic elements and conventions function within filmic adaptation to shift perspective from a late-Victorian readership to a contemporary, mastery gaze on to the historical past.

In his first appearance after nearly eight years, in *The Hound* Holmes continued to mediate the cultural anxieties of a Victorian readership; today, he presents Victorian culture as an artefact to be studied and as an icon of adaption. Firmly rooted in Gothic imagery and conventions, Mills's adaptation creates a landscape typical of the urban Gothic and shifts the viewer's perspective between Holmes's panoptic, masterly gaze to Watson's view of the urban explorer at street level. Mills emphasises and augments existing parallels between Baker Street and Dartmoor to elicit in a new light the connections between urban and rural, internal and external, and to find new perspectives for reader and viewer alike. Through windows and the camera lens Mills shifts perspective to bridge the fissure between period and medium as anxiety becomes interest, culture becomes artefact, and Sherlock Holmes retains his status as the pre-eminent Victorian detective.

Notes

1. An abridged version of this chapter was initially published in *The Baker Street Journal*, Spring 2010.
2. Walkowitz bases this idea on her analysis of Dore and Jerrold's *London: A Pilgrimage* (1872).

4
The Curious Case of the Kingdom of Shadows: The Transmogrification of Sherlock Holmes in the Cinematic Imagination

Harvey O'Brien

When the Lumière cinematographe made its debut in 1895, Sherlock Holmes was on hiatus.[1] By the time he returned in print, he had already made at least one cinematic appearance. In *Sherlock Holmes Baffled* (1900),[2] Holmes is frustrated by a burglar who is able to appear and disappear at will. It is a straightforward trick film, using stop-motion to make the burglar disappear. This gimmick was popular in early cinema, forming part of the link between the theatre of the nineteenth century and the development of a continuity system of cinematic narration.[3] The 'shock' of the trick made people laugh, but it showed them what the cinema could do. There is something significant in the inclusion of Sherlock Holmes as the 'dupe', though. Holmes is evoked only in the title of the film and in the fact that the unknown actor portraying him is tall and wears a three-quarter length smoking jacket. Yet we are invited to recognise 'Sherlock Holmes' as an icon of late nineteenth-century popular culture: a symbol of empiricism and rationality, and a fictive detective who had been able to unravel every forensic detail of the world of his time. The collision between Holmes's steadfast rationality and the capacity of the cinema to make magical things happen made clear to audiences that the impossible is no longer something that must be ruled out.

This chapter is not about the classical Holmes, or canonical adaptations of Doyle stories. It examines films in which Holmes represents a point of origin, but in which variances on the classical in some ways revise, and in other ways complement, the construction and deployment of this iconic figure. In *The Private Life of Sherlock Holmes* (Wilder, 1970) we find Holmes doubted: facing scepticism and anachronism in Billy Wilder's delicate blend of parody and homage. In *The Seven-Per-Cent Solution* (Ross, 1976) we have Holmes delirious: a drug-addled Holmes for the 1970s, exploring the roots of his obsessions in the dreamscapes of guided therapy from Sigmund Freud. In *Murder by Decree* (Clark, 1978) we have Holmes defeated: 'solving' the case of Jack the Ripper but unable to challenge the true social evils behind the Royal/Masonic conspiracy that explains who the Ripper truly was. These three films from the 1970s are excellent examples of the intellectually revisionist tendencies of that era, reflecting an ever-widening sense of ideological disillusionment. This chapter also examines three films from the 1980s, in which we see the assertive spectacularism of the Reagan and Thatcher era, not devoid of complication or doubt, but pursuing a consciously youth-oriented 'escapist' path that invites us to evaluate that from which we are escaping. In *Young Sherlock Holmes* (Levinson, 1985) we encounter Holmes regressed: Barry Levinson's Steven Spielberg-produced vision of a juvenile Holmes for a juvenile audience. In *The Great Mouse Detective* (Clements, Musker 1986) we have Holmes miniaturised: a deployment of the iconography of Holmes in an animation. Finally, in *Without a Clue* (Eberhardt, 1988) we discover Holmes simulated: a different order of scepticism in tune with the 1980s fascination with surface gloss and celebrity, as Holmes is revealed to be nothing but an actor hired by the genius Dr Watson.

What is of most interest across all of these films is the ways in which Holmes, sometimes against 'himself', sometimes with surprising sympathy for what he had come to represent, becomes a means by which a changed and changing world can be imagined through the movement of shadows. Writing in 1896, young Maxim Gorky famously described his first encounter with the cinema as being in 'the kingdom of shadows'.[4] He described the sensory and emotional immersion provided by the new medium, the terror and wonder of seeing 'not life, but its shadow' (1996: 6), not so much reality as a kind of ghostly analogue. Gorky was here identifying the first principle of the cinema; it is an illusion that transmogrifies recognisable matter into an imagining: reality into a representation, life into a shadow. The same can be said of the films of Sherlock Holmes, cast as shadows from the 'point of origin': that is, the (literary) Holmes mythos. In these films the literary (and often cinematic – either way, the classical) Holmes provides thematic and ideological grounding for historically contextual apposition. From within a nexus of morality, ethics, politics, sociology and psychology particular to the moment of realisation, Holmes again becomes a kind of 'dupe', or at least a focal point for orienting the audience towards societal shifts in perception. Holmes's very fixedness as an idea serves the reimagining of the fixity of his image. In 1900 those laughing at Holmes's inability to apprehend or comprehend the cinematic thief found themselves inadvertently learning what editing could do. In a similar manner, so might audiences encountering the cinematic iterations of Sherlock Holmes throughout the twentieth century ask what *purpose* Holmes serves in terms of mediating an experience *of* the cinema.

The classical Holmes

There are numerous books which chart the appearances of Sherlock Holmes on film and television. These books engage in degrees of debate across a range of adaptations, but tend to confine analysis to matters of fidelity. The very word 'adaptation' tends to ascribe a kind of *apriori* pejorative assessment to a lesser copy, rather than to explore the transformative qualities of movement from one medium to another. Granted, sometimes the median point of reference is actually not the literary source, but it is a 'classical' Holmes nonetheless: usually either (or both) Basil Rathbone and Jeremy Brett's portrayals of the character. As Barnes remarks though, 'the idea of Sherlock Holmes has become far larger, and now means far more, than the letter of the texts that inspired it' (Barnes, 2008: 8). Here we duly step beyond the canon into the murk of cinematic re-imagination – the idea of Holmes – but it is worth briefly reviewing one or two points regarding the canonical cinematic, or at least imagistic, Holmes.

We might begin with Sidney Paget's illustrations from *The Strand*, which remain an important frame of reference for production designers and casting directors. *The Seven Per-Cent Solution* actually begins with a montage of these images, marking designers Ken Adam's and Peter Lamont's awareness of these 'points of origin'. Doyle does provide a description of Holmes, of course: a tall man who seems taller because he is lean, with sharp eyes, a hawk-like nose and a prominent chin, with stained but delicate hands.[5] D. H. Friston was the first artist to illustrate a Holmes story,[6] but it is Paget's sketches, which began with 'A Scandal in Bohemia' (1891), that become the first of our shadows cast from that point of origin: they define how we begin to *see* Holmes.

Yet even here we have points of debate. Doyle was known to have been unhappy with Paget's rendering of Holmes, and a piquant case of sibling rivalry between Walter and Sidney Paget around the original commission took on greater import with the obvious physical similarity between Walter Paget and Holmes as drawn by Sidney. To this day, the official position (Milner *Oxford Dictionary of National Biography*) is that Walter was not the model for Holmes, but, semantically speaking, this only asserts that Walter did not actively consent or pose. Frankly, any cursory comparison of Sidney's unpublished 1904 'Portrait of Sherlock Holmes' and images of Walter reveals the legacy of this 'canonical' visualisation of the stern, balding Holmes as rooted in reality, yet refracted and recast to create an imaginative representation of a person who did not exist.[7] Consider also how Doyle's own father, Charles, contributed a bearded Holmes to the first book edition of *A Study in Scarlet*, not out of fidelity to his son's description of the character, but to his own countenance. Artistic reflexivity in portraiture has a way of making the impersonal extremely personal.[8]

Moving swiftly through the initial cinematic representations, we encounter the 'canon' again with Basil Rathbone. For many years Rathbone remained the defining screen Holmes, and with some fourteen films in the classic series, this is no wonder. Worth bearing in mind, though, is that in this 'classical' Holmes there are only two stories set within the original literary–historical period. Pitting Sherlock Holmes against the Nazis was nonetheless a restatement of classicism. Holmes's absolute devotion to the pursuit of justice from a standpoint of moral rightness rooted in Victorian self-assurance was seen to be the way to outwit and defeat the irrational, atavistic forces against which the Anglo-American Alliance fought in World War II. As Bosley Crowther put it in a review of *Sherlock Holmes and the Secret Weapon* (Neill, 1942) in *The New York Times*, Holmes and Watson are 'set to chasing Nazi villains in the war-consumed London of today with the same hale and vigorous tenacity as they showed towards opium smugglers years ago' (Crowther, 1943). Though the forensic and logistical details of the world in these films differ from those of the stories, the shadowy contours of Rathbone's Holmes are entirely classical in this sense.

Then we have Jeremy Brett as Holmes in the long running Granada TV series that most consider both classical and canonical, not least in the conscious attempt to adapt the entire literary source. Again, though, the shadow of imagining falls from unexpected angles. Canonical as the Rathbone films may have been, it was simply not possible to represent Holmes's darker side in the moral climate within which those films were produced. Freed from this and other constraints, and also able to use the serial format of television to keep a constant focus on development and continuity, the Granada series was able to firmly establish a classical, median image against which any subsequent representations would be measured. What is most important about *this* 'classical' Holmes is the very conscious attempt to integrate more of Doyle's conception of a man with demons and vices, including drug addiction and a certain disdain for women. The darkness of the interpretation was, of course, also fed by the well-publicised personal demons of the actor portraying Holmes, who had almost as much of a love–hate relationship with the character as Doyle had had. As Barnes reports, 'at his best, he [Brett] was touched by genius, at his worst, simply touched' (2004: 113). Watching Brett's Holmes stare down both friend and adversary from dark-rimmed eyes, the viewer is invited to contemplate the soul from which the desire for resolution stems.

Doubt, delirium, and defeat: the shadow of the 1970s

The cinema of the 1970s was one of doubt and disillusion, marking, on one hand, the restructuring of the economics of film production as the studio system finally gave way completely, and, on the other hand, a free-for-all in content terms as the Production Code collapsed (Leff, 1980: 41–55). The nett effect was the legitimising of an adult cinema capable of directly addressing darker material. There was also a corresponding shift towards the political left as a reaction to the perceived failure of the conservative agenda. This created a climate for realism, revisionism, and self-doubt in which an 'establishment' character like Sherlock Holmes, you would imagine, would be out of his depth, or simply entirely anachronistic.

The Private Life of Sherlock Holmes is actually a keystone film of this period. It was directed by industry veteran Billy Wilder, known for acerbic films such as *Double Indemnity* (Wilder, 1944) and *The Apartment* (1960). Though some at the time – and since – saw his Holmes as a bitter parody, Wilder's affection for the subject had sustained him through some fifteen years of development. As George Morris would observe in *Film Comment*, the film's conscious concern with anachronism mirrors Wilder's own sense of disconnection from the new Hollywood: 'The tragic aura of melancholy that suffuses this film is not confined to the romance at its center. *The Private Life of Sherlock Holmes* is also an elegy for the values of honor and fair play that died with the passing of the nineteenth-century' (1979: 37).

The film sets itself up as anti-classical from the outset, using the framing device of a locked box containing manuscripts describing cases considered too embarrassing to publish. The film was originally supposed to run for three hours with four separate stories, but ended up featuring just two – one in which Holmes (Robert Stephens) extricates himself from an invitation to impregnate a Russian ballerina by intimating that he is homosexual, and one in which Gabrielle Valladon (Genevieve Page), an Irene Adler-type character who is secretly a spy, outwits him, earning his admiration (love?) and driving him to despair when she is executed. Here, three important things are happening. Firstly, by attempting to present a multi-part narrative, director Billy Wilder and writer I.A.L. Diamond were attempting to defer to the canon while also revising it, indicating a connection with, but not necessarily an adherence to, the narrative frameworks of the past. This is an example of what Vera Ditka identifies as 'discontinuous movement' (2003: 56) in genre cinema, where the conscious signalling of formal distance also marks ideological disparity. In breaking up the narrative and drawing attention to its construction, the film is addressing the totalising function of narrative itself, and indicating its potential unreliability (as Watson's 'secret' account of events). Secondly, the overall satirical tone of the film purports to revise the image of Holmes by dwelling on his failure or discomfort. In the second of the two stories, self-conscious absurdity is deployed in having Holmes searching for the Loch Ness monster, which turns out, in fact, to be an experimental British submarine, and Holmes's bafflement is suggested to be founded both in the seeming inanity of the case and in his fascination with Gabrielle Valladon. Thirdly, however – and this is the most interesting thing about the film – in making such a conscious and evident effort to question the validity of the image of Holmes as invincible, the film actually presents another type of classical shadow.

Where Mycroft (Christopher Lee) comes to represent the voice of the establishment and legitimate espionage, Sherlock stands apart from the mechanisms of power. This effectively exempts him from the status quo. It liberates him, in fact, from expectation, and this Holmes becomes surprisingly rich in counter-cultural energy. Thus Wilder creates a sense of subversion in the film's view of Holmes's world perfectly in keeping with the era's confusion about authority. Even the suggestion of homosexuality (which inspires violent outrage in Watson [Colin Blakely] whom, naturally, Holmes suggests is his lover), does not demonise or criticise either homosexuality or Holmes himself. Instead, it proves a means to allow him to avoid being defined, and the audience is thereby forced to ask themselves who Holmes might be on a fundamental human level – one of 'us', not 'them', in a time of divisive images of self and other. This actually works extremely well, and the film becomes, in its own way, affectionate in its embrace of a Holmes who no longer stands for Queen and Country, but for the problem of identity faced by many people with reference to a world without role models in the shadow of 1968.

The Private Life of Sherlock Holmes ends with a scene in which Holmes, upon hearing of the execution of Gabrielle Valladon, takes his cocaine kit into his bedroom and closes the door on Watson, who begins to write. This is a resonant moment, calling to mind the famous conclusion of John Ford's *The Searchers* (1956) in which the hero Ethan's exclusion from civilisation is signalled by a door closing on his silhouette. Holmes closes the door on the audience, leaving us only with Watson and his writing as our key to understanding him as he escapes into cocaine. Wilder here brings literature and cinema into deliberate collision, asking the audience to evaluate the authority of narrative (and narrational, or explicative) voice, and inviting us to withhold judgment.

Holmes's use of drugs is also central to *The Seven Per-Cent Solution*. The film presents the tragic side of Sherlock Holmes – a brilliant mind corrupted by addiction – as a shadow cast from the real-life context of the use of hard drugs in the 1970s. By centrally confronting Holmes's addiction to cocaine (anchored by a brilliantly edgy performance by Nicol Williamson, whose wild eyes and rapid, almost gabbling speech give a real impression of narcotically-fuelled manic energy), the film is also able to deploy an element of cinematic realism such as is visible in dramas on drug addiction such as *The Panic in Needle Park* (Schatzberg, 1971) and *French Connection II* (Frankenheimer, 1975), while also deploying comedic high adventure in a more familiar generic mould. Again, a classical image is consciously challenged and a new set of epistemological parameters is put in place, another shadow from the point of origin that illuminates rather than obscures the world in which it has been produced.

The film has two narrative threads, one surrounding the treatment of Holmes's addiction, the other an adventure of kidnapping and murder in which he becomes embroiled while being treated. In both cases the underlying question of why Holmes does what he does is central. When presented with the case, Freud (played by Alan Arkin) dismisses the Doyle-based rationale that Holmes turns to cocaine out of boredom and frustration (a common explanation for inner city drug abuse in the later-twentieth century), saying a man of his intelligence would never do such a thing. Freud turns instead to Sherlock's childhood. Using hypnosis, he examines Holmes's obsession with Professor Moriarty, played by Laurence Olivier as a harmless and genteel old man harassed by the agitated, paranoid Holmes. The two things are ultimately shown to be interrelated, as Holmes's repressed childhood memories show that the reason he has become a detective – to punish the wicked – is because he saw wickedness at first hand as a boy. A flashback sequence is revealed piecemeal throughout the film as a kind of 'primal scene' playing out in Holmes's mind, and is then finally shown entirely after the adventure plot is resolved. It shows that Moriarty, who was Sherlock and Mycroft's mathematics tutor in their youth, had an affair with Mrs. Holmes. Sherlock witnessed her death at the hands of his father, who found the couple in bed together. In this, Holmes's persistent persecution of Moriarty and his taking of drugs are both symptoms of a desire for punishment and resolution stemming from a traumatic incident over which he had no control.

Importantly here, we see that the Victorian desire for social justice rooted in moral rightness is supplanted by a more old-school personal vendetta, rationalised through denial into a legitimate cause, both motivated by enduring trauma. This reading of the 'cause' of Holmes's addiction reflects a deep scepticism with moral authority, in keeping with *The Private Life of Sherlock Holmes*, and also an even greater assertion of Holmes's outsider status by making him a junkie. The 'cause' of problems (social and personal) runs deep and the resolution requires the application of purposeful intelligence. This is the other key element of the film: a comparison of Holmes's deductive reasoning with the methodologies of psychoanalysis. It is this that creates a bond between Holmes and Freud, and allows the audience to enjoy the byplay between Nicol Williamson as Holmes and Alan Arkin as Freud. In one key scene, as Holmes is about to explain how he has deduced the perpetrator of a kidnapping from forensic detail, Freud interjects and explains it all in terms of psychological motivation. Holmes is enthralled and thoroughly enjoys the recitation, which Freud delivers with a detective-like monologue that both he and the audience recognise as crossing generic boundaries. It also deepens the sense of the meaning behind (criminal) motivation, which we must also consider when understanding Holmes's problem. The result is a cogent argument in favour of understanding crime not as a forensic puzzle, but as a deeply-rooted consequence of enduring psychological and sociological traumas. The film addresses all of this with a light touch, freely mixing tones and touching on the comic scepticism of Billy Wilder, but embracing a much broader sense of adventure. In doing so, the film avoids the trap described by James Monaco as weighting down so many films of the period, where 'an overlay of erstwhile mythic significance' (1979: 274) often smothered the nostalgic pleasures of genre.

The issue of motive is also central to *Murder by Decree*, but not that of Holmes. This film determinedly shifts the focus away from Holmes's demons and onto those of society as he pursues Jack the Ripper against a backdrop of social injustice, anarchy, and conspiracy. The story of Holmes versus the Ripper was previously explored both on stage and in print by non-Doyle authors, and was also the subject of a 1965 film *A Study in Terror*. *Murder by Decree* is more ideologically specific in its application of the Ripper to the Holmes universe, using it in the same way that psychoanalysis is used in *The Seven Per-Cent Solution* and that revisionism frames *The Private Life of Sherlock Holmes*, as a means of undermining the comfortable frameworks of the classical Holmes. The Ripper plot in *Murder by Decree* follows the outlines of the Masonic/Royal conspiracy outlined in the theories of John Lloyd and Elwyn Jones and later elaborated by Steven Knight.[9] In plot terms, the Ripper is ultimately revealed to be a two-man team: a fanatical royalist abetted by the royal surgeon, both of them trying to cover up the fact that the Prince of Wales has fathered a Catholic child with a woman of the lower orders. This fact is known to both the highest governmental authorities, who are also Freemasons, and to a sinister group of anarchists who are attempting to use the case to overthrow the Government. Holmes ends up confronting both factions, almost dying at the hands of the rippers in the process.

Holmes's alignment with the forces of authority is therefore in focus again, and this time he is firmly placed within them at the outset, only to be, by the end of the film, thoroughly disillusioned. It begins with Holmes (Christopher Plummer) and Watson (James Mason) attending a performance at the Royal Opera House in full evening dress, with Watson staunchly defending the Prince of Wales, who arrives late and is booed and jeered by the lower-class audience in the gods. The film's awareness of social class is pronounced, as is its sense that social distinctions are illusory, if not downright destructive. Throughout the film there is antagonism between Holmes and the police only because they seem determined to keep him off the case, but he is otherwise generally seen as a team player who will do the right thing by the status quo, namely what is expected of him as a gentleman. This becomes crucial to the film's intense scepticism of moral authority, as Holmes finds himself manipulated by the forces both of order and of anarchy.

It is exactly this that gives the film its dark heart. The Ripper is an ill that can never be cured, not even as easily as a schism caused by trauma like in *The Seven Per-Cent Solution*, because his emergence is the result of inherent social failure. Underlying the Royal/Masonic conspiracy is deep social dysfunction, rooted in class distinction (a clear mirror of contemporary twentieth-century ideological struggles between models of socialism and capitalism), and Holmes discovers, ultimately, that he is powerless to really resolve anything. He fails to prevent any of the murders and his defeat of one of the two rippers in the film's climactic fight scene takes place when Holmes is actually lying on his back on the ground. He is essentially beaten, but the killer stumbles backwards into a cargo net and is strangled. This is not Holmes triumphant, but Holmes defeated: able to 'detect' crime, but not to solve it. His pyrrhic victory over the perpetrator is shown to be even more hollow when he is forced to cover up the facts in the concluding scene. He is confronted by the Prime Minister (Sir John Gielgud) and forced to conceal the truth to protect the Realm. There is an attempt to give Holmes the moral high ground by having him barter the life of the Royal child for his silence, but it is a symbolic gesture in an image of Holmes as completely out of his depth in a society that is clearly unjust, imbalanced, and, ultimately, insane.

Regression, miniaturisation, and simulation: the shadow of the 1980s

As the blockbuster evolved through the 1970s and 80s, so did the technical capacity of cinematic special effects of increasing 'realism' (compared to the theatrical imaginings of early cinema) to blend the more outlandish and spectacular imaginings of film-makers with identifiable physical reality. This had the effect of partly grounding fantasy in reality, and allowing the recognition of the boundaries of reality and the suspension of disbelief to become much less pressing, enabling 'escapism'. This brings us back to Gorky, who in 1896 wrote of losing your sense of reality in the face of the Kingdom of Shadows: 'You are forgetting where you are. Strange imaginings invade your mind and your consciousness begins to wane and grow dim...' (1996: 8). The point is that, again, this is not a new experience as such, but it is a neoclassical experience in the 1980s, especially following on as it does from the 1970s. As David A. Cook remarks, it is also representative of the failure of a different kind of cinema: the introspective, auteurist New American cinema that had washed up on the shores of the disaster of Michael Cimino's *Heaven's Gate* (1980). Instead, eyeing the profits gleaned from *Star Wars* (1977) and *Superman* (1978), the corporate decision-making process turned towards bankable 'kidpix' trading on nostalgic, almost regressive, views of cinema as toybox.[10] Stephen Prince summarises that cinema moved from being 'films' to 'filmed entertainment': 'setting the industry on a course towards globalization and a new oligarchy of planetary media titans' (2000: xii).

Young Sherlock Holmes is a very good demonstration of this process, and like *The Private Life of Sherlock Holmes*, the use of Holmes in particular is revealing. It is a much-criticised film, dismissed by the trade publication *Variety* (31 December 1984) as 'another Steven Spielberg film corresponding to those lamps made from driftwood and coffee tables from redwood burl and hatchcovers. It's not art but they all serve their purpose and sell by the millions'. It features spectacular digital imaging, and was instrumental in the development and acceptance of CGI for rendering special effects in Hollywood, but the plot is more classical than one might think. Although it features flying gargoyles, a roast pheasant coming to life and, famously, a stained glass Knight attacking a Parson, each of these images is a visualisation of hallucinations triggered by an old-school poison dart. The plot has young Holmes (Nicholas Rowe) still at school, where he meets young John Watson (Alan Cox),[11] becoming embroiled in a mystery where, curiously, Egyptian (as opposed to Indian like in *The Sign of Four*) villains are seeking revenge on a covenant of British adventurers who have wronged them. This does not become clear for a while, as the film enjoys checkmarking aspects of the Doyle canon within the framework of an account of Holmes's adolescence: showing us the formative experiences that honed his intellect, refined his methodology, and even touched his heart.[12]

One key element of the plot is its 'explanation' for Holmes's later relative disinterest in romance. In this film Holmes is a typically love-lorn adolescent, and the object of his affections is one Elizabeth Hardy (Sophie Ward). In ways similar to both *The Private Life of Sherlock Holmes* and *Murder by Decree*, Holmes's failures, or perceived failures, come to define his character, as ultimately young Sherlock is unable to prevent Elizabeth's death at the hands of the villainous Professor Rathe (Anthony Higgins). Holmes's personal devastation at the loss causes him to consciously choose never to love again (rather than retreat into drugs), a conveniently adolescent construction of character that also nonetheless feeds the model of psychoanalysing Holmes and plumbing his 'hidden' past to understand his reasoning, as seen in *The Seven Per-Cent Solution*. Not unlike Ross's earlier film, this is also playful in tone, freely mixing the genres of adventure and detection, but overlaid with the unreconstructed appeal to wonder and spectacle.

What is significant here is the conscious address to a juvenile audience. One could, maybe overly reductively, call it condescension, and there is a feeling of contrivance in the way it represents its villains in a heavily over-determined Orientalist mode that makes it more a homage to *Indiana Jones and the Temple of Doom* (Spielberg, 1984) than to Doyle. But, it is also representative of the general shift in cinema in that period, towards a younger audience, doing what George Lucas said he wanted to do with *Star Wars* in 1977: give fairytales to a generation that had none. The recourse to classical figures or classical archetypes as part of this was actually quite natural, and bearing in mind that Tarzan, Allan Quatermain, Superman, and Flash Gordon had all been given new effects-driven treatments aimed at a youth audience through a veil of nostalgia on the part of their makers, it was probably inevitable that this would also happen to Sherlock Holmes. In this address to the young (or to a sense of child-like wonder) we have a demonstration of the perceived need on the part of cinematic storytellers to visualise their wildest imaginings with as much bombast as the screen could hold, a kind of cinematic 'shock and awe' that recalls Singer's account of the Victorian Press where 'Modernity ushered in a commerce of sensory shocks. The "thrill" emerged as the keynote of modern diversions' (1995: 88). Ironically though, the point of the film is the way in which Holmes transcends these wonders and becomes a mature (and traumatised) young adult. It is a contradictory message, perhaps, but one given force by the end-of-credits gag in which Professor Rathe is revealed to be alive and living in Switzerland under the assumed name 'Moriarty'. The (classical) adventure has just begun.

A step further backwards in demographic appeal was taken in *The Great Mouse Detective*. Based on Eve Titus's *Basil of Baker Street* (1958), the film is aimed squarely at children. It literally miniaturises the Holmes mythos. No need to be overly concerned even with the motivations of an adolescent here as Holmes becomes not a man, but a mouse. The film is, as noted, based on a novel (a series of novels, actually), and though it might seem a contrivance of the Disney machine, you have to bear two things in mind: first, at that time the Walt Disney company had not yet regained its hold on the popular audience (this would come in 1989 with *The Little Mermaid*), and second, the novel itself was not criticised as illegitimate in paralleling the adventures of Sherlock Holmes in the story of a mouse who emulates Holmes's techniques in order to solve problems in the rodentine world. It is important to understand it in the context of this overall sense of demographic reframing in the era and the recourse to classical models to provide the basis of new fairytales. Essentially, a child watching *The Great Mouse Detective* will get many of the pleasures of an adult watching Basil Rathbone, complete with the assurance of a moral universe defined in clear terms of good and evil, decent and depraved, asserting yet another classical model in which even the intertextuality is irrelevant (from the point of view of the child), but in which the world must be believable and comprehensible. Interestingly, like *Young Sherlock Holmes*, *The Great Mouse Detective* also deployed computer graphics as part of the otherwise classical animation style in rendering some of the mechanical settings in the film such as the interior of a clock, making it something of an aesthetic signifier of things to come in the form.

If the previous two films were concerned with escaping from the reality of the 1980s by way of juvenile spectacle, *Without a Clue* consciously, if gently, asks its audience to question the surface appearance of things in something of an echo (shadow?) of the sceptical 70s. The story revolves around a Holmes who is, in fact, an actor named Reginald Kincaid (Michael Caine) hired by Dr. John Watson (Ben Kingsley) as a front for his investigative activities. This contrivance mirrors the plot of the popular television series *Remington Steele* (TV 1982–7), of course, so no great claim to originality is made in admitting to some enjoyment of the premise. It also has the additional classical connection in symbolically elevating Dr Joseph Bell, by making a brilliant doctor the hero instead of a made-up 'consulting detective'. The television series *Murder Rooms* (TV 2000–1) would later do this also, but in a very different way.

The issue at the heart of *Without a Clue* is again a recognition of the intertextual, in that audiences will recognise a fusion of realities in an in-jokey tale of the egos of actors and the image of classical authority projected by Victorians in a film in which two Oscar winning British actors fill the lead roles. It is hard not to listen to Caine and Kingsley's exchanges about acting, performance, and illusion and not feel the audience is being addressed directly and begged for their indulgence. In an early scene Holmes complains to Watson about the difficulty of memorising endless 'twaddle', by which he means the jargon-heavy detail upon which Watson's deductions are made. It's a mild type of reflexivity, yes, but it is knowing, and contributes to the overall sense that the film is consciously unmasking its own artificiality while addressing the mechanics of the genre. In casting Caine the film also consciously engages a social agenda already seen in action in *Murder by Decree*, whereby the conceits of the upper classes are shown to be remote from the realities of the proletariat. As Sherlock Holmes, Caine is all authority, clarity, and class, but it is, of course, a front. As Reginald Kincaid, Caine deploys his usual repertoire of comic cockney conceits, and by doing so neatly summarises his own career, which has allowed him to move between both registers. As Watson, Kingsley presents a unique redemption of the Watson figure, arguably by way of Dr. Joseph Bell, and thereby intertextually addressing the artificiality of the Holmes mythos itself. This Watson is also reflexive of Doyle himself though, in that as the author of the Holmes stories, he finds himself unable to create an alternative character 'John Watson: The Crime Doctor' when he fires Kincaid in anger and frustration, and the publisher of the stories threatens to sue him unless he brings Holmes back.

Without A Clue is a very mild piece of cinematic craft, feeling more like a television production for the most part and modest in its ambition, yet by virtue of its central conceit and its casting, it does achieve some rhetorical effect in its deployment of 'Sherlock Holmes', a very apt illustration of the era's concern with surface gloss. This is the world of the glitz and glamour of the 1980s, where Reaganite 'morning in America' misinformation, Thatcherite hard-sell advertising, spin doctors, media consultants, and the paparazzi seemed to mediate and even define the boundaries of perceived reality. It is given a Victorian analogue in a film inhabited by a Sherlock Holmes who is all image and no substance, barely controlled by an unlovable professional who stays hidden in his shadow.

It is, in some ways, an apologia for this world in that Kincaid is able to come good on the basis of his actual training in swordplay (for a play meaningfully entitled 'Shadow of Death') to defeat Moriarty (Paul Freeman), who knows Kincaid is an idiot actor and underestimates him as a result. In some ways the film is therefore as profoundly occupied with epistemological doubt as any of the 1970s films, but in common with the others of its era, it offers a happy resolution. In this case it is self-reflexivity and comedy rather than spectacle *per se*, although comedy does involve a high degree of spectacle in terms of visual and verbal gags that break the calm surface of reality with the unexpected. It also plays to the classic (and only partially tongue-in-cheek) observation by Ronald A. Knox that Holmes's penchant for theatricality and his taste for epigrams reveal something profoundly and believably human at the heart of the character (1928: 145–75). *Without a Clue* ends with Kincaid, having saved the day, proclaiming the case closed to the assembled press with a warm, wry grin that is every inch Michael Caine and not a bit Sherlock Holmes, and the result is that we smile too. As the 1970s left us with a strong sense of doubt, the 1980s left us with an illusion of reassurance in our recognition of the pervasiveness of artifice.

Conclusion

The iconic classical image of Sherlock Holmes comes with such a pre-loaded set of ideas around knowledge, reason, and justice that the deployment of Holmes enables film-makers to ask audiences to question the very basis of these things as much as it enables them to simply assert them. In viewing Holmes framed by doubt, disillusion, despair, irrationality, and wonderment, audiences are given a particular, powerful, and identifiable median point of reference rooted in a literary point of origin that remains untarnished by the revision. On the contrary, intertextual recognition of the source is essential to understanding the meaning and value of the rendering of the character. In the films of the 1970s and 80s, we see very particular demonstrations of this, bearing in mind that classical adaptations continued to be made throughout both periods. In examining these few and particular films, I am not suggesting that these alone represent either the best or the whole of a preferred reading of Sherlock Holmes. On the contrary, I am suggesting that they simply demonstrate the sense of possibility that comes with entry to the Kingdom of Shadows. By way of a brief conclusion, it is worth nothing that Guy Ritchie's 2009 rendering of the character through the prism of the 'new ladism' and 'bromance' is another clear example of the enduring appeal of the character, as is the 2010 BBC TV series *Sherlock*, where the technology and culture of the twenty-first century equally prove to be merely a veil through which to evaluate the virtue of intellectual interrogation and a desire for justice rooted in a point of origin that remains firmly canonical.

Notes

1. Doyle famously 'killed' the character in the short story 'The Final Problem' (1893).
2. Various sources date the film differently.
3. See Kramer and Grieveson (eds), *The Silent Cinema Reader* (2004); Thomas Elsaesser (ed.), *Early Cinema: Space, Frame, Narrative* (1990); Ben Brewster and Lea Jacobs, *Theatre to Cinema* (1997).
4. See Maxim Gorky, 'The Kingdom of Shadows' in Kevin Macdonald and Mark Cousins (eds), *Imagining Reality: The Faber Book of Documentary* (1996: 6–10).
5. This is a summary/paraphrase of Watson's description of Holmes in *A Study in Scarlet*.
6. For Friston's illustrations see *Beeton's Christmas Annual* of 1887, from engravings by W. M. R. Quick.
7. Images of both can be accessed online at http://www.artintheblood.com/greensherlock.htm
8. See Owen Dudley Edwards (1983: 35).

9. In *Jack the Ripper, The Final Solution* (1976), and fuelling renewed debate on the Ripper case. This is a vast area of research (known colloquially as 'Ripperology'). Donald Rumbelow's very useful summary book *The Complete Jack the Ripper* (1987) examines many of the fictive refigurations of the Ripper.

10. See David A. Cook, *A History of Narrative Film*, 3rd edn (1996: 944–8); Steven Bach, *Final Cut* (1985).

11. The very fact that this is so particularly non-canon is part of the point. We know explicitly from *A Study in Scarlet* how Holmes and Watson met. It doesn't matter. The film distils the essence of the mythos, repurposing it because it is *expected* that Holmes will have Watson by his side.

12. There had in fact been a short-lived *Young Sherlock* TV series in 1982. In 2010 Anthony Lane began a new *Young Sherlock Holmes* series of novels (not contiguous with the film).

5

Sherlock Holmes, Italian Anarchists and Torpedoes: The Case of a Manuscript Recovered in Italy[1]

Claudia Capancioni

In Arthur Conan Doyle's adventures of Sherlock Holmes, Italy is not a country for the iconic British detective to visit. John Watson considers Holmes's journeys to Tibet, Iran, Arabia and Sudan but rarely dwells on trips to continental Europe: there are only references to France, Switzerland, and (what was then) Imperial Russia.[2] Nonetheless, as Michael Kaser explains, Sherlock Holmes had 'many clients from across the Channel' (Haining, 1980: 94), including personalities such as the kings of Scandinavia and Bohemia, as well as the Pope.[3] However, Holmes's international reputation has inspired a number of European writers to relocate Doyle's hero in other countries. Singularly attractive to Italian writers, however, is the character's supposed fondness for Italian culture. Holmes escapes 'from [the] weary workaday world by the side door of music' (Doyle, 1951: 244), by listening to opera and frequenting 'garish' Italian restaurants (Doyle, 1997: 103). His knowledge of the Italian language, as Enrico Solito suggests,[4] is good and 'The Adventure of the Red Circle' (1911) demonstrates his ability to decipher a coded light signal in Italian. Whereas, in *The Alternative Sherlock Holmes: Pastiches, Parodies and Copies* (2003), Watt and Green simply state that 'probable visits to Italy are well supported by references in the Canon' (89), Solito eloquently investigates an unchronicled visit to Italy which Holmes refers to in 'The Adventure of the Empty House' (1903), the story that ends the Great Hiatus, in which Watson discovers that Holmes reached Florence a week after his fight with Moriarty on the Reichenbach Falls, on 4 May 1891.[5]

Since the beginning of the twentieth century, Italian writers have appropriated Holmes and relocated him in Italy through parodies and pastiches. Contemporary Italian writers, in particular, have created literary afterlives of Holmes worthy of attention, such as Umberto Eco's *Il nome della rosa* (1980, *The Name of the Rose*, 1983). Like Eco, other Italian writers appropriate Doyle's character, or his archetypal features, in order to give life to historical detective stories. This chapter analyses an original Italian period apocryphal narrative, Joyce Lussu's *Sherlock Holmes: anarchici e siluri* (1982, 'Sherlock Holmes: Anarchists and Torpedoes'),[6] in which Holmes is the epitome of deductive, scientific reasoning and impartial acumen, of the pursuit of justice more than of the law, and of the British Victorian gentleman. *Sherlock Holmes: anarchists and torpedoes* recreates the historical and geographical domains of Doyle's canon and transports Holmes to Italy on the basis of an international case of espionage. The date is 1908 and Holmes is personally entrusted with an investigative case in the Italian central Adriatic region of the Marche by the Minister of War, Richard Burton Haldane (1856–1928), and the Prime Minister, Henry Campbell-Bannemann (1839–1908). This British secret mission involves international politics and military projects implicated in the development of new technological weapons: torpedoes for submarines. Holmes must investigate the presence of a secret Austro-Hungarian plant in Ancona, Marche's larger city and sea port. He succeeds in his mission with the help of local anarchists and socialists; then, back in London, he disappears, leaving his account of this case with Watson.

The novel ends with an unexpected postscript where Lussu declares that her story is in fact based on Holmes's autobiographical account: she found his journal among the manuscripts and documents of her grandmother, the British novelist Margaret Collier (1846–1928). Collier kept Holmes's manuscript together with three pages of her own diary sealed in an envelope. The pages of her diary entries describe Watson's visit to her home in Plymouth and his decision to leave Holmes's journal with her. Thus, Lussu's novel openly signals its parodic nature in a postmodern sense: *Sherlock Holmes: anarchists and torpedoes* is a postmodern parody as defined in Linda Hutcheon's words, 'a value-problematizing, de-naturalizing form of acknowledging the history (and through irony the politics) of representations' (1989: 94). In using parody, Lussu destabilises the readers' expectations in relation to a Sherlockian story and to the authorship of such a story. She subverts historical and literary representations by casting the famous fictional British detective as a 'misunderstood character' (211), and transforming common people into the heroes and heroines of a detective story. Moreover, she grants Holmes a voice: free from 'his biographers, Watson, Arthur and Adrian Conan

Doyle' (211), he is able to express a troubled conscience as he is significantly changed by the sacrifice of an anarchist. In Lussu's novel, this icon of Britishness and the British Empire articulates a pacifist view and moves towards expressing a postcolonial perspective.

Sherlock Holmes's Italian afterlives

The Alternative Sherlock Holmes: Pastiches, Parodies and Copies (2003) specifies that '[t]he writing of pastiches and parodies began within five years of the first Sherlock Holmes story' (1), but in Italy the phenomenon began later. In 1887, the publication of the very first Italian detective story, Emilio De Marchi's *Il cappello del prete* ('The Priest's Hat'), coincided with the publication of Doyle's *A Study in Scarlet*. Nevertheless, the first Italian translation of Doyle's stories only appeared in 1895, when the publishing house Verri collected three stories in a single volume entitled *Le avventure di Sherlock Holmes* ('The adventures of Sherlock Holmes'). Italian readers waited until 1899 to be able to read Holmes's adventures in Italian on a regular basis, and almost simultaneously with the British readership, when they were finally published in the *Corriera della sera* weekly magazine, *La Domenica del Corriere*. Since then, Doyle's canon has not been out of print; even when the Fascist dictatorship censored detective fiction as immoral, and ostracised English and French literature in general, detective stories were available underground. The name of Doyle's character has made it into the Italian language by means of the expression *essere uno Sherlock*, defining a person with deductive skills comparable to Holmes.[7] Many Italian writers have paid literary homage to Holmes with pastiches and parodies, beginning with Dante Minghelli Vaini who, in 1902, celebrated Holmes as the archetype of the perfect detective gentleman with a collection of six stories set in Italy and narrated by Dr Maltson entitled *Shairlock Holtes in Italia* ('Shairlock Holtes in Italy'), published under the obvious pseudonym Donan Coyle.[8]

Lussu's *Sherlock Holmes: anarchists and torpedoes* appeared in print at a time when Italian detective fiction had achieved a high popular and academic profile. In recent years, this national attention has become international with Andrea Camilleri's Inspector Salvo Montalbano series, in which the eponymous detective is a civil servant who, like Holmes, pursues justice beyond the law. Luca Crovi (*Tutti i colori del giallo* 2002, 'All the Shades of Yellow') affirms that, in the 1980s and 1990s, many writers of detective fiction won literary prizes and obtained a wider readership.

Sherlock Holmes: anarchists and torpedoes has not yet been translated into English, but Italian Sherlockians have shown an increasing interest in Lussu as a member of the community of authors who are devotees of Doyle's canon and endeavour to keep it alive.[9] The novel is often cited in the context of Italian studies of Holmes's afterlives and her name circulates on the World Wide Web as the author of an unusual Italian apocrypha in which Doyle's private detective is transported into the Italian political context at the beginning of the twentieth century.[10]

The Italian location of *Sherlock Holmes: anarchists and torpedoes* is of historical relevance. In 1908, this region captured the historical, political and cultural complexities of the country. Before Italy's unification in 1861, the Marche reflected the peninsula's division: the Pope ruled over most of the region while the south was part of the Kingdom of the Two Sicilies. In 1860, near Ancona, the militia of Giuseppe Garibaldi (1807–82) defeated the Papal States' forces, supported by France and Austria. This victory marked the end of Italian Risorgimento, the Italian struggle for unification. This Italian region also resonates with autobiographical intertexts for Lussu. Both her British maternal grandmother, Margaret Collier, and her paternal great-grandmother, Ethelin Welby (1817–95), married into the local gentry of the Marche area. As a result, this region is for her a space of encounter where a plurality of stories is 'absorbed and transformed' (Roudiez, 1980: 66). Her multinational family's commitment to British and Italian political, artistic and scientific fields intertwines with their involvement in the lives of the local inhabitants of the Marche and their participation in anarchist, pacifist and socialist movements. In the first instance, *Sherlock Holmes: anarchists and torpedoes* is an anomaly in her writing career: in fact, it is her only detective story. Born into an Anglo-Italian anti-fascist family, Lussu (1912–98) lived an intense political and intellectual life as a Resistance fighter, a feminist, a pacifist, and an environmental activist. Her oeuvre spans a wide range of genres and subject matters from 1939 to 1998, including poetry, prose, political and historical essays, as well as translations. When she moved from Rome to the Marche in the later part of her life, she developed an interest in her ancestral home and the role her family played in this region's historical and cultural heritage.[11] This region is therefore a unique source for her interweaving of historical and fictional characters, of international and local events, as well as public and personal stories.

At an autobiographical intertextual level, *Sherlock Holmes: anarchists and torpedoes*, is informed by her Anglo-Italian heritage: Holmes is an acquaintance of her grandmother and her uncle, the portraitist John

Collier (1850–1934). The Colliers have been defined as 'an interesting dynasty' (Jenkins, 1995: 369) founded by Lussu's great-grandfather, Robert Porrett Collier, first Baron Monkswell (1817–86), who was appointed to the Judicial Committee of the Privy Council by Gladstone in 1872. It was a progressive, liberal, intellectual and political family closely linked to the Huxley family.[12] On the way to Ancona, Holmes befriends Lussu's grand-uncle Tommaso Salvadori (1835–1923), an eminent ornithologist who worked at the British Museum from 1890 to 1894. He was among the one thousand volunteers who, led by Garibaldi, landed in Sicily in June 1860. In the Marche, Holmes interacts with real-world historical local figures such as the painter Sigismondo Nardi (1866–1924) and the scientist Luigi Paolucci (1849–1935). Moreover, in this Italian afterlife, the archetypal British Victorian gentleman meets members of Lussu's family who experienced Victorian London and the Marche at the turn of the century. Through their Anglo-Italian point of view, Holmes reflects on the limits of imperialist politics as being disrespectful of the value of differences at international, or local, level. Lussu constructs her family as Holmes's unique opportunity to examine the value of pacifism and multinationalism.

The Case of a Manuscript Recovered in the Marche

Sherlock Holmes: anarchists and torpedoes was published in 1982. A second edition was included in the collection entitled *Storie* ('Stories') which was published in 1986. While the general narrative frame remains the same, the text in the second edition has been extensively revised: there is a further final chapter and the discussion of Holmes's state of mind is expanded as Lussu develops a psychoanalytical aspect to Holmes's encounter with Italian anarchists. The postscript is followed by historical notes on events related to the First World War and an alphabetical list including all the real-world historical characters with brief biographical and bibliographical details, entitled 'Personaggi e interpreti' ('Characters and cast'). The second edition was republished in a commemorative new anthology, *Opere scelte* ('Selected Works'), in 2008. This chapter focuses on the second edition and its subversive postmodern nature which claims a new political voice for Holmes. The protagonist of this detective fiction is not a ready-made transposed Holmes, but a fictional character unfolding his personality as a result of the liberating absence of Watson's narrating voice.

In comparison with the international context of alternative stories of Holmes, *Sherlock Holmes: anarchists and torpedoes* is a new story that directly refers to the original canon. In the second chapter, Holmes is introduced as a man of about fifty years of age who 'was born twenty years previously, in 1887, at the age of thirty, in the exuberant imagination of the English doctor and historian Arthur Conan Doyle' (127).[13] Lussu adapts Holmes as the protagonist of a story of international espionage in which the Italian anarchists' political stand against Austro-Hungarian imperial oppression slowly becomes his ulterior motive for investigation. As a period parody, it recalls Doyle's stories set in the early twentieth century in which the detective becomes an unofficially claimed national hero who defends the country from a foreign threat. Lussu's re-creation is mainly influenced by the atmosphere of some of the adventures, such as 'His Last Bow' (1917), in which England is not ready to step into the conflict to support France or Belgium because it is not prepared 'for submarine attack' in 1914 (Doyle, 1997: 184), and 'The Adventure of the Bruce-Partington Plans' (1908), whose title refers to the secret plans of the Bruce-Partington submarine. In *Sherlock Holmes: anarchist and torpedoes*, the characters discuss the Triple Alliance and the inevitably approaching war but, in the end, the British national hero discovers a different image of war and its consequences. The war does not simply demand the sacrifice of those who want to defend their countries voluntarily, but also of innocent citizens including children.

In relation to Doyle's narrative frame, the adventure of Holmes in the Marche precedes the events described in 'His Last Bow'. Holmes does not spend his retirement in Sussex in 1908, but instead is in London. After Watson's marriage, he is a regular guest at the Stephens' salon where the fictional protagonist interacts with real-world historical figures of the Bloomsbury Group, 'instead of relieving his melancholic solitude simply by playing his Stradivarius or injecting himself with morphine' (126).[14] The list includes the philosopher Bertrand Russell, the economist John Maynard Keynes, and writers such as Edward Morgan Forster, Herbert George Wells, and Rebecca West, as well as Vanessa Bell and Virginia Woolf. After the mission in the Marche, Holmes spends only twenty-four hours in his flat; then, in 1909, he is reported missing by members of the Bloomsbury Group.

In *Sherlock Holmes: anarchists and torpedoes* the anonymity of the third-person narrator is complicated by the final meta-narrative twist. In line with a biographical tradition which aims to prove the existence of Doyle's character, Lussu does not doubt the reality of Holmes's person but challenges the authority of Holmes's biographer, Watson, and by extension Doyle himself. She questions the conformity of the official portrayal of Holmes by claiming his independence from Doyle's authority. In the postscript, she creates a link between her parody and the original by assuming the role of Holmes's biographer instead of Watson. She is his biographer in a way in which Watson could not be as she describes Holmes's development of a different understanding of nationalism in his encounter with Italian anarchists. In Lussu's literary creation, Watson does not want to keep Holmes's personal journal in his dispatch box 'located at the Charing Cross branch of the Cox and Co. bank' (Doyle, 1951: 134), but cannot destroy it. He does not accept Holmes's 'sympathy for anarchists and socialists' (213),[15] and therefore he cannot narrate his Italian adventure. Instead, he entrusts Lussu's grandmother with Holmes's manuscript. In recognising Watson's role as a 'friend and biographer' (211) of Holmes,[16] Collier adds:

> I must say that I had a very good impression of Holmes when we talked at length about Italy and the Marche, ... On the contrary, I have always had a much worse opinion of the stories of his biographers, Watson, Arthur Conan Doyle and all the others who have tried to narrate the adventures of this nice character, who is, in my opinion, largely misunderstood (211).[17]

Lussu's grandmother questions the authority of previous works by real and fictional Holmes's biographers. She perceives the importance of the story in understanding Holmes, but she does not narrate it. It is Lussu who takes responsibility for telling a story in which Holmes's political views are redefined.

In *Sherlock Holmes: anarchists and torpedoes*, the narrator affirms that Holmes has a 'manic-depressive' disposition:

> Dr Sigmund Freud, the renowned psychologist from Vienna, defined, by using modern terms, as 'manic-depressive'; in other words Holmes went from periods of frenetic and very lucid activities, in which he showed extraordinary mental and physical energies, to periods of stillness, of almost lethargy, marked by sceptical and sarcastic pessimism (127).[18]

The hero of logical deduction and scientific method is now qualified by both his rational *and* his irrational powers. Psychoanalysis is used to clarify behaviours described – but not explained – by Watson in the original stories. Rather than discussing the nature and the ethical implications of Holmes's conduct, he reduces them to eccentricities. Lussu explains them by alluding to the unconscious side of Holmes's mind, and the unpredictability of human behaviour. In her story, the narrator does not sympathise with Watson's vagueness, omissions and silences, but examines explicitly what has been suppressed: Holmes's sexuality and his consumption of stimulant drugs. Her portrayal praises his exceptional deductive skills but also takes into account his contradictory tendencies towards irrationality and excess. The narrator is interested in highlighting the contradictions between Holmes's rational and Romantic qualities, and the ways in which he has been trying to reconcile them. Holmes has, in fact, attempted to improve his social skills, albeit with difficulty. Instead of escaping to the isolation of drugs, he enjoys the company of other exceptional figures of his time in the Stephens' salon. He does not simply cite literary works but, as an acquaintance of the Bloomsbury Group, he is well informed about contemporary literary and art movements, and contemporary social and philosophical research.

In the fifth chapter, a confident Holmes admits to his homosexuality and the use of morphine; he also suggests that others read Freud's essays in order to study the subject better. In his discussion of masculinity in the work of Doyle, Joseph Kestner argues that Doyle's hero is an icon possessing all of the qualities defined as masculine in Victorian society, such as 'observation, rationalism, factuality and logic, comradeship, daring and pluck' (Kestner, 1997: 2). In Lussu's text, however, the exceptionality of Holmes's deductive skills does not conflict with a sexuality that could define him as an outsider. His otherness as a homosexual and a drug taker is significant to Lussu's Holmes because it provides a level of understanding between him and the anarchists he meets in the Marche. This representative of Victorian masculinity is up against a female legend of the early twentieth century, Mata Hari, who represents the myth of the female spy, the *femme fatale* who uses her sexuality as a weapon. She appears as a mysterious woman who is not successful in attracting Holmes's attention. Here, Lussu has interpreted the incongruity and silences surrounding the *sexual* identity of Doyle's fictional hero in order to direct the spotlight onto other problematic issues relating to identity, such as moral values and patriotism. The attention is solemnly and centrally on the issues of war in moral terms and Holmes's 'otherness' is functional to his interest and sympathy towards one anarchist in particular, Giovanni Lupis, who is the character who argues against war most strongly in the text. Lupis is an engineer turned anarchist who articulates the ethical concerns and the consequences of the use of scientific progress for military purposes. While Holmes has a complex and conflicting personal identity, Lupis has a complex national identity that creates for him a difficult, conflicting political position.

Fiction and history intermingle in the creation of the character Lupis, based on Giovanni Luppis (1813–75), an engineer who collaborated with Robert Whitehead (1823–1905) in the creation of the first torpedo, called Whitehead-Luppis, at the Stabilimento Tecnico Fiumano, a technical plant in Fiume (currently Rijeka in Croatia). In 1908, Fiume was an Austro-Hungarian city with a large Italian ethnic minority, which is why Luppis served in the Austrian navy despite his Italian origins. In Lussu's fictional world, the engineer who invented a prototype of a military weapon becomes an anarchist who regrets his invention because he fears its future use as an instrument of death:

> I hate war, sir, this terrible devastation which takes us back in history and causes unspeakable suffering. But the war will occur and I will not be able to be an impassive and impartial witness (142).[19]

An old and sick Lupis expresses his opinion on war and political activism to the British consul in Ancona, Edward Kane, after having clarified the difference between his Italian origins and his citizenship. Although he has 'Italian language and nationality' (138),[20] he is an Austrian citizen. He solves the case by sacrificing his life in order to destroy the secret military plant. Holmes compares him to Saint George, highlighting their similar 'fight against imaginary and real monsters' (182).[21]

The traditional Sherlockian plot is modified as the famous detective does not reach the solution alone. In Ancona, Holmes shares his investigation with Kane, Lupis, and a young orphan called Domenico. Thirteen-year old Domenico helps Lupis in finding the location of the plant by telling him a story of secret passages, and 'very beautiful silver fish which are tapered and as big as whales with a little house on their backs which reminded me of the ones carried by elephants' (194).[22] In his young mind, the torpedoes become 'sparkling' fish (194).[23] However, Lupis recognises them as military weapons and explains to the child:

> [W]ar is the most horrific thing humankind invented. My son, I wish you would never experience war. Look always for people who hate war and love peace, and stay close to them, work with them (196).[24]

As an engineer who is conscious of his role in creating military weapons, Lupis advises Domenico to be a pacifist. He is concerned with the forthcoming war and wants to transmit a message of peace.

He invites Domenico to tell his story; he then executes his plan and dies destroying the plant.

The case is solved, but it is no longer the main subject of the story. The plot is complicated by the death of Domenico, who is killed by a stray bullet and, in Holmes's own words, becomes 'the first victim of the great world war' (202).[25] Holmes rhetorically asks Kane, 'Don't you know that you win a war by killing old anarchists and young thirteen-year old boys?'(202).[26] Domenico's story signifies the death of many unknown, unaware citizens who happen to be inadvertently involved in a war. The loss of soldiers' lives symbolised by monuments dedicated to the 'Unknown Warrior' is here replaced by the image of Domenico's dead body held in Holmes's arms. Domenico's story is a testimony to an unofficial history of those lives that remain untold and unrecognised, especially the old and the children who die as victims of a decision made by a minority.

The final chapter of *Sherlock Holmes: anarchists and torpedoes* expands on the psychological effects of the tragic deaths of Lupis and Domenico on the British detective. Holmes returns to London traumatised. Leonard Huxley, Virginia and Vanessa Stephen, and Leonard Woolf visit Holmes's flat and discover his drawings of an old man and a young boy in conversation. Holmes's traumatic memories create symbolic images of this dialogue, of explosions and blood, in which a black tie symbolises Lupis's anarchism and scary silver fish describe Domenico's fantastic adventure. The narrator points out an old man's face which variously expresses happiness and pain; his mouth is at times 'half open as if he spoke, at times torn by red strokes of blood' (205).[27] This half-open mouth symbolises Holmes's struggle as much as Lupis's struggle. Holmes listened to the dialogue between Lupis and Domenico and would be able to pass their story on himself, but his memories appear to be unspeakable. The story ends without certainties regarding Holmes's location and activities. There is no explanation regarding the connection between the account of this adventure of Sherlock Holmes and its narrator; the readers are left with an open ending. It is the post-script that uncovers Holmes's original autobiographical account of this story.

In *Sherlock Holmes: anarchists and torpedoes* Lussu adapts Holmes as the protagonist of a story in which an Italian anarchist's political act provokes a reconsideration on the nature of war. In the postscript, she claims Holmes's autobiographical voice. He was able to put his memories in writing but, in the case of this adventure, Watson leaves them unchronicled. As Collier's diary explains, Watson believes Holmes's journal 'provides clear evidence of Mr Holmes's patriotic values darkening, even a lack of respect towards our most sacred institutions, our glorious Army and our glorious Navy' (213).[28] This patriotic Watson cannot represent a new Holmes whose pursuit of justice has taken him on a life changing journey and who now identifies with anarchic and socialist views. Only Virginia Woolf is not troubled by Holmes's change of heart: in the last chapter, she asks the novel's most topical question, '[w]hat is unusual about Holmes making friends with anarchists?'(205).[29] She supports Holmes's pacifist afterlife, disregarding the archetypal Victorian imperialist Britishness in Holmes in order to celebrate him as the archetype of British acumen that pursues justice beyond nationalist values.

In the interweaving of family history, fiction and espionage, the issue of authorship loses relevance as Holmes's journal passes from hand to hand in Lussu's family. It is the survival of the story which it tells that matters. Holmes's testimony of Lupis and Domenico's story survives and can be passed down in the written form. It is translated, interpreted, and manipulated, but it is not forgotten. As Brian McHale argues, a detective story is 'the epistemological genre *par excellence*' (McHale, 1987: 9). In her Italian Holmes pastiche, consequently, Lussu extends the epistemological themes of this literary genre to comprise history itself, investigating and analysing past history but from a pacifist perspective. She sets out to 'free' Holmes's unauthorised voice from the repressive narratives of Watson/Doyle. In *Sherlock Holmes: anarchists and torpedoes*, moreover, Doyle's fictional hero takes on the duty of transmitting the anarchic and socialist pacifist legacy of the Marche. In this Italian postmodern afterlife, Holmes is cast to signify a commitment to justice without frontiers.

Notes

1. As Joyce Lussu's *Sherlock Holmes: anarchici e siluri* has not been translated, all translations from the original Italian are mine.
2. See Roberts (1984) A Biographical Sketch of Sherlock Holmes. In: Shreffler, ed. *The Baker Street Reader: Cornerstone Writings about Sherlock Holmes*; Haining (ed.) *Sherlock Holmes Compendium*.
3. In *The Hound of the Baskervilles* (1901–2), Holmes investigates the Vatican cameos; in 'Black Peter' (1904) the case concerns the death of Cardinal Tosca.
4. Solito is one of Italy's major experts on Doyle's canon, and is the author of parodies and pastiches such as *Sherlock Holmes e le ombre di Gubbio* (2006) and *Sherlock Holmes e l'orrore di Cornovaglia* (2008). He is a leading member of the Sherlock Holmes Society of Italy, *Uno Studio in Holmes* (A Study in Holmes). This society publishes *Sherlock Magazine* [http://www.unostudioinholmes. org]. Solito also edits the society's journal, entitled *The Strand Magazine*.

5. See Solito, E. & Salvatori, G. (eds) (2010) *Italy and Sherlock Holmes* [http://www.bakerstreetjournal.com].
6. In this chapter, I refer to *Sherlock Holmes: anarchici e siluri* by using the title's translation into English. All quotations are from its second edition, as included in the anthology Lussu published in 1986 entitled *Storie* ('Stories').
7. See Pirani, R. (ed.) (1999) *Le piste di Sherlock Holmes*.
8. See Crovi, L. (2000) *Delitti di carta nostra: una storia del giallo*.
9. Lussu's personal membership card for 'The Sherlock Holmes Society' of London is kept with her documents by her son.
10. See 'Sherlock Holmes e il Conero' (2005) and 'Ancona, nuova musa degli autori polizieschi' (2005). They show an interest in Lussu's work based on its location in the *Sherlock Magazine* [http://www.sherlockmagazine.it/giornale.php].
11. See *Le inglesi in Italia: storia di una tribù anglo-franco-marchigiana in un angolo remoto degli Stati Pontifici* (1970, 'English Women in Italy: The Story of an Anglo-French Family from the Marche in a Remote Corner of the Papal States'); *Margaret Collier. La nostra casa sull'Adriatico: diario di una scrittrice inglese in Italia (1873–1885)* (1981, 'Our Home by the Adriatic: The Italian Diary of an English Woman Writer, 1873–1885'); *La storia del fermano: dalle origini all'unità d'Italia*, (1982, 'The History of Fermo: From its Origin to the Unification of Italy').
12. John Collier was married first to Marian Huxley and, after her death, to Ethel Huxley. They were Thomas Huxley's daughters.
13. *Era nato venti anni prima, nel 1887, già quasi trentenne, dalla fervida fantasia del medico e storico inglese Arthur Conan Doyle.*
14. *invece di alleviare le malinconie della solitudine soltanto con gli esercizi al suo stradivario o con le iniezioni di morfina.*
15. *delle simpatie per gli anarchici e per i socialisti.*
16. *amico e biografo.*
17. *Debbo dire che Holmes mi aveva fatto un'ottima impressione e avevamo parlato a lungo dell'Italia e delle Marche, ... Impressione molto meno buona mi hanno fatto invece i racconti dei suoi biografi, da Watson a Arthur Conan Doyle a tutti gli altri che hanno voluto descrivere le avventure di quel simpatico e, secondo me, largamente incompreso personaggio.*
18. *il dottor Sigmund Freud, il noto psicologo di Vienna, definiva in termini moderni 'manico-depressivo'; ossia Holmes passava da periodi di frenetica e lucidissima attività, in cui esprimeva energie mentali e fisiche al di sopra del normale, a periodi di stasi quasi sonnolenta, tinti di scettico e sarcastico pessimismo.*
19. *Io odio la guerra, signore, questo immane sconvolgimento che ci riporta sempre indietro nella storia e causa sofferenze inenarrabili. Ma la guerra ci sarà, e non potrò assistervi impassibile al di sopra delle parti.*
20. *di lingua e nazionalità italiana.*
21. *i mostri fantastici e reali.*
22. *bellissimi pesci d'argento tutti affusolati, grandi come balene, con sulla schiena una specie di casetta che mi fece pensare a quelle che portano gli elefanti.*
23. *luccicanti.*
24. *la guerra è la cosa più orrenda che l'uomo abbia inventato. Ti auguro di non conoscere mai una guerra, figlio mio. Cerca sempre le persone che odiano la guerra e amino la pace, e sta vicino a loro, lavora con loro.*

25. *primo caduto della grande guerra mondiale.*
26. *Non lo sa che le guerre si vincono ammazzando i vecchi anarchici e i ragazzi tredicenni?*
27. *bocca dischiusa come se parlasse, ora lacerata da rossi tratti di sangue.*
28. *c'è un evidente oscuramento dei sentimenti patriottici del Signor Holmes, addirittura una mancanza di rispetto verso le nostre istituzioni più sacre, il nostro glorioso Esercito e la nostra gloriosa Marina...*
29. Che c'è di strano se Holmes ha fatto amicizia con gli anarchici?

6
Sherlock's Progress through History: Feminist Revisions of Holmes

Sabine Vanacker

> I fear that Mr. Sherlock Holmes may become like one of those popular tenors who, having outlived their time, are still tempted to make repeated farewell bows to their indulgent audiences. This must cease and he must go the way of all flesh, material or imaginary. One likes to think that there is some fantastic limbo for the children of imagination, *some strange, impossible place* where the beaux of Fielding may still make love to the belles of Richardson, where Scott's heroes still may strut, Dickens's delightful Cockneys still raise a laugh, and Thackeray's worldlings continue to carry on their reprehensible careers. Perhaps in some humble corner of such a Valhalla, Sherlock and his Watson may for a time find a place, while some more astute sleuth with some even less astute comrade may fill the stage which they have vacated. (Doyle, 1981, *The Case-book of Sherlock Holmes*: 983)

In 1927 Arthur Conan Doyle published *The Case-Book of Sherlock Holmes*, his fifth and final collection of short stories about the iconic detective. Tellingly, he uses the preface to invoke a fictional ending for his protagonist and an afterlife, an imaginary universe where heroes and their fictional narratives can endure. At the same time, however, he pictures an alternative future in which a defiant Holmes might stage an 'unauthorised' return like an aging, needy tenor conspiring with his indulgent audience. Of course, the author had already tried to murder the character in 'The Final Problem' (1893) – the Reichenbach Falls, a desperate struggle and a watery death – but Holmes had swiftly revealed himself to be a fictional monster that could not be contained. Doyle soon experienced what Martin Priestman has called the 'raw power' of series fiction (Priestman, 2000: 54), the readers' desire for more stories and their refusal to let a fictional universe end. Twenty-thousand cancelled *Strand* subscriptions later, Doyle gave in to public demand and his own financial needs by resurrecting Holmes in 'The Adventure of the Empty House' in *The Strand Magazine* (October 1903; Pugh, 2005: 18). For a brief period, two opposing potentialities now coexisted. In one narrative strand, Sherlock Holmes is catastrophically dead at Reichenbach. Watson is heart-broken; we sense the pathos of a tragic, dark and finite universe. Simultaneously, there is Holmes resurrected, comic, inviolate and unending; the universe imperfect and flawed but forever open to resolution. In his own writing practice Doyle would continue to perform this narrative ambiguity, constantly shelving Holmes for other projects and then resurrecting him to knit yet another mystery into his hero's fictional life. Encountering a living Holmes in 'The Adventure of the Empty House', Watson faints in the presence of this *revenant* but the mystery is soon explained: Holmes has been away to draw out his remaining enemies, travelling through Italy, Tibet, Persia, Sudan and France in an absence that Holmesian folklore has since termed his 'hiatus' (Doyle, 1981: 485–8).

For Doyle, resurrecting Holmes meant re-entering a known fictional universe, with familiar characters, recognisable mysteries, methods and solutions. Priestman has pointed to Doyle's early mastery of the series phenomenon as crucial to his long lasting and pervasive success. The format Doyle developed is indeed both paradoxical and compelling: as part of a series, the individual stories are governed by repetition, featuring the same characters performing 'the same kind of action in roughly the same narrative space or time-slot' (Priestman, 2000: 50). Holmes and Watson are forever setting off from and returning to 221b Baker Street; their unequal relationship is restated throughout; Doyle regularly repeats Holmes's scenes of instruction on observation and deduction. Besides this static quality, this 'endlessly repeating present' (Priestman, 2000: 54), at the heart of the Holmes canon there is a yearning for change, for additional information about Holmes, for growth and development in the character and a narrative arc that outstretches the limited plot line of each adventure. It is this fundamental tension that has generated so many Holmes stories and has, ever since, left readers wanting more. Grafting additional, complementary stories onto an existing corpus – some set after the 'hiatus', some represented as the collection of earlier adventures – Arthur Conan Doyle, post-Reichenbach, in fact became the first contributor to Holmes's cultural 'afterlife'.[1]

Since Doyle's own death this fictional afterlife has – not surprisingly – continued. The many writers who have since contributed Holmes stories and 'apocrypha'– Richard Lancelyn Green, David Stuart Davies and William Baring-Gould, to name but a few – have between them filled out the titillating details Doyle provided about the biography of his hero. We know about his early career, his spying brother Mycroft and his French ancestry. This corpus of canonic and 'unauthorised' Holmes stories has expanded exponentially with so-called fan fiction. Largely (but not exclusively) internet-based, fan fiction collects stories by reader–writers, fans of Sherlock Holmes who continue the Holmes environment by writing their own narratives. The fan fiction sites devoted to Holmes join with others – sites devoted to Jane Austen's fiction, for instance, to the Harry Potter phenomenon, to *Star Trek* or *Blake's Seven* – in demonstrating the fictional drive and potential of fans, whose writing exists on the same spectrum between repetition and continuation on the one hand, and innovation and development on the other. Fan fiction writers and readers treat an author's fictional universe as a narrative playground, 'part of a resource that belonged to all' (Stasi 2006: loc. 1799). It is a fascinating new phenomenon that might have appealed to Doyle's more entrepreneurial instincts: readers who enjoy the fiction so much that they write to prolong its life.

However, Holmes has undergone an even more radical transformation. In yet another demonstration of readers' creative potential the two long-established detective series that are the subject of this chapter – Laurie R. King's 'Mary Russell' series and the 'Irene Adler' series of Carole Nelson Douglas – present the Holmes world as a woman-centred universe. This chapter will consider these feminist revisions of the Holmes myth using the critical perspective developed for the collaborative, democratic and ever-open phenomenon of fan fiction and other so-called 'archontic' literature. The first section will consider how these feminist stories are grafted onto the Holmes canon. For instance, in Douglas's series, Holmes himself appears, but the stories focus on his famous adversary from 'A Scandal in Bohemia' (1891). Here Irene Adler is still an American 'contralto' opera singer who, like her Doyle counterpart, enjoys a liaison with a boorish Bohemian king. Unlike Doyle's 'deceased' Irene, she is very much alive and married to Godfrey Norton. Laurie King's transformation of the Holmes myth, moreover, feels even more piercing: her Holmes meets a feminist Jewish Anglo-American girl, Mary Russell. In the course of the first novel he trains Mary as a detective and they fall in love. With Mary as his sidekick, the pairing with Watson – the 'great male dyad' – is subverted, the male-centred

Holmes myth fundamentally altered (Pugh, 2005: 103). As a result, the feminist revisions by Douglas and King 'actualise' situations that 'A Scandal in Bohemia' only touches upon tentatively and temporarily: Holmes defeated by Irene Adler or Holmes in love with a woman who is his equal. In *Difference and Repetition* Gilles Deleuze famously emphasised the 'reality' not only of what actually happens, but also of any event that could *potentially* take place: 'The virtual is fully real in so far as it is virtual' (Deleuze, 1994: 208; quoted in Stasi, 2006: 1049–52). With the virtual feminist potential of the Holmes stories thus actualised, the final section of this chapter will investigate the ambiguous function of history in the two series.

Finding the narrative gaps and feminising the Holmes myth

The Doyle pastiches by King and Douglas are explicitly and playfully intertextual projects. They share this feature with all the amateur and professional writers of Holmes stories, and indeed with the serial author Arthur Conan Doyle himself, as he fixed yet another Holmes adventure within the existing body of work. In an article that attempts to relate fan fiction theoretically to its source texts, Abigail Derecho reflects on the terminology for this phenomenon. Rejecting terms such as 'derivative' or 'appropriative' literature, Derecho suggests the Derridean term of 'archontic' fiction.[2] As a neutral term 'archontic fiction' favours neither source text nor target text, while at the same time it highlights the *intentionally* allusive nature of fan fiction. Archontic fiction, in this context, is all fiction committing itself to establishing a dialogue with a source text that is culturally central and resonant (Derecho, 2006: 1047–8). Doyle's Holmes stories do indeed constitute such a master text, testifying to the centrality of Doyle's detective in late-Victorian and Edwardian British culture. They effectively and reiteratively perform the power of rationality, the power structures of Britishness, Empire and the hegemony of the gentleman. Holmes is his successful embodiment, a role model for boys and men, what Diana Barsham called a 'mentor of manhood' (2000: 11). King and Douglas, American female writers both, target some of the blind spots, gaps, omissions and repressions in the Holmes myth.

> For these gaps may only become visible – may only, indeed, be gaps – when the text is read from a position that refuses the illusion of continuity; and textual gaps are filled in according to an associative, not a deductive, logic. (Willis, 2006: 2273–4)

From their mainstream feminist perspective, King and Douglas seek to 'correct' certain aspects of the Holmes myth, disentangling it from the late-Victorian ideology to which it subscribes and which it naturalises, giving it a woman-friendly, modestly liberal feminist tendency. Like fan fiction writers, they love the canon on which they base their texts, but they critique what Ika Willis has called the 'docility' of the intertext, seeking to open up the Sherlock Holmes universe to alternative, possibly subversive, cultural and ideological codes (Willis, 2006: 2273–4).

Archontic writers, such as Douglas, King, Baring-Gould and the fan fiction writers, approach the Holmes canon obliquely: 'Fanfic happens in the gaps between canon, the unexplored or insufficiently explored territory' (Pugh, 2005: 92). Fan fiction writers often choose to focus on scenes not described in the canonic stories, or develop and speculate on certain characters. Laurie King makes such use of Holmes's brother Mycroft, who features in a few stories of Doyle's canon – 'The Greek Interpreter' (1893), 'The Final Problem' (1893), 'The Adventure of the Empty House' (1903) – but who plays an increasingly central role in King's series. Alternatively, similar to the debates often taking place in Sherlockian journals, archontic writers may 'mine' the Doyle canon searching for its gaps, omissions or contradictions. They focus, for instance, on explaining the mystery of Watson's war wounds (a Jezail bullet to the shoulder in *A Study in Scarlet*, 1887), an injured leg in *The Sign of Four* (1890), or on the lack of clarity about his marriage(s) (Campbell, 2007: 157). Even a renowned detective writer such as P. D. James cannot resist fan fiction behaviour in *Talking about Detective Fiction* (2009), playfully wondering about the other unfortunate tenants of Baker Street, those inhabiting a flat '221A, and possibly a 221C', speculating about Watson's bull pup and about the contradiction between Holmes's obvious success as a consulting detective and his modest accommodation (2009: 38).

Laurie King opts to set her Mary Russell series after the chronology constructed in Doyle's stories, rooting her opening novel onto a whimsical Doylean joke: the detective as retired beekeeper on the Sussex Downs as mentioned in both 'The Adventure of the Second Stain' (1904) and 'His Last Bow' (1917). King makes Holmes's beekeeping into the central metaphor of her series: *The Beekeeper's Apprentice* (1994) is later followed by *The Language of Bees* (2009) and *The God of the Hive* (2010). Carole Nelson Douglas, on the other hand, splices her detective stories into the story sequence created by Doyle: *Good Night, Mr Holmes* (1990), for instance, lodges itself in the undefined narrative space between *A Study in Scarlet* and 'A Scandal in Bohemia'. Early on in the novel, Irene Adler and her sidekick Nell Huxleigh meet Jefferson Hope – Holmes's tragic antagonist in

A Study in Scarlet – and the story ends with Irene, now married to Godfrey Norton, departing for France at the end of 'A Scandal in Bohemia'.

In all its manifestations, the archontic universe created around Doyle's original Holmes is a surprisingly successful form of 'collective authorship', Barthes's death of the author predicating the creative rise of the reader/interpreter. Consequently, the series by Douglas and King challenge their readers to be vigilant textual detectives, alert for clues to the numerous allusive games. Only a proficient Doyle reader will pick up the initial clue to the central antagonist of *The Beekeeper's Apprentice*, linking Mary's female mathematics tutor at Oxford with 'Professor Moriarty of mathematical celebrity' (Doyle, 1981: 471). Their reader-ship must also be sufficiently well-read to recognise where the fictional world of Doyle merges with that of Kipling (as occurs in King's *The Game*, 2004) or with the equally virulent cultural myths circulating around Jack the Ripper (Douglas's *Castle Rouge*, 2002).

Both authors also engage explicitly with the Holmes apocrypha, most notably in their references to William Baring-Gould, who wrote an early fictional 'biography' of Sherlock Holmes using his grand-father's life as source material for the description of Sherlock's youth (King, 2002). In *The Moor*, Laurie King returns the favour by pressing William's grandfather, the Reverend Sabine Baring-Gould, into service as Sherlock Holmes's 'godfather'. The factual-fictional family relation-ship between Holmes and the Baring-Goulds strengthens and deepens in texture, as Baring-Gould is now himself pulled into the fictional realm. Carole Nelson Douglas plays a similar game with Baring-Gould: in the scholarly apparatus with which she surrounds her Irene Adler novels, the fictional scholar Fiona Witherspoon reacts with outrage to Baring-Gould's speculation of a marriage between Holmes and Adler (Douglas, 2005: 393). Laurie King's series, on the other hand, opts for actualising Baring-Gould's suggestion: in *The Language of Bees* (2010) the two detectives discover that Holmes has indeed had a son by Irene Adler, and even has a (dead) daughter-in-law and a granddaughter. Like the competing, alternative story lines proliferating in internet fan fiction archives, King and Douglas colonise different plot lines and construct their novels in these alternative versions of fictionality.

Critics of fan fiction and other archontic narratives are very clear about the Barthesian impulse behind all this writing. Fan fiction is the unambiguous, dynamic and active expression of reader desire:

> We had a canon of stories invented by others, but we wanted more, sometimes because the existing stories did not satisfy us in some

way, sometimes because there are simply never enough stories and we did not want them to come to an end. So we invented the ones we wanted. (Pugh, 2005: 9)

As Willis reminds us, archontic writers take the 'immoral right' of Barthes' projected reader 'to make and circulate meanings' (Willis, 2006: loc.). Rudely re-orienting Doyle's world, King and Douglas perform the modern reader's desire, creating a Holmesian world that is no longer the homosocial late-Victorian environment but a recreated fictional past now profoundly sympathetic to women and to a feminist view. Both Irene Adler and Mary Russell parallel the utopianism personified in Doyle's Holmes: fantasies of female power for the late-twentieth-century female reader as Holmes was for his original audience. Both retain the Doylean aspiration to complete self-control; both novels pastiche Doyle's scenes of instruction, where an astounded Watson is taught to observe and deduce. Indeed, Mary 'out-sherlocks' Holmes: their first meeting is a dialogue of mutual readings, both protagonists confidently expounding the other's secrets based on their body language and dress (King, 1996: 8–9, 19–20). In Douglas's work too, there is often a flurry of such diagnostic Holmesian readings, regularly performed against Holmes himself, as when Godfrey Norton deduces Holmes's character from his look for the benefit of Irene (Douglas, 2005: 320). Carole Nelson Douglas constitutes a competing constellation of detective and sidekicks. Irene Adler too is on a hiatus and presumed deceased – Watson mistakenly reports her death in 'A Scandal in Bohemia', so the reasoning goes (Douglas, 2005: 2–3). Like Holmes, she is a shape shifter and actor, a cross dresser for detective purposes, adept at dialects. Her mobility and public presence – not expected in Doyle's period – results from her career as an opera singer and actress. In this feminist alternative universe, indeed, Holmes is frequently the antagonist, feared and disliked by the prim and partial Nell, a competitor from whom clues have to be hidden and solutions snatched.

The decline of a hegemonic detective

Both series, however, move beyond merely incorporating a female utopian figure into the Holmes myth. The entry of Mary Russell and Irene Adler coincides with the diminishment of the great detective. In the Mary Russell novels King introduces clear overtones of an (unfeminist) old-fashioned romance – the world's most hegemonic man falling for a sixteen-year old girl, the rational detective betrayed by his emotionality.[3] However, with the narrative focus on Mary, Holmes is assigned a secondary role in what are, at times, psychologically inflected novels, removing Holmes far from the rationalist fantasy of Doyle. Moreover, in her first novel, *The Beekeeper's Apprentice*, King develops a motif of old age around Holmes, then apparently (only) 54 (1996: 24). When Mary and Holmes first meet he is a man locked into the psychology of depression, as Mary explains: 'He was stagnating – yes, even he – and would probably have bored or drugged himself into an early death. My presence, my – I will say it – my love, gave him a purpose in life from that first day' (34). Indeed, King has Watson thanking Mary Russell for giving renewed energy and life to the detective, who appears so enfeebled that Watson feared 'he would not see a second summer, possibly not even the new year' (37). He even needs to be shielded from the loss of confidence attendant on encroaching old age: 'I said nothing, because he would hear only: Holmes, you're slipping' (265). More seriously still, the central threat in this novel is presented by a woman, the daughter of Holmes's old adversary Moriarty. Patricia Moriarty is so dangerous, so knowledgeable about Holmes and his methods that, so the story explains, the great detective has to be sidelined.

> A woman! She has turned my own words against me, ... you know ... this ... person has even penetrated into one of my bolt-holes! Yes, today, there were signs ... I still cannot believe that a woman can have done this, deducing my deductions, plotting my moves for me, and all the time giving the impression that to her it is a deadly but effortless and highly amusing game. (1996: 272)

Thus the story effectively turns into a battle between Mary Russell and Patricia Moriarty. For Moriarty's plot to be foiled Holmes is required to simulate weakness and humiliation as he pretends to pine for Mary Russell. Indeed, as he appears weaker, Mary Russell's role makes her stronger until 'I became, in other words, more like Holmes than the man himself: brilliant, driven to the point of obsession, careless of myself, mindless of others' (1996: 332). King defiantly mixes her metaphors in this novel, linking the fight between the old and young queen bees in a hive with the queens of a chess game, Holmes now the vulnerable king, surrendered in order to allow Mary to win the game.

Carole Nelson Douglas, on the other hand, undermines the Holmes myth by reading the Doyle universe as an act of patriarchal suppression. Douglas's series frames Irene's adventures with a faux-academic commentary by the American scholar 'Fiona Witherspoon, Ph. D, F.I.A'.

Her comments position Penelope Huxleigh's diaries about Irene as examples of a rediscovered and re-valued women's history: 'From her first outing, Douglas's Witherspoon raises issues of suppression, of who is allowed to tell the stories and of what stories get told' (Johnsen, 2006: 92). The Doyle manuscript is now read for its palimpsested underlying meanings; in the Douglas universe this suppressed feminist material is actualised and called forth. A minor Doyle character appearing in only one story, Irene Adler is famously called *'the'* woman by a half-regretful Holmes, in what Rosemary Johnsen notes is 'a key text for any feminist rewritings of Holmes' (2006: 95). 'A Scandal in Bohemia' is presented as the story of a near-miss romance for Holmes. Significantly, in this early story Doyle had simultaneously raised and foreclosed a plot line. With Irene Adler – whose portrait Holmes so famously keeps – he calls up the 'virtual reality' of a possible romantic story line and a possible major character. As Watson comments so evocatively, the event had the potential of undoing Holmes, of removing the source of his superiority – his rationality. Love and emotionality, says Watson, would be to Holmes like '[g]rit in a sensitive instrument, or a crack in one of his own high-power lenses' (Doyle, 1981: 161). However, by the start of his story, we are carefully assured, the danger has already been avoided, the rational identity is intact and only a photograph of Irene Adler remains. The photograph serves as a reminder, a warning but also as an amulet for protection: 'In his eyes she eclipses and predominates the whole of her sex' (Doyle, 1981: 161). Irene Adler's photograph presents *the* woman, a female ideal to which all other women are inferior. Her elevation predicates their subordination, her idealised, impossible picture a patriarchal fetish for the protection of Holmes. Into this narrative crevice, both signalled and denied by Doyle, into this small gap with potential for subversion, Carole Nelson Douglas wedges her Irene Adler stories.[4] By resurrecting Irene Adler, she not only revives the romantic danger to Holmes, but also threatens his narrative universe.

The feminist revisions by Douglas and King look for such traces of a potential story, for such narrative virtualities in the Doyle canon and in the apocrypha, unpicking Doyle's tale in order to weave a counter-discourse. *Good Night, Mr. Holmes* (2005) re-tells the story of Irene's shady love affair with the Bohemian king but from a female perspective, re-actualising what Watson and a fictional Doyle have redacted. In this female re-narration, Irene's stay in Bohemia is governed less by her love affair with the crown prince and more by her desire to sing at the Prague opera and pursue her artistic career. A more sinister figure than Doyle's pompous foreigner, the king attempts to entrap and detain

Irene, so keeping the photograph is not a case of blackmail but one of legitimate self protection. While staying close to the events described in the Doyle text, Douglas performs a 'resignification' of the central events and characters (Willis, 2006: 2286–7), effectively undermining the authority of Doyle's story as limited and male-centred. Holmes, the panopticist of the Doyle narratives, is demonstrated as having only limited vision, 'his extraordinary powers' of deduction resulting in only a partial explanation (Doyle, 1981: 161).

A neo-Victorian Holmes

Doyle's Holmes stories are fairly a-historical narratives. While they at times refer to contemporaneous events or anxieties – the Ku Klux Klan in 'The Five Orange Pips' (1891), the Molly Maguires in *The Valley of Fear* (serialised in 1914–15) – and are ready to exploit aspects of modernity – newspapers, type-writers, telegrams and train travel – they feel situated in a notional Victorian context that would become increasingly nostalgic as Doyle's series developed over time. Even *The Valley of Fear*, published in 1916, is a story that denies its First World War context; the action is placed in an almost mythological pre-war environment, sequestering the reader from the historical realities. In their feminist revisions of Holmes, however, both Douglas and King engage with history in a number of ways. Consequently, the many references to contemporary Victorian and Edwardian events and historical figures link the Holmes series of Douglas and King with the neo-Victorian novel. Cora Kaplan has highlighted the neo-Victorian novel's engagement with this period as a 'discourse through which both the conservative and progressive elements of Anglophone cultures reshaped their ideas of the past, present and future' (2007: 4).[5] In their recent definition of this popular new genre, Ann Heilmann and Mark Llewellyn emphasise the self-reflexive and self-conscious aspects of the genre (Heilmann and Llewellyn, 2010: 4). Part of the project shared by these archontic feminist revisions of Holmes involves a representation of the (late-) Victorian period as productive of the modern world, almost using the Victorian age as an explanatory origin myth for the complex modern world of the millennial society.

Rosemary Johnsen has suggested that King persistently presents the Holmes character in relation to historical change (Johnsen, 2006: 86–8) and indeed her series, which starts with Holmes and Mary meeting in 1915, explicitly positions Sherlock Holmes as an exponent of the (late-) Victorian era now increasingly out of his time. The paradigm of late

Victorian and Edwardian masculinity, this Holmes has outlived his age and exists in a state of belatedness, out of synch with the rest of history: 'the world was a different place from that of Victoria Regina' (King, 1996: xx). There is quite a bit of unease in *The Beekeeper's Apprentice* around Holmes's beekeeping in Sussex during the Great War despite the 'distressing presence' of 'a silent, rigid, shell-shocked young man – a boy, really, but for the trenches' (King, 1996: 105). Although he has been spying against the Kaiser (1996 : 26) and is acting in 'an advisory function' (1996: 45), Holmes now remains in Sussex far from the trenches:

> In the short view, with some minor exceptions, we are sitting this war out. We are leaving it to the buffoons in power and the faithful sloggers who march off to die. And afterwards, Russell? Are you able to take the long view, and envisage what will take place when this insanity comes to an end? (King: 46)

This Holmes is at odds with the ideological context of World War I, where the national story is one of solidarity and togetherness.[6] Likewise, *The Moor* (2002), Laurie King's pastiche of Doyle's 'The Hound of the Baskervilles' (1901–2), is couched in an argument concerning old age and nostalgia for the bygone Victorian era. Gothic Dartmoor still provides a fluid and shifting reality,[7] as in Doyle's original tale; gender relationships are equally abusive and family traits again pierce through the conspiracy, as in the earlier story. But reality is altered in a different, more fundamental way: Ketteridge, the current owner of Baskerville Hall (who has bought the Hall from Stapleton's impoverished daughter) has introduced electricity to 'startling' effect, resulting paradoxically in the apparent 'unreality' of the ancient building, as Mary considers: 'Baskerville Hall, on the other hand, was the real thing. A structure grown slowly over the centuries...Why then did the substantial Baskerville Hall linger in the mind as somehow ethereal, unreal, and slightly "off"?' (King, 1996: 225–6). Laurie King's novel focuses on another survivor of a bygone Victorian era. Sabine Baring-Gould, the author of 'Onward Christian Soldiers' (King: 10) is portrayed as an arch-Victorian polymath, expert in a wide variety of sciences and the typical Victorian 'scientist'/ collector (King: 10), but he is now extremely elderly and close to death. Set later than Doyle's version, the story is couched in nostalgia for a bygone, Victorian era, as the elderly Baring-Gould mourns the Victorian era when 'there were men and women who stood out' (King: 346).

Interestingly, both King and Douglas add further, crucial corrections to the official late-Victorian histories in their feminist revisions. In *The*

Moor, King also includes a spoiler to Doyle's own preoccupations with Empire, Englishness and the suggestions of reverse colonisation in his fiction – the many murder plots that have their origin in the US, India or Australia.[8] Richard Ketteridge, the new American owner of the Hall, is of mixed race: 'Our dusky host had made for himself a Moorish retreat in the midst of Dartmoor' (King, 1996: 132). Now a mixed-race owner of Baskerville Hall is to be protected by Holmes and Russell, in yet another late-twentieth century ideological correction of Doyle's world. *Good Night, Mr Holmes* similarly corrects the Anglo-centred world view of 'A Scandal in Bohemia' by removing Doyle's story from London to alternative, forgotten centres of culture: Milan, Warsaw and Prague. Irene Adler is not only distracted by her love affair and her career, but also by 'the joyous spring of Czech cultural revival', her acquaintance with the composer Dvořák and the rising protest against hereditary rulers (Douglas, 2005: 217–18). In Doyle's adventure, Bohemia is a country on the margin of European identity. The text very much stresses the stolid, pompous un-Englishness of a prince on the fringes of the English world. In *Good Night, Mr Holmes,* Bohemia is a country at the centre of its history, an exciting core of cultural revival and rebellion against the idea of Empire. The Austro-Hungarian Empire is corrupt, represented by the complicit Bohemian rulers who would rather cover up the murder of a king than risk undermining their power.

In the Laurie King novels, another country proves far more central than Doyle's English heart of the British Empire. Mary is not only a detective but also a Talmudic scholar and she lectures a sceptical Holmes about the fundamental ties to rationality within her own Jewish identity. When the two detectives are forced to leave England, Mary chooses to travel to what is then Palestine. When Mary first sees Jerusalem in the distance the Doyle universe is again re-oriented, away from London and the British centre.

> There before us she rose up, the city of cities, the umbilicus mundi, centre of the universe, growing from the very foundations of the earth, surprisingly small, like a jewel. My heart sang within me, and the ancient Hebrew came to my lips. (King, 1996: 292)

Moreover, both series are characterised by a very particular treatment of history. As Holmes, Irene Adler and Mary Russell go forth, their fictional universe is pierced by a large amount of 'historical' events and characters. Both King and Douglas emphasise the synchronicity and serendipity of their historical world and Holmes's contemporaneity with the historical characters who are, as it were, 'sucked' into Doyle's fictional world. Thus, Douglas's female detectives encounter the great and the good of this edited, fictionalised Victorian period: Whiteley's Emporium, the jeweller Tiffany, Oscar Wilde and his wife Constance, Bram Stoker, Henry Irving and Antonin Dvořák. *Spider Dance* (2004) introduces Joseph Pulitzer and the Vanderbilts, and moves into Edith Wharton terrain in discussing the early twentieth-century development of New York: the Vanderbilt mansion and its new white style rather than the brownstone older buildings (Douglas, 2005: 22). In *Good Night, Mr. Holmes*, 'the grandes dames of American commerce – the Mmes. Pulitzer, Vanderbilt, Astor and Stanford – proceeded to snap up the best of the French crown jewels' (Douglas, 2005: 323). Mary Russell's American heritage leads to a novel centred on the San Francisco earthquake (*Locked Rooms*, 2005). *The Language of Bees* (2009) is thronged with early twentieth-century bohemians: the surrealist poet André Breton and the sculptor Jacob Epstein are name-checked (King, 2010: 61), when Mary visits London's Café Royal she encounters Augustus John, the sculptor Alice Wright (King, 2010: 163; 167), while the novel is dominated by the sinister figure of the occultist Aleister Crowley. This is a representation of recent history that turns away from the sociological, from the discussion of material circumstances or social context, to embrace a perspective on history seen again through the lens of 'the agency of individuals' as Deborah Cartmell points out (Cartmell et al., 2001: 2).

It is also a perspective on the historical Victorian age that is closely allied to archontic story telling itself. In 'The Problem of Thor Bridge' (1922) Sherlock Holmes scathingly criticises Watson's 'involved habit...of telling a story backward' (Doyle, 1981: 1056), a self-reflexive reference to Doyle's own frequent comments about his own approach to storytelling. The appearance of Holmes, Watson, Russell and Adler within a historical context results in a similar teleological effect: all the fictional detectives' actions help to bring history about. Irene Adler's wearing of the striking but artistically challenging brooch constructed by the younger Tiffany helps cement the jeweller's fame. In *Spider Dance* Irene Adler assists Lola Montez, while in *Good Night, Mr. Holmes* she is involved in the Czech cultural revival with her work for the composer Antonin Dvořák. Characterised by 'popular culture's playful and opportunistic treatment of history', both series consequently treat history 'as a dynamic resource for exciting stories and poetic, morally uplifting untruths' (Cartmell et al., 2001: 2). Of course, these are postmodern games, but their effect is the treatment of history as yet another fictional universe, itself now open to archontic re-narrativisation. In both cases, events and 'real' figures are drawn into a fictional world. The effect is at once alienating, rich and suggestive of a deeper, more satisfying historical reality. These 'historical' characters mix confusingly with fictional ones since their referentiality to a historical 'reality' approaches the way Watson and Holmes 'resonate' in readers' memories, to paraphrase Rosemary Johnsen (Johnsen, 2006: 86). Indeed, the presence of Breton, Tiffany, the Vanderbilts, Bram Stoker, and indeed Arthur Conan Doyle himself in these novels 'actualises' Holmes, while his status renders the historical characters fictional. It is a history being helped by the detectives towards its utopian future, a history with the chaotic, messy and meaningless reality removed, a Victorian age with added fictional causality and meaningfulness.

What the feminist series around Mary Russell and Irene Adler, and their introduction of historical material, suggest is the polyphonous potential already present in the intertext of the Doyle stories. Their revisions unearth not just the ideological perspectives that were present, but also those that were absent and could have been present. In this sense, King, Douglas and their fan fiction colleagues actualise the 'virtual' possibilities within the Holmes canon and in history, even. In fact, Sherlock Holmes himself has always sounded very much like a Deleuzian *avant la lettre*, when, explaining the science of deduction to a baffled Watson, he evokes the improbable-possible: 'It is an old maxim of mine that when you have excluded the impossible, whatever remains, however improbable, must be the truth' (Doyle, 1981: 315). Like a fan fiction writer, Holmes only believes in the unreality of the impossible: what is possible is 'real' in the sense that the potential is there for it to exist, to be actualised.

Conclusion: Arthur Conan Doyle diminished

Finally, we must briefly consider the appearance of Arthur Conan Doyle himself in these two series and the issue of the author's own fictional afterlife. In novels that consistently, and evocatively, blur the boundary between historical characters and fictional characters even Doyle himself, confusingly, becomes fictionalised. Holmes's displeasure with Arthur Conan Doyle is regularly reiterated in Laurie King's series, where Doyle is characterised as 'Dr. Watson's literary agent and collaborator' (King, 2002: 23). Holmes complains bitterly about Doyle's publications, referring to 'Conan Doyle and his accomplices at *The Strand*' (King, 2002: 24) and Mary comments on his use of 'extravagant phrases'

(King, 2002: 34). In this parallel world both Holmes and Watson make jokes at the expense of the spiritualist Doyle, as when Holmes describes the credulous Sabine Baring-Gould: 'Revelations, visitations, spooks, you name it – he's worse than Conan Doyle, with his fairies and his spiritualism' (King, 2002, 30). As Rosemary Johnsen points out, Doyle's appearances in the series of Douglas and King occur in order to prove verisimilitude (2006: 86–7). It is as a comic figure that Doyle appears in the series of both King and Douglas. He is the suppressor of feminist truth and a gullible spiritualist in Douglas; in King's series, he is the mercantile editor of Watson, co-responsible at least for the romantic inflection of the stories that Holmes so dislikes. When Doyle decided to resurrect Holmes after the Reichenbach Falls, he could not have foreseen his own fictional afterlife. If Doyle's fictionalisation 'proves' Holmes's existence, then Holmes's existence, his 'actualisation' has rendered Doyle fictional.

Notes

1. In 1901 Doyle published 'The Hound of the Baskervilles' but he sets this story before Holmes's disappearance. Holmes does not 'return' until 'The Adventure of the Empty House' in 1903.
2. Derecho derives this term from Derrida's concept of the archive, never closed and always receptive to new and transformative content, as expressed in his *Archive Fever* (1995).
3. Indeed, Rosemary Johnsen clearly points out an underlying, more conservative strain in King's work and has criticized King's female characters, apart from Mary, as being distinctly traditional, a result of creating Mary as a female Holmes (2006: 100). There are other conservative elements: King may be aiming for historical correctness but Mary's response to the first Labour government in *The Language of Bees* is surprisingly negative.
4. Irene Adler has recently appeared in Series Two of the BBC's *Sherlock*. In 'A Scandal in Belgravia' (2012) Doyle's adventuress has been turned into a professional dominatrix, advertising her services on her own website – complete with photograph – which Sherlock eagerly scans. In another witty, literal actualisation performed upon the Doyle story, the 'mistress' of the King of Bohemia has become a sexual 'mistress' to her clients, one a female member of the royal family.
5. Both Douglas and King employ a frame narrative and the convention of the 'found manuscript' to relate their narratives to their historical contexts (Johnsen, 2006: 88). Laurie King writes herself into the novels as the unwilling, intrigued recipient of an unwanted manuscript in an apparently wrongly delivered DHL parcel containing the elderly Mary Russell's own accounts of the past. Carole Nelson Douglas employs the scholarly corrective commentary of 'Fiona Witherspoon, Ph.D., F.I.A.', a member of the Friends of Irene Adler.

6. Doyle published 'His Last Bow' (1917) in the middle of the Great War, yet he sets the story on the eve of war, possibly to distance his protagonist from the war narrative.
7. The misty, shifting moor as an almost mythological site of gothic unease in Doyle's work is discussed in Catherine Wynne's book *The Colonial Conan Doyle: British Imperialism, Irish Nationalism and the Gothic* (2002).
8. In stories such as 'The Adventure of the Speckled Band' and *The Valley of Fear*, Doyle's implicit concerns about Britain's colonial empire and the late-Victorian anxiety of reverse-colonisation are often expressed in the American, Australian and Irish references echoed in the stories (Wynne, 2002).

7
Sherlock Holmes Reloaded: Holmes, Videogames and Multiplicity

Souvik Mukherjee

After disappearing in the Reichenbach Falls while grappling with Professor Moriarty in 'The Final Problem' (1893), Holmes re-emerges in 'The Adventure of the Empty House' (1903), supposedly having spent three years (in the Holmesian time-scheme) disguised as the Norwegian explorer Sigerson so as to fool Moriarty's dangerous minions. Since then, Holmes has continued to return in many different places and times. In the world of Holmesian pastiche, he lives myriad lives in stories by enthusiasts all over the world. The Mary Russell novels, Anthony Burgess's short story 'Murder to Music' (1989), Caleb Carr's *The Italian Secretary* (2005) and films such as *Murder by Decree* (1980) are just a few examples. This narrative multiplicity of the Holmes stories is intriguing, and there are few parallels in literature. Like Lord Blackwood, Holmes's antagonist in the recent *Sherlock Holmes* (2009) film, Holmes too is continually resurrected, almost as if by magic.

A similar phenomenon, however, can be observed in a more recent narrative medium. Videogames such as *Prince of Persia: The Sands of Time* (Ubisoft 2003; *Sands of Time* hereonwards) are also characterised by narratives where the *telos* or 'ending' keeps changing, a phenomenon of which the game is self-aware. *Sands of Time* tells the story of a Persian prince who accidentally unleashes a horrific sandstorm that plunges the flow of time into chaos and turns his companions into sand monsters. With the help of a mythical weapon, the Dagger of Time, he has to overcome numerous challenges in order to finally restore normalcy. It is possible to 'die' in the game at any point in the story, but if this happens the protagonist exclaims 'no no...this is not how it happened at all' (Ubisoft 2003). Like Holmes in the Reichenbach Falls, the Prince too can return to his story, but in this case by using the Dagger of Time, which allows him to rewind time and to 'replay' the story from a certain point at which it was saved on the computer's memory. In effect, this creates the possibility for a multiplicity of narratives within what is assumed to be a single story.

Traditional frameworks of critical analysis, such as Structuralist discourse, struggle with plots that do not conform to a linear chronology or where it is possible to go back in time to follow a different course of events, as seen in videogames such as *Sands of Time* and arguably, in the complicated time scheme(s) of the Holmes stories. Further, both videogames and the Holmes stories link their storylines to a vast range of other stories and events, thus creating a complex narrative structure that traditional literary criticism cannot analyse. A different framework of analysis based upon multiplicity is therefore required. Through a comparison with the complex narrative multiplicity of videogames, the following sections will analyse how the story of Sherlock Holmes keeps being 'reloaded' and replayed – almost like a videogame.

Digital games researcher Janet Murray started a major debate in Game Studies[1] research regarding whether videogames were purely games or whether they were stories as well. Although Murray's position has since been challenged as being too extreme, the fact that videogames tell stories is one that cannot be ignored.[2] One of the main difficulties with perceiving videogames as stories was that videogame narratives, instead of conforming to traditional narrative structure with a beginning, middle and end, have many middles and many endings. Responding to this, recent research has focused on the multi-telic and complex temporality of videogames and argues that the complex narrative structure in videogames is not unique to the medium, but rather is a persistent characteristic of narrative itself.

To return, however, to the canonical Holmes and his 'final' problem: if one is to consider the number of different opinions on his survival, an easy comparison could be made with the multi-telic plots of games such as *Prince of Persia: The Sands of Time*. In 'The Empty House', Holmes's 'dramatic reappearance' gives a serious shock not only to Watson, but also to the entire literary world and some purist Holmes fans. As late as 1966, *The Times* reported:

> The Final Problem, which brought Holmes and Moriarty to their fatal confrontation, was so apparently conclusive that to this day there are many who find Holmes's explanation of how he escaped unsatisfactory. Father Knox distinguished between those international scholars who thought that Watson faked The Final Problem for his

own purposes, and those who 'regard The Final Problem as genuine and the Return-stories as fabrication.' (Haining, 1973: 122; original formatting)

In the Holmes pastiches, this takes a more complex turn. Jamyang Norbu's *The Mandala of Sherlock Holmes* (1999) claims to be based upon the discovery of a manuscript that Hurree Babu from Rudyard Kipling's *Kim* (1901) is supposed to have written, detailing the hitherto unknown adventures of Holmes in Tibet. Hurree Babu recounts in his manuscript:

> Over coffee Mr Holmes told us the story of the great deception he had performed on the world.
>
> 'You have by now heard of Professor Moriarty,' said Sherlock Holmes, pushing his chair away from the table and stretching his long legs.
>
> 'The Times of India carried an article about his criminal empire simultaneously with your obituary,' I ventured.
>
> 'We received information from London about the Professor and his gang,' Strickland said. 'I also read quite a lively story about the whole business in the Strand Magazine!' (Norbu, 1999)

Hurree Babu's account of Holmes in India and, later, in Tibet adds another new strand to the story of Holmes. At the other extreme, *The Seven-Per-Cent Solution* (1974), by Nicholas Meyer, dismisses 'The Final Problem' and 'The Empty House' as fabrications by Watson, thus illustrating an even greater variety in the versions of Holmes's survival after his ordeal at the Reichenbach.

The plots of the pastiches are too numerous to list, but some key themes emerge among the favourites. One of these is Holmes's investigation of the Whitechapel murders of five prostitutes by the so-called Jack the Ripper; the other is his involvement with the Cthulhu 'mythos', which is a framework of common fictional elements that appear in H. P. Lovecraft's stories. Besides being recreated in the later Holmes novels and in films, both of these themes have inspired videogames on Holmes.

The Ripper murders have remained unsolved and still give rise to much speculation about possible culprits. The Metropolitan Police narrowed their suspects down to four names from a total of around 176, and the Holmes pastiches based on the murders reflect this variety of explanations and conjectures (Doyle and Crowder, 2010: 239–40).

Edward B. Hanna, in his Holmes novel *The White Chapel Horrors* (1993), describes a profile of the Ripper that the FBI put up as an exercise:

> He was a white male, single, in his mid or late twenties, of average intelligence, who in all probability lived alone. 'He was not account-able to anyone' and could therefore come and go as he pleased at all hours. He lived in the area of the killings and had an intimate know-ledge of its geography. (1993: 359)

Almost Holmesian in detail, this description is still a very open one and could fit multiple suspects. Although Hanna himself leaves the reader without a clear solution, he seems to favour the theory that there is some involvement of the royal family behind the murders. The film, *Murder by Decree*, ends with a similar conclusion; only here, the crimes are directly connected with the royal household and are concealed by important government officials belonging to the Masonic order. On an extremely different note, Michael Dibdin's *The Last Sherlock Holmes Story* (1978) claims that Holmes himself is the Ripper and, bored after of years of solving crimes, he is now bent on committing the perfect crime. There are also other versions by Ellery Queen (1944) and M. J. Trow (1998), where diverse figures like Ellery Queen or Inspector Lestrade are shown as being cleverer at detection than Holmes. Whitechapel itself figures again in the film *The Case of the Whitechapel Vampire* (2002), which is set in an abbey in Whitechapel but has nothing to do with the Ripper stories. Adding to this list of Holmes stories involving the Ripper and Whitechapel is a recent videogame, *Sherlock Holmes vs. Jack the Ripper* (Frogwares 2009), which also has the Whitechapel investiga-tion as its backdrop.

Another popular theme, the Lovecraftian mythos, is the subject of a videogame called *Sherlock Holmes: The Awakened* (Frogwares 2006; henceforth referred to as *The Awakened*). As Brett Todd, reviewer for GameSpot.com, describes it:

> Both true to the character of Sherlock Holmes and a rip-roaring pulp adventure in its own right, *The Awakened* is a must-play game. Mystery lovers with a taste for the supernatural will feel right at home with this slice of Cthulhu-infused Victoriana. (2007)

Lovecraft's tales are about a series of fearsome deities from outer space called the Great Old Ones, and in the stories Lovecraft and other writers, such as Robert Howard and August Derleth, used elements from each other's work to interlink the tales. Carrying on the tradition, developers of the videogame *Call of Cthulhu: Dark Corners of the Earth* (Bethesda Softworks 2006) use these themes to build a survival-horror game experience. Perhaps not coincidentally, the protagonist in the game is also a private investigator who, like Holmes in *The Awakened*, challenges Cthulhu cultists.

The Cthulhu–Holmes connection, however, is not unique to videogames. *Shadows over Baker Street* (Reaves and Pelan, 2003) contains a series of stories by writers such as Neil Gaiman, wherein Holmes and the mythos come together. Linking his story to the events around *A Study in Scarlet* (Doyle, 1929), Gaiman brings the Cthulhu mythos into the early part of Holmes's career. Other authors in the anthology set their stories much later; so, in terms of the time when Holmes comes across the Cthulhu mythos, the collection itself is a multiplicity.

In a way, the Holmes stories have their own mythos and this makes it easy for other narratives to introduce Holmes as a key character within them. The multiplicity of the linkages – as in the examples of the Cthulhu mythos and the Whitechapel murders – are made possible only because the canon itself is characterised by a high degree of multiplicity. Even the chronologies constructed by Doyle, and later by Holmes scholars, it must be observed, are quite varied. The adventures in the canon are not chronologically ordered: some, like the 'The Adventure of the "Gloria Scott"', although published in 1893, date back to Holmes's early life. *The Hound of the Baskervilles* (Doyle, 1928) is similarly published after Holmes's purported death in 'The Final Problem', and before the 'The Empty House', where he returns. In his chronology on the 'Sherlock Peoria' website, Brad Keefauver (2001) disagrees with the authoritative version drawn up by William S. Baring-Gould. Laurie King (2010), supplementing her Mary Russell novels, provides a different chronology to both of the above. The narrative multiplicity of the stories, however, does not stop at the discussion of the problematic chronology of the stories.

Geographically too, Holmes's stories map a huge and varied area, from Agra to the wastelands of Utah. Often, Holmes's tales interweave with very different and almost independent stories, such as the story of the Pinkerton detective Birdie Edwards in *The Valley of Fear* (1915) and that of the Mormons in *A Study in Scarlet* (1887). These variations, which are already extant in the canonical Holmes stories, create a very complex temporal, spatial and narrative structure when coupled with those in the many Holmes pastiches. The collective range of Sherlockiana, both canonical and non-canonical, plugs into different areas of enquiry, and the result of trying to chart the narrative progression of Holmes's stories is as chaotic as the usual mess in his room at 221b Baker Street.

Traditional theories of narrative struggle to cope with the phenomenon of multiplicity. The purported death and the return of Sherlock Holmes have had their share of critical attention, but these accounts do not go far enough in exploring the temporal complexity of the Holmes narratives. Michael Harrison's *The World of Sherlock Holmes* (1975), almost biographical in detail, has no mention of 'The Final Problem' and 'The Empty House'. Samuel Rosenberg's book (1974), although subtitled 'The Death and Resurrection of Sherlock Holmes' is essentially a treatment of the Holmes stories as allegories or as representations of certain important real-life contemporaries of Holmes.

A later essay by John A. Hodgson addresses the issue in some depth and discusses the 'Final Problem' as being, *per se*, 'an alternative retelling of a story' (1994: 348). Hodgson observes that two extremely condensed accounts of Holmes's death are provided, and while one of these is the story told by Watson, there is a different version by Moriarty's brother, Colonel James Moriarty, which actually maligns Holmes. However, there is a further multiplicity in the whole episode: Watson's account of Holmes's demise, as the abovementioned article from *The Times* states, seems quite conclusive; of course, it is totally subverted by Holmes's own account of his survival. For Hodgson this is a discourse with multiple stories and he attempts to analyse it based on a Structuralist analysis of the detective novel and on Roger Caillois's reading of detective fiction as a rule-based game. As the following argument illustrates, both of the above frameworks encounter significant problems as Hodgson's analysis reveals the inherent multiplicity of the events in the Holmes timeline.

Tzvetan Todorov's (1975) Structuralist analysis sees the detective story as a duality: the story of crime (that Hodgson reads as *fabula*, the 'story' that the reader interprets) and the story of the investigation (for Hodgson, this is *syuzhet*, the 'discourse' or the unchanging plot written by the author). Finding deeper implications in the Holmes stories, Hodgson then introduces a further complexity with Jonathan Culler's argument that the discourse tells the story in a double sense: the events of the story where they are independent of anything else, and where they are products of signification. Hodgson interprets this to mean that the story has multiple discourses and also that the discourse itself has multiple stories.

From the duality of the fixed categories of *fabula* and *syuzhet*, Hodgson's analysis seems to be moving towards a notion of multiplicity. His observations on the events (or discourse) in separate Holmes stories can be complicated much further if one is to look at the multiplicity of the broader chronologies that interweave each other in a fuller overview at Sherlockiana. It might be useful to note that videogames also problematise the *fabula-syuzhet* duality as they can have many *syuzhets* where the sequence of events depends on the *fabula,* or on how the reader/ player plays out the story.

The other perspective from which games have been compared to Holmes stories by Hodgson, draws on Caillois's essay, 'The Detective Novel as Game' (1983). Caillois states of the detective novel that

> It is not a tale but a game, not a story but a problem. This is why just at the moment when the *novel* is freeing itself from all rules, the *detective novel* keeps inventing stricter ones. Its interest, its value, and even its originality increase with the limitations it accepts and the rules it imposes on itself. (1983: 10; original emphasis)

He goes on describe the detective novel as a jigsaw puzzle which one puts together to make a complete and simple picture from incomprehensible fragments. Caillois was not familiar with digital games, but his sweeping generalisation is too simplistic for any kind of games, and therefore also for detective fiction. The way in which the Holmes stories interweave with each other is not considered here: given the mesh of complexity that this interweaving of the pastiches and the canon creates, the picture in the Holmes stories is far from simple and complete.

As far as games are concerned, digital games researcher Jesper Juul, commenting on Caillois's categorisations of games in *Man, Play and Games* (Caillois, 1961), concludes that 'It is unclear to what extent Caillois's categories ultimately include or exclude each other, and some of the general claims made about their possible combination are at odds with most contemporary games' (Juul, 2005), and goes on to observe that Caillois's conception of the ruled nature of games 'is contradicted by most commercial board games, almost all video games, and generally all rule-based games that include a *fictional* element' (Juul, 2005; original formatting).

Both Structuralist narrative analysis and Caillois's rule-bound model for detective fiction are found wanting if the Holmes stories are considered in their totality and multiplicity. The comparison between the multiplicity of videogames and the Holmes stories is obviously more useful; however, a more robust theoretical framework is required to understand it. Gilles Deleuze's conception of multiplicity can prove useful in this context. As Manual DeLanda states, multiplicity is a Deleuzian concept 'that stands out for its longevity' (2002: 9). As pointed out so far, both the Holmes stories and most storytelling videogames have a chronology and narrative structure that can be nonlinear and can overlap or interweave. Sometimes the same stories are retold, but with a difference that makes it difficult to distinguish between the difference and the repetition. Further, they also 'plug in', as it were, to other narrative multiplicities (the Cthulhu mythos, for example).

The multi-telic is always a point of difficulty for narrative media. Therefore, when Holmes baffles everyone with his dramatic return in 'The Empty House' there is much doubt as to which version of the same story is the real one. A similar question arises when the player reloads an instance of *The Awakened* and replays from the point he or she has been killed: is the reload a return to the same narrative or the construction of a different one? Seen in this way, Holmes's return in 'The Empty House' can be viewed as a 'reload'; therefore, the problem cannot be said to be unique to videogame narratives but is, arguably, true of the conception of narrative itself.

In Deleuzian philosophy, it is possible to view the multi-telic as being various actualisations of a virtual possibility. Deleuze speaks of a 'real virtuality' rather than a virtual reality. In these terms, both the death and the re-emergence of Sherlock Holmes are equally real; they are actualisations of a mesh of possibilities influenced by their temporal environment. According to Deleuze:

> The virtual is not opposed to the real but to the actual. The virtual is fully real in so far as it is virtual. ... Indeed, the virtual must be defined as strictly a part of the real object – as though the object had one part of itself in the virtual into which it plunged as though into an objective dimension. ... The reality of the virtual consists of the differential elements and relations along with the singular points which correspond to them. (1994: 208)

As actualisations occurring within a mesh of possible events, all of these instances are valid events that have been formed under the influence of various factors which Deleuze terms 'singularities'. It might be useful to clarify, as DeLanda does, that 'Deleuze's speculation about virtuality is guided by the closely related constraint of avoiding typological thinking, that style of thought in which individuation is achieved through the creation of classifications and of formal criteria for membership in those classifications' (DeLanda, 2002: 34). So the actualisations mentioned above are not marked by their being individual instances within a particular category. Events in a videogame or in Holmes's narratives are never defined absolutely – there is always the possibility that the event in the videogame is viewed differently when a parallel or a different event takes place in the game. Using a Holmesian analogy, the same fall into an abyss might stop signifying death when, in another replay, the player emerges from it after finding a 'power-up' that proves vital for dispatching the main 'boss' (or antagonist) in the game. For Deleuze, the understanding of individuation of the actualisations is based on the notion 'that resemblances and identities must be treated as mere results of deeper physical processes' (DeLanda, 2002: 39). Using a ludic metaphor, Deleuze states that, 'since each is a passing present, one life may replay another at a different level' (Deleuze, 1994: 105). The Holmes mythos and the gameplay instances in videogames can, therefore, both be better understood as ongoing processes rather than discrete events.

Simply analysing the multiplicity of events *within* a story, however, leaves some of the larger connections unanalysed. Within the canon, the Holmes stories constantly link to other cases, whether recorded by Watson or otherwise. For example, Moriarty appears to have a direct hand in the events of *The Valley of Fear* (Doyle, 1929) and Holmes mentions Moriarty reminiscently in other stories such as the 'The Empty House', 'The Norwood Builder', 'The Missing Three-Quarter', 'The Illustrious Client' and 'His Last Bow' (Doyle, 1928). The pastiches make the links more complex by interlinking with the canon and with other narratives, as mentioned earlier.

This aspect of the Holmesian capacity to fit into multiple narrative contexts, judging from the popularity of the spin-offs and other responses to the so-called 'after-lives of Holmes', clearly necessitates further analysis. Again, in the absence of adequate tools from traditional narrative theory, Deleuzian multiplicity could provide another useful analytical framework. According to DeLanda, the Deleuzian idea of assemblages was 'meant to apply to a wide variety of wholes constructed from heterogenous parts' (DeLanda, 2006: 3) and it might be worth considering this in order to explain the multiplicity both in the Holmes stories and in videogames.

As the network of ideas that constitutes the rudiments of assemblage theory is scattered in the work of Deleuze (and Felix Guattari) and is characterised by hermeneutic puzzles, DeLanda adapts this into a more clarified version that he calls 'neo-assemblage theory' or 'assemblage theory 2.0', in order to mollify Deleuzian purists. Although there are occasional references to the original Deleuzoguattarian discussion in *A Thousand Plateaus* (Deleuze and Guattari, 1987), this essay will mainly follow DeLanda's formulation.

As opposed to organic totalities (as conceived in, say, Hegelian philosophy), assemblages are characterised by a relation of exteriority. DeLanda states that

> A component part of an assemblage may be detached from it and plugged into a different assemblage in which its interactions are different. In other words, the exteriority of relations implies a certain autonomy for the terms they relate, or as Deleuze puts it, it implies that 'a relation may change without the terms changing'? Relations of exteriority also imply that the properties of the component parts can never explain the relations which constitute a whole. (2006: 10)

Consider then, the Holmes assemblage where many different elements link with each other and constitute a whole despite remaining separate. Norbu's book, for example, 'plugs in' to the canon while still remaining exterior to it. Simultaneously, it can be said to be 'plugged in' to the Kipling assemblage (where it relates to Rudyard Kipling's Indian stories), and so on.

'Plugging in', in the Deleuzoguattarian sense, means a multidirectional process wherein any entity may form flexible and variable attachments with others. In DeLanda's terms, 'Assemblages may be taken apart while at the same time ... the interaction between parts may result in a true synthesis' (2006: 11). In the Deleuzoguattarian notion of the assemblage, the processes for forming assemblages either stabilise the identity of the assemblage, by increasing its degree of internal homogeneity or the degree of sharpness of its boundaries, or destabilise it. The former are referred to as processes of territorialisation and the latter as processes of deterritorialisation.

Coincidentally, Deleuze and Guattari express this process through a lecture given by Doyle's other famous creation, Professor Challenger. In what is almost a Professor Challenger pastiche, they depict Challenger as lecturing on the deterritorialisation and reterritorialisation of the Earth 'after mixing several textbooks on geology and biology' (Deleuze and Guattari, 1987: 45). Following the above discussion of the multiplicity in Holmes, perhaps Deleuze and Guattari's mention of Challenger in this context is not that coincidental if we consider how both of Doyle's creations lend themselves so effectively to multiple assemblages.

The linking of the Holmes stories to the Cthulhu mythos or the Ripper murders, as described earlier, are other examples of this 'plugging in'. In videogames too, the multiple narratives 'plug in' to each other and to a series of other multiplicities. Generally speaking, videogames can be seen to 'plug in' to the narrative assemblage, to the ludic, the machinic and social assemblages, as I have discussed in depth elsewhere (Mukherjee, 2012). In terms of the narrative, the individual instances of gameplay 'plug in' to the total narrative of the game – they are exterior in the sense of being discrete actualisations, and at the same time they are definitely part of the total experience of play. With the above in mind, it will be instructive to see how the Sherlock Holmes games behave as multiplicities.

Most Sherlock Holmes videogames are like the jigsaw puzzle detective fiction that Caillois describes and are usually far less interesting than the stories in the canon. Two recent titles, however, are of interest: as discussed earlier, they plug into the multiplicities of the Cthulhu mythos and the Ripper tales. While the saving and reloading at different points does give the narrative its peculiar structural complexity, this can easily be ignored because of the repetitiveness and linearity of *The Awakened*. Although interesting in the way in which it follows other pastiches and links Holmes to the Cthulhu mythos, the game can be quite boring when the player does not take the right step. There are virtually no choices in the game and the player will often hear characters repeating the same lines unless a specific action has been completed. The designer, Frogwares, prefers the adventure game genre, and this in itself might be thought to limit the possibilities of the game when compared to other genres which involve more freeform movement and sophisticated Artificial Intelligence (AI). However, adventure games like *Blade Runner* (Westwood Studios 1997), which also incorporates detection, have far greater choices and possibilities, so it is the treatment of the story rather than the genre that is the main factor.

The plot of *The Awakened* plugs into many Holmesian tropes from the canon and the pastiches: there is an escaped Maori, a visit to an asylum in Switzerland and even symbols like those in 'The Dancing Men' (Doyle, 1928). Structurally, however, the game seems little more than a jigsaw puzzle and might easily tempt a response such as Caillois's. Moreover, the game's design does not improve much on that of older Holmes games such as *Sherlock Holmes: Mystery of the Mummy* (Frogwares 2002) and *Sherlock Holmes: Nemesis* (Frogwares 2008). Therefore, in both technical and narrative terms it compares poorly to other videogames that involve detective stories, such as *Max Payne*

(Remedy Entertainment 2001) or the more recent *Heavy Rain* (Quantic Dreams 2010).

Both *Max Payne* and *Heavy Rain* are heavy in narrative and dependent on pathways that the player follows. *Max Payne* is quite linear, but the much greater freedom of movement that the third-person shooter genre allows gives the impression of much more control and choice than *The Awakened*. The protagonist, Max Payne, an NYPD officer, is out to find the killers of his family and to explore the origins of a major drug racket. In his investigations, Max can move back and forth between places; the player is able to control his character to a much greater degree than the point-and-click mechanism of *The Awakened* allows. Consequently, while playing Sherlock Holmes in the Frogware games feels like solving a jigsaw puzzle, in *Max Payne* the involvement is such that often the player feels that he or she *is* Max. The apparent choices that the player makes seem almost real.

Heavy Rain is about finding the mysterious 'origami killer', a serial killer who uses extended periods of rainfall to drown his victims. The game is designed so that the chapters in the story change with changes in the fates of the characters. Therefore, should a character die, then the chapters about him or her do not appear. As IGN.com's walkthrough (the step-by-step guide to the game) states, 'certain chapters occur only under certain conditions' (IGN.com 2010). The walkthrough also describes seven different endings, all of which lead to different combinations of epilogues. The IGN guide calls it a cinematic adventure game (note the similarity with the genre of Frogwares's Holmes games), but the genre is given a new character as the game's website describes:

> As you play the game, your actions and choices will have a tangible impact on the fates of these characters, and the way that the plot unfolds. Your every decision can have significant and unforeseen consequences – making the gameplay experience uniquely dramatic and engrossing. To take an extreme example, if one of your characters dies during the game due to your actions, it isn't 'Game Over'. Instead, the plot continues using the other characters, and that character's death becomes part of the story – influencing the attitudes of other characters and affecting what leads and paths can be taken. (*Heavy Rain* website 2010)

The narrative multiplicity to which *Heavy Rain* aspires is indeed impressive. However, open-world games such as *Fallout 3* (Bethesda Softworks 2008) offer even more narrative possibilities, complex chronologies, and connections to more assemblages. To oversimplify, *Fallout 3* is the story of a son's search for his father's secret in a hostile post-apocalyptic wasteland. However, it can also be read as a detective story where the protagonist has to collect various clues to piece together enough information to find many of the governing secrets of the wasteland. Further, there are some side quests that resemble detective fiction – for example, one where the protagonist needs to find a runaway android disguised as a human (somewhat reminiscent of *Blade Runner* perhaps). Finally, characters with names like Pinkerton and Moriarty also hint at how the game plugs into the detective fiction assemblage. In *Fallout 3*, the wasteland is a vast, explorable area where the player can travel back and forth, investigate, take up side quests and even rest.

Although in comparison with the above games the Holmes games appear to be badly wanting, the most recent title by Frogwares is a significantly better attempt. *Sherlock Holmes vs. the Ripper* has a very convincing environment and more possibilities for action than its predecessors. As Holmes, the player still has to solve many puzzles within the game and collect numerous clues to be able to determine the correct identity of the Ripper from the five suspects. However, instead of making the gameplay so linear, perhaps future designers of the Holmes games could design game-mechanics like those of *Heavy Rain* (which even has a similar context to *Sherlock Holmes vs. the Ripper*) or those of an open-world game with more freedom to explore and investigate, thus reflecting the multiplicity of the Holmes mythos. Through their shortcomings, however, the Sherlock Holmes videogames draw attention to what larger and more flexible game-systems are capable of and to what this means for the Holmes mythos itself. Seen in these terms, perhaps the analysis of temporality and multiplicity can provide a more accurate overview.

Despite its different iterations and ramifications, one event in the Holmes stories has proved crucial in problematising the plot (the *syuzhet*, in Structuralist terms) and has upset any possible temporal schema that might have been imposed by any biographer of Holmes. This, obviously, is Holmes's return from supposed death and his purported survival of the lethal grapple with Moriarty. The problem with the temporal schema also applies to videogames although, here, players are more accustomed to reloading back into 'life' after in-game 'deaths' as part of the process.

Another problem for videogames and Holmes stories is the vast multitude of areas to which they link – forming part of the totality and yet maintaining their distinctiveness. Videogames are increasingly opting for more multiple and open-world designs rather than the linearity that characterised earlier adventure games. A parallel may be drawn with more traditional approaches to Sherlock Holmes's return and to the many parallel lives that Holmes is seen to live in the pastiches. Not being able to cope with the multiplicity, these accounts then resort to a discussion of authenticity – whether it is to ask if Holmes really survived the Reichenbach, or whether he ever faced the Ripper or Cthulhu. However, in the same way as the Holmes videogames cannot but prefigure an open-world videogame based on Sherlockiana, binary positions in Holmes scholarship will hopefully adapt to a more inclusive theoretical framework that accounts for the inevitable multiplicity of the stories. The concept of multiplicity, as illustrated through DeLanda's reading of Deleuzian ideas of assemblage and temporality, is one such framework.

To sum up, the Holmes stories in older narrative media are clearly much closer to videogame systems with more advanced AI and gameplay options. As already illustrated, Sherlockiana keeps reinventing itself, and more and more narrative strands plug into the assemblage. The following example is symptomatic. This essay began with a reference to the *Sherlock Holmes* film released in December 2009. Within months of its release the BBC series *Sherlock* (BBC 2010) was broadcast, where a twenty-first century version of Holmes solves crimes aided by sophisticated computers and has his clues marked out by a digital text overlay, almost as if it were a videogame. Obviously, with Holmes transcending temporal boundaries in all of these various ways, the chronology of his narrative is problematised. Using the Deleuzian framework described above, together with a comparison with similar occurrences in videogames, it is possible to get a feel of the multiplicity that the Holmesian assemblage constitutes. One does not need a computer game to load the adventures of the great detective. Holmes's narrative is constantly being saved and reloaded from a mesh of possibilities: in themselves, the plural and multiple assemblages of Holmes's story are already a videogame that has been played out long before the technology for digital games was even conceived of.

An episode in *Star Trek: Next Generation* (1988) shows the spaceship's Holodeck computer program generating new Holmes stories in virtual environments in which the user can participate seamlessly. Perhaps with recent developments in gaming technology, the Holodeck version of Holmes – where people can solve their customised Holmes adventures – is not too distant. Irrespective of narrative technologies, the inherent multiplicity and the ability to plug into different assemblages are the reasons why the Holmes stories always remain so current and relevant, whether in videogames or for Lt. Commander Data, *Star Trek*'s android Holmes admirer.

Notes

1. Game Studies is a relatively young discipline informed by interdisciplinary research on games, especially digital games, from perspectives such as the Social Sciences, Humanities and Informatics.
2. This is especially the case with the clear storytelling intention of games like *Sands of Time* and the way in which they tell different stories, depending how they are played out.

8
Sherlock Holmes Version 2.0: Adapting Doyle in the Twenty-First Century

Bran Nicol

A decade into the twentieth century, Sherlock Holmes seemed to have entered a kind of semi-retirement. In 'The Devil's Foot', published in *The Strand* in December 1910, Watson explains that the reason he has provided his readers with so few new case studies over recent years is because of his friend's 'aversion to publicity'. It is certainly not, he continues – protesting perhaps a little too much – because of 'any lack of interesting material' ('The Devil's Foot', *His Last Bow*: 153). Instead of a new case, Holmes has suggested that he write about a case which happened in Cornwall some 13 years previously. Even then, Holmes seems to have been a little the worse for wear, and is away from London to recuperate on the advice of his doctor:

> It was, then, in the spring of the year 1897 that Holmes's iron constitution showed some symptoms of giving way in the face of constant hard work of a most exacting kind, aggravated, perhaps, by occasional indiscretions of his own. (153)

Work and occasional indiscretions. These elements are crucial to the enduring appeal of the character of Holmes – despite the hint of decline in this story and others in *The Last Bow* – and, as this essay will highlight, are central to the most recent adaptations.

Fast forward one hundred years, and Sherlock Holmes has been injected with a new energy. In 2009 we are just as likely to find him waking up naked while tied to a bedpost following a night of (heterosexual) passion, or swinging on a chandelier to escape in the Lord Chief Justice's palace in London, as assessing incriminating evidence. A year later, and perhaps even more improbably, we see him checking the weather forecast on his smartphone and quoting the 1970s children's TV series *Jim'll Fix It*. These references are from two of the most recent and successful updatings of Sherlock Holmes: the $500m-grossing Guy Ritchie movie of 2009, starring Robert Downey Jr. as Holmes and Jude Law as Watson, in which Holmes is rewired as blockbuster action hero, and *Sherlock*, the critically-acclaimed three-part BBC series of 2010, which transposes Holmes consulting-detective business to present-day London, and stars Benedict Cumberbatch and Martin Freeman as the main characters. Perhaps inevitably, both projects justified their innovations by claiming that they return us to something essential yet frequently overlooked in the original Doyle canon. Ritchie noted of his film that '[t]here's quite a lot of intense action sequences in the stories, sometimes that hasn't been reflected in the movies' (*Telegraph* 2008), while Mark Gatiss, the co-creator (along with Steven Moffat) of the BBC series, stated that the motivation behind their updated Holmes was to 'blow[-] away the fog' from what had become an overly reverential approach to adapting Doyle, whereby earlier film-makers had tended to place the emphasis on 'the trappings, the Hansom cabs, the costume, the fog' (BBC DVD) and so forth, at the expense of what was the source of the original's appeal. He leaves unspoken exactly what this is but, as deduced from his own series, he means the brilliance of 'the Holmes method', the relationship between Holmes and Watson, and, most of all, the peculiarities of Holmes's personality.

For all their status as specific reworkings of the Holmes stories, both, too, are symptomatic of how the classic 'logic-and-deduction' model of detective fiction, which Doyle was so instrumental in establishing, has, on screen, mutated into a variety of 'crime thriller' which blends the traditional indulgence in esoteric puzzles with dramatic action and suspense.[1] In fact, the solving of puzzles is reduced in comparison to the action in Ritchie's film, and turned into a kind of thrilling drama of its own in the BBC series. According to Martin Rubin, the thriller as a category is predicated upon suspense, and continually evokes fear and anxiety. This is true of these rebooted Sherlock Holmes thrillers. But in the case of the superior BBC version, the suspense is accompanied by a focus on Holmes's own tendency towards what we might call 'sociopathology', or his disregard for the feelings of others in attempting to get his way.[2] In what follows I want to contend that this combination invites a response from the viewers which is itself curiously 'sociopathological' in its attitude to the characters on screen, and thus symptomatic of the pleasure the crime thriller affords us in the early twenty-first century.

'Malignant enemy or guardian angel'?

Screen versions of Sherlock Holmes have created iconic and memorable figures which are symptomatic of the age in which they were produced: the irreverent Basil Rathbone/Nigel Bruce pairing in the films of the late 1930s and 1940s, the decadent anachronism of Robert Stephens in Billy Wilder's 1970 *The Private Life of Sherlock Holmes*, the dark severity of Jeremy Brett in the Granada TV series from 1984–94. The two adaptations in question here are no different in this respect. But perhaps the most appropriate Holmes for the late-twentieth and early twenty-first centuries is one who does not share his name, nor is he even a detective. In Hannibal Lecter, the former psychiatrist and serial killer at the heart of Jonathan Demme's 1991 film of Thomas Harris's novel *The Silence of the Lambs* (1988), we are given an insight into what might be considered a parallel universe where the cold, incisive personality and methodology of someone like Holmes had fermented in the febrile, violent, morally bankrupt atmosphere of our age: a man whose 'high-powered perception' is geared towards self-gratification. As in the Holmes stories, Lecter works alongside the police, sometimes helping them, sometimes keeping things from them. And, like Holmes, he is able to construct personalities and hypotheses from almost imperceptible details. In the movie's famous Baltimore jail scene, in which the young apprentice FBI agent Clarice Starling confronts the notorious killer behind his glass-walled cell, Lecter engages in an unmistakably Holmesian 'introductory exercise' to demonstrate how he is able to penetrate the very core of her identity: 'You use Evyan skin cream, and sometimes you wear L'Air du Temps, but not today. You brought your best bag, though, didn't you?' From this deduction it takes only a few short steps for him to recognise what has driven her to escape her humble upbringings and move up, 'all the way to the F...B...I'.

In her book *Twentieth-Century Crime Fiction: Gender, Sexuality and the Body* (2001) Gill Plain argues that a profound shift took place in crime fiction as it moved towards the end of the twentieth century. While in the nineteenth and early-twentieth centuries crime fiction was about 'confronting and taming the monstrous' (3) this task has become much more complex as the genre has developed. Crime fiction originally kept 'the other' (especially sexuality and the body) at bay, but recent innovations (Plain focuses in particular on the rise of the lesbian detective and the serial killer narrative) confirm that what was previously 'other' or monstrous to the detective universe is now incorporated within. There is consequently an *absence* of the truly monstrous, rather than an excess of it. The Hannibal Lecter series provide a good example. In each of the three novels (*Red Dragon* [1981], *The Silence of the Lambs,* and *Hannibal* [1999]), the serial killer is not simply a monstrous outsider to be contained, but is firmly *inside* the narrative, and indeed for much of it we are taken inside his mind. Moreover, the proximity between hunter (detective) and killer which is accentuated throughout the Hannibal series means, Plain argues, that 'the killer rather than the detective [is] the point of identification for the reader' (227). In *Hannibal*, in particular, we have the eponymous 'monster of the contemporary psyche ... not below but above ground' (Plain: 227), free to roam and therefore no longer contained by the insulating conventions of the detective narrative.

The way Doyle's stories contain monstrosity verifies Plain's argument about the original paradigm which twentieth-century crime fiction progressively collapses. What is 'other' in the Sherlock Holmes canon – frequently suggested by the arresting, disturbing narratives or 'scenes' (the creeping man, the yellow face, and so forth) at the heart of what Thomas Sebeok has called the 'inner story', around which Holmes and Watson's investigations (the main story) revolve (1997: 277) – is always explained and ultimately eliminated by Holmes's confident detective work. Nevertheless, there is something monstrous about Sherlock Holmes himself, which remains after the cases are solved – precisely because of his inhuman capacity for intellectual endeavour. Nowhere is this clearer than in *The Hound of the Baskervilles* (1901–02), a novel which, in its middle section, sees Holmes terrorise Watson by wandering around the moor at night when he has told his friend he has gone back to London. Even though Watson notes that 'the man on the tor' is extremely tall and thin, the process of uncanny defamiliarisation means he is unable to guess his identity until Holmes chooses to reveal himself. Watson feels as if he is in the grip of an 'unseen force' and worries, 'Was he our malignant enemy, or was he by chance our guardian angel?' (Doyle *Hound*: 120). Here, Holmes himself generates one of the uncanny scenes around which the narrative is constructed. The strange episode, while ostensibly the result of a conviction that the case can only be solved once the criminal lets down his guard in the detective's apparent absence, shows Holmes's potential to elude the strictures of normality and inhabit the 'monstrous' zone in the story's location in a way that links him powerfully with the mythic hound.

It is notable that, on three occasions during this episode, Watson describes the strange man as 'dogging' him (Doyle *Hound*: 100; 114; 119). Canine references in a novel of this title surely cannot be ignored: here they underline the fact that there are not one, but two monstrous creatures upsetting the natural order of things: the hound, and the great detective.

The problem faced by any Sherlock Holmes adaptation which seeks to resist falling into mere historical pastiche is not so much how to follow the great Holmeses of the past, such as Rathbone or Brett, but how to present an appealing yet reassuring picture of the eccentric genius who does not conform to social norms after the Other has become integrated in crime fiction, as Plain argues, and after the serial killer narrative in particular. This is something, I shall argue in what follows, which has shaped the two recent adaptations in focus here. Our culture instinctively finds the excessive abilities and personality traits of a man like Holmes suspicious at best, and dangerous at worst. Downey Jr. said of preparing to play the part in the film, 'The more I look into the books, the more fantastic it becomes. Holmes is such a weirdo' (BBC News Online 2008). In the BBC series, Holmes is repeatedly addressed as 'freak' by police sergeant Sally Donovan, who is forced by her superior, Inspector Lestrade, to allow him to work alongside her. In the first episode, *A Study in Pink* (first aired on 25 July 2010), as they stand at a crime scene, she warns Watson about Holmes:

> Stay away from that guy.... You know why he's here? He's not paid or anything. He likes it. He gets off on it. The weirder the crime, the more he gets off.... One day we'll be standing around a body and Sherlock Holmes will be the one who put it there.... Because he's a psychopath. Psychopaths get bored.

Holmes, inevitably overhearing the conversation, acknowledges that sometimes people do assume he is the murderer, and insists that he is not a psychopath but 'a high-functioning sociopath'.

This remark may be tongue-in-cheek, but it is a significant departure for Sherlock Holmes adaptations to explicitly define Holmes as pathological. The BBC series does not shy away from presenting its Holmes as comparable to the obviously unhinged villains he confronts. By contrast, Ritchie's film version carefully keeps its Holmes on the merely eccentric or 'weird' side of abnormal. He is a reckless risk-taker and thrill-seeker, devoid of the carefully sustained balance between asceticism and excess which defines the original. He is a variation on Robert

Stephens's decadent aesthete in Wilder's *The Private Life of Sherlock Holmes* (1970), but swashbuckling instead of languid. That his abnormality does not extend into the pathological is conveyed through the comparison the film sets up with its master-criminal Lord Henry Blackwood (Mark Strong). Blackwood is a backwards-engineered psychopath in the grip of a God delusion, and he exhibits no empathy at all with his victims ('Five otherwise meaningless creatures called to serve a greater purpose'). Holmes speculates that if he and Watson were to dissect Blackwood's brain after he is hanged they would find 'some deformity that'd be scientifically significant'. That Holmes does not approximate Blackwood's monstrosity is made clear in a curious intertextual reference during the scene in which Blackwood summons Holmes to his cell before he is hanged. The scene is a clear echo of Starling's Baltimore visit to Lecter in *The Silence of the Lambs*. Holmes is directed down a corridor remarkably similar in scale, architecture and lighting to the one in Demme's film, the guard warning him that many of the prisoners have had to be moved away because Blackwood 'has a peculiar effect on the inmates, as though he can get inside their heads'. Blackwood's cell is adorned with inscriptions and pictograms,[3] and even some of the close-ups, in which the faces of criminal and detective appear in the same frame, eliminating the protective bars between them, resemble the previous film. Whether or not this is a deliberate echo is not the point; rather, so iconic is the Hannibal Lecter scene in cinematic history, the source of numerous parodies in popular culture, that it is difficult for the viewer not to be reminded, at some level, of the most famous serial-killer film of all. In this way, Ritchie's movie conveys to its viewers the fact that, despite its Victorian London setting (albeit one rendered in a hyper-real style[4]), Holmes is dealing with a phenomenon we are familiar with from our own cultural landscape: the psychopathic mass killer. It also provides the film's viewers with a kind of insurance policy, a guarantee that, unlike *The Silence of the Lambs*, it is not the Holmes-figure who is the dangerous intellectual schemer, but his adversary.

The film's containment of Holmes's power is achieved by effectively reducing the significance of his intellect in favour of emphasising his physical bravery and skill. It downgrades the famous 'Holmes method' – the quasi-scientific procedure for deduction based on observation which is, Pierre Bayard has remarked, 'the primary reason that these texts have become famous' (2008: 30) – to a mere incidental quirk of nature. In order to acknowledge its credentials as an authentic Sherlock Holmes movie, the method is duly foregrounded early in the film. Mary Morstan (a character who featured in *The Sign of Four* and here is Watson's fiancée) remarks to Holmes that making 'grand assumptions out of such tiny details' seems 'far-fetched', only for the detective to counter that 'In fact the little details are by far the most important'. But his actual deployment of the method is confined to showy set-pieces, such as proving his point by cruelly shattering Morstan's self-esteem by deducing facts about her previous marriage in front of Watson, or, later, being able to pinpoint exactly which place in London he has been taken by Hansom cab although blindfolded. Solving the real mystery – an elaborate series of illusions fuelled by the Biblical delirium of Blackwood and his acolytes – requires a more general combination of sharp reasoning and inspired research with extreme bravery and physical prowess – the kind of methodology deployed by any number of cinematic blockbuster heroes faced with a supervillain, like Batman[5] or Indiana Jones. Even though Ritchie's Holmes is able to determine how Blackwood has managed to pull off such terrifying illusions (the plot here is reminiscent of Holmes's exposure of the supernatural sham in *The Hound of the Baskervilles*), in this movie Holmes essentially comes across as a clever, eccentric action hero, a figure who does for the detective story what Captain Jack Sparrow of the *Pirates of the Caribbean* franchise (2003–11) does for the pirate adventure, rather than the pioneer of a new, historically-specific system for solving crime. Ritchie may have been correct when he implied that the original stories were as much melodramas as crypto-criminological case studies (*Telegraph* 2008), but there is no reason for this to be Sherlock Holmes, for the job could have been done by any other hero.

'Data, data, data': Holmes rebooted

'Data, data, data – I cannot make bricks without clay' ('The Adventure of the Copper Beeches' [*Adventures of Sherlock Holmes*: 289])

In Ritchie's *Sherlock Holmes*, the distinctive Holmes method becomes transmuted into eccentricity, the potentially disturbing power of the intellect safely channelled into physical power, as Holmes fights, jumps and shoots his way to solving the crime. This marks an interesting change from the way the body figures in Doyle's original stories. In *Detective Fiction and the Rise of Forensic Science*, Ronald R. Thomas's study of how detective fiction supported criminology in making the 'nineteenth-century person legible for a modern technological culture' (2004: 17), Holmes is described as a machine which makes the body tell the truth, a literary counterpart of contemporary devices used in crime detection, such as the lie detector or the camera. But in Ritchie's film it is the effect on Holmes's *own* body of his profession and lifestyle which is continually foregrounded – most indulgently in a bare-knuckle boxing scene (perhaps reflecting Doyle's own love of pugilism) where Holmes and an opponent fight bare-chested in front of a baying audience. The function of this emphasis on the detective's body displaces Holmes into the kind of universe inhabited by the noir private eye rather than the gentleman detective. More significantly, though, it has the effect of domesticating the power of his intellect. The mind is directed towards the needs of the body in this Holmes film, rather than the other way around. We can see this even more clearly in *Sherlock Holmes*'s distinctive, videogame-esque, approach to combat sequences. The conceit is to show a fight twice in quick succession: the second in 'real time', as it would have actually happened, but the first a slow-motion close-up depicting how Holmes's brain visualises each stage of his attack in advance in order to take advantage of his opponent's weaknesses. This is accompanied by an interior monologue which conveys his logic as he assesses his enemy:

> Head cocked to the left: partial deafness in ear: first point of attack. Two, throat. Paralyze vocal chords. Stop screaming. Three, got to be heavy drinker. Floating rib to the liver. Four, finally, dragging left leg. Fist to patella. Summary of prognosis, conscious in 90 seconds. Martial efficacy, quarter of an hour. Full faculty recovery, unlikely.

In this way the 2009 movie envisages Holmes as a figure just as 'computerised' as the gaming action heroes who feature increasingly in popular cinema, such as the Prince of Persia or Neo from *The Matrix*, and transmogrifies the Holmes method into a kind of onboard computer geared up to enhance bodily performance.

The comparison between Holmes and a computer is an inevitable refiguration of the original idea of Holmes as a 'machine' which is more in tune with the tropes of postmodernity. It is also made in the 2010 BBC series, but this time in a way which properly recontextualises the Holmes method rather than reducing it – giving it a full 'system update', in other words. Moffat and Gatiss's BBC series is one of the most ambitious re-imaginings of Holmes ever attempted. Three episodes were shown in July and August 2010: 'A Study in Pink', 'The Blind Banker' and 'The Great Game'. These managed to plausibly transpose the distinctive features of the original stories into the twenty-first century world. In the opening episode, for example, the re-styled Watson – a forty-something, slightly disaffected man searching listlessly for a fulfilling job and relationship – has just returned from the recent 'war against terror' in Afghanistan, just as the original incarnation served there during the second Anglo-Afghan war of 1878–80. This Watson keeps a blog instead of writing his memoirs, while Sherlock Holmes maintains a website, 'The Science of Deduction', and uses a nicotine patch instead of a pipe (one case is, inevitably, 'a three-patch problem' ['A Study in Pink']). Other features are cleverly preserved and updated, such as the duo repeatedly hailing taxis to hurtle from one city location to another, or enlisting the help of a graffiti artist just as the original Holmes called upon the 'Baker Street Irregulars'. Some amusingly plausible interactions with contemporary culture are suggested, as when Holmes passes the time by solving the 'mysteries' on *The Jeremy Kyle Show* ('course he wasn't the boy's father! Look at the turn-ups on his jeans!'). Most impressively, though, the series manages to sustain the parallel between Holmes's technique and character and the high-tech digital world of the twenty-first century.

At the beginning of 'A Scandal in Bohemia' Watson describes Holmes as 'the most perfect reasoning and observing machine that the world has seen' (Doyle, 'Scandal': 3). Thomas quotes the line often in support of his argument that Holmes is best understood as a fictional machine rather than a literary character (Thomas, 2004: 32, 119). But Benedict Cumberbatch's 2010 Holmes is more like a version of the machine which drives twenty-first century crime investigation: the computer. Presented with a crime scene, this Holmes processes the information rapidly and accurately, circumventing the laborious process of collecting and then analysing forensic, ballistic, or biographical data. Here we have the Holmes for our age: a central processing unit. This is conveyed most obviously by the scenes in which Holmes surveys and analyses a body or a crime scene. Accompanied by dramatic music, *CSI*-style high-definition 'dolly-zooms' provide close-ups of objects while Holmes intones a breathless kind of forensic poetry to his mesmerised audience, Lestrade and Watson:

> I found this inside his trouser pockets. Sodden by the river, but still recognisably … ticket stubs. He worked in a museum or gallery. Did a quick check. The Hickman gallery has reported one of its attendants as missing, Alex Woodbridge … ('The Great Game')

To underline the idea of Holmes as wired into some mysterious vast crime-solving mainframe, during such episodes the screen is overlaid with text showing the menus of a smartphone or the content of SMS messages as he searches for information.

This parallel is explicitly made in the third of the episodes, 'The Great Game'. Early in the episode there is an exchange which updates Watson's famous expression of amazement from *A Study in Scarlet* about how Holmes's 'ignorance was as remarkable as his knowledge', namely that he knows almost nothing about 'contemporary literature, philosophy and politics' and is even 'ignorant of the Copernican Theory and of the composition of the Solar System' (Doyle: 17). The Watson of 123 years later comments on his companion's 'spectacular ignorance', his inability to name the prime minister or know 'whether the earth goes round the sun', and exclaims, 'It's primary school stuff. How can you not know that?!' Holmes's reply replaces Doyle's original, rather awkward, analogy between an empty attic which a workman needs to carefully stock with 'nothing but the tools which may help him in doing his work' (Doyle 17) with a more predictable but quite accurate comparison: 'Well, if I ever did, I've deleted it. ... Listen. [pointing to his head] This is my hard drive, and it only makes sense to put things in there that are useful' ('The Great Game').

That the link between forensic technology and the Holmes method is made as easily in the twenty-first century as it was in the nineteenth is not surprising because when it comes to investigation the latter age is, in crucial respects, simply a development of the one which provided Holmes's original context. Ours is a more advanced and accelerated form of the system Jean Baudrillard described as 'production', which emerged with the scientific, positivist ethos of the nineteenth century. Production is a process by which everything can 'be produced, be read, become real, visible, and marked with the sign of effectiveness; ... transcribed into force relations, into conceptual systems or into calculable energy; ... said, gathered, indexed and registered' (1977: 21–2). What is created by this process, for Baudrillard, is precisely 'reality' – that is, a system of values, rules, and perceptions that we all subscribe to. Reality is thus 'coded' in Baudrillard's terms according to what is essentially a binaristic system where everything has a value, an opposite, and a meaning. Our contemporary digital culture makes this 'productive' basis for modern existence – and the 'hyperreality' it engenders due to its special ability to produce copies that are themselves originals – even more pervasive. Without drawing on Baudrillard (the kind of reference best left to *The Matrix*), the 2010 *Sherlock Holmes* nonetheless subtly demonstrates that this binaristic, digital world of value is a more important background for its narratives than London. In the second episode, 'The Blind Banker', Holmes tells Watson:

> The world's run on codes and ciphers, John. From the million pound security system at the bank to the PIN machine you took exception to [at the beginning of the episode Watson's card is refused by an automatic supermarket till]. Cryptography inhabits our every waking moment. But it's all computer generated – electronic codes, electronic ciphering methods. ('The Blind Banker')

The specific context for this declaration is to compare modern coding with the more 'ancient' kind of cryptography they have come up against in this case (a complex yarn about a Chinese drug-smuggling ring which communicates through obscure messages inscribed on artworks and antiques) but, more generally, it describes the environment of the whole series. It is a computerised world, conveyed visually by the brief speeded-up transitional shots of London which punctuate the narratives of the series; a 'clean' London – quite the opposite of the traditional 'Holmesian' world of shadows and fog, which was much-exaggerated in Ritchie's film – going about its unceasing business, all bright lights and speeding cars, like the circuitry of a gigantic computer. It is natural that such a computerised world would produce a computerised detective. While his eccentricities make him, on the face of it, an anomalous figure in this world, in fact this Sherlock Holmes is perfectly in keeping with it, and its personification. The police officers he works beside openly despise this 'freak' who intrudes into their own carefully-controlled environment, but this is no doubt because he is the walking incarnation of the systems they adhere to rather than a disturbing alternative to them. Moffat and Gatiss's Holmes is the symptom of the postmodern age of production.

This is also how we must account for his sociopathy. A repeated refrain in the series is Holmes's apparent inability to empathise with others on an emotional level. At one point in 'A Study in Pink' Watson is appalled that Holmes has difficulty grasping the fact a mother might still be 'upset' by the memory of her stillborn daughter 14 years later. A running joke in the series is the preposterous idea of Holmes having friends. As it is in the original, emotion would seem to be a threat as dangerous to the smooth-functioning of the Holmes method as a virus is to a hard drive: after comparing Holmes to a 'perfect reasoning and observing machine' Watson goes on to note that '[g]rit in a sensitive instrument, or a crack in one of his own high-power lenses, would not be more disturbing than a strong emotion in a nature such as his' ('Scandal', *Adventures*: 3). Yet besides the fact that it is essential in order that his system will not malfunction, Holmes's lack of empathy is also the natural product of the 'sociopathic' world represented by modern crime drama. Crime narratives in popular fiction and television present us with a world in which emotion has been sidelined. It is a world in which the 'waning of affect' which famously typifies postmodernity according to Fredric Jameson (1991: 61), is inscribed in every scene. Not that the depiction of emotion is absent from the contemporary crime thriller. Far from it: characters cry at the death of a loved one, rage at someone who stands in the way of their desire, express terror as they are persecuted or tortured, and so on. We watch such expressions of emotion on screen continually in every crime drama. But we do so largely unmoved, because we know that what really matters is the plot. More precisely, detective fiction is itself symptomatic of the modern scientific, positivist, digitised universe, all ones and zeroes and positive values. It too (as I have argued elsewhere [Nicol 2011]) is an exemplary expression of the modern 'project' of production, in Baudrillard's terms: the job of the detective is to bring what is hidden or obscured or mysterious into the light, make it readable, intelligible, real, so it can be interpreted, judged, brought to account. Watching detective drama puts the viewer in the position of the high-functioning sociopath: we recognise emotion but we do not really empathise with those who suffer from it, for we are coldly interested in getting to the bottom of the mystery.

'Give me work' (*The Sign of Four*)

> The work itself, the pleasure of finding a field for my peculiar powers, is my highest reward. (*The Sign of Four*: 8)

It is possible to read the BBC series as a comment on the 'sociopathy' of the detective and detective fiction as a genre, a parallel perhaps to Mark Haddon's novel *The Curious Incident of the Dog in the Night-time* (2003), which tells the story of a 15-year-old boy with an unspecified autistic disorder, who uses the techniques he has gleaned from reading the Holmes stories to investigate the death of a neighbour's dog and eventually stumbles upon the key to the *real* mystery (his mother's disappearance) after a long and difficult process of trying to decode adult emotion. There is something 'autistic' or even 'sociopathic' about detective work: it can effectively sift through the facts, but it is not equipped to deal with emotion.

But lack of empathy and limited emotions are not the only pathological traits exhibited by the 2010 Sherlock Holmes. He experiences two more extreme kinds of emotion, both of which are linked with each other: boredom, and the thrill of making cognitive connections. Boredom is fundamental to the constitution of Doyle's original Holmes. In another of the early myth-creating tales, *The Sign of Four* (1890), a concerned Watson confronts his friend with the risk posed to his great intellectual powers by persisting with the 'pathological and morbid process' of taking cocaine. Holmes replies

> My mind...rebels at stagnation. Give me problems, give me work, give me the most abstruse cryptogram, or the most intricate analysis, and I am in my own proper atmosphere. I can dispense then with artificial stimulants. But I abhor the dull routine of existence. I crave for mental exaltation. (Doyle: 8).

Boredom is the opposite of work for Holmes, and the intolerable gap between the two is filled by the temporary high provided by 'artificial stimulants'. Given the care with which the Moffat/Gatiss series transposes many of the original elements of Doyle's stories into early twenty-first century equivalents, it is surprising that Holmes's use of drugs is not something it has chosen to update (though there is a staged drugs bust at the detective's home in 'A Study in Pink').[6] But Holmes's boredom is still there, and arguably even more important. The third episode, 'The Great Game', begins with Holmes alone in his apartment, so intensely bored that he fires a number of gunshots into his wall, then looks out of the window and observes how 'quiet, calm, peaceful' it is, only to conclude, 'Isn't it *hateful*?' Mrs Hudson points out that he will soon be cheered up if a 'nice murder' comes along. This is another sociopathic element of Holmes which raises the spectre of criminality: psychopaths, as Sergeant Donovan says, get bored. Sure enough, later in the episode when Lestrade asks Holmes why in the world would anyone torture a woman by strapping explosives to her, Holmes replies, 'Oh...I can't be the only person in the world that gets bored'. Soon after, the criminal in question – revealed as Moriarty, recast as a besuited psychopathic middle manager – admits that he has embarked upon his campaign of destruction 'because I'm bored'. 'We were made for each other, Sherlock', he remarks.

Work has always been central to the crime thriller, especially the hard-boiled/noir tradition of private eye movies, from *The Maltese Falcon* (1941) to *Zodiac* (2007). The private eye, as John Irwin has argued, symbolises the significance of work in modern American constructions of masculinity (2006: 36). He typically lives for his work, and chooses work over love. This is not usually the case in the classic 'logic-and-deduction' detective story. Although the detective works relentlessly, he does so in the name of pleasure or justice, not because he needs to make a living. (Where private eye movies are upfront in dealing with the issue of the detective's payment for work rendered, the idea of a monetary reward is treated with scorn by Sherlock Holmes.) Nevertheless, Holmes's plea 'give me work' shows that he provides an important tangent to the function of work in detective fiction and films, one not considered by Irwin – and this too is central to the BBC *Sherlock Holmes*. The Moffat/Gatiss Holmes is a man for whom the very idea of a life without work makes little sense. He spends the spare time he has alone, conducting experiments which will advance his 'science of deduction'. On two occasions in the series, Watson opens the fridge to find human body parts (eyes, and then a head). A comic sub-story in 'The Great Game' is about Watson's attempts to start a relationship up with Molly Hooper only for Holmes to prevent them from enjoying any time together by constantly engaging Watson in work.

Work in the series is not about economics, as it is in hard-boiled fiction – or at least it has more to do with a libidinal economy than a monetary one. Work provides the antidote to the intense boredom Holmes experiences in that it promises the *jouissance* he craves from intellectual endeavour. The exquisite pleasure Holmes derives from his method is conveyed brilliantly by Cumberbatch when he drama- tises the method 'in action', namely when Holmes makes a connection between apparently unassociated facts or discovers a new piece of infor- mation. His face lights up, and he exclaims 'ohhhh!' or 'ahhhh!' The state of mind he conveys resembles what Freud termed 'epistemophilia', or when

[t]he thought process itself becomes sexualized, for the sexual pleasure which is normally attached to the content of thought becomes shifted on to the act of thinking itself, and the satisfaction derived from reaching the conclusion of a line of thought is experi- enced as a *sexual* satisfaction. (Freud, 1984: 124)

As one of the 'component instincts', epistemophilia – the drive to know – is a normal part of subjectivity, as it is central to children's formative research into sexual identity. But Freud insisted that the epis- temophilic drive may be pathological (a feature of obsessional neurosis,

for example, as in the case of his patient 'The Rat Man'). The extreme
pleasure Cumberbatch's Holmes takes from the thought process is
clearly not normal. Indeed his epistemophilia might be perversely
considered the most *sexualised* aspect of the BBC series, despite the clever
red herrings it lays down with regard to the possibility of homosexual
attraction between Holmes and Watson – a compelling skein of pink
running through the series (and far more in keeping with the homosocial nature of the original stories than the heteronormative exploits
of Robert Downey Jr. in *Sherlock Holmes*). The closest thing on screen
to an exhibition of sexual desire – certainly more erotic than Watson's
laborious courtship of Molly Hooper – is the *jouissance* of Holmes's
cognitive activity.

This is, finally, another way that the updated Sherlock Holmes, for all
his abnormality, for all his monstrosity, is actually symptomatic of the
postmodern sensibility. Just as he is uninterested in others and unable
to empathise with them, he is also subject to highs and lows, alternating
between periods of extreme boredom and moments of euphoria – the
kind of mood swings which postmodern culture induces in its subjects
as a result of its characteristic 'waning of affect', which Jameson (appro-
priating an idea in Lyotard's *Libidinal Economy* [1974]) terms 'intensities'
(Stephenson, 1989: 4). But Holmes is not just typical of the age in this
respect; he is also the counterpart of the viewer of the series itself, and
the genre it represents more generally: the contemporary crime thriller.
It is a commonplace of criticism on detective fiction that the detective
is the reader's textual surrogate, someone who is engaged in a parallel
process to that of the reader as s/he decodes the text: interpreting signs,
piecing together the narrative. In Tzvetan Todorov's neat formulation,
'author: reader = criminal: detective' (1977: 49). A variation on this
parallel relationship pertains in the crime thriller which combines – as
the BBC Sherlock Holmes series does so effectively – the action of the
hard-boiled thriller with the cerebral puzzle-solving of the classic 'logic
and deduction' detective story. As we watch we surrender ourselves to
the emotions traditionally generated by the thriller (fear, suspense)
while also periodically indulging in the pleasures of cognition, along
with the detective. This means that just as we assume the non-empa-
thetic demeanour of the sociopath as we watch the suffering of others,
just as we ironically seek to escape routine existence by watching a form
which revolves around work, so we also become – while immersed in
the drama – subject to similar mood swings to those of the most pathological Sherlock Holmes yet. It seems appropriate that the crime thriller
has achieved a seemingly unassailable dominance among the various

genres of popular culture. More than its capacity to incorporate 'the other' within its examples, might this be because it parallels the depiction of the volatile 'intensities' of our age by the very way in which we are invited to enjoy the text? Where the realist novel was once valued for the 'love' which conditioned the empathetic approach to characters by both author and reader (Bayley, 1960), the crime thriller is typified by an attitude of cold disregard. For all its undoubted verve, the BBC series, in contrast to the limited videogame action hero of the Ritchie film, brings a very nineteenth-century creation – Sherlock Holmes – perfectly into line with the character of our times.

Notes

1. Martin Rubin argues that 'The concept of "thriller" falls someway between a genre proper and a descriptive quality that is attached to other, more clearly-defined genres – such as spy thriller, detective thriller, horror thriller. ... The thriller can be conceptualized as a "metagenre" that gathers several other genres under its umbrella, and as a band in the spectrum that colors each of those particular genres' (1999: 4).
2. The term 'sociopathy', now generally preferred amongst psychiatrists to 'psychopathy', is, like many terms in the discourse of psychiatry, rather loosely defined. The DSM-IV (*Diagnostic and Statistical Manual of Mental Disorders, Fourth Edition* [1994]) describes it as 'a pervasive pattern of disregard for and violation of the rights of others occurring since age 15 years' which is evidenced in at least three out of seven behavioural traits: failure to conform to social norms by acting unlawfully, deceitfulness, impulsivity, irritability and aggression, reckless disregard for safety of self and others, consistent irresponsibility, lack of remorse. I am using the term here in the more general sense that features in works which diagnose 'cultural psychopathology', such as Martha Stout's *The Sociopath Next Door* (2005) and Paul Babiak's and Robert Hare's *Snakes in Suits: When Psychopaths Go to Work* (2007), as an attitude towards the other person which is characterised by a lack of empathy and remorse.
3. The lines Blackwood quotes are from *The Book of Revelations* and relate to the figure of the Red Dragon, a myth favoured by another psychopath in Harris's first Lecter story, of this title.
4. Jean Baudrillard's term for the effect of the real (which is always already simulated) being reproduced so effectively that it comes to seem imaginary, or more real than real (1994). This is the effect of Ritchie's larger-than-life, CGI-enhanced London.
5. Warner Brothers took on the Sherlock Holmes project after perceiving it had similar revisionary potential to *Batman Begins*.
6. Ritchie's film also leaves out the drug-taking element in favour of suggesting that Holmes has a fondness for alcohol, though this is perhaps more understandable given the movie's status as family blockbuster.

9
The Strange Case of the Scientist Who Believed in Fairies

Andrew Lycett

In writing the life of Sir Arthur Conan Doyle, with its riveting mix of domestic incident and great external events, I was fascinated throughout by one particular aspect – how this medically trained creator of the supposedly super-rationalist detective Sherlock Holmes could become an apostle for spiritualism – to the extent that, in 1920, slightly more than three decades after launching his famous detective, he lent his considerable support to two young Yorkshire girls who manifestly conned the world into believing that they had photographed fairies in their back garden: the famous Cottingley Fairies.

To understand this intellectual journey, it is necessary to know something of Conan Doyle's background. He was born in Edinburgh in May 1859 into a family which hailed from Ireland on both sides, was staunchly Roman Catholic and had a deep artistic streak. And art in the blood, as Sherlock Holmes once remarked, 'is liable to take the strangest forms' (Doyle 1981: 435).

His uncle Richard (or Dicky) Doyle was perhaps the best-known artist among them. He worked for *Punch* (contributing the iconic image of Mr Punch and his dog which graced the magazine's cover for over a century) and was also well-known for his genre paintings of fairies. Arthur's father, Charles, also had artistic leanings, but he did not have the drive of Dicky and his other brothers. When, as a young man, he was sent up to Edinburgh to serve his apprenticeship as a clerk in the Office of Works, he became depressed and took to the bottle. Although he had the good sense to marry a spirited woman called Mary Foley, he eventually had to be institutionalised as an alcoholic – a great blight in Arthur's life. As a result, the rest of the family rallied around and helped to send Arthur to board at school with the Jesuits at Stonyhurst in Lancashire.

After completing his education there in 1875 Arthur did not really know what to do with his life. A family friend, Dr Bryan Waller, who was a student, and later a lecturer, in Anatomy at Edinburgh University, encouraged the young man to follow his lead and read medicine at the university in his home town.

This proved to be a turning point for Conan Doyle, who quickly grew beyond his Jesuit education and learnt to think in a sceptical and analytical way. The city itself was known as the Athens of the North, reflecting its position in the vanguard of the empirical tradition of the Scottish enlightenment. There he studied under teachers such as Joseph Bell, the professor of surgery, whose precise observation of his patients was to be so influential in the make-up of Sherlock Holmes.

Even as a student of medicine, Conan Doyle began to turn out regular stories. One, 'The Mystery of Sasassa Valley', was published by *Chamber's Magazine* in September 1879. And like much of Conan Doyle's early output, it had a ghostly or occult theme, showing the forces of reason and progress triumphing over those of darkness and superstition. So, even in these early days, contrasting strands were developing in Conan Doyle's life. One was his juggling of the medical and the literary. For the time being these coexisted quite easily, but in later years they would become less comfortable bed-fellows. And the same would be true of the other strand – the distinction between the rational and supernatural in Conan Doyle's life and in his writings.

On the surface there was no conflict here. I have stressed the empiricism he picked up at Edinburgh. This scientific approach was to dominate not just his professional work, but also his more general philosophy, for this was the age of Darwin and other debunkers of the divine order. During his undergraduate years, Conan Doyle dropped his Catholicism and, to the horror of his family, began to describe himself as an agnostic.

However, Conan Doyle could not quite give up his sense that there was a higher being in the universe, and so he began describing himself as being 'in a broad sense' Unitarian – a self-professed rationalist religion which discarded the trappings of organised Christianity. However, his beliefs were closer to the American transcendentalism espoused by Ralph Waldo Emerson – a mixture of German idealism (of a type Conan Doyle had come across while taking a gap year in Austria in 1875–6), New England practicality and British romanticism. In this context, he was particularly attracted to the writings of the New Englander Oliver Wendell Holmes, who managed to combine being a writer and a doctor, as Conan Doyle hoped to do. And, as would later become clear, that surname would stick.

After graduating Conan Doyle initially flailed around, unsure of what he should do. Eventually, in mid-1882 he found himself on the south coast of England, where, at the age of twenty-three, he established himself as a doctor in a single-handed general practice in Southsea, a suburb of Portsmouth.

His seven years there were to prove very important in the development of both his career and his ideas. Since life was initially hard, he asked his mother for help from the family. Since his sisters were otherwise occupied (earning money for the family purse as governesses), Arthur was joined by his nine-year-old brother Innes, who acted as his receptionist. Gradually, as he became successful in his practice, he developed into an established member of the local community, trading on his practical scientific approach to problem solving.

Nevertheless, despite having lost his religion and committed himself to an empirical approach to knowledge, he found himself increasingly at odds with the uncompromising materialism of the medical profession. He remained convinced there was another dimension to life – and this made him sympathetic to the late-Victorian fascination with paranormal activities and to scientific attempts to explain them rationally. This was a cultural response to the 'death of God' which followed Darwin's publication of his theory of evolution. As quickly as mediums came up with feats of levitation and extra-sensory perception, scientists tried to explain them. Conan Doyle was fascinated, taking heart from the encouragement of a Portsmouth friend, General Alfred Drayson, a former army officer who was an early member of the Society for Psychical Research (founded in 1882).

At the same time, blessed with abundant energy, the young doctor continued to write stories which he sent to outlets such as *Blackwoods Magazine* in his home town of Edinburgh and to the *Cornhill* in London. As before – and in keeping with his interests – his style was generally an adventure tale with a ghostly or occult twist. An early example is 'The Captain of the Polestar' (1882), which pitted a rational medical student against the unhinged captain and superstitious crew of an Arctic whaler in a powerful story about the clash of reason and the paranormal in the 'white desert' of Arctic icebergs. There he has his fictional student joke with the ship's captain about 'the impostures of Slade' (Doyle, 2010: 14).

Here he was referring to Henry Slade, one of the many American mediums who, in the wake of the table rapping of the Fox sisters in the middle of the century, had come over to Britain. Slade had introduced automatic writing into the mix, but he had been challenged by

E. Roy Lankester, a young professor of zoology, who had snatched away his slate, leading to a prosecution for fraud. Interestingly Lankester was later to contribute ideas to Conan Doyle's novel *The Lost World* (1912).

As a doctor, Conan Doyle could claim a particular professional interest in paranormal matters. For along with the more esoteric ideas of levitation and haunting, there was, from a medical point of view, a practical side to this kind of research. For many years scientists had been looking into mesmerism (and later hypnotism) as a therapeutic tool to heal people with afflictions – usually mental illness.

So, at the same time as writing stories about weird happenings, Conan Doyle began to write tales of people with mesmeric powers. One is 'John Barrington Cowles' which was published in *Cassells Saturday Journal* in 1884. It is interesting for several reasons, not least that it was one of his few stories to deal with Edinburgh. It tells of a promising student who falls in love with a cold but beautiful woman with sinister mesmeric powers. His friend, the narrator, discovers that she comes from an exotic background, her father being a former Indian army officer with a reputation for the evil eye and for having 'having theories of the human will and of the effect of mind over matter' (Doyle, 2010: 153). After falling under her spell the student wastes away and dies. However, although he was clearly interested in this subject matter, Conan Doyle was careful to maintain the scepticism which came with his training as a scientist, and therefore at this stage his involvement with the paranormal remained merely a personal interest.

In 1885 his existence was changed when he married Louise Hawkins. This came about because Conan Doyle had taken in a young patient who was terminally ill with cerebral meningitis. The lad was Louise's brother and, after he died, Arthur found himself attracted to the mourning Louise. This was not necessarily the basis for a firm relationship, but Arthur had mentioned in several of his regular letters to his mother that he needed a wife. Louise fitted the bill.

Domestic life suited him because, two years later, he turned his hand to another writing genre – crime fiction – that was to make his name. He had read earlier detective story writers such as Edgar Allan Poe and the Frenchman Emile Gaboriau, and he thought he could do better. Feeling, as he put it, the need to see his name on the back of a volume, he penned *A Study in Scarlet*, a gory story about a London murder with North American antecedents. This did the rounds of several publishers before finding a home in *Beetons Christmas Annual* of 1887.

It was a significant story because it introduced the consulting detective Sherlock Holmes and his sidekick and biographer Dr Watson. In an early draft he described Holmes as having 'analytical genius' (quoted in Nordon: 212). In other words, he was designed to bring a scientific approach to the business of solving murders. (This, of course, was in keeping with the questing, investigative spirit of the age.)

Initially Conan Doyle cast his mind back to his professor, Joseph Bell, with 'his eerie trick of spotting details' (Doyle, *Memories and Adventures*: 74) and convinced himself, 'If he were a detective he would surely reduce this fascinating but unorganised business to something nearer an exact science. I would try if I could get this effect' (74–5). Thus he imbued Sherlock Holmes with Bell's powers of observation, but also with insights from the latest crime-fighting techniques such as advanced forensics and anthropometrics – the science of predicting criminality from a person's features (drawing on the work of the Frenchman Alphonse Bertillon, who introduced the police mug shot).

In this respect the detective became a symbol of scientific knowledge bringing order to the muddled universe. But that did not mean that Conan Doyle was giving up his fascination with the paranormal. While writing his biography, I travelled to the home of an eminent cardiologist in New Jersey, where I was given access to his superb collection of Sherlockian books and manuscripts. These included three notebooks in which Conan Doyle had recorded his first séances. As I wrote in my book:

> On 24 January 1887 Arthur and his architect friend Henry Ball found themselves in a group of five people sitting nervously round a dining room table at Kingston Lodge in the north of Portsmouth. As candidates for spiritual enlightenment, they seemed eager but slightly out of their depth. Not knowing precisely how to conduct a table-rapping session, they had decided to follow a set of instructions published by Light, the magazine of the recently formed London Spiritual Alliance. To get themselves in the mood, they intoned the first chapter of the Book of Ezekiel where a spirit appears to the Prophet in dramatic forms: "And I looked, and, behold, a whirlwind came out of the north, a great cloud, and a fire infolding itself, and a brightness was about it, and out of the midst thereof as the colour of amber, out of the midst of the fire. Also out of the midst thereof came the likeness of four living creatures. And this was their appearance; they had the likeness of a man. (Southsea Notebooks, private collection)

In all, Conan Doyle went to around twenty such sessions, trying different approaches, without gaining much enlightenment. At one he tried to see if he could summon up some automatic writing – but to no avail. At another he was excited to find that when he thought of his wife, the table began to rap out TO. Expecting this to carry on to spell his wife Louise's nickname, TOUIE, he struggled not to touch the table top with anything but his finger tips. But the next few letters turned out to be MMY (Lycett: 125).

Despite such setbacks, Conan Doyle's interest remained strong. In one of these notebooks, he noted how General Drayson had been converted to spiritualism after getting a message from his dead brother. Underneath he carefully listed the names of several eminent scientists who had embraced spiritualism, as well as some weighty books he intended to read: Carl von Reichenbach's *Abstract of Researches on Magnetism*, William Gregory's *Letters on Animal Magnetism*, Robert Dale Owen's *Footfalls on the Boundary of Another World*, Robert Hare's *Experimental Investigation: the Spirit Manifestations* and even David Dunglas Home's *Incidents of my Life*. This was a crash course in science and the paranormal, so far as it was then known.

Conan Doyle also gave an insight into where he was coming from personally. He had long convinced himself intellectually that there was a world of the spirit, but he had not experienced it personally. Here worries about his father weighed upon him. By then Charles Doyle had succumbed to alcoholism and had been committed to an institution in Scotland. His son Arthur could not understand what happened to the spirit or 'soul' of a man who cracked his skull or became addicted to alcohol or drugs. So far as he could make out from his father, 'his whole character would change, and a high nature might become a low one'. This was the rational doctor's point of view: at this stage the 'soul' was simply a physical entity to him – 'the total effect of all the hereditary or personal functionings of the mind' (*Memories and Adventures*: 83). But he was beginning to discern that there might be another reality. As he later put it, 'It had never struck me that the current of events might really flow in the opposite direction, and that the higher faculties could only manifest themselves imperfectly through an imperfect instrument. The broken fiddle is silent and yet the musician is the same as ever' (*Memories and Adventures*: 84).

With his concern to ensure that any position he took was backed by adequate scientific evidence, he was encouraged by the work of the newly formed SPR. Although he does not mention it, he was almost certainly buoyed by the Society's massive study *Phantasms of the Living*, published in 1886, which catalogued the stories of people who claimed to have felt, seen or otherwise experienced the deaths of others who were far away from them. Frederick Myers, one of the authors (and one of the founders of the SPR), stated that the book's aim was to move away from the 'ghoulies and ghosties' image of extra-sensory perception and establish it as simply another form of communication. For this he coined the term 'telepathy'.

This was the cue for Arthur to attempt his own experiments with Henry Ball. The two of them would sit in Ball's house and try to project their thoughts to each other. Although Arthur divulged little about this, he did say, 'Again and again ... I have drawn diagrams, and (Ball) in turn has made approximately the same figure. I showed beyond any doubt whatever that I could convey my thought without words' (*Memories and Adventures*: 84).

By early 1887 Arthur's investigations into the paranormal were being conducted on at least three separate fronts: there was this rather prosaic experimentation into thought transference; there were further séances at General Harward's, another of the somewhat esoteric retired military men who populated the town; and, leaving nothing to chance, he had also joined the freemasons – his initiation into Phoenix Lodge No 257 in Southsea coming on 26 January, only two days after his first table rapping session, and so suggesting he wanted to tap into the store of occult knowledge which traditionally stood at the heart of freemasonry.

Before long Arthur dashed off a letter to the spiritualist magazine *Light* about his experiences. He described how 'after many months of enquiry' he had come to discover that 'it was absolutely certain that intelligence could exist apart from the body' (Lycett: 131). This, he had decided, was not explicable 'on any hypothesis except that held by Spiritualists' (131).

Frederic Myers at the SPR was delighted to read of this new scientifically literate recruit to psychic research. The very next day he wrote asking if Arthur could now help him and the Society with further investigation into the phenomenon he had experienced. 'Your profession has doubtless accustomed you to weighing evidence, and you will recognise that inquiries like the above are dictated by no idle curiosity' (Nordon: 150).

Doyle responded with a short novel, initially called *The Problem*, then *The Mystery, of Cloomber*, which explored the ever-fascinating theme of reincarnation and karma. Written between April and July 1888, this told the story of a former army General who, having been cursed after killing a Buddhist adept in India, is forced into a life of terrified seclusion on his estate on the west coast of Scotland, as he awaits the fated appearance of three of his victim's associates intent on retribution.

Despite some slapdash detail, such as giving Sikh and Moslem names to Buddhists, Conan Doyle's aim was clear: he wanted an excuse to explore some of the more esoteric ideas he had recently encountered. So, his so-called Buddhists go into flashy trances and talk of out of body experiences. When one of them expands on astral projection, he uses the language of experimental physics being carried out at that time by scientists such as the future Nobel Prize winners Lord Rayleigh and Joseph John Thompson (both of them supporters of spiritualism): 'This is accomplished by our power of resolving an object into its chemical atoms, of conveying these atoms with a speed which exceeds that of lightning to any given spot, and of there re-precipitating them and compelling them to retake their original form' (Doyle, *Mystery of Cloomber*: 169). Doyle put this into his own context at the end of this short book, when his main narrator signs off:

> Science will tell you that there are no such powers as those claimed by the Eastern mystics. I, John Fothergill West, can confidently answer that science is wrong. For what is science? Science is the consensus of opinion of scientific men, and history has shown that it is slow to accept a truth. Science sneered at Newton for twenty years. Science proved mathematically that an iron ship could not swim, and science declared that a steamship could not cross the Atlantic. (240)

Far from being a denial of science, this was Arthur's statement of his belief that Western science was not yet equipped to understand some of the complexities of Oriental religion.

But Conan Doyle was now committed to another part of his life. His Sherlock Holmes stories were beginning to take off, and his career took on a different trajectory, as he moved from Portsmouth to London, was able to give up medicine, and devoted his time to writing ever more lucrative adventures of his consulting detective.

In late 1893 he experienced a setback when his wife Louise was diagnosed with tuberculosis. He did his best to prolong her life, taking her for winter holidays in the sun (in Switzerland and Egypt) and moving the family home from South Norwood to Hindhead which was supposed to have better air.

Around the same time his father died, and this seems to have led to some sort of spiritual crisis in Arthur's life. This is the evidence of a curious semi-autobiographical novel he wrote in 1893–4 called *The Stark Munro Letters*, in which he explored his ideas about science, the universe and religion. Drawing on Arthur's relationship with his university friend George Budd, this book tells of a young doctor's growing awareness of divine purpose in the universe as he tries to find a way between the conflicting demands of science and religion.

Looking back to his earlier concerns about materialism (which had been articulated in *The Narrative of John Smith*), this later volume shows how he had been affected by the recent death of his father in its feverish debate about how a man's essence or soul cannot be crushed by alcoholism, madness or even death, because it does not lie in his material form, but in something more intangible – one of the issues he had been interested in Southsea.

Around the same time he dashed off another novel, *The Parasite*. This time his subject matter was more sensational – the enslavement of a young physiologist, Professor Gilroy, by a female mesmerist, Miss Penclosa. Having written a broad-ranging metaphysical book, he had decided to look more closely at the fundamentals of scientific investigation – one of the issues thrown up by his membership of the Society for Psychical Research.

While in Switzerland, Arthur had been in touch with Professor Oliver Lodge, a leading physicist who kept up the tradition of prominent scientists investigating the paranormal. Lodge was no fanciful paranormal researcher, but a hard-headed scientist making significant discoveries about the capacity of electromagnetic waves to send messages without wires. He saw correspondences between this and the extra-sensory communication at the centre of modern psychical research. Arthur was fascinated by such findings because they seemed to prove his hypothesis about the close links between science and religion. However, he apologised to Lodge for being only a novice in this field, adding that his curiosity was greater than his understanding.

His new novel, *The Parasite*, suffered from being a fictional vehicle for ideas as he explored how the new science of psychology was developing in parallel with the study of the paranormal. Arthur made much of the contrast between Gilroy's dogged materialism ('Show me what I can see with my microscope, cut with my scalpel, weigh in my balance, and I will devote a lifetime to its investigation') and the excitement of the research conducted by his psychologist colleague which 'strikes at the very roots or life and the nature of the soul!' (2009: 5, 15).

Arthur remained obsessed by what happened to the soul in mesmerism, madness and death. When Gilroy's girl friend is mesmerised, he notes that, 'Her organs were acting – her heart, her lungs. But her soul! It had slipped beyond our ken. Whither had it gone? What power had dispossessed it?' (2009: 10) Miss Penclosa explains her powers by saying 'practically, you send your soul into another person's body' (2009: 17) When Gilroy's mind is taken over by her, he has a breakdown and spouts 'silly jokes' during a lecture, 'sentiments as though I were proposing a toast, snatches of ballads, personal abuse even against some member of my class' (2009: 39). As a result of this, and of the demands of his literary career, Doyle had little opportunity to develop his interest in the paranormal. He did not give up completely, but he was marking time when, for example, in June 1894 he joined Frank Podmore and Dr Sydney Scott of the SPR on a field trip looking for ghosts in a house in Charmouth, Dorset. Strangely I could find no specific record of this investigation in the archives of the SPR in Cambridge. However, it seems from various reports that the team may have been the victims of a hoax by someone in the house, perhaps the Irish maid. Strangely, however, when Doyle described this incident thirty years later in his autobiography, he suggested that the whole experience had had something to do with the skeleton of a child which was later dug up in the garden in Charmouth.

'There is a theory' he wrote in 1924, when he was more deeply committed to spiritualism and had come to abhor the SPR's and Podmore's impartial, so-called scientific approach to such phenomena,

that a young life cut short in sudden and unnatural fashion may leave, as it were, a store of unused vitality which may be put to strange uses. The unknown and the marvellous press upon us from all sides. They loom above us and around us in undefined and fluctuating shapes, some dark, some shimmering, but all warning us of the limitations of what we call matter, and of the need for spirituality if we are to keep in touch with the true inner facts of life (*Memories and Adventures*: 148).

But that was later. At this stage in 1894 the fact was that his sceptical side still did not allow him to go beyond this kind of quasi-scientific research into the paranormal. Despite his strange utterance at the time of his earlier séances in Portsmouth – that 'This message marks in my spiritual career the change of "I believe" into "I know"' (Southsea Notebook, privately held) – he had not reached the stage of experiencing communication with the dead, the fundamental belief of the growing religion of spiritualism.

Meanwhile, friends in the SPR, such as Frederic Myers, continued with their experiments into other states of consciousness. In 1903 Myers produced his magnum opus, *Human Personality and Its Survival of Bodily Death*, which posited that personality was something like the electromagnetic spectrum, capable of survival after death, with some 'subliminal' parts only communicable to people with special powers. Conan Doyle remained interested enough in the subject to forecast gamely in *Through the Magic Door* that this would 'be recognized a century hence as a great root book, one from which a whole new branch of science will have sprung' (1907: 253).

Interestingly, at much the same time, Sigmund Freud was developing his rather more influential ideas about the subconscious in human personality. To arrive at his theories he had studied in Paris with the Frenchman Jean-Martin Charcot, who had been researching hypnotism as a cure for hysteria.

So, there you have two differing approaches to human consciousness – one which was essentially spiritual and the other which was mechanistic – from the same rational school as Sherlock Holmes when he was trying to gather together all the evidence in a particular case.

For Conan Doyle, however, it would soon be time for him to make up his mind where he stood. For years he had straddled the fault line between these two approaches. So long as the SPR was doing credible research into consciousness, he was happy. He could support it and maintain his scientific credibility. At the same time he could continue to dabble with séances and other paranormal experiments, which were occasionally reflected in his writings.

At the time there was a fashion for more esoteric magic associated with the Order of the Golden Dawn. But, despite being approached, Doyle rejected such groups – largely because they had no interest in the scientific tradition he still held close to him.

His institutional sympathies were clear from entries in his diary from the autumn of 1896, detailing the substantial regular payments he made to *Light*, the magazine of the London Spiritual Alliance – an organisation founded by the remarkable English medium and Anglican churchman the Reverend William Stainton Moses in 1884 (Conan Doyle Diaries, British Library).

Hitherto, Doyle's financial outgoings in this field had been limited to his regular two guinea subscription to the Society for Psychical Research. But now he began disbursing sums of a different order – £300 here, £500 there, adding up to £4250 over a seventeen month period – in ordr to ensure the survival of this minority interest magazine.

So by supporting the LSA and *Light*, Doyle demonstrated where his sympathies were beginning to turn – to those who believed in spiritualism and acted out their lives according to its precepts, rather than the scientists who continued to experiment into the paranormal in so-called laboratory conditions.

He continued in this vein for some time. But with the onset of the First World War the equation changed, and he found he could no longer keep his scientific detachment. Louise had died and he had married a younger woman, Jean, and moved to Sussex. Following the deaths of family and other friends in the trenches, he and Jean felt the need to test some of the hypotheses he had been dabbling with. He claimed that when he tried to get in touch with loved ones he was successful. This personal experience proved to him that the research which had been carried out into the paranormal had been correct.

After he became a committed spiritualist in 1916 he still liked to say that his knowledge of life beyond death was based on scientific principles. And for the remaining fourteen years of his life he sought to prove this, as he continued to give credence to, for example, experiments in spirit photography – the idea that you could capture the image of a spirit on film. In his book *The Case for Spirit Photography* he endorsed the research of William Hope's Crewe Circle, which had experimented widely in this field.

But, as I have noted, this interest got him into trouble in 1920 when he promoted the case of the Cottingley Fairies, as evidenced in photographs purportedly taken by two young Yorkshire girls. To even the untrained eye these seemed bogus – as was admitted by the girls much later in life. But Doyle regarded them as evidence that a new age had dawned.

He began writing books about his beliefs, such as *The New Revelation* and *The Vital Message*. Drawing on ideas he had discussed with his friend Sir Oliver Lodge, these referred to communication with another world through the ether. But he had abandoned what is generally regarded as scientific objectivity, making clear that his sympathies were wholly with the spiritualist rather than the psychical researcher. 'It takes a most powerful medium to get results when the surrounding atmosphere is tainted by doubt and scepticism and criticism', (Lycett, 2007: 379) he wrote.

In March 1920 a new challenge unexpectedly arose when the famous American illusionist Henry Houdini sent Conan Doyle a copy of *The Unmasking of Robert-Houdin*, his book about the French conjuror from whom he had taken his name. This started as a history of magic and ended as a disillusioned exposé of Robert-Houdin's trickery. Included in it were some observations on the Davenport Brothers, a couple of Americans whose successful stage show had reproduced the table-tappings and other spiritualist phenomena of the mid-nineteenth century.

In his polite letter of thanks, Conan Doyle queried whether the Brothers were really the tricksters Houdini implied; he was convinced that they had supernatural powers, but had been traduced by opponents who liked to claim they had been 'exposed'. 'Some of our people think that you yourself have some psychic powers' (qtd. in Kalush and Sloman: 382), Doyle added in a comment which was to lead to an interesting liaison between the two.

When Houdini came to Britain later that year, Conan Doyle invited him to séances. Houdini had just enough interest to play along with this. But when Doyle visited the United States a couple of years later the relationship began to unravel. One incident occurred at a séance in Atlantic City, where Jean Conan Doyle claimed to convey a message from Houdini's mother. This was expressed in English, but Houdini later revealed she could not speak English, only her native Hungarian.

Thus, Houdini retreated into his position of being a materialistic magician who performed tricks. He became an outspoken opponent of any aspects of spiritualism which claimed communication with other dimensions. As such, he clashed with Conan Doyle over a Boston medium called Mina Crandon, known as Margery. She claimed to be able to do all sorts by psychical means, including causing flashes of light, manifesting ectoplasm (often from her vagina), ringing bells, levitating tables, moving objects round a room, and communicating through a control who was her late brother, Walter. She had convinced a group of Harvard academics of her claims, and seemed well on course to win a prize put up by *Scientific American* for this. But Houdini saw through one of her tricks and denounced her as a fraud.

Conan Doyle did not seem to be worried. He had become the acknowledged leader of the spiritualist movement at home and abroad. He lectured round the world, undertaking tours centred on his beliefs not only in Britain, but also in Australia and New Zealand, the United States and Canada, South and East Africa, Scandinavia and other parts of Europe. He was, by now, Honorary President of the International Spiritualists Federation.

He, or rather his wife Jean, began receiving messages through a Mesopotamian spirit guide called Pheneas, who became the guiding force of his life. He collected Pheneas's sayings in a book called *Pheneas Speaks*. As token of his commitment he set up a Psychic Library and related Museum in London's Victoria Street. The Museum housed a collection of spirit photographs, aports, and other items associated with séances including 'psychic gloves'. Its telegraphic address was 'Ectoplasm Sowest London'.

Conan Doyle also became president of the London Spiritualist Alliance, which had benefited from a memorial fund for war dead and had been able to buy new headquarters in Queensberry Place, South Kensington. The top floor was rented out to Harry Price's National Laboratory for Psychical Research, which Doyle supported, while he was also President of the British College of Psychic Science in Holland Park.

All the while, Sherlock Holmes survived mishaps such as his creator's attempts to kill him off at the Reichenbach Falls. But whereas Conan Doyle was tempted to introduce his spiritualism into other later stories such as the Professor Challenger series, and in particular a story called *The Lost Mist*, he resisted any such suggestions with Sherlock Holmes. When presented with evidence of vampirism in the story 'The Sussex Vampire' (1924), the great detective tells Dr Watson defiantly, 'This agency stands flat-footed upon the ground and there it must remain. The world is big enough for us. No ghosts need apply' (1981: 1034).

By now, Conan Doyle's physical strength was fading. As the head of British spiritualists, his last public act before his untimely death in July 1930 was to lead a delegation of interested parties to the Home Office to protest against harassment of mediums by the police using Witchcraft and Vagrancy Acts dating back to the eighteenth century. (Only a couple of years earlier The LSA's very own Mercy Phillimore had been arrested at the Alliance's premises on these charges. Sir Arthur had been incensed to learn that the police had used agent provocateurs, having sent three women there to have their fortunes told.)

Sadly, by this time (1930) Conan Doyle had fallen out with the LSA. He had reluctantly resigned his position following some internal squabbles – though this was not known at the time. A few months earlier he had also resigned from the Society for Psychical Research, but this was more obviously on the cards as the Society had failed to back him on matters such as 'Margery'.

On the morning of 7 July 1930 he died in his bed at his home, Windlesham, in Sussex. A spiritualist funeral was held at the property, followed by a memorial service at the Royal Albert Hall, attended by 6000 people. On the platform there was an empty chair beside Jean: this was where Doyle was expected to come back. During the proceedings Estelle Roberts, a clairvoyant, announced dramatically 'He is there' (Lycett, 2007: 433) and went across to whisper something to Jean. She later explained: 'He gave me a message – a personal one, which I gave to Lady Doyle, but am unable to repeat publicly. I saw him distinctly he was wearing evening dress' (Lycett, 2007: 433). Since then, Conan Doyle's legacy has inspired generations of spiritualists. His own messages from the other side have provided the basis for the teaching of the White Eagle Lodge founded in 1936.

During – and indeed after – his lifetime he donated money to all sorts of spiritualist causes, including churches. One of these, at Rochester Square in Camden, is close to where I live. When I was writing my book, I went there a couple of times, hoping to get some sort of message from him. I thought I would make it easier for him, since I was carrying a letter in his own hand in my pocket, but nothing came.

Nevertheless, the story of Conan Doyle's highly individualist quest for truth and understanding about the mysteries of the universe remains inspiring, and, for all its absurdities, a testament to the tenacity and inquisitiveness of his peerless creation, Sherlock Holmes.

10
Channelling the Past: *Arthur & George* and the Neo-Victorian Uncanny
Patricia Pulham

In his 2005 novel, *Arthur & George*, Julian Barnes centres on a specific form of cultural afterlife: neo-historical biofiction. This emergent literary genre, which fuses fact and fiction, has achieved increasing popularity in recent years, resulting in bestsellers and prizewinning novels such as Colm Tóibín's *The Master* (2004) and David Lodge's *Author, Author* (2004), both of which offer fictionalised versions of the life of Henry James and the Victorian milieu in which he lived and wrote. Like Tóibín's and Lodge's works, *Arthur & George* appropriates historical figures – in this case, Arthur Conan Doyle and George Edalji – and uses factual knowledge and fictive reconstruction to re-present known events through an imaginative lens. In 1903 Edalji, a young solicitor of Parsee extraction, was found guilty and condemned to seven years' penal servitude for mutilating cattle. In choosing the Edalji case as his topic, Barnes – while explicitly writing of Doyle, who took up Edalji's case and campaigned for a reversal of this judgement – also implicitly resurrects Sherlock Holmes, as it is in response to this case that Doyle dons his creation's mantle and turns detective.[1] The background to Doyle's involvement with Edalji is outlined by Martin Booth, who explains that late in 1906, Doyle came across the case in an article entitled 'Edalji Protests His Innocence' which appeared in an edition of *Umpire*, a sports-based magazine that included general news items (1997: 263). Following the publication of Edalji's side of the story, Doyle became convinced of his innocence and later wrote, 'the unmistakeable accent of truth forced itself upon my attention, and I realized that I was in the presence of an appalling tragedy, and that I was called upon to do what I could to set it right' (qtd. in Booth 1997: 265). From December

1906 to August 1907, he responded to that call and conducted a detailed investigation into the matter.

In a review which appeared in *The Spectator* on 9 July 2005, Sebastian Smee describes *Arthur & George* as 'a crime novel, a two-person biography, a romance, a historical novel, and a philosophical speculation all rolled into one' (2005: 34). The ambiguous nature of Julian Barnes's novel comes as no surprise to his readers; as Bianca Leggett notes, he is known as 'a novelist whose form is not fixed, but characterised by new and hybrid forms that accommodate the ideological concerns of his narrative' (2009: 27). This chapter explores key aspects of the novel's hybridity and attempts to identify the 'ideological concerns' that inform it; it considers *Arthur & George* in the context of the detective novel, biofiction, spiritualism, and the neo-historical novel, while pointing to Barnes's implicit interest in and deployment of the Freudian uncanny, invoked in the novel via allusions to blindness, doublings, and spectrality.

Detection

As Martin Booth has noted, Doyle, like Sherlock Holmes, was frequently asked to solve crimes or mysteries, and was even sent clues to help him (1997: 259). By the time Doyle became interested in the Edalji case, he had already (unknowingly) been approached by the defendant. Given the volume of such correspondence (Edalji's letter to Doyle was one among many), Alfred Wood, Doyle's secretary, had opened the letter and kept it from him, supposedly due to Doyle's low spirits following the loss of his first wife, Louise (Booth, 1997: 259). Interestingly, Booth argues that Doyle was well-equipped to act as a substitute for his creation. He writes:

> As a doctor, he possessed many of the attributes of a good detective. His memory was exceptional, his powers of observation finely sharpened, and his ability to assimilate and co-ordinate random information superb. Writing the Sherlock Holmes stories had sharpened his deductive skills, although he was always quick to point out that in these the solution came before the mystery unfolded or the crime was committed, at least on paper. (1997: 259)

The conflation between author and character which Booth hints at is something I discuss later in this chapter, but, at present, I want to concentrate on his reference to Doyle's 'powers of observation'

(1997: 259). 'Observation', the ability not simply to 'see' but to note and analyse what is seen, is posited as a key attribute of the successful detective. In *A Study in Scarlet* (1887), Watson reads an article written by Sherlock Holmes in which he discovers that the 'Science of Deduction' requires acute attention to visual detail.[2] On 'meeting a fellow mortal' the student of this science is instructed by Holmes to 'learn at a glance to distinguish the history of the man, and the trade and profession to which he belongs'; he continues:

> Puerile as such an exercise may seem, it sharpens the faculties of observation, and teaches one where to look and what to look for. By a man's finger-nails, by his coat-sleeve, by his boot, by his trouser-knees, by the callosities of his forefinger and thumb, by his expression, by his shirt-cuffs – by each of these things a man's calling is plainly revealed. (Doyle, 1993: 19)

In *A Study in Scarlet*, Holmes explains that he has a 'turn both for observation and for deduction'; that, for him, observation is 'second nature', traits he considers vital in a 'consulting detective' (1993: 19–20). He proceeds to prove his point, engaging in what is commonly called the 'introductory exercise' as he explains the 'train of reasoning' which led to his knowledge that Watson had come from Afghanistan:

> Here is a gentleman of a medical type, but with the air of a military man. Clearly an army doctor then. He has just come from the tropics, for his face is dark, and that is not the natural tint of his skin, for his wrists are fair. He has undergone hardship and sickness, as his haggard face says clearly. His left arm has been injured. He holds it in a stiff and unnatural manner. Where in the tropics could an English army doctor have seen much hardship and got his arm wounded? Clearly in Afghanistan. (Doyle, 1993: 21)

Hearing his explanation, Watson compares him to Edgar Allan Poe's Monsieur Dupin. While Holmes disparages his French counterpart, it is evident from Poe's narrator in 'The Murders in the Rue Morgue' that Dupin is equally adept at observation. In Poe's story, Dupin appears to 'read' his companion's mind, but reveals that his 'reading' is simply a question of deduction made possible by acute observation. In the preamble to his story, the narrator asserts that 'To observe attentively is to remember distinctly' and that the gifted analyst makes 'a host of observations and inferences' (Poe, 1972: 96), a process we see at work not only in Doyle's Sherlock Holmes stories, but also in Barnes's *Arthur & George*.

The question of 'observation' and 'seeing' becomes particularly important in regard to the Edalji case: the fact that George is myopic – a fact uncovered by Doyle's professional scrutiny – is cited as a key reason why he could not have committed the crime for which he was imprisoned. In a letter to the *Daily Telegraph*, dated 9 January 1907, Doyle requests that the editor publish the results of his enquiry into the case and asks that the statement be headed 'No Copyright', so that other papers – especially the Midland papers in the area in which Edalji was convicted – 'would copy it in extensor', as he believed that only an appeal to the public could put an end to what he considered to be 'a national scandal' (Gibson and Green, 1986: 124–5). In the letters to the editor that follow over a period of months, the matter of Edalji's myopia is raised on numerous occasions. In one, dated 13 January 1907 and dedicated to 'The Question of Eyesight', Doyle writes:

> To my mind it was as physically impossible for Mr. Edalji to have committed the crime as it would have been if his legs, instead of his eyes, were crippled. I have asked the editors of three of the leading medical papers to put the question of possibility before those of their readers who practise eye work. When the replies have come in we shall see what the opinion of the occulists of Great Britain is upon the subject. (qtd. in Gibson and Green, 1986: 125)

In his letter of 26 January 1907, headed 'The Edalji Case: Summing Up', he lists as one of his key points[3] 'The physical disability produced by myopia from which Mr Edalji suffered' and in a later letter, dated 11 March 1907, he states that 'The opinion of some twenty experts upon the question of eyesight and its relation to the crime' will be presented as evidence before the Committee of Inquiry for consideration (qtd. in Gibson and Green, 1986: 127–8).[4]

Doyle's concern with the nature of seeing is observed by Julian Barnes and features as a form of leitmotif in *Arthur & George*. The novel opens with a scene from Arthur's childhood which introduces the theme:

> A child wants to see. It always begins like this, and it began like this then. A child wanted to see. … What he saw there became his first memory. A small boy, a room, a bed, closed curtains leaking afternoon light. … A small boy and a corpse … and the body that of Arthur's

grandmother, one Katherine Pack.... Grandmother's soul had clearly flown up to Heaven, leaving only the sloughed husk of her body. The boy wants to see? Then let the boy see. (Barnes, 2005: 3–4)

In Barnes's novel, as in Doyle's correspondence to the *Daily Telegraph*, much is made of Edalji's myopia. Arthur's first meeting with George at the Grand Hotel, Charing Cross, in January 1907 is described in language that points to the importance of seeing:

Arthur is late for his appointment with George Edalji.... Now he enters the foyer at speed, and looks around. It is not difficult to spot his waiting guest: the only brown face is sitting about twelve feet away from him in profile. Arthur is about to step across and apologize when something makes him hold back. It is, perhaps, ungentlemanly to observe without permission; but not for nothing was he once the out-patient clerk of Dr Joseph Bell. So: preliminary inspection reveals that the man he is about to meet is small and slight, of Oriental origin, with hair parted on the left and cropped close; he wears the well-cut, discreet clothing of a provincial solicitor. All indisputably true, but this is hardly like identifying a French polisher or a left-handed cobbler from scratch. Yet still Arthur continues to observe, and is drawn back, not to the Edinburgh of Dr Bell, but to his own years of medical practice. Edalji, like many another man in the foyer, is barricaded between newspaper and high-winged armchair... he holds the paper preternaturally close, and also a touch sideways, setting his head at an angle on the page. Dr Doyle, formerly of Southsea and Devonshire Place, is confident in his diagnosis. Myopia, possibly of quite a high degree. And who knows, perhaps a touch of astigmatism too. (Barnes, 2006: 293–4)

The passage is not unlike an exercise in Holmesian deduction, and its semantic field also draws attention to the question of 'seeing' and 'sight': Doyle 'looks around'; he 'spot[s]' Edalji; he 'observe[s]' him; he 'inspect[s]' him in order to identify his 'myopia' and 'astigmatism'. Significantly, the novel also ends as it begins, with a focus on 'sight', this time in relation to a 'clairvoyant', one who has 'clear sight', engaged in an attempt to channel the ghost of Doyle. Its closing pages envisage Edalji's attendance at a Spiritualist meeting held at the Albert Hall on Sunday 13 July 1930 as a public farewell to Arthur Conan Doyle, which George attends, at which an empty chair placed on the stage symbolises Arthur's 'presence' (Barnes, 2006: 457–58). The chairman of the meeting, 'Mr George

Craze of the Marylebone Spiritualist Association' reads a statement on behalf of Lady Conan Doyle, which states: 'Although our earthly eyes cannot see beyond the earth's vibrations, those with the God-given extra sight called clairvoyance will be able to see the clear form in our midst' (Barnes, 2006: 481). Following the singing of the Spiritualist hymn 'Open My Eyes That I May See Glimpses of Truth', Estelle Roberts, Doyle's 'favourite medium', takes centre stage (Barnes, 2006: 486–7). She channels the spirits of the dead and conveys messages to the living. As she does so, Edalji, watching, analyses the ways in which this might be done. He decides that the most probable explanation is that someone who knows each of the bereaved audience members passes private details onto the séance organisers, thus providing them with 'evidence' of an existence beyond death, and concludes: 'As with perjury, it works best when there is a clever mixture of the true and the false' (Barnes, 2006: 491). At the end of the séance, following the medium's claims that Doyle's spirit has indeed been in their midst, Edalji cannot decide 'whether he has seen the truth or lies, or a mixture of both' (Barnes, 2006: 500). As he leaves the hall, 'He focuses once more on the plat-form' and looks at the empty chair 'where Sir Arthur has, just possibly, been' (Barnes, 2006: 501). The narrator tells us that he 'gazes through his succession of lenses, out into the air and beyond' and asks us:

What does he see?

What did he see?

What will he see?

On the face of it, the three different tenses which Barnes uses to end his novel are perhaps 'symptomatic of the uncertainty regarding not only the Edalji case, but historical events in general' (Berberich, 2011: 128). However, the importance given in the text to questions of sight, seeing, observation, and analysis compels one to modify the narrator's questions and to ask what do we see when we read *Arthur & George*; what can we see that was once hidden; and what will we see when the hidden comes to light? Like Edalji, we too look through a 'succession of lenses': through Barnes's wide-angled lens we see the development of parallel lives from childhood to adulthood; through his telescopic lens past events are brought into focus; and a microscopic view of interior thoughts allows us to sympathise with each character. But, like Edalji, it is difficult for us to decide whether we have 'seen the truth or lies, or a mixture of both' (Barnes, 2006: 500).

Biofiction

This complex combination of 'truth or lies, or a mixture of both' also informs biofiction. In her recent book, *Victoriana: Histories, Fictions, Criticism*, Cora Kaplan defines biofiction as a 'hybrid genre' that can be 'interpreted in various ways, as highlighting the tension between biography and fiction, as well as marking the overlap between them' (2007: 7). She argues that 'biography has become the new novel' and writes: 'If so, it is the new – superficially at least – as retro, its blockbuster proportions reminiscent of the Victorian three-decker, as are the more traditional examples of its narrative form' (Kaplan, 2007: 37). For Kaplan, biography's 'triumphal moment' in the twenty-first century 'might seem...like the crude revenge of nineteenth-century realism on the cool ironies, unfixed identities and skewed temporalities of the postmodern' (2007: 37). However, as she goes on to explain, in her view biography's 'return is inevitably a return with a difference' and one whose prominence constitutes 'an argument *within* rather than simply *with*...postmodernity' (2007: 37–8; original emphasis). This genre, itself a form of 'revenant' concerned with lives lived in the past, contributes to what Christian Gutleben has referred to as 'nostalgic postmodernism'; writing specifically about novels that engage with the Victorian period, Gutleben contends that 'retro-Victorian fiction displays signs of nostalgia in its very principle...in the conservatism of certain Victorian precepts and the imitation of a language of the past' (2001: 193). However, that does not mean that such works cannot be informed by a postmodern playfulness that questions even as it engages with the past; Kaplan's argument is supported by the fact that Barnes's own interest in 'biofiction' is signalled in an earlier – clearly postmodern – novel, *Flaubert's Parrot* (1984), which blends 'fiction, biography, and literary criticism' (Sesto, 2001: 33). Here, as Bruce Sesto comments, '"biography" is interwoven with fictional narrative; the life of Flaubert unfolds in fits and starts, zig-zagging tentatively through the mind of Barnes's main character and occasional first-person narrator [Geoffrey Braithwaite]'(2001: 41). In addition, Braithwaite becomes increasingly aware that his own life parallels events in Flaubert's novel *Madame Bovary* (1857), and begins to realise that 'he and his wife have already been written' (Sesto, 2001: 51). This conflation between the 'facts' of Braithwaite's life (which, in *Flaubert's Parrot*, are already fiction), and a fictional construct points to the illusory nature of biography's 'truth' and, like biofiction, highlights the 'tension between biography and fiction' and 'overlap between them' which Kaplan observes in her analysis of the genre.

Arthur & George is a novel which similarly blends the 'facts' of Doyle's and Edalji's lives with a fictional interiority. Moreover, it is a novel that represents a factual personage (Doyle) who was often conflated with his fictional construct (Holmes), and whose creation seemed to acquire a factual persona. In her brief critique of Barnes's novel, Kaplan asserts that he does not 'give in to the temptation of making Conan Doyle into his celebrated sleuth' (2007: 158). Yet, I would argue that this is not entirely the case, and that Barnes draws subtle attention to the parallels between author and character by alluding to others' conflation of the two figures and by, as we have seen, drawing on the Holmesian lexicon of deductive processes. As the Edalji story spreads in newspapers across the world, the narrator notes that Doyle grew used to the repeated headline 'Sherlock Holmes Investigates'; at one point, Edalji considers that 'Sir Arthur had been too influenced by his own creation'; and when Doyle declares himself a 'fully-fledged' spiritualist, newspaper headlines shriek 'Has Sherlock Holmes gone mad?' (Barnes, 2006: 398, 426, 461).

The neo-victorian uncanny

While Doyle's investigation of the Edalji case takes place in Edwardian England, in focusing on an episode in Doyle's life during which he takes on the mantle of his fictional detective, and in beginning and ending his novel with scenes of death and afterlife respectively, Barnes is surely asking us to consider his novel and the complex relationship between Doyle and Sherlock Holmes in the light of neo-Victorianism. Doyle himself arguably engaged in a form of Victorian revival when he resuscitated Holmes in 1902 after his plunge into the Reichenbach Falls in 1893 (Saler, 2003: 608); T. S. Eliot associated Holmes with 'the pleasant externals of nineteenth-century London' and for Vincent Starrett, Holmes and Watson 'still live…in a nostalgic country of the mind: where it is always 1895' (qtd. in Saler, 2003: 608). Starrett's reference to 'the nostalgic country of the mind' is pertinent given that the issue of 'nostalgia' has been hotly debated in relation to neo-Victorianism. If one considers the word's etymology, the nature of our imaginary return to the Victorian appears to be somewhat complicated; its original meaning – that is, homesickness (often manifested in physical symptoms), formed from the Greek words *nostos* meaning 'homecoming' and *algos*, meaning pain, grief or distress (Banhart, 2006: 710) – suggests that the neo-Victorian engagement with the past is a kind of return 'home'. As I have written elsewhere, this return 'home' posits neo-Victorianism as a form of the uncanny.[5] In his 1919 essay, 'The Uncanny', Freud refers to what he describes as the 'joking saying' that 'Love is a home-sickness', which suggests that 'whenever a man dreams of a place or country and says to himself, while he is still dreaming: "this place is familiar to me, I've been here before", we may interpret the place as being his mother's ...body' (1955: 245). Given Elizabeth Barrett-Browning's description of the Victorian age in *Aurora Leigh* (1857) as maternal: 'full-veined' and 'double-breasted' (1993: 201; V. 1. 216), the nostalgic return to the Victorian textual 'body' implied by neo-Victorian fiction underlines a simultaneous longing and anxiety, which manifests itself in a series of recognisable features which Freud describes as uncanny. Freud's list of psychological triggers for uncanny sensations include the double; repetition; the animation of the seemingly dead or, conversely, the death-like nature of the seemingly animate; ghosts or spirits; and the familiar made strange. Moreover, in his reading of E.T.A. Hoffmann's 'The Sand-Man', Freud locates a key source of the uncanny in a fear of blindness, more specifically in a fear of losing one's eyes that is linked via the Oedipus complex to a fear of castration. He argues that 'The Sand-Man' makes it clear 'beyond doubt that in Hoffmann's tale the sense of the uncanny attaches directly to the figure of the Sand-Man, and therefore to the idea of being robbed of one's eyes' (Freud, 2003: 138). If we consider these uncanny triggers in relation to *Arthur & George*, its deployment of the neo-Victorian uncanny proves clear: it 'doubles' Doyle and Holmes; it reanimates Victorian genres, for example the realist text, detective fiction, and the Victorian ghost story; and it plays with death, ghostliness, and spectrality, seemingly animating the dead and, in doing so, posits Barnes himself as a form of 'medium' who channels past events and spectral entities. More importantly, however, it uses vision as a trope which asks us to examine both physical and textual 'blindness' – blind spots and narrative blinds that involve the reader in an intricate and potentially castrative game of detection.

If we return, for a moment, to the opening of the novel, it is evident that we are presented with a form of 'primal scene': 'It always begins like this' we are told, 'A child wants to see...What he saw there became his first memory'; what he sees is 'a bed, closed curtains leaking after-noon light...and a corpse' (2006: 3–4). Barnes's scene setting – the child looking, the bed, the closed curtains – all lead us to expect a sexual encounter, one correlative to the Freudian primal scene in which the child witnesses or fantasises that he has seen his parents engaging in copulation, an act that he interprets as an act of violence committed by the father against the mother, and which may later unconsciously inform the onset of the child's Oedipal stage in which the mother becomes the prime object of desire. What the young Doyle sees in *Arthur & George*, however, is not the sexual act, but his grandmother's corpse. Nevertheless, the key to this scene, I would argue, is the sentence: 'The boy wants to see? Then let the boy see' (Barnes, 2006: 4). It is precisely this sentiment that informs Hoffmann's 'The Sand-Man', in which Nathaniel's discovery of the dangerous truth about his love-object, Olympia, is permitted. Not only does he find that she is an inanimate, corpse-like doll, he also finds that 'Olympia's deathly-white face possessed no eyes' and that 'where the eyes should have been, there were only pits of blackness', thus contributing to Freud's assessment of the tale as an instance of the uncanny that posits an association between blindness and the fear of castration (Hoffmann, 1982: 119–20); Nathaniel's initial pleasure in looking is here complicated by that look's castrative property. However, according to Freud, 'Visual impressions' nevertheless 'remain the most frequent pathway along which libidinal excitation is aroused' and become associated with a 'pleasure in looking [scopophilia]' (Freud, 2001: 156–7). Moreover, as Peter Brooks argues, this desire to see – and to obtain pleasure by looking, namely scopophilia – is inextricably linked to a desire to know. Brooks writes:

> As the fictions most consciously concerned with the epistemology of observation demonstrate, scopophilia is inextricably linked with epistemophilia, the erotic investment in the desire to know. The inherently unsatisfiable desire resulting from the drive to know, as from the drive to see, tends to make the objects of knowledge graspable, and visible, only in parts, never in the wholeness of vision and understanding that would fulfil the observer-knower's quest. (Brooks, 1993: 122)

One might argue that, in Barnes's novel, the desire to see, and the pleasure or sexual excitement that might be roused in the young Doyle as a result of the primal scene, is undermined by the fact that what the child sees is not the sexual act, but his grandmother's corpse. Nevertheless, the scene is posited as significant in terms of what was to become a key concern for Doyle; Barnes writes:

> An encounter in a curtained room. A small boy and a corpse. A grandchild who, by the acquisition of memory, had just stopped being a thing, and a grandmother who, by losing those attributes the child was developing, had returned to that state. The small boy stared; and over half a century later the adult man was still staring. Quite

what a 'thing' amounted to – or, to put it more exactly, quite what happened when the tremendous change took place, leaving only a 'thing' behind – was to become of central importance to Arthur. (Barnes, 2006: 4)

Barnes, here, is of course referring to Doyle's involvement with spiritualism, yet the impact of this primal scene also seems inherently related to looking, to curiosity and the desire to know which is associated with the processes of detection. The adult Doyle is 'still staring', he wants to know what happens after death, and the 'thing', the trace of existence that is left behind, becomes of vital significance. Building on Marie Bonaparte's earlier identification of the murder in Poe's 'The Murder's in the Rue Morgue' as a form of 'primal scene', in her 1949 essay, 'Detective Stories and the Primal Scene', Geraldine Pederson-Krag suggests that the 'primal scene' lies at the heart of all detective fiction's appeal. According to her formulation, 'the victim is the parent for whom the reader (the child) has ... oedipal feelings'; the child becomes the detective, and the detective mystery allows a trauma-free re-enactment of the primal scene (qtd. in Cohen, 2000: 158). Featuring a corpse (albeit one that died of natural causes), the 'primal scene' in Barnes's own 'detective novel' seemingly becomes the implicit focal point for a complex nexus of narrative strands and highlights the importance of looking, or curiosity, which becomes a thematic motif. In doing so, it associates that curiosity explicitly with Doyle's investigations into spiritualism, and implicitly with the processes of detection which, in the text, are carried out by Doyle doubled by (or possibly possessed by) the spectral presence of his own creation. At the same time, the reader is also implicated in the desire to know, and in due course I will suggest just what it is that the reader discovers by the end of *Arthur & George*. However, for the moment, I want to return to what Barnes refers to as the 'thing' that is left behind by death and how this relates to Arthur's desire for knowledge.

Spiritualist traces

The examination of the 'thing' or 'trace' that is left behind is key to Doyle's scientific endeavours, in terms of both spiritualist investigation and Holmesian detection. Initially, as Chris Willis notes, the idea of 'any link between spiritualism and detective fiction seems totally contradictory' (2000: 60). 'Classic detective fiction' she argues 'is a literature of logic in which everything has a scientific explanation. It is concerned with hard facts and encourages scepticism' (Willis, 2000: 60). Spiritualism, on the other hand, 'involves suspension of logical faculties to believe in events and phenomena that cannot be explained in scientific or logical terms' (Willis, 2000: 60). However, as Willis points out there are interesting parallels:

> [T]he rise of the fictional detective coincided with the rise of spiritualism. Both began in the mid-nineteenth century.... Both attempt to explain mysteries. The medium's role can be seen as being similar to that of a detective in a murder case. Both are trying to make the dead speak in order to reveal a truth. (Willis, 2000: 60)

It is perhaps unsurprising, therefore, that the creator of the rational detective Sherlock Holmes also became, in his later years, a staunch supporter of spiritualism. Moreover, as Alex Owen notes, spiritualism 'was itself the child of scientific naturalism and rational explanation...steeped in the scientism of the [Victorian] period' (2004: n.p.), and Doyle himself made a more explicit connection between detection and spiritualism when he referred to 'clairvoyants as detectives' in an article that appeared in the *Sunday Express* on 22 October 1921.[6]

In *Arthur & George*, we simultaneously witness and participate in a detective mystery and a spiritualist meeting at which Barnes functions, as stated above, as a kind of 'medium' who channels past events and the spirits of the dead. Opening with a primal scene, the novel positions the reader in the role of inquisitive child, one who has the desire to see and to know. However, the fact that the novel ends with a spiritualist meeting suggests that our medium (Barnes) is engaged in an act of misdirection. In *The Truth about Spiritualism* (1934), Carl Bechhofer-Roberts explains how closely related some forms of mediumship were to conjuring. According to Bechhofer-Roberts, 'ghostly' effects were often achieved by misdirecting the sitter 'by causing him to look where the medium wanted him to look' (2007: 73). Interestingly, such tricks sometimes relied on the concealment of an accomplice behind a curtain. This method was of particular use in the process of 'spirit writing'; describing a séance with the medium Henry Slade, Todd Jay Leonard explains:

> His technique involved using two small framed chalkboards. First, he would have the sitters come in and he would show clearly that the boards were indeed blank with no writing on either one. He would place the boards together, slate to slate, and ask the spirit to write a

message. The sitter would audibly hear the sound of chalk striking the slate. Next he would pull the chalkboards apart and a message would be visible. ... Initially, he had written a message on a separate chalkboard which fit snugly on the back of the top board. When he placed the two boards together, the loose one (from the back) would fall down over the blank portion of the bottom board. The accomplice would then mimic the sound of chalk writing on a slate from behind a curtain. When Slade lifted the top board, a pre-existing message would be visible from the loose slate that now fit on top of the bottom board. (2005: 127–8)

Similarly, in Barnes's novel we are provided with the illusion that the protagonists' stories are unfolding as the novel develops, whereas in fact we are reading the pre-existing text of their already-lived lives and actions. I suggest that, in *Arthur & George*, Barnes, like Slade, is engaged in an act of misdirection, and his readers, like Slade's sitters, look where Barnes wishes them to look, rather than acting independently. What we *think* we see are Doyle and Edalji's lives and Doyle's successful campaign to release George. What we do not see, however, but what is perhaps implicit in the continual invitation to look, is that Doyle himself suffered a form of myopia where Edalji was concerned. As Bozena Kucala notes, the Edalji case was a complex one: George only obtains a partial pardon; the authorities refuse to pay compensation for wrongful imprisonment; the identity of the true criminal remains uncertain; and Edalji's sister casts doubts on her brother's mental stability (2009: 63). Moreover, as Martin Booth comments, subsequent research has revealed that 'George was not all he seemed to be' (1997: 266). While he may have been innocent of animal mutilation, it has been suggested that he was involved in financial embezzlement and that, rather than being 'gentle and self-effacing', he may have been 'the owner of a devious and vicious mind' (1997: 266). Whether Doyle knew of these rumours remains unclear. What is certain, however, is that in adding an 'Author's note' to his novel, Barnes is at pains to suggest the 'authenticity' of his sources. He writes that, 'Apart from Jane's letter to Arthur, all letters quoted, whether signed or anonymous, are authentic; as are quotations from newspapers, government reports, proceedings in Parliament, and the writings of Sir Arthur Conan Doyle' (2005: 505). Nevertheless, what we learn from Barnes's novel is that however 'authentic' these may be, the truth remains elusive. The novel begins with a 'primal scene' that elicits a desire to see and to know (associated with detection) and ends with a performance of clairvoyance (associated with spiritualism) in which what is seen remains unknowable. The questions on which Barnes's novel ends – 'What does he see? What did he see? What will he see?' – invoke the present, the past, and the future, suggesting that his text is a meditation on knowledge, time, and secrets. In merging detection and spiritualism – both Victorian constructs – Barnes, while inviting us to look behind the curtain that obscures the past, simultaneously points to the void we might find there – the past castrates. In invoking the neo-Victorian uncanny, *Arthur & George* posits our knowledge of the Victorian period as a form of trauma[7] and demonstrates that any engagement with the past is a potentially castrative process, that its blinds and our own blind spots will continually affect our ability to resurrect it. In art as in life, afterlives, whether that of Doyle, or his literary creation, must always possess the air of inexplicable mystery.

Notes

1. The Edalji case is the first instance of Doyle's own detective work; the second relates to 'The Case of Oscar Slater' (1912), in which Doyle examined the brutal murder of a Glasgow woman, Marion Gilchrist, and posited the innocence of the accused, Oscar Slater, a German Jew.
2. The 'Science of Deduction' is the title of Chapter 2.
3. Seventh of seven.
4. In *Criminal Man* (*L'uomo delinquente*, 1876), Cesare Lombroso listed 'acute eyesight' as one of the criminal's features. See Lombroso (2006: 340).
5. See introduction to Arias and Pulham (2009).
6. See James Douglas, 'Are the Dead Alive: A Week-End with Conan Doyle', *Sunday Express*, 22 October 1921.
7. For a discussion of neo-Victorian fiction and trauma, see Kohlke (2008).

11
Arthur Conan Doyle's Appearances as a Detective in Historical Crime Fiction

Jennifer S. Palmer

'Come, Watson, come! ... The game is afoot. Not a word! Into your clothes and come!' cries Sherlock Holmes in 'The Adventure of the Abbey Grange', first published in *The Strand Magazine* in September 1904 (Doyle, 1971: 833). Within ten minutes, an enthusiastic Watson is in the cab with Holmes en route for Charing Cross Station. In the years since Doyle's death, Holmes's clarion call appears to have sounded for his creator as well. Numerous writers have followed the path of creating further literary adventures for Holmes, such as the collaboration between Doyle's son Adrian and John Dickson Carr with their collection *The Exploits of Sherlock Holmes* (1954).[1] Indeed, 'Arthur Conan Doyle' himself appears to have become embroiled in such adventures: in various recent detective stories, the successful author of the Sherlock Holmes canon has now, surprisingly, been transfigured into a fictionalised, sleuthing character, at the behest of various authors of historical crime fiction.

Over the last thirty years the so-called history–mystery genre has become a major force in crime fiction. Historical mysteries like A. S. Byatt's *Possession* (1990) and Julian Barnes's *Arthur & George* (2005)have achieved critical acclaim and won major literary prizes. Like all crime stories they 'combine the power of narrative, often suspenseful narrative, and a focus on circumstantial detail' (Johnsen, 2006: 19), but combine this with a fascination for a historical period and a commitment to historical accuracy. The complex relationship between fact and fiction is at the heart of the appeal of history–mysteries. One popular development within this genre sees a 'real-life' historical figure pressed into service as the *detective*. This very particular and paradoxical conflation of fact and fiction stretches the generic conventions of the historical mystery to its limits. As Diana Wallace remarks, 'the very term "historical fiction" is a kind of oxymoron, joining "history" (what is "true"/ "fact") with "fiction" (what is "untrue"/ "invented")' (2008: x). It raises questions about historical and narrative boundaries: can a historical figure be employed fictionally? Can a real person be made to assume a role – that of detective or sidekick – which may be totally at variance with the attitudes of their own time?

These issues can be addressed by considering the detectives of some of these historical mysteries. Some writers use obscure figures as detectives, for instance Liselotte, second wife of Philippe, Louis XIV of France's brother, in Stephane Daimlen-Vols's *Hour of the Wolves* (2001); some consider a young, as yet unknown figure, as in Andrew Taylor's *The American Boy* (2003), which concerns Edgar Allan Poe's education in England. Other crime writers opt for a person with a documented role in law and order, like Sir John Fielding, the blind magistrate in eighteenth-century London in Bruce Alexander's John Fielding mysteries or, more bizarrely, Queen Elizabeth I in Karen Harper's mysteries. In the twentieth century such choices reflect a media-dominated society by including film stars, such as Ron Goulart's Groucho Marx and Bill Crider's Humphrey Bogart. The popularity of such real historical figures as literary detectives can be attributed to a contemporary celebrity-obsessed society that regards the famous as valid material for entertainment. Appearing in barely-factual gossip magazines and sensational newspaper stories, the famous have become crossover figures, already existing on the boundary between fact and fiction. Their deployment as detectives in historical factual-fictional narratives completes their status in that shadowy realm.

The growing phenomenon of historical figures as detectives – ninety-five in my sample – includes rulers, artists, philosophers, film stars and actual law enforcers.[2] Writers are by far the most recurrent among these unusual detective figures, with more than thirty featuring in my sample. Here, again, the protagonists come from a wide spectrum; the earliest is Pliny in 83AD, who is aided by Tacitus in *All Roads Lead to Murder* (Albert Bell 2002), while, in 1942, Agatha Christie assists the pathologist Sir Bernard Spilsbury in *The London Blitz Murders* (Max Collins 2004). Undoubtedly the detective writer's keen observational skills qualifies them as a sleuth. Unsurprising, the individuals most used as detectives are the seminal figures in crime fiction: Poe and Doyle. Doyle's excursions into crime solving are more numerous than Poe's, attributable in part to Doyle's longer, more public life, which included investigations of the spirit realm, as well as Holmes's iconicity. In her article on two history–mystery writers – Carole Nelson Douglas (who follows the career of Irene Adler) and Laurie King (who has invented Mary Russell as the wife of an elderly Holmes)[3] – Rosemary Johnsen makes a comment that is equally valid for those stories presenting Doyle as a detective: 'King and Douglas have taken up a universally known figure...each reference to Conan Doyle, Watson, or Holmes's "reality" resonates with readers' knowledge' (2006: 86).

This chapter examines twelve authors who feature Doyle as a detective at various stages in his life. As detailed in Andrew Lycett's biography and elsewhere, between 1876 and 1881 Doyle trained as a doctor in Edinburgh under Doctor Joseph Bell. This period of the writer's life is used by Howard Engel (1997), David Ashton (2009) and David Pirie (2001, 2004, 2006), while Doyle's early career as a doctor in Plymouth and Southsea from 1882 to 1886 is the background for Roberta Rogow's novels (1998, 1999, 2001, 2002). Detective stories focusing on the young Doyle from 1876 to 1886 play on the formative influences that may have contributed to his writing. Incidents and encounters in the life of the later Doyle form the 'excuse' or the 'space' where crime stories are inserted. Gyles Brandreth's series of books featuring Oscar Wilde as a detective include appearances by the younger Doyle in the early years of his fame as author of the Holmes stories (Brandreth, 2007, 2008, 2009, 2010). Of course, Doyle did become involved in the investigation of real-life criminal cases: in 1905 he investigated the case of George Edalji, and his efforts in tackling that miscarriage of justice formed the basis of Barnes's *Arthur & George* (Stashower, 2000: 254–5), although it is not a crime fiction novel. Doyle investigated other real life crimes such as the 'Brides in the Bath' murders (Costello, 1991), and in *The Sherlockian* Graham Moore shows Doyle attempting to prove that a serial killer was responsible for the murders (Moore, 2010: 102, 118). The text alternates chapters about the fictional Doyle's adventures in 1900 with the efforts of the modern hero, Harold White (just inducted into the Sherlock Holmes Irregulars in New York) in 2010 to find a famous document relating to Doyle. Although he was a convert to spiritualism in 1916, it was after the First World War that Doyle's active interest in the religion developed, with the involvement of his second wife, Jean (Stashower, 1999: 64–367). His friendship with Houdini began in 1920 (Lycett, 2007: 401), but it ended when they feuded over spiritualism (Lycett, 2007: 422). The magician features in four books (William Hjortsberg, 1994; Walter Satterthwait, 1995; Thomas Wheeler, 2004; Barbara Michaels, 1999). Hjortsberg's *Nevermore*, set in New York in 1921, concerns a series of terrifying murders which Houdini and Doyle investigate. Houdini is 'Holmes' at an English country house party at which a murder occurs in Satterthwait's *Escapade* – Doyle has a small role since a fictional Pinkerton detective, Phil Beaumont, does the Watsonian legwork. Wheeler's *The Arcanum*, set in New York in 1919, is a thriller in which four members of the eponymous society apparently investigate horrific events. The novel combines Doyle and Houdini as detectives with the Louisiana Voodoo practitioner Marie Laveau (who died 1881) and H. P. Lovecraft (1890–1937), the American writer of horror, fantasy and science fiction. Michaels puts a group of historical figures – Houdini, Doyle, Nandor Fodor and Frank Podmore – in a room together in order for them to discuss their views on several well-known ghost cases. To complete this list of twelve books are two novels by Mark Frost, set in 1884 and 1894 respectively, with an emphasis on occult events. These are thrillers in which bizarre things happen to Doyle, who is accompanied in his adventures by Jack Sparks, a fictional secret agent for Queen Victoria.

All of these writers draw accurately upon events in Doyle's life. Doyle acknowledged Bell's influence on the development of his diagnostic skills, and claims in his 1924 autobiography that he 'used and amplified [Bell'] methods' in the creation of a 'scientific detective' (*Memories and Adventures*: 26). The novels involving strange spirit manifestations relate to Doyle's belief in spiritualism. Only Hjortsberg changes occurrences in Doyle's life to suit his narrative, and he explains exactly which events he has moved into 1923 from earlier or later in Doyle's experiences in the USA (Hjortsberg, 1994: Author's note). Crucially, all of these writers affect our perception of the historical Doyle. By fictionalising his words, actions and attitudes, the twenty-first century Doyle is being shaped as much by these narratives as he is by biographical explorations into his life and work.

These detective novels are also examples of neo-Victorian fiction. In the recent surge of neo-Victorian novels, Doyle, a stalwart late-Victorian/ Edwardian, becomes an attractive figure. The rise of neo-Victorianism is more than conservative nostalgia for the past; its success can also be attributed to a feature held in common with the fictionalised use of the Doyle character: the 'overlap between fact and fiction in so many neo-Victorian novels in the use of real-life personalities from the period' (Heilmann and Llewellyn, 2010: 19). Cora Kaplan's definition relates neo-Victorianism to a postmodern play with pastiche and literary self-consciousness at the heart of this fictionalisation of historical characters:

> Borrowing postmodern styles but adapting them to retro genres and themes, the hallmark of innovative historical fiction in the

last third of the twentieth century was a juxtaposition of heavily ironised late twentieth century commentary and the self-conscious cleverness of the Victorian reference, as imitation, citation or rewrite. (Kaplan, 2007: 88)

Kaplan also highlights the variety of neo-Victorian fiction, 'a genre that has become so capacious and lucrative that it contains several mini-genres, including pastiche Victorian crime fiction and mass-market romance' (2007: 88). As historical crime novels, all must fulfil Wallace's statement that 'historical fictions are often judged on their perceived "authenticity", not only whether they get their "facts" right but also whether they are imaginatively "true" to the period' (Wallace, 2008: xi). At the same time, however, as examples of pastiche Victorianism they engage their audience in a conspiratorial relationship, whereby the readers' enjoyment stems from their recognition of these novels as a dialogue between fantasy and historical fact, and from their knowledge of the Holmes canon.

The representations of the fictional Doyle

There are various key groupings or clusters within this body of Doyle-featured novels; these are not mutually exclusive – some appear in more than one cluster. Firstly, there are the novels about a young, enthusiastic and impressionable Doyle, set before he had published his first Sherlock Holmes story *A Study in Scarlet* (1887). Howard Engel and David Pirie show Doyle as the Watson to Bell, who chose the medical student to be his out-patient clerk at the Infirmary in 1878 (Doyle, *Memories and Adventures*: 25; Lycett, 2007: 53). This key relationship in Doyle's life inspires a number of detective stories. Engel's *Mr. Doyle and Dr. Bell* (1997) is set in 1879 as Bell and Doyle investigate an Edinburgh case; Bell's deductive powers eventually solve it. Both Engel and Pirie postulate an uncertain Doyle who is impressed, often unwillingly, by Bell. In Engel's novel, Doyle undertakes the legwork for Bell in a case in which the corrupt establishment is attempting a cover up. The side-kick Doyle describes Bell listening to his observations in a mimicry of Watson's narrative style: 'he pulled the roasted chestnuts of significance from the red coals of my narrative' (Engel, 1997: 79). The first novel in Pirie's trilogy, *The Patient's Eyes*, is mainly set in 1882 in the Portsmouth area; *The Night Calls* is set in 1883 in London; and *The Dark Water* moves from London through Edinburgh to Dunwich. *The Patient's Eyes* shows Bell solving the case of a female cyclist who feels she is being followed

(Pirie, 2001). Whereas Doyle is cynical about Bell's claims at first, in successive books the narratives become darker and Doyle's belief in Bell gets much stronger as they work together in pursuit of the nefarious Neill Cream.[4] The novels' Gothic character is marked and Cream is created as an evil Moriarty-like figure.

Both Engel and Pirie endow Bell with the Sherlockian ability to draw conclusions from small indications: Engel cites Bell's deductive skills, much admired by his Edinburgh students. He recognises that a patient had been recently discharged from the army and had served in a Highland regiment in Barbados as a non-commissioned officer:

> Dr Bell...placed a friendly hand on the man's shoulder. 'You see, gentlemen,' he said to all of us in the crowded room, 'the man was respectful, but he did not remove his hat upon entering. They do not uncover in the army. Had he been out of uniform for a long time, he would have learnt our ways. So, his discharge is of recent date. He has the air of authority, and he is obviously a Scot. As to Barbados, I see from the book that his complaint is elephantiasis, which is a complaint of the West Indies.' (Engel, 1997: 9)

Pirie, in *The Patient's Eyes*, presents a sceptical Doyle asking Bell to deduce information from his father's watch:

> The watch is about fifty years old. Its owner is a man of untidy habits – very untidy and careless. He was left with good prospects but threw away his chances. He has lived for some time in relative poverty with a few short intervals of prosperity. After that he took to drink and his mind went. That is all I can honestly tell you. (Pirie, 2001: 85)[5]

Doyle is horrified. For knowledgeable Holmesians this is an intertextual reference to *The Sign of Four* (1890), in which Holmes deduces from Watson's pocket-watch that it originally belonged to his alcoholic brother.

A Trick of the Light by David Ashton (2009) is one of a series, originally episodes in a BBC radio series, about Inspector James McLevy of the Edinburgh police. In this story, set in 1881, the imaginary police detective is assisted by a fictional Doyle. Like Bell, McLevy is also represented as a role model for Holmes and his remarks follow the Holmesian style: 'There are three intelligences we must bring to a crime, Mister Doyle. Forensic, intuitive and experiential' (2009: 243). Ashton's character further pastiches the great detective when he recognises the boxer in Doyle:

'The skin on the knuckles of your right hand is somewhat abraded,' McLevy remarked. 'Of course ye could have received such chasing a ball, but there is also a bruised discolouration indicating impact and I also note the marking of a mouse under your left eye'. (2009: 30)

Holmes's boxing prowess, noted in *A Study in Scarlet* (1973: 13), is based on Doyle's own pugilistic skills. Lycett describes the boxing match between Doyle and the steward Jack Lamb on the S.S. Hope in 1881 (Lycett, 2007: 70).

The above novels demonstrate the prevalence of Holmesian behaviour by those who detect with Doyle. Many of these writers use Doyle as the Watson to their Holmes. To this deployment of the real Doctor Bell can be added the imaginary Inspector McLevy, Rogow's Lewis Carroll, Brandreth's Oscar Wilde, Satterthwait's and Hjortsberg's Houdini, and Frost's imaginary Jack Sparks. For example, in Frost's *The List of Seven* (1993) comments are made on Jack's violin playing ability and his knowledge of make-up and disguise, and we learn later that Jack has been addicted to cocaine. All of them function in a Holmes-like manner, making deductions from the evidence which usually eludes Doyle, and taking responsibility for the elucidation of the crimes.

A second clearly-defined category among the Doyle pastiches consists of a cluster of stories featuring other historical Victorians, often contemporaneous writers. Roberta Rogow's four volumes, all titled beginning with *The Problem of...*, follow Doyle's career in 1885–6 in Brighton, Portsmouth, London and Oxford. Here the detective is Charles Dodgson (Lewis Carroll);[6] Doyle provides him with assistance, often of a muscular nature, and finds some clues, while Dodgson solves the crimes. In Brighton, Dodgson is initially presented as a doddery old man, but the keen detective skills that he demonstrates belie this persona. In *The Problem of the Spiteful Spiritualist* he remarks, 'I applied the rules of logic. When one has eliminated that which is impossible, what remains, however improbable, must be the truth' (1999: 241). Then there is the following exchange: '"Indeed," Mr. Dodgson remarked. "But recall, sir, the footsteps on the carpet in the hall." Dr Doyle frowned. "But there were no signs of footsteps on the carpet." "Precisely what was so interesting." Mr Dodgson said.' (241). This fictionalisation of Doyle draws on the 1892 Holmes story 'The Adventure of Silver Blaze'. Brandreth's Oscar Wilde (presented as a Sherlockian reasoner *par excellence*) solves cases in 1883, 1889, 1890 and 1892, and here Doyle's involvement is tangential. Wilde's assistant detective and narrator is Robert Sherard, who in reality was a biographer of Wilde.[7] In *Oscar Wilde and the Ring of Death* Wilde identifies the boy who drives a pony and trap in Eastbourne as a budding actor:

> Oscar ... smiled. 'The boy was familiar with the word "consanguin-eous" – and proud to be. It's a word that features prominently in Shakespeare's *Twelfth Night* but not, I imagine, in the daily discourse of the average East Sussex stable lad ... I jumped to a happy conclu-sion, that's all – prompted no doubt by my seeing a poster adver-tising the Eastbourne Vagabonds' production of the play displayed in the foyer of the Devonshire Park Theatre'. (2008: 155)

Here Doyle merely makes a Watsonian remark: 'Oscar you amaze me. Nothing passes you by' (99). In his biography, *Memories and Adventures* (1924), Doyle recalls his meeting with Wilde in 1889:

> His conversation left an indelible impression upon my mind. He towered above us all, and yet had the art of seeming to be interested in all we could say.... He took as well as he gave, but what he gave was unique. (1989: 78)

In *Oscar Wilde and the Nest of Vipers* Wilde convinces the Prince of Wales that his new chef must come from Madagascar because his cheese straws are flavoured with a unique cinnamon. He later reveals to Doyle that he was guessing, and Doyle records Wilde saying, 'the party piece reas-sured him (the Prince of Wales)...made him feel he did indeed have Holmes on the case' (Brandreth, 2010: 33–4).

Moore's *The Sherlockian* highlights another of Doyle's literary acquaint-ances. Doyle sent a play to the actor-manager Henry Irving, whose busi-ness manager was Bram Stoker (Stashower, 2000: 174–5) and this became the start of a friendship with Stoker (Moore, 2010: 40).[8] The Houdini of Satterthwait's book, set in 1921, is the investigator into a death at a house party who explains the whole story in the novel's denouement (1995: 339–43). Here Doyle has little to do and fails to realise what the solution is. In *Nevermore* Houdini shows Doyle some of his skills, but is still able to amaze him with tricks such as deducing what Doyle had written while several streets away from Houdini's house:

> The knight [Sir Arthur] was back in the Houdini parlour before ten minutes had elapsed ... [Houdini said] 'Good, I have devised this test,

Sir Arthur, to teach you what can be done in the realm of the miraculous by means of pure trickery. The illusion you are about to see is
one to which I've dedicated a lot of thought...I assure you it's accomplished entirely through natural means. (Hjortsberg, 1994: 60–1)

The obvious third grouping incorporates novels concerning the occult
and spiritualism. *The Arcanum* (2004) features a quartet of real life individuals, including Doyle, Houdini, Lovecraft and Laveau, who are attacked
as they struggle to vanquish a diabolic secret threat. In Michaels's *Other
Worlds* (1999) two well-known nineteenth-century American ghost
stories are related to a group comprising Doyle, Houdini, Fodor and
Podmore, who give their interpretations of the events after each story.
Podmore was an investigator into alleged psychic phenomena for the
Society for Psychical Research, and Fodor was a leading authority on
poltergeists and other paranormal phenomena. These detective novels
all present a detecting Doyle in a Gothic setting, linking him with
themes of the occult and/or spiritualism. The occult examples differ
from the mainly rational explanations found in the other novels,
and although Pirie's trilogy adopts a Gothic style, it does not eschew
rational explanations. These works were written over the same time
frame as the 'rational' novels and present another view of Doyle as a
believer in spiritualism, while also reflecting the Gothic elements in
some of Doyle's own fictions. In Mark Frost's *The List of Seven* (1993)
Doyle is threatened by a Satanic coven in London and tracks them with
Jack Sparks, Queen Victoria's secret agent. The three thrillers employ
features such as ghostly, fiendish manifestations, séances, individuals with extraordinary mind powers, and trained attackers with no
concern for their own lives. Horrific and impossible events occur in *The
List of Seven*. Doyle remarks that 'there were bloodless blind men with
Oriental daggers stalking London trying to carve him like a Christmas
goose' (47), and that '[e]very square inch of his [Doyle's] room looked to
have been drooled or saturated with a clear, viscous fluid...the surface
of every object in the room had been partially liquefied, then cooled
and hardened' (39). The unreality of what Madame Blavatsky describes
as 'ectoplasmic detonation' might be enough to discourage a reader who
prefers ratiocination (Frost: 64). In *The Arcanum*, Doyle fights demons
on top of a New York subway train, and the creatures

swayed forth from the stygian darkness, lithe robed bodies with
drooping hoods conceal[ed] long faces with glowing red rubies
instead of eyes. Thin stalks of wood, like beaks, substituted for noses.

Clutched in their gloved fists were enormous scythes gleaming silver.
(Wheeler: 82)

In *The Six Messiahs* Doyle and Jack Sparks return in a religious cult
thriller in which the enemy is a man who can keep a mass of followers
under mind control. Here, rampaging men of single-minded violence
feature, but not the ectoplasmic emanations of Frost's first thriller.

A further section of this group reflects Doyle's real-life interest in spiritualism. In Satterthwait's *Escapade* Houdini and Doyle deal with the
appearance of family ghosts and the death of a family member; Doyle's
role, really, is confined to the promotion of spiritualist methods to detect
the ghosts. Though the murder and other ghostly manifestations prove,
as Houdini demonstrates, to be totally explainable by rational means
Doyle is unwilling to accept that no magic is involved. He tells Beaumont
that he believes that Houdini can dematerialise (131). In *Nevermore*
Doyle is on a speaking tour of America in 1923 when a series of murders
occur which copy those of Poe's fictions. For instance, a woman's body
is found in a bricked-up closet with a howling, black cat on her shoulder,
copying Poe's 'The Black Cat'. Houdini solves the mystery and Doyle
provides Watson-like assistance while having strange encounters with
Poe's ghost: 'Arthur returned the specter's stare. He knew those doleful
mourner's eyes, the ironic brow and clipped moustache.... It was Poe'
(Hjortsberg, 1994: 73). Hjortsberg uses the famous, and genuine, story
of Houdini's scepticism when Jean Doyle produces messages in automatic writing allegedly from Houdini's mother (Hjortsberg, 1994: 130–1;
Lycett, 2007: 412). In the discussions about ghost stories in *Other Worlds*
(1999) the four protagonists give us their interpretations concerning the
American tale of the Bell Witch. While Doyle suggests that one of those
involved is a medium channelling spirits, Podmore sees the ghost as a
mischievous child poltergeist, Houdini presents the sceptical interpretation of fraud, and Fodor, the explanation of multiple personalities. All
explanations are consonant with the interests of these men. Doyle sees
young Betsy Bell as the centre of the happenings in the Bell household:

> Why, gentlemen, isn't it obvious that Betsy was a powerful natural
> medium? That is proved beyond the shadow of a doubt by her
> convulsive seizures. I have seen the same thing happen when a spir-
> itual entity attempted to gain control of an inexperienced medium.
> (Michaels: 89)[9]

Referring to their second case, Fodor describes how the group is 'at
our usual impasse – Doyle maintaining the spiritualist interpretation,

Houdini pinning the blame on the naughty kiddies' (Michaels: 215). Rather bizarrely, these real-life figures from different times and places are pursuing their discussion in a comfortable room akin to a gentlemen's club in some other universe. In the finale to *Arthur & George*, Barnes emphasises Doyle's spiritualist dimension as the novel ends with an historical event, a recreation of the actual spiritualist meeting held by Doyle's family after his death at which communication with Doyle was attempted.

The cultural afterlife of Doyle in the Doyle pastiches

How valuable is the fictional Doyle? What does he contribute to these novels? Is his presence 'merely corroborative detail, intended to give artistic verisimilitude to an otherwise bald and unconvincing narrative?' (Pooh-Bah in Gilbert & Sullivan *Mikado*, Act II, Vol. 2: 56). As I demonstrate, there are reasons for the fictional Doyle's presence in these novels as a doctor, as a man of action, as an observer of the puzzle presented for elucidation, and, occasionally, as a significant participant in the detection. As the inventor of Sherlock Holmes, his presence provides the reader with a frisson of excitement.

Doyle's medical knowledge is frequently employed in these novels. At the beginning of *The Problem of the Missing Hoyden* Doyle takes care of an elderly man who has collapsed and who turns out to be the distressed Lewis Carroll (Rogow: 12). In *The Six Messiahs* Doyle recognises that his friend Jack Sparks is suffering from a profound mental condition and uses his skill to persuade Jack to reveal his malaise (Frost: 232). In *Arthur & George* Doyle, with his training in ophthalmology, is able to show the impossibility of Edalji committing the crimes of cattle mutilation due to his poor eyesight, and this is corroborated historically as Doyle used his ophthalmic training to assist Edalji (Lycett: 169).

Doyle was a lover of sports and the outdoors, and this well-known aspect of his life is deployed in his fictional representations. In *Trick of the Light* he throws a missile to aid a dazed McLevy who has fallen while fighting a murderer on a roof:

> Conan Doyle had a mighty arm. He fielded on the boundary of life and his motto was *steel true, blade straight*. The cricket ball is a hard, dangerous object and has killed more men than might be supposed by those who see only fellows dressed in white upon green grass. It flew through the night air of Edinburgh like an arrow and smashed into the head of the beast as it prepared to crash down its clasped fists in a deadly strike. (Ashton: 248)

Indeed, Doyle often provides the legwork in these books while his companion does the thinking. In *Escapade*, after Houdini has explained who the murderer is, it is Doyle who prevents him from escaping: 'Doyle was ready and he grabbed the man's hand with his own left and he popped him a very good right on the point of his chin and the man went crashing to the floor' (Satterthwait: 343). In the thrillers Doyle must fight against the villains (as in the example of demons on a subway train) and does so with gusto, even in his sixties.

He contributes to the elucidation of mysteries, although he is not the key detective. In *The Problem of the Surly Servant* Doyle is able to give the police inspector some valuable information, informing him 'I've made something of a study of cigars' and identifying a stub as an American stogie (Rogow: 192–3). This, of course, is an intertextual reference to *The Sign of Four*, in which it is revealed that Holmes has written a monograph on tobacco ash. Most significantly, Doyle can, with inadvertent remarks, aid the Holmesian figure, and in *The Patient's Eyes* he draws Bell's attention to the wind howling in the chimney while Bell is investigating the cause of a woman's death. Bell realises that the woman had been gassed from an adjoining room and the flue operated so that the gas was then dissipated. Doyle attempts to investigate the case of the lady cyclist on his own and tells Bell that he 'followed [Bell's] precepts to the letter. Investigation, Observation, Deduction, Conclusion. What could possibly be wrong with that?' (Pirie: 170). Unfortunately, Bell's reply is 'Almost everything' as he points out Doyle's errors (171).

Doyle acts as a Holmes-figure in *The Sherlockian* and wants Stoker as his Watson; Stoker observes that 'you think because you squirted life into Holmes from the tip of your pen, you might become him yourself. So you need a Watson and – you've chosen me' (Moore: 77). Stoker's comment on Holmes's fictionality 'proves' the factuality of Doyle the detective. Perhaps to show how detective abilities have been transferred to this fictional Doyle, or to illustrate his greater maturity, by 1894 he manages a Sherlockian feat of observation in *The Six Messiahs*, when he describes the man who has approached him for aid:

You were born and raised on the Lower East Side of New York City. The oldest son of Russian immigrant parents. You are a secular Jew, thoroughly and wilfully assimilated into American culture. That you have rejected the religious observances of your father has been a matter of no small dispute between you. You sailed to London approximately six weeks ago from Spain ... where, over a period ... you negotiated a complicated transaction involving the purchase of an extremely rare and valuable book which you are now transporting to America. (Frost, 1995: 53)

In all of these novels Doyle provides verisimilitude by his presence and those of the real people with whom he was associated. Two factors apply specifically to Doyle: the first is the knowledge all readers have of Sherlock Holmes, which leads them to an interest in how Doyle came to invent Holmes and the influences in his own life which produced this figure. That means that Doyle's training, activities as a doctor, private life and beliefs are all germane. Furthermore, the writers exploit incidents and characters that occur in the Holmes stories as the basis for their stories: when a historical crime writer has Doyle trying to interpret a cipher (Pirie, 2006: 258–65) the initiated reader is reminded of 'The Dancing Men' (Doyle, 1971: 610); Doyle's visit to an opium den (Pirie, 2004: 406–11) recalls 'The Man with the Twisted Lip' (Doyle, 1971: 124); and meeting a man with a collection of poisonous creatures (Pirie, 2001: 198) plays on 'The Speckled Band' (Doyle, 1971: 173). In the second of Brandreth's Oscar Wilde novels a jaded Doyle is already planning to kill off his Sherlock Holmes character (2009: 102). Likewise, the second sentence of the *The Sherlockian*'s prologue in 1893 is: 'I'm going to kill him' (Moore: 1). The reappearance of Sparks in *The Six Messiahs* – after a ten year gap – prefigures the return of Holmes in Doyle's own oeuvre, 'The Adventure of the Empty House'. When the Sherlockian characters in the various novels show their abilities to reason from often limited evidence, the Holmes stories are recalled. The character of Sherlock Holmes occupies the centre of these writers' interest in Doyle and this is why Doyle is, in nearly all of them, not the major detective. As the creator of Holmes he must continue to be the narrator of the adventures and therefore the Watson figure. His contributions as doctor, man of action and occasional discoverer of information all fulfil the Watsonian template. The exceptions to this representation of Doyle as Watson occur in *Arthur & George* and *The Sherlockian*, in which he sometimes acts as a Holmes-type figure. In *Arthur & George,* Arthur discusses the evidence against George Edalji with Chief Constable Anson, who says, in response to a question from Doyle:

'What, in your opinion, really happened?...Most crimes, Doyle – almost all crimes, in fact – occur without witnesses...Forgive me for lecturing you about the real world.' Doyle wondered if he would ever cease being punished for having invented Sherlock Holmes. Corrected, advised, lectured, patronized – when would it ever stop? (Barnes: 272–3)

Here, as so often, Doyle's ambivalent relationship with Holmes is exploited and his synonymy with Holmes is reiterated. In *The Sherlockian* Doyle is a detective in the Holmesian mould, and this makes an interesting counterpoint to the other books. He muses as he tries to piece together some clues:

> If he could not do it he wouldn't be merely a failed detective – he'd be a failed writer as well. He and Holmes would go down as charlatans together. Arthur's 'science of deduction' ... would prove but a dreadful sham. (Moore: 149)

He visits murder sites and makes inferences as his own creation would have done, but he is uneasy about this and eventually says 'no more playing detective' (Moore: 252). Again, his love–hate relationship with his creation is illustrated: 'murder taste[s] sweet on Arthur's lips' as he pens the death of Holmes (Moore: 9). Both Lycett, Doyle's biographer and Moore, the novelist, quote Doyle's diary entry 'Killed Holmes' (Lycett: 207; Moore: 12).

The use of Doyle adds to the complexities of producing the stories. All history–mysteries have to function on two levels – establishing both a criminal investigation and a viable historical background. The historical crime fictions featuring Doyle which are highlighted in this chapter all establish viable historical background details from Doyle's life, but they also build on fictional images from the Holmes stories. The novels are all securely rooted in the events and the attitudes of Doyle's life and in the mindset of the period in which he lived. Doyle is a good choice as a detective in historical crime fiction because of his and his detective's cultural significance in the modern world. As a man tells Doyle in *The Sherlockian* 'There's no-one wants to think of Holmes as being dead – We want Mr. Holmes to live forever' (Moore: 83). This could be expanded to include Doyle himself as an icon who, as creator of Holmes, almost merges with his creation in popular memory. Moore illustrates the confusion between Doyle and Holmes in a comment by Harold White on the views of the Baker Street Irregulars. A speaker has referred to Doyle's biographers as having 'crafted masterful portraits of John Watson's friend and literary agent' (Moore: 31):

> Most Sherlockians sort of ... uh, *pretend* ... that Holmes was real and that Conan Doyle had his adventures published as fiction to preserve his privacy. The rival Doyleans, as they call themselves, think the Sherlockians are stupid. If Jeffrey [the speaker] had acknowledged

Doyle as the *author* of the stories, half the room would bleat blasphemy. Better to side with the Sherlockians. The Doyleans are less prone to rebellion. (Moore: 32)

D. Michael Risinger comments in his article on *Arthur & George* that 'what we are to examine is art imitating life imitating art imitating life' (2007: 2). Rich layers continue to be added to the Holmes and Doyle oeuvre, showing that Doyle is becoming as powerful an icon as his famous creation.

Notes

1. See Peter Ridgeway Watt and Joseph Green, *The Alternative Sherlock Holmes* (2003).
2. This information is based on my unpublished paper, presented at 'The Literary Art of Murder Conference' (4–6 April 2008), Newcastle University.
3. See Sabine Vanacker's chapter in this volume.
4. Neill Cream was a doctor who trained at Edinburgh during the same period as Doyle (1878). He was found guilty and executed in 1892 for the 'Lambeth poisonings' and is thought to have committed other poisonings.
5. See also the BBC's 'The Patient's Eyes' in which Bell deduces information about Arthur's father.
6. Dodgson is the only major personality used about whom I can find no evidence that he and Doyle knew each other.
7. A friend of Oscar Wilde, Robert Sherard published the first accounts of the life of Oscar Wilde, *Oscar Wilde: The Story of an Unhappy Friendship* (1902), *The Life of Oscar Wilde* (1906), and *The Real Oscar Wilde* (1916).
8. *The Sherlockian* differs from the other books listed because it has rigidly alternating chapters – one story describes Doyle's apparent investigations around 1900, and the other investigations in 2010 of Doyle's activities in 1900.
9. In *The New Revelation and the Vital Message* Doyle recalls that he investigated an allegedly haunted house with Podmore for the Society for Psychical Research in 1894 (1938: 22–3).

12
Sherlock Holmes in Fairyland: The Afterlife of Arthur Conan Doyle

Clive Bloom

There is a conundrum inside Arthur Conan Doyle and inside Sherlock Holmes. Why did the creator of the master of deduction turn to a belief in fairies and all things invisible: Sherlock Holmes contra his creator? Why did a rational man (who in his very actions and hobbies defined the age in which he lived), with the most rational of heroes, turn to the 'invisible', and why do we still refuse to see that the author's swerve into esoteric belief is at one with the nature of his creation? Why was Doyle condemned for a naivety that Sherlock Holmes was never subject to? Indeed, how did Doyle come to stand for the opposite values of his own creation?

The last two decades of the nineteenth century were a period of both intense complacency and intense doubt. A type of deep-seated neurosis seemed to grip those for whom the long Victorian age was in its twilight years. It was a period exemplified by its 'isms'. Indeed, the late-nineteenth century was marked by its search for a way of life different from that inherited from the past and which those very 'isms' embodied. At the margins, antithetical systems gestated and waited to be born. Ideas heralded coming times and the new person whose modernity was expressed by adherence to one or more of the following: anarchism, hedonism and individualism, bohemianism and avant-gardism; collectivism and syndicalism; communism and socialism; vegetarianism, nudism and sun worship; atheism and secularism; spiritualism, and social Darwinism; demon worship, free love and drug addiction; fairies and woodcraft – powerful and sometimes eccentric ideologies in which Victorians and Edwardians found meaning in experiences seemingly more complex than those of their forbears. You chose your necessary poison, and consequently your damnation or salvation.

It is against such rapid changes in experience that Sherlock Holmes must be seen. He is, despite his quirky love of old shag, drugs, avant-garde art and strange violin music, a bulwark against the damnable 'isms' of the age. Holmes may be a detective, but he is a detective who is unique in vocation and whose powers of deduction, are based not on intuition but on observation and logical deduction. What cannot be seen cannot be explained. He is, in short, a materialist whose very materialism gives assurance of a greater good beyond the material realm. Holmes put back what was missing from the puzzle of existence in order to reassure the world of the continuity of the status quo and the rightness of reason's rule. Whether the enemy is a vampire in southern England or a hell-hound in Devon, the explanation is consistently rational, material and mundane. Everything is reduced to what may be observed and consequently to the assertion that human beings wear their motives in their clothing and their innermost thoughts in the torn scraps of detritus that cling to them: literally, for Holmes, manners maketh the man. One only has to read the opening deductions regarding Dr Mortimer in *The Hound of the Baskervilles* to see the absurdity of the position. In Holmes's world there is only the behaviour of social beings, but social beings whose actions are perverted and who therefore have to be eliminated from society.

Although Doyle was tinkering with Holmes in 1886, the detective finally came to the public's notice in 1887, a year marked by bloody clashes with those godless socialists so threatening to Victorian sobriety. If the Church could no longer assuage middle-class doubts, Holmes could at least protect against existential fears, a talisman against change in a godless universe, a universe where, a year later, the likes of Jack the Ripper stalked like an invisible 'terrorist' (to use George Bernard Shaw's colourful description). The police were flatfoots precisely because the society that they protected was no longer stable, no longer grounded. Holmes is really not a detective; rather, he is the high priest of stability in a destabilised world.

The Greenwich explosion of 1894 and the death of the anarchist Martial Bourdin reinforced the idea of irrationality at the heart of the empire. It is interesting that the idea of a random force that is inherently evil starts to infiltrate popular fiction after 1894. From now on, an ideological counter weight to law and order that had not existed before the explosion would prove irresistibly attractive to readers. The fascination with the anti-matter of evil was most famously mooted by Doyle in 'The Final Problem', which introduced Dr Moriarty to readers in *The Strand Magazine* in December 1893. The introduction of the 'Napoleon of Crime' (1981: 471) was to 'kill off' the perfect Holmes through the appearance of his nemesis. Holmes himself, long separated from Watson (who has married), is reunited for one last time, but Holmes is 'paler and thinner', his 'nerves...at the highest tension' (469). Against him is ranged the genius of evil whose 'hereditary tendencies' (470) are of 'the most diabolical kind' (470–1). Indeed, Moriarty is the antithesis and the double of Holmes, for if Holmes is the presiding genius of law and order, Moriarty is, in essence, the coming corporate genius who was more than 'an individual' and more like a 'mighty organisation' (472) dedicated to urban chaos and whom Holmes must stop in order to save London. 'The air is sweeter in London for my presence' (477) says Holmes, but Moriarty will poison that air with the criminality which was a euphemism for moral corruption:

> His career has been an extraordinary one. He is a man of good birth and excellent education, endowed by nature with a phenomenal mathematical faculty. At the age of twenty-one he wrote a treatise upon the binomial theorem, which has had a European vogue. On the strength of it he won the mathematical chair at one of our smaller universities, and had, to all appearances, a most brilliant career before him. But the man had hereditary tendencies of the most diabolical kind. A criminal strain ran in his blood, which, instead of being modified, was increased and rendered infinitely more dangerous by his extraordinary mental powers…. He is the organizer of half that is evil and of nearly all that is undetected in this great city. He is a genius, a philosopher, an abstract thinker. He has a brain of the first order. He sits motionless, like a spider in the centre of its web, but that web has a thousand radiations, and he knows well every quiver of each of them. He does little himself. He only plans. But his agents are numerous and splendidly organized. (470–1)

Moriarty heads the first great fictional crime syndicate; he is the first of those invisible criminal masterminds who rule the world from behind the scenes and who have fascinated generations of writers ever since. Great crime, Doyle avers, is closer to great philosophy than mere criminality; closer, indeed, to an aesthetic and academic exercise:

> [Moriarty] is extremely tall and thin, his forehead domes out in a white curve, and his two eyes are deeply sunken in his head. He is clean-shaven, pale, and ascetic-looking, retaining something of the professor in his features. His shoulders are rounded from much

study, and his face protrudes forward and is forever slowly oscillating from side to side in a curiously reptilian fashion. (472)

The final confrontation at the Reichenbach Falls is both a cleansing and an annulment. Watson gloomily reflects that 'there deep down in that dreadful cauldron of swirling water and seething foam, will lie for all time the most dangerous criminal and the foremost champion of law' (480). Of course, the corpse of Sherlock Holmes would not remain dormant for long, but nor would that of Moriarty, who becomes a symbol for the coming age, reappearing in abstracted and occult form in films like Fritz Lang's 'Dr Mabuse' series of 1922 and 1933 and in the spy novels of Ian Fleming in the 1950s.

There was perhaps, if not approval of, then at least a fascination with moral decay in some literary quarters, and there was certainly an abiding interest in the clandestine world of anarchism in general and what it said about modern life and those people so alienated that only wholesale destruction could save the world. For a few, anarchism represented the possibilities of emancipation and freedom from hardship, for others it showed the way into the new socialist republican future, but for the many it was nothing but an invitation to a future both chaotic and murderous; that such men were out there in the streets of Britain's major cities prophesying such ideas was incomprehensible and terrifying. Holmes was indispensable, the latter half of the nineteenth century unthinkable without him. Holmes was the last defence against a lawless and indifferent world. Indeed, for two brief periods during 1907 and 1912, Doyle convinced himself that he actually was Holmes, using the detective's methods of observation and deduction to argue the case for justice for George Edalji and Oscar Slater respectively, and in so doing exposed the corruptions of imperialism and the justice system. Holmes, and then Doyle himself, were the final bulwarks against corruption and social injustice, with Doyle writing up both cases for the public just as Watson publicised the exploits of his friend.

Doyle was acutely aware of the duplicitous nature of his society. Moriarty is the double of Holmes, the schizoid other which Holmes might just become. The double haunts Victorian Britain, exemplified by the appearance of Robert Louis Stevenson's schizoid protagonist in *Dr Jekyll and Mr Hyde* in 1886, with its play upon the closeness of moral being and the ideas of the new psychology which conceived of multiple selves competing for the ego's attention. For the most part, such ideas concentrated on the split personality. This dualism at the heart of the ego was best exhibited by the playful appearance of E. W. Hornung's sportsman-thief, the raffish and charming A. J. Raffles in *Cassell's Magazine* in 1898. Hornung was Doyle's brother-in-law, and Raffles and his side kick Bunny a type of family joke at the expense of Holmes and Doyle. Unlike Moriarty, however, Raffles has a perverse conscience which sees him sacrifice himself in the Boer War as an act of 'atonement'. Nevertheless, it was George Orwell who detected something new in Raffles: 'Raffles... has no real moral code, no religion, certainly no social consciousness. All he has is a set of reflexes: the nervous system, as it were, of a gentleman' (quoted in Hornung, 1996: ix). All that is left of the Victorian male by the end of the century is a set of cynical reflexes and nervousness which reflects a crisis of self and confidence in the solidity of what is around you. All that is left, in the last defence, is a gentleman who may be a thief, but is not a cad.

The nineteenth century was a period where opposites might be reconciled without any sense of contradiction. On the one hand the period was notable for its material, technological and scientific sense of progress, whilst on the other, it was a period filled with forebodings of moral decay and physical disaster. The Victorians lived their lives as much in the material here-and-now as in an hallucinatory elsewhere exemplified by their obsession with the spirit realms of drugs, fairies and ectoplasm. Doyle and Holmes stand at the heart of the debate.

As the nineteenth century wore on, personal or identity 'politics' came to the fore, driven by industrialisation, the overwhelming weight of the metropolis, the burden of empire and immigration, technological advances and the significance of an ever-present and fully-functioning capitalism which exposed divisions in society that were explained by the 'survival of the fittest' social Darwinism that had grown up to account for what seemed to be an age that had lost its meaning in the scramble for money and social position. For many, this meant an existential crisis that went to the heart of both the individual and their status and presence, and the sociological dimension in which they functioned.

This change of mental landscape could not have happened without a radical shift in attitudes, not least of which was a 'new' ideology of death, an ideology that at its height amounted to a metaphysical politics. The dead were swiftly becoming the companions of the living. Indeed, trips out of town to the fashionable private cemeteries around London were accompanied by a morbid obsession with death itself, an obsession started by the Queen whose unearthly shrieks on the death of Prince Albert had started the cult of mourning and her own state of perpetual purdah.

The modern form of spiritualism which evolved in the Victorian era to accommodate this interest in the recently deceased represented a decisive break from all previous supernaturalism: a revolutionary leap from an essentially archaic, religious belief system concerned with the limits of sin and redemption (and fear of the dead) to one that was, in most of its features materialist, religiously ambivalent or agnostic (and fascinated with the dying and the dead). The development of carefully constructed mourning rituals and the belief that the dead were only 'asleep' and not departed went hand in hand with a new gothic monumentality in funereal sculpture and private cemetery gardens. The dead were not to be quarantined, but embraced in monumental architecture and symbolism which clearly demonstrated that the deceased were not gone forever, but merely asleep or 'living' on another plane of existence parallel to ours.

In many of its more theorised aspects it was engaged in an aggressive debate with Darwinism or the consequences of Darwinism, and Darwin himself took a lively interest in the doings of clairvoyants. This 'revolution' was driven by the belief that contact with the dead and other disembodied spirit entities was a desirable thing. It was in direct opposition to the archaic belief that such contact should be feared and shunned and its practitioners treated as necromancers. The new 'rational' supernatural was believed to go beyond religion and science, and explain both. Although this advance was supposedly based on 'natural law' and a type of spiritualised universal mechanics, it was founded on one central dogmatic assertion: *survival after death* as proven 'beyond doubt' through the increasing activities of mediums. For spiritualists, 'spiritualism' was a 'science', half way between religion and scientific enquiry.

Despite the importance of science and technology in the Western world and the advances of rational thought, a general belief in the paranormal remained both widespread and deeply felt. Curiously, this shift in attitudes towards the dead was the product of the neuroses of a technological modern society. If there is a story to be read in this ethereal realm, it is not that of the eternal return of the non-living, but rather the narration of a progressive and inclusive modernity in which supernaturalism was an integral part of the contemporary experience of the Victorian and Edwardian mind. In this regard, Doyle was only the most vocal and high-profile believer.

Doyle had, after a long search, at last found the truth which reconciled the spiritual with the material:

I seemed suddenly to see that this subject with which I had so long dallied was not merely a study of a force outside the rules of science, but that it was really something tremendous, a breaking down of the walls between two worlds, a direct undeniable message from beyond, a call of hope and of guidance to the human race at the time of its deepest afflictions. (quoted in Miller, 2008: 350)

Doyle had, of course been born into a period of intense spiritual change. By the time of his birth in 1859, more than half the population of America believed in spiritualism and there were 25,000 practising mediums; séances and levitations were all the rage amongst crowned heads and society notables (Miller: 352). In his twenties, Doyle was still a 'convinced materialist', but was becoming more fascinated by the subject, attending séances and table tipping sessions between 1885 and 1888 (355). Some prominent scientists were also becoming convinced of the reality of an 'unseen universe of Spirit', as Alfred Wallace put it, and even Darwin was less than sceptical.

At the very point at which Doyle was thinking about the first Holmes story, he was also wondering about faith. He refused to accept organised religion, and although not an atheist, was attracted to spiritual theories which kept an idea of God, but ditched the paraphernalia of worship. From the late 1880s Doyle was reading mystic literature, but writing rationalist detective fiction. By 9 May 1889 Doyle was a convinced spiritualist actually signing a letter to *The Portsmouth Evening News* 'a Spiritualist' (Miller: 360). His friends drew back, yet he advanced, becoming more embroiled with spiritualism-minded people to the exclusion of others. In 1916 Doyle suggested that spiritualism was a 'revolution' in thought more profound than any political revolution, looking towards a new millennium of hope and consolation where the living could commune with the dead, and by 1917 Doyle had joined Sir Oliver Lodge in the London Spiritualist Alliance. By 1920, and against the evidence of his own eyes (or expressly because of it), Doyle had embraced the fairies of Cottingley and written several articles saying so, articles that simply brought ridicule.

The editor of *The Strand* begged Doyle to desist, seeing the devaluation of all that Holmes stood for and all that Doyle epitomised as the pipe-smoking 'embodiment of common sense' (Miller: 372). For E. T. Raymond, writing in *The Living Age* in 1920, Doyle had now become a 'fictional' character whose views were opposed to those of Holmes; 'instead of common sense' there was the 'wildest mysticism', but when had Holmes ever been common sense? (Miller: 380). *Punch*, meanwhile, ribbed Doyle with a ditty:

> If you, Sir Conan Doyle, believe in fairies,
> Must I believe in Mister Sherlock Holmes?

> If *you* believe that round us all the air is
> Just thick with elves and little men and gnomes,
> Then must I believe in Doctor Watson
> And speckled bands and things? Oh, no! My hat!
> Though all the t's are crossed and i's have dots on
> I simply can't. So that's that! (Miller: 408)

Yet fairies, elves and gnomes were the staple of much mid-Victorian art and belief: Tinker Bell arrived in 1904, and Doyle's uncle made a living out of painting them. Doyle became progressively convinced of the materialisation of the hitherto unseen in this world. A revelation was at hand. Materialism had given way to a new amalgam, not because of the dubious activities of mediums, but because of the tested methods used by scientists to prove mediumship authenticity and show their access between 'two worlds' to be a real phenomenon.

> [Death] makes no abrupt change in the process of development, nor does it make an impassable chasm between those who are on either side. No trait of the form and no peculiarity of the mind are changed by death but all are continued ... in recent years there has come to us from divine sources a new revelation ... by far the greatest religious event since the death of Christ ... it is a revolution in religious thought, a revolution which gives us as a by-product an utter fearlessness of death. (Doyle, quoted in Miller: 350)

Doyle always had a rocky relationship with organised religion: he believed in divorce on equal terms and was open to non-orthodox spiritual explanations of the universe. For weeks on end he pondered the mystery of spiritualist belief.

The Edwardian world had inherited the Victorian militarist whirlwind and an apocalyptic war with France, Germany or Russia seemed inevitable. It was in this atmosphere of anxiety that Doyle moved closer to the spirit world. In the latter half of his life, however he turned increasingly towards an interest in life after death and used the science fiction tales of his new hero, Professor Challenger, to explore the conundrum, especially Challenger's penultimate novel of 1926, *The Land of Mist*, where the Professor's best friend and daughter go on a spiritual adventure in order to reveal the truths of spiritualism. Challenger is no longer the explorer of lost realms, but merely an old-fashioned materialist refusing to acknowledge the new revelation: 'this soul talk is the Animism of savages. It is superstition, a myth ... [humans are] four buckets of water and a bagful of salt...when you're dead you're dead' (2006: 15–16). His friend Malone disagrees on philosophical lines and is slowly convinced that even 'ectoplasm' (250) has a material basis; by turns, Malone comes to the conclusion of life after death as a reality, material science giving way to 'spiritual progress' (44), all, nevertheless, repressed by the vindictive nature of the police and the ignorance of judges. Spiritualism was not only revelation, it was also revolution.

The arguments of the time are not debates between faith and reason, but are rather two forms of logic based on quite unrelated conceptual systems. Indeed, most writers of the occult insisted upon the conspiratorial nature of both conventional science and established religion which (against the evidence of history) had worked together in order to *conceal* a set of truths they only dimly understood but which they, nevertheless, fully comprehended would destroy their power should such truths be revealed to a wide public. 'Illuminated knowledge' would, Doyle believed, soon replace both science and religion; séances and clairvoyance were the portals to a new revelation.

If science emphasised effect (not self-based) then 'magical' encounters emphasised affect (where subjectivity is a necessary corollary of determination: the self as conduit). Spiritualist encounters were suffused with an over-abundance of affect, where a 'fact' in the world was determined by the presence of subjectivity and then returned as an effect (bells ringing, levitation, spirit hands). Spectators at such events were not mere onlookers, but were in fact witnesses of a new revelation of history in which time itself was abolished, and with it the linear idea of events.

Such visionary experience 'in the world' aspired to the conditions of history, and yet was excluded, not only by outside derision, but by its own incapacity to conform to historical determination (nor yet to the theological determination of the miraculous – of which it fell short). Excluded from history although experienced as an event, the supernatural was relegated by its own processes and procedures to pseudo-history and the marginal: *confronting* history, but incapable of being incorporated within it. Supernatural experience occurred *within* history but lacked significance: the effort of becoming an event was too great for the weight of its signification, leaving it only a mere anecdotal status. It is this dislocation that makes an hallucination an event, but prevents it from becoming history. Instead, all is determined by a certain *scenario*, a theatre of staging, witnessing and participation, at once cerebral and visceral. This scenario, according to its script, setting and direction, created a framework whose dynamic tended towards zero: a trajectory out of time altogether into the ritualistic and mythic, or precisely the plane upon which Holmes operates.

The new arts were not immune from the influence of the spirit world. Photography, that most scientific of art forms, was soon to be put to use in trying to capture the aetherial world of spirits conjured by the occultists. In photography it was felt that the fleeting and invisible would become visible and permanent. In capturing the spectral on what was already a spectral apparatus (later Doyle would hope to talk to spirits through the telephone), photographers would redeem their medium from one that was only good for recording the mundane. It happened as an accident, when William H Mumbler caught the fleeting trace of a (real) woman on his photographic plate, but others thought that this was the way into the spirit world. The loss of life in inexplicable catastrophes, such as the Commune of Paris, the American Civil War and the Great War, prompted collusion with mediums as well as experimentation with the medium.

Spirit photography took off in America, wafted to France and thence to Britain. It was most popular during the 1860s and 1870s and, curiously, it accompanies that other foray into the unknown, the pornographic photo.[1] Both were aimed at large commercial profit, and whilst some photographers were genuinely interested in ectoplasm and spiritualism most were happy to produce spoof photos of shrouded spectres and ectoplasmic extrusions. The use of white sheets to produce 'ghosts' as well as the use of 'ghost stamps'(a technical device to distort a normal picture by adding a light source not present) kept an avid public more than happy. The exhibitionist spirit medium 'Eva P' sat for nude photographs with ectoplasm coming from her vagina and sliding over her breasts, in so doing creating a spectacular and legitimated pornographic theatre of which photography became the accomplice. And yet, belief in spirit photography remained high up to the 1920s, as the only verifiable way of exhibiting the scientific proof of spiritualist phenomena. Doyle was convinced that the technology of the camera could prove the spiritual presence of the dead:

By the way, you should try for a psychic picture. ...

I always thought that that at least was fraud.

On the contrary, I should say that it was the best established of all phenomena, the one which leaves the most permanent proof. (132)

Socialism and spiritualism formed two means whereby the masses made their revolt. Yet the problem was how to reconcile these apparently opposite ideologies. Both provided for refusal and rebellion and both led to a restored harmony 'on the other side' – the other side of capitalist history. If the socialist revolution itself led to emancipation from the thrall of history, then for the spiritualist that emancipation or release came through death. Both sets of beliefs emancipated their believers into the freedom of a future as yet unrealised. The twin knowledge of death and of history, their secret occulted meanings finally revealed, allowed those who truly understood to rise above the mundane and achieve full consciousness. Such consciousness was the result of understanding the hidden processes of life and its universal or cosmic determinants.

The steady decline in established religious belief during the Victorian period amongst intellectuals, on the one hand, and the working masses, on the other, did not halt the various forms of religiosity. These were reinvented in the congruence of some sort of spiritual belief and the belief in the inevitable rise of socialism. For years non-conformism had been the backbone of Liberalism, but Liberalism (the very backbone of Doyle's beliefs) was in decline (at first very slowly), as non-conformism itself declined and the secular 'religion' of socialism took hold. Most members of the working classes did not go to any form of worship, let alone that of the very people who oppressed them; intellectuals became increasingly outspoken critics of religious superstition. The reaction of Church leaders and congregations was an important factor in modelling the collectivist tendencies in socialism into a working and coherent ideology with which to challenge Liberalism and finally defeat it.

The first specific conjunction of socialism and the Church was in 1877, when Stewart Headlam, curate of St Matthew's Bethnal Green, London (an area in the heartland of socialist concerns regarding poverty and deprivation) set up the Guild of St Matthew in order to combat the secular propaganda of people like Charles Bradlaugh, then speaking regularly in the same area for the National Secular Society. Headlam, however, did not object to Bradlaugh or his followers and regularly spoke at their venues and worked alongside them. Indeed, he vexed the Anglican establishment more than he ever worried a freethinker.

The Labour Church Movement, as such, was the creation of John Trevor, a Unitarian preacher. He finally abandoned the Bible in his early twenties, but returned with a newly-blended faith in socialism and in Christ. Trevor slowly came to the belief that a new type of religion was needed for the humble of the nineteenth century. He attended the Unitarian conference of 1885 and heard Ben Tillett talk of the lack of response from churches to what the working class needed in their lives. The workers, Tillett told the conference, were not irreligious, just spiritually ill led. To help propagate this new vision of socialist Christianity, partly inspired by the Fabian economic group to which Trevor belonged, partly by the work and organisation of the Salvation Army, and partially by the idea of a 'New Theology of Modernism', he decided to hold his first Christian experiment in Manchester in October 1891. A huge audience turned up to see trade unionist leaders Ben Tillett and Tom Mann (almost persuaded to become a preacher by Cardinal Manning, before actually becoming a communist) preach the good word. It was said that when Christ was mentioned by name there was cheering from the audience.

Doyle embraced the sense of equality and levelling of those churchmen who had effectively broken away from the orthodox Church. Nevertheless, he rejected their collectivism. Instead, for Doyle, spiritualism was essentially about individual salvation, thus reconciling the new revolution in spirituality with the status quo. He remained a Liberal at heart:

> There is no such leveller of classes as spiritualism, and the char woman with psychic force is the superior of the millionaire who lacks it. [The poor] and the aristocrats fraternize instantly. The Duchess [asked] for admission to the grocer's circle. ... It makes me see red when I remember these folk, Lady This and Countess That, declaring all the comfort they have had [from spiritualism], and then leaving those who gave it to die in the gutter or rot in the work house. (134; 164–5)

Just as Doyle tried to reconcile the supposed opposites of rationalism and spiritualism in a new unity, so Headlam and Trevor were trying to reconcile the Christian message with that of materialist socialists. Far from being deluded or a freak, Doyle was again at the centre of Victorian debate.

The reconciliation of materialism and spiritualism in Doyle's work was not, after all, the aberration of a deluded man, but was instead the fulfilment of much that Holmes stood for (and much that the age stood for, too), a rational explanation of inexplicable phenomena in a confused world. In spiritualism, Doyle reconciled his lapsed Catholicism with a new religious conviction of the survival of life after death which itself ironically confirmed and upheld his belief in the reality of the nature of material evidence, even if that material was now invisible and strange. This new revelation would kill off Holmes more surely than a fall from a high cliff because Holmes would no longer be needed to reassure us.

Of course, Doyle was often naïve, too gullible and too easily convinced, too willing to grasp at straws to prove a slim theory, but in all this he shared the delusions of his age rather than stood against them; stood, indeed, for the Victorian he was and remained 'the one fixed point in a changing age' (1981: 980), remarks Watson in the midst of the First World War. Doyle was a patriotic Liberal and imperialist, but he shared more than he realised with the anarchists and socialists whom Holmes constantly defeated, and with a Church that Doyle himself had long since forsaken. What Doyle saw was a new world order and a new beginning, not so much socialist and Christian as personal and spiritual, the final reconciliation of opposites. To him, his delusions were certainties, spiritualism the one veil Holmes could not penetrate: the final problem, finally solved.

Note

1. A longer version of this argument is to be found in Clive Bloom, *Gothic Histories* (2010). See Chapter 7.

Bibliography

Stories by Arthur Conan Doyle Cited

A Study in Scarlet (Nov. 1887)
The Sign of Four (Feb. 1890)
A Scandal in Bohemia (July 1891)
The Five Orange Pips (Nov. 1891)
The Man with the Twisted Lip (Dec. 1891)
The Adventure of the Blue Carbuncle (Jan. 1892)
The Adventure of the Speckled Band (Feb. 1892)
The Adventure of the Beryl Coronet (May 1892)
The Adventure of the Copper Beeches (June 1892)
The Adventure of Silver Blaze (Dec. 1892)
The Greek Interpreter (Sept. 1893)
The Adventure of the Naval Treaty (Oct.–Nov. 1893)
The Final Problem (Dec. 1893)
The Hound of the Baskervilles (1901–2)
The Adventure of the Empty House (Oct. 1903)
The Adventure of the Dancing Men (Dec. 1903)
The Adventure of the Solitary Cyclist (Jan. 1904)
The Adventure of the Abbey Grange (Sept. 1904)
The Adventure of the Second Stain (Dec. 1904)
The Return of Sherlock Holmes (1905)
The Adventure of the Bruce-Partington Plans (Dec. 1908)
The Adventure of the Devil's Foot (Dec. 1910)
The Adventure of the Red Circle (Mar.–Apr. 1911)
The Valley of Fear (Sept. 1914–May 1915)
His Last Bow (Sept. 1917)
The Problem of Thor Bridge (Feb.–March 1922)
The Adventure of the Sussex Vampire (Jan. 1924)
The Adventure of the Retired Colourman (Dec. 1926)
The Adventure of the Veiled Lodger (Feb. 1927)
All short stories and novellas can be found in Doyle, A. C., 1981. *The Complete Sherlock Holmes*. London: Penguin.

Feature Films, Television Programmes and Games Cited

Blade Runner, 1997. [PC Game] Westwood Studios: Virgin Interactive Entertainment.
Call of Cthulhu: Dark Corners of the Earth, 2006. [PC Game] Headfirst Productions, Bethesda Softworks.
Fairy Tale: A True Story, 1997. [Film] Directed Charles Sturridge. Paramount.
Fallout 3, 2008. [PC Game] Bethesda Game Studios, Bethesda Softworks.

French Connection II, 1975. [Film] Directed by John Frankenheimer. USA: Twentieth Century Fox Film Corporation.

Heaven's Gate, 1980. [Film] Directed by Michael Cimino. USA: United Artists Corporation, Ltd. Partisan Productions, United Artists.

Heavy Rain, 2010. [Playstation 3] Quantic Dreams, Sony Computer Entertainment.

Indiana Jones and the Temple of Doom, 1984. [Film] Directed by Steven Spielberg. USA: Paramount Pictures, Lucasfilm.

Max Payne, 2001. [PC Game] Remedy Entertainment, Gathering of Developers.

Murder by Decree, 1978. [Film] Directed by Bob Clark. UK/Canada: Saucy Jack Inc, Highlight Theatrical Production Corporation Ltd, Murder by Decree Productions, Canadian Film Development Corporation, Famous Players, Wow!!! Entertainment, Robert A. Goldston.

Murder Rooms: Mysteries of the Real Sherlock Holmes: The Dark Beginnings of Sherlock Holmes 2000. [TV] Directed by Paul Seed. London: BBC.

Murder Rooms: Mysteries of the Real Sherlock Holmes: The Photographer's Chair, 2001. [TV] Directed by Paul Marcus. London: BBC.

Murder Rooms: Mysteries of the Real Sherlock Holmes: The Patient's Eyes, 2001. [TV] Directed by Tim Fywell. London: BBC.

Photographing Fairies, 1997. [Film] Directed by Nick Willing. London: Dogstar.

Prince of Persia: The Sands of Time, 2003. [PC Game] Ubisoft Montreal, Ubisoft.

Remington Steele, 1982–1987. [TV Series] USA: MTM Enterprises.

Sherlock, A Scandal in Belgravia, 2012. [TV Programme] BBC, BBC Three, 7 January 2012, 21:00, Season 2, Episode 1, written by Steven Moffat and Mark Gatiss and directed by Paul McGuigan.

Sherlock, A Study in Pink, 2010. [TV Programme] BBC, BBC One, 25 July 2010, Season 1, Episode 1, written by Steven Moffat and Mark Gatiss and directed by Paul McGuigan.

Sherlock, The Hounds of Baskerville, 2012. [TV Programme] BBC, BBC One, 8 January 2012, Season 2, Episode 2, written by Mark Gatiss and Steven Moffat and directed by Paul McGuigan.

Sherlock Holmes, 2009. [Film] Directed by Guy Ritchie. USA: Warner Bros.

Sherlock Holmes and the Secret Weapon, 1942. [Film] Directed by Roy William Neill. USA: Universal Pictures.

Sherlock Holmes: Nemesis, 2007. [PC Game] Frogwares, Focus Home Interactive.

Sherlock Holmes: The Awakened, 2006. [PC Game] Frogwares, Focus Home Interactive.

Sherlock Holmes: The Mystery of the Mummy, 2004. [PC Game] Frogwares, Focus Home Interactive.

Sherlock Holmes vs. Jack the Ripper, 2009. [PC Game] Frogwares, Focus Home Interactive.

Star Trek: The Next Generation, Elementary, Dear Data, episode 3, 1988. [TV Programme] CBS Television, 5 December 1988.

Star Wars, 1977. [Film] Directed by George Lucas. USA: Lucasfilm, Twentieth Century Fox Film Corporation.

Superman, 1978. [Film] Directed by Richard Donner. USA: Alexander Salkind, Dovemead Films, Film Export A.G.

The Adventures of Sherlock Holmes, 1984–92. [TV Programme] Granada, 1984–92.

The Adventure of Sherlock Holmes' Smarter Brother, 1975. [Film] Directed by Gene Wilder. USA: Jouer Films, Twentieth Century Fox Film Corporation.

The Case of the Whitechapel Vampire, 2002. [Film] Directed by Rodney Gibbons. UK: The Hallmark Channel.

The Great Mouse Detective, 1986. [Film] Directed by Ron Clements and John Musker. USA: Walt Disney Pictures, Silver Screen Partners II.

The Hound of the Baskervilles, 1988. [TV Film] Directed by Brian Mills. UK: Granada Television, WGBH.

The Hound of the Baskervilles, 1978. [Film] Directed by Paul Morrissey. UK: Michael White Productions.

The Hound of the Baskervilles, 1939. [Film] Directed by Sidney Lanfield. UK: Twentieth Century Fox Film Corporation.

The Panic in Needle Park, 1971. [Film] Directed by Jerry Schatzberg. USA: Gadd Productions Corp., Didion-Dunne.

The Private Life of Sherlock Holmes, 1970. [Film] Directed by Billy Wilder. UK/USA: Phalanx Productions, Inc. Mirisch Productions, Mirisch Films Limited, Sir Nigel Films, The Mirisch Production Company.

The Searchers, 1956. [Film] Directed by John Ford. USA: Warner Bros. Pictures, C.V. Whitney Pictures.

The Seven-Per-Cent Solution, 1976. [Film] Directed by Herbert Ross. UK/USA: Herbert Ross Productions, Universal Pictures.

The Silence of the Lambs, 1991. [Film] Directed by Jonathan Demme. USA: Strong Heart/Demme Production, Orion Pictures Corporation.

Without a Clue, 1988. [Film] Directed by Thom E. Eberhardt. UK: Incorporated Television Company.

Young Sherlock Holmes, 1985. [Film] Directed by Barry Levinson. USA: Amblin Entertainment, Industrial Light & Magic, Paramount Pictures.

Works Cited

Alexander, B., 1995. *Blind Justice*. New York, Berkley Prime Crime.

Arias, R. and Pulham, P. (eds) 2009. *Haunting and Spectrality: Possessing the Past*. Basingstoke: Palgrave Macmillan.

Ashton, D., 2009. *A Trick of the Light*. Edinburgh, Polygon.

Auden, W. H., 1988 (1962). The Guilty Vicarage. In: R. W. Winks (ed.) *Detective Fiction: A Collection of Critical Essays*. Woodstock, Vermont: Countryman Press.

Bach, S., 1985. *Final Cut: Dreams and Disaster in the Making of Heaven's Gate*. London and Boston: Faber and Faber.

Bailey, P., 1994. Holmes Flares up Again. *The Guardian*, 8 March, p. 9.

Balio, T., 1985. *The American Film Industry*. Revised edn. Madison, Wisc. and London: University of Wisconsin Press.

Banhart, R. (ed.) 2006. *Chambers Dictionary of Etymology*. New York: Chambers.

Banks-Smith, N., 1993. Snapshots. *The Guardian*, 28 January, p. 10.

—— 1992. Holmes and the Playful Dowager. *The Guardian*, 3 January, p. 28.

Baring-Gould, W. S., 1962. *Sherlock Holmes: A Biography*. London: Rupert Hart-Davis.

Barnes, A., 2004. *Sherlock Holmes on Screen*. London: Reynolds and Hearn.

Barnes, J. 2005. *Arthur & George*. London: Vintage.

Barsham, D., 2000. *Arthur Conan Doyle and the Meaning of Masculinity*. Aldershot: Ashgate.

Batory, D. M., 1988. 'Was Watson an Uncle?' *The Baker Street Journal: An Irregular Quarterly of Sherlockiana*, June, 38 (2), 78–81.

Baudelaire, C., 2010 (1863). *The Painter of Modern Life*. Translated from French by P.E. Charvet. London: Penguin.

Baudrillard, J., 1977. *Forget Foucault*. Translated from French in 1987 (translator not cited). New York: Semiotext(e).

Baudrillard, J., 1994. *Simulacra and Simulation*. Translated from French by S. Glaser. Ann Arbor: The University of Michigan Press.

Bayard, P., 2008. *Sherlock Holmes Was Wrong: Re-opening the Case of the Hound of the Baskervilles*. London: Bloomsbury.

Bayley, J., 1960. *The Characters of Love*. London: Constable.

BBC News Online, 2008. Law to Star in Ritchie's *Sherlock*. [BBC News Online]. 1 October 2008. Available at: http://news.bbc.co.uk/1/hi/entertainment/7646463.stm [Accessed 4 July 2011].

Bechhofer-Roberts, C. E., 2007. *The Truth about Spiritualism*. Whitefish, MT: Kessinger Publishing.

Benzikie, S., 1992. Analysts Fear New Drama at Granada. *Daily Mail*, Wednesday 5 February, p. 39.

Berberich, C., 2011. 'All Letters Quoted are Authentic': The Past after Postmodern Fabulation in Julian Barnes's *Arthur & George*. In: S. Groes and P. Childs (eds) *Julian Barnes: Contemporary Critical Perspectives*. London and New York: Continuum, 117–28.

Binyon, T. J., 1989. '*Murder Will Out*': The Detective in Fiction. Oxford and New York: Oxford University Press.

Biressi, A., 2001. *Crime, Fear and the Law in True Crime Stories*. Basingstoke: Palgrave.

Bloom, C., 2010. *Gothic Histories: The Taste for Terror, 1964 to the Present*. London: Continum.

Bonner, H., 1992. Why Shock Sacking of Granada's Boss Poses Threat to ITV. *Daily Mirror*, Wednesday, 5 February, p. 6.

Booth, M., 1997. *The Doctor, the Detective, and Arthur Conan Doyle*. London: Hodder & Stoughton.

Brandreth, G., 2010. *Oscar Wilde and the Nest of Vipers*. London: John Murray.

—— 2009. *Oscar Wilde and the Dead Man's Smile*. London: John Murray.

—— 2008. *Oscar Wilde and the Ring of Death*. London: John Murray.

—— 2007. *Oscar Wilde and the Candlelight Murders*. London: John Murray.

Brewster, B. and Jacobs, L., 1997. *Theatre to Cinema*. Oxford and New York: Oxford University Press.

Broadcasting Research Unit, 1989. Quality in Television. London: John Libbey.

Brooks, P., 1993. *Body Work: Objects of Desire in Modern Narrative*. Cambridge, Mass.: Harvard University Press.

Brown, P. and Sparks, R., 1989. *Beyond Thatcherism: Social Policy, Politics and Society*. Milton Keynes: Open University Press.

Browning, E. B., 1993. *Aurora Leigh*. Oxford: Oxford World's Classics.

Brunsdon, C., 1990. Problems with Quality. *Screen*, 31 (1) Spring Issue, 67–90.

Burgess, A., 1989. *The Devil's Mode*. London: Hutchinson.

Byatt, A. S., 1990. *Possession*. London: Chatto & Windus.
Caillois, R., 1983. The Detective Novel as a Game. In: G. W. Most and W. W. Stowe (eds) *The Poetics of Murder: Detective Fiction and Literary Theory*. San Diego, CA: Harcourt Brace Jovanovich.
—— 1961. *Man, Play, and Games*. Translated from French by M. Barash. New York: Free Press of Glencoe.
Calanchi, A. (ed.) 2007. *Linguæ &: Rivista di lingue e culture moderne*, 2. Urbino: University of Urbino. [online] Available at: http://www.ledonline.it/linguæ/
Campbell, M., 2007. *Sherlock Holmes*. Harpenden, Herts.: Pocket Essentials, Kindle edition.
Carr, C., 2005. *The Italian Secretary: A Further Adventure of Sherlock Holmes*. New York: Carroll & Graf.
Carr, John Dickson, 1949. *The Life of Sir Arthur Conan Doyle*. London: John Murray.
Cartmell, D., Hunter, I.Q. and Whelehan, I. (eds) 2001. *Retrovisions: Reinventing the Past in Film and Fiction*. London: Pluto Press.
Cavalcanti, A., 1938. Comedies and Cartoons. In: C. Davy (ed.) *Footnotes to the Film*. London: Lovat Dickson Ltd., Reader's Union Ltd.
Charney, L. and Schwartz, V.R. (eds) 1995. *Cinema and the Invention of Modern Life*. Berkeley, Los Angeles, and London: University of California Press.
Clover, C.J., 1992. *Men, Women, and Chainsaws*. London: BFI.
Cohen, M., 2000. *Murder Most Fair: The Appeal of Mystery Fiction*. London: Associated University Presses.
Cook, D. A., 2000. *Lost Illusions: American Cinema in the Shadow of Watergate and Vietnam 1970–1979*. Berkeley, Los Angeles, London: University of California Press.
—— 1996. *A History of Narrative Film*. 3rd edn. New York and London: W.W. Norton and Co.
Costello, P., 1991. *The Real World of Sherlock Holmes*. London: Robinson Publishing.
Cox, M., 1997. *The Baker Street File: A Guide to the Appearance and Habits of Sherlock Holmes and Dr Watson, Specially Prepared for the Granada Television Series*. Chester: Calabash Press.
Crider, B., 2004. *We'll Always Have Murder*. New York: New York Books.\
Crovi, L. 2002. *Tutti i colori del giallo: il giallo italiano da De Marchi a Scerbanenco a Camilleri*. Venice: Marsilio Editori.
—— 2000. *Deliti di carta nostra: una storia del giallo italiano*. Bologna: Puntozero Editrice.
Crowther, B., 1943. Sherlock Holmes and the Secret Weapon. *The New York Times*, 5 January.
Davies, D. S., 2007. *Starring Sherlock Holmes*, with a foreword by I. Richardson. London: Titan Books.
Davy, C. (ed.) 1938. *Footnotes to the Film*. London: Lovat Dickson Ltd., Reader's Union Ltd.
DeLanda, M., 2006. *A New Philosophy of Society: Assemblage Theory and Social Complexity*. London: Continuum.
—— 2002. *Intensive Science and Virtual Philosophy*. London: Continuum.
Deleuze, G., 1994. *Difference and Repetition*. Translated from French by P. Patton. London: The Athlone Press.

Deleuze, G. and Guattari, F., 1987. *A Thousand Plateaus : Capitalism and Schizophrenia.* Translated from French by B. Massumi. London: Continuum.

Derecho, A., 2006. Archontic Literature: A Definition, a History, and Several Theories of Fan Fiction. In: K. Hellekson and K. Busse (eds) *Fan Fiction and Fan Communities in the Age of the Internet: New Essays.* Jefferson, NC and London: McFarland & Company, Kindle edition.

Derrida, J., 1995. Archive Fever: A Freudian Impression. Translated from French by Eric Prenowitz. *Diacritics*, 25, 9–63.

Dibdin, M., 1978. *The Last Sherlock Holmes Story.* New York: Pantheon Books.

Ditka, V., 2003. *Recycled Culture in Contemporary Art and Film: The Uses of Nostalgia.* Cambridge: University of Cambridge Press.

Douglas, C. N., 2005 (1990). *Good Night, Mr. Holmes.* New York, NY: Forge Books.

—— 2005 (2004). *Spider Dance.* New York, NY: Forge Books.

—— 2002. *Castle Rouge.* New York, NY: Forge Books.

Douglas, J., 1989. Review: The Changing Tide – Some Recent Studies of Thatcherism. *British Journal of Political Science*, July, 19 (3), 399–424.

Doyle, A. C. Diaries (unpublished). British Library Manuscripts.

—— 2011. *The Narrative of John Smith.* London: British Library.

——2010. The Captain of the 'Pole-Star'. In: *The Captain of the Polestar and Other Tales.* London: The British Library.

—— 2006. *The Land of Mist.* London: Dodo Press.

—— 2002. *The Hound of the Baskervilles.* New York, Modern Paperback Editions.

—— 1997. The Adventure of the Bruce-Partington Plans. In: *His Last Bow.* London: Penguin Books.

—— 1989 (1924). *Memories and Adventures.* Oxford: Oxford University Press.

—— 1981 (1930). Preface to *The Case-book of Sherlock Holmes.* In: *The Complete Sherlock Holmes.* 1981. London: Penguin, 983–4.

——1973 (1929). *Sherlock Holmes: A Study in Scarlet; The Sign of Four; The Hound of the Baskervilles; The Valley of Fear: The Complete Long Stories.* London: Murray.

—— 1971 (1928). *Sherlock Holmes: His Adventures; Memoirs; Return; His Last Bow and The Case-book: The Complete Short Stories.* London: Murray.

—— 1951. The Retired Colourman. In: *The Case-Book of Sherlock Holmes.* London: Penguin Books.

—— 1938. *The New Revelation and The Vital Message.* London: Psychic Book Club.

—— 1912. *The Lost World.* London: Hodder & Stoughton.

—— 1907. *Through the Magic Door.* London: Smith, Elder.

—— 1895. *The Mystery of Cloomber.* New York: R. F. Fenno.

—— Southsea Notebooks (unpublished). Private Collection.

Doyle, A. and Carr, J. D., 1954. *The Exploits of Sherlock Holmes.* London: J. Murray.

—— 1954. *The Exploits of Sherlock Holmes.* London: J. Murray.

Doyle, A. C. and Stoker, B., 2009. *The Parasite* and *The Watter's Mou',* edited by C. Wynne. Kansas: Valancourt.

Doyle, S. and Crowder, D. A., 2010. *Sherlock Holmes for Dummies.* Indianapolis, IN: Wiley Pub., Inc.

Dudley Edwards, O., 1983. *The Quest for Sherlock Holmes.* London: Penguin.

Duncan, A., 2008. *Eliminate the Impossible.* London: MX Publishing.

Eco, U., 1989 (1985). *Reflections on The Name of the Rose.* Translated from Italian by W. Weaver. London: Secker & Warburg.

Eco, U. and Sebeok, T. A. (eds) 1983. *The Sign of Three: Holmes, Dupin, Peirce.* Bloomington, Ind.: Indiana University Press.

Edginton, I., 2011. *Victorian Undead: Sherlock Holmes vs. Dracula.* London: Titan.

Ellis, J., 1992. *Visible Fictions: Cinema, Television, Video.* London: Routledge.

Elsaesser, T. (ed.) 1990. *Early Cinema: Space, Frame, Narrative.* London: BFI.

Engel, H., 1997. *Mr. Doyle and Dr. Bell. Woodstock* New York: Overlook.

Estleman, L. D., 1978. *Sherlock Holmes vs. Dracula or The Adventure of the Sanguinary Count.* London: New English Times Mirror.

Evans, S., 1997. Thatcher and the Victorians: A Suitable Case for Comparison? *History,* 82 (268), 601–20.

Field, A. J., 2009. *England's Secret Weapon: The Wartime Films of Sherlock Holmes.* London: Middlesex University Press.

Fiske, J., 2003. *Television Culture.* London: Routledge.

Freud, S., 2003. *The Uncanny.* Translated from German by D. McClintock. London: Penguin.

—— 2001. *A Case of Hysteria, Three Essays on Sexuality, and Other Works.* In: *The Standard Edition of the Complete Psychological Works of Sigmund Freud.* Translated from German by J. Strachey. Vintage: The Hogarth Press, VII (1901–1905).

—— 1984. Notes upon a Case of Obsessional Neurosis ['The Rat Man']. In: *Case Histories II,* Pelican Freud Library, vol. 9. Harmondsworth: Pelican, 36–128.

——1955. The Uncanny. In: *The Standard Edition of the Complete Psychological Works of Sigmund Freud, Vol. XVII (1917–1919): An Infantile Neurosis and Other Works,* 217–53. Translated from German by James Strachey. London: The Hogarth Press and the Institute of Psychoanalysis.

Frost, M., 1996. *The Six Messiahs.* New York: Avon.

—— 1993. *The List of Seven.* New York: William Morrow.

Fry, S., 2008. The BBC and the Future of Public Service Broadcasting, 7 May. [online] Available at: http://www.bbc.co.uk/thefuture/transcript_fry2.shtml [Accessed 17 July 2009].

Gay, P., Johston, J., Waters, C. (eds) 2008. *Victorian Turns, Neo-Victorian Returns.* Newcastle: Cambridge Scholars.

Genette, G., 1982. *Palimpsests: Literature in the Second Degree.* Translated from French by C. Newman and C. Doubinsky, foreword by G. Prince, 1997. Lincoln and London: University of Nebraska Press.

Gibson, J. M. and Lancelyn Green, R. (eds) 1986. *Letters to the Press: The Unknown Conan Doyle:* London: Secker & Warburg.

—— 1982. *Essays on Photography: The Unknown Conan Doyle.* London: Secker & Warburg.

—— (eds) 1982. *Uncollected Stories: The Unknown Conan Doyle.* London: Secker & Warburg.

Gorky, M., 1996. The Kingdom of Shadows. In: K. MacDonald and M. Cousins (eds) *Imagining Reality: The Faber Book of Documentary.* London and Boston: Faber and Faber.

Goulart, R., 1998. *Groucho Marx, Master Detective.* New York: St Martin's Press.

Grann, D., 2004. Mysterious Circumstances. *The New Yorker,* 13 Dec.

Greene, H. (ed.) 1971. *The Rivals of Sherlock Holmes.* London: Bodley Head.

Gurney, E., F. W. Myers and F. Podmore, 1886. *Phantasms of the Living.* London: Trübner and Co.

Gutleben, C., 2001. *Nostalgic Postmodernism: The Victorian Tradition and the Contemporary British Novel*. Amsterdam: Rodopi.

Haddon, M., 2003. *The Curious Incident of the Dog in the Night-time*. London: Jonathan Cape.

Haining, P., (ed.) 1980. *A Sherlock Holmes Compendium*. London: W. H. Allen.

—— 1973. *The Sherlock Holmes Scrapbook; Fifty Years of Occasional Articles, Newspaper Cuttings, Letters, Memoirs, Anecdotes, Pictures, Photographs and Drawings Relating to the Great Detective*. London: New English Library.

Hall, S., 1983. The Great Moving Right Show. In: S. Hall and M. Jacques (eds) *The Politics of Thatcherism*. London: Lawrence and Wishart.

Hanna, E. B., 1993. *The Whitechapel Horrors*. New York: Carroll and Graf.

Harper, K., 1999. *The Poyson Garden*. New York: Dell Books.

Harris, P., 1984. Sherlock Holmes Returns to Uncover Foul Deeds. *The Globe and Mail* (Canada), Saturday 11 August.

Harris, T., 1999. *Hannibal*. New York: Delacorte Press.

—— 1988. *The Silence of the Lambs*. New York: St. Martin's Press.

—— 1981. *Red Dragon*. New York: G.P. Putnams, Dell Publishing.

Harrison, M., 1975. *The World of Sherlock Holmes*. New York: Dutton.

Healey, M., 2008. *What is Branding?* Mies, Switzerland: Rotovision.

Heavy Rain official website. [online] Available at: http://www.heavyrainps3.com [Accessed 29 July 2010].

Heilmann, A. and Llewellyn, M., 2010. *Neo-Victorianism: The Victorians in the Twenty-first Century, 1999–2009*. Hampshire: Palgrave Macmillan.

Higson, A., 2006. Re-presenting the National Past: Nostalgia and Pastiche in the Heritage Film. In: L. D Friedman (ed.) *Fires Were Started: British Cinema and Thatcherism*, 2nd edn. London: Wallflower.

Hjortsberg, W., 1994. *Nevermore*. New York: St Martin's Press.

Hodgson, J. A., 1994. The Recoil of 'The Speckled Band': Detective Story and Detective Discourse. In: J.A. Hodgson (ed.) *Sherlock Holmes: The Major Stories with Contemporary Critical Essays*. Boston, MA: Bedford Books.

Hoffmann, E. T. A., 1982. The Sandman. In: *Tales of Hoffmann*. Translated from German by R. J. Hollingdale et al. London: Penguin, 85–125.

Holt, D. B., 2004. *How Brands Become Icons*. Harvard: Harvard Business School Press.

Hornung, E. W., 1996. *The Collected Raffles Stories*. Oxford: Oxford University Press.

Horowitz, A., 2011. *The House of Silk: The New Sherlock Holmes Novel*. Kindle edition.

House of Commons, 1999. *A Century of Change: Trends in UK Statistics Since 1900*, House of Commons Research Paper 99/111, 21 December 1999 (14). Available at: http://www.parliament.uk/commons/lib/research/rp99/rp99–111.pdf. [Accessed 09/12/2010].

Hutcheon, L., 1989. *The Politics of Postmodernism*. London and New York: Routledge. IGN.com. [online] Available at: http://uk.guides.ign.com/ guides/811232 [accessed 29 July 2010].

Irwin, J. T., 2006. *Unless the Threat of Death is behind Them: Hard-boiled Fiction and Film Noir*. Baltimore, MD: The Johns Hopkins University Press.

Itzkoff, D., 2010. For the Heirs to Holmes, A Tangled Web. *New York Times*, 19 January.

Jackson, K., 1993. Underrated: A Jigger of Remorse, a Dash of Lunacy; Overdue Credit Where Credit's Due. *The Independent*, 20 October, p. 26.

Jacques, M., 1983. Thatcherism – Breaking out the Impasse. In: S. Hall and M. Jacques (eds) *The Politics of Thatcherism*. London: Lawrence and Wishart.

James, P. D., 2009. *Talking about Detective Fiction*. Oxford: The Bodleian Library.

Jameson, F., 1991. *Postmodernism, or the Cultural Logic of Late Capitalism*. Durham, NC: Duke University Press.

Jeffords, S., 1994. *Hard Bodies: Hollywood Masculinity in the Reagan Era*. New Brunswick, NJ: Rutgers University Press.

Jenkins, R., 1995. *Gladstone*. London: Macmillan.

Jhally, S., 1990. *The Codes of Advertising: Fetishism and the Political Economy of Meaning in the Consumer Society*. New York: Routledge.

Johnsen, R. E., 2006. *Contemporary Feminist Historical Crime Fiction*. New York: Palgrave Macmillan.

Joyce, S., 2007. *The Victorians in the Rearview Mirror*. Athens, OH: Ohio University Press.

Juul, J., 2005. *Half-real: Video Games between Real Rules and Fictional Worlds*. Cambridge, Mass. and London: The MIT Press.

Kalush, W., and Sloman, L. R. 2006. *The Secret Life of Houdini*. London: Atria.

Kaplan, C., 2007. *Victoriana: Histories, Fictions, Criticism*. Edinburgh: Edinburgh University Press.

Kayman, M.A., 1992. *From Bow Street to Baker Street: Mystery, Detection and Narrative*. London: Macmillan.

Keay, J., 1987. *The Spy Who Never Was: The Life and Loves of Mata Hari*. London: Michael Joseph.

Keefauver, B., 2001. *Sherlock Peoria website. Chronology*. [online] Available at: http://www.sherlockpeoria.net/Who_is_Sherlock/SherlockTimeline.html [Accessed 29 July 2010].

Kestner, J.A., 1997. *Sherlock's Men: Masculinity, Conan Doyle and Cultural History*. Vermont and Aldershot: Ashgate.

Kidd, C. and Williamson, D. (eds) 2000. *Debrett's Peerage and Baronetage*. London: Debrett's Peerage.

King, L.R., 2010. *The God of the Hive*. London: Allison and Busby.

—— 2010. LRK on: Sherlock Holmes. Laurie R. King Website. [online] Available at: http://www.laurierking.com/etcetera/lrk-on-holmes [Accessed 29 July 2010].

——2010 (2009). *The Language of Bees*. London: Allison and Busby.

——2006 (2005). *Locked Rooms*. New York, NY: Bantam Books.

—— 2005 (1994). *The Beekeeper's Apprentice or On the Segregation of the Queen*. New York and London: Bantam Books.

—— 2004. *The Game*. London: Allison and Busby.

—— 2002 (1998). *The Moor*. London: Harper Collins Publishers.

Kingsley, H., 1986. In My View. *Daily Mirror*, Thursday, 7 August, p. 19.

—— 1984. In My View: It's Not So Elementary. *Daily Mirror*, Wednesday, 25 April, p. 19.

Kipling, R., 1901. *Kim*. London: Macmillan.

Knight, S., 1976. *Jack the Ripper: The Final Solution*. London: Harrap.

Knight, S. T., 1980. *Form and Ideology in Crime Fiction*. Basingstoke: Macmillan.

Knox, R. A., 1928. Studies in the Literature of Sherlock Holmes. In: *Essays in Satire*. London: Sheed and Ward, 145–75.

Kohlke, M. L., 2008. Speculations in and on the Neo-Victorian Encounter. *Journal of Neo-Victorian Studies* [online], 1 (1). Available at: http://www.neovictorianstudies.com/ [Accessed 31 July 2010].

Kramer, P. and Grieveson, L. (eds) 2004. *The Silent Cinema Reader*. London and New York: Routledge.

Krueger, C.L. (ed.) 2002. *Functions of Victorian Culture at the Present Time*. Athens: Ohio University Press.

Kucala, B., 2009. The Erosion of Victorian Discourses in Julian Barnes's *Arthur & George*. *American, British and Canadian Studies, Special Issue: Worlds within Words: Twenty-first Century Visions on the Work of Julian Barnes*, 13, 61–73.

Lamond. J., 1931. *Arthur Conan Doyle: A Memoir*. London: John Murray.

Lancelyn Green, R. and Gibson, W. M. (eds) 2000 (1983). *A Bibliography of A. Conan Doyle*. Boston: Hudson House.

Lancelyn Green, R. (ed.) 1985. *Letters to Sherlock Holmes*: Selected by Richard Lancelyn Green. London: Penguin.

Leff, L. J., 1980. A Test of American Film Censorship: *Who's afraid of Virginia Woolf?* (1966). *Cinema Journal*, Spring, 19 (2), 41–55.

Leggett, B., 2009. Alternatives to Metanarrative in the Work of Julian Barnes. *American, British and Canadian Studies, Special Issue: Worlds within Words: Twenty-first Century Visions on the Work of Julian Barnes*, 13, 26–38.

Lejeune, A., 1991. *The C. A. Lejeune Film Reader*. Manchester: Carcanet.

Lellenberg, J., D. Stashower and C. Foley (eds) 2007. *Arthur Conan Doyle: A Life in Letters*. London: HarperPress.

Leonard, T. J., 2005. *Talking to the Other Side: A History of Modern Spiritualism and Mediumship*. Lincoln: iUniverse.

Lombroso, C., 2006. *Criminal Man (L'uomo delinquente)*. Translated from Italian by M. Gibson and N. Hahn Rafter. Durham, NC: Duke University Press.

Lussu, J., 2008. *Opere scelte*. Ancona: Il Lavoro Editoriale.

—— 1986. *Storie*. Ancona and Bologna: Il Lavoro Editoriale.

—— 1982. *Sherlock Holmes: anarchici e siluri*. Ancona and Bologna: Il Lavoro Editoriale.

Lycett, A., 2007. *Conan Doyle: The Man Who Created Sherlock Holmes*. London: Weidenfeld & Nicolson.

Maugham, W. S., 1967. *On Literature*. London: New English Library.

McFarlane, B., 1996. *Novel to Film: An Introduction to the Theory of Adaptation*. Oxford: Clarendon.

McHale, B., 1987. *Postmodernist Fiction*. New York and London: Methuen.

Meyer, N., 1974. *The Seven-per-cent Solution: Being a Reprint from the Reminiscences of John H. Watson, M.D.* New York: Dutton.

Michaels, B., 1999. *Other Worlds*. New York: Harper Collins.

Miller, C., 1994. Last Night's TV. *Daily Express*, Tuesday, 8 March, p. 47.

Miller, R., 2008. *The Adventures of Arthur Conan Doyle*. London: Harvill Secker.

Milner, J. D., 2004. Paget, Sidney Edward (1860–1908), rev. Mark Pottle, *Oxford Dictionary of National Biography*. Oxford: Oxford University Press. [On-line] Available at: http://www.oxforddnb.com/view/article/35359 [Accessed 27 Jan 2012].

Monaco, J., 1979. *American Film Now*. New York, London and Scarborough, Ont.: New American Library.

Moore, G., 2010. *The Sherlockian*. New York: Twelve, Hachette Book Group.

Morley, C. (ed.) 1981. *The Penguin Complete Sherlock Holmes*. Harmondsworth: Penguin.

Morris, G., 1979. The Private Films of Billy Wilder. *Film Comment*, Jan/Feb, 15 (1), 34–9.

Mosley, C. (ed.) 2003. *Burke's Peerage, Baronetage and Knightage, Clan Chiefs, Scottish Feudal Barons*. Wilmington, Del: Burke's Peerage & Gentry.

'Mr Punch's Personalities': *Punch or the London Charivari* 170 (12 May 1926), 517.

Mukherjee, S., 2012. EgoShooting in Chernobyl: Identity and Subject(s) in the S.T.A.L.K.E.R Games. In: J. Fromme and A. Unger (eds) *Handbook of Digital Game Cultures*. Dordrecht: Springer Netherlands.

Murray, J., 1997. *Hamlet on the Holodeck: The Future of Narrative in Cyberspace*. New York and London: Free Press.

Nadel, A. , 1997. *Flatlining on the Field of Dreams*. New Brunswick, New Jersey and London: Rutgers University Press.

Nead, L., 2000. *Victorian Babylon: People, Streets and Images in Nineteenth-Century London*. London: Yale University Press.

Nicol, B., 2011. Detective Fiction and the 'Original Crime': Baudrillard, Calle, Poe. *Cultural Politics*, November, 7 (3), 445–63.

Nollen, S. A., 2004 (1996). *Sir Arthur Conan Doyle at the Cinema: A Critical Study of the Film Adaptations*. London: McFarland and Co.

Norbu, J., 1999. *The Mandala of Sherlock Holmes: The Adventures of the Great Detective in Tibet*. New Delhi: Harper Collins Publishers.

Nordon, P., 1966. *Conan Doyle*, trans. Frances Partridge. London: John Murray.

Oak Taylor-Ide, J., 2005. Ritual and Liminality of Sherlock Holmes in *The Sign of Four* and *The Hound of the Baskervilles*. *English Literature in Transition, 1880–1920*, 48 (1), 55–70.

Osborne, R., 1995. Crime and the Media: From Media Studies to Post-Modernism. In: D. Kidd-Hewitt and R. Osborne (eds) *Crime and the Media: The Post-Modern Spectacle*. London: Pluto.

Owen, A., 2004. *The Darkened Room: Women, Power, and Spiritualism in Late Victorian England*. Chicago and London: University of Chicago Press.

Paterson, P., 1994. Definitive My Dear Holmes. *Daily Mail*, 8 March, p. 29.

Paton, M., 1994. Last Night's TV. *Daily Express*, 22 March, p. 29.

Perdue, P., 2009. Did You Notice Nothing Curious about That Advertisement. *Baker Street Journal Christmas Annual*. Indianapolis: BSJ.

Pirani, R. (ed.) 1999. *Le piste di Sherlock Holmes*. Pontassieve, Florence: Pirani Bibliografica Editrice.

Pirie, D. 2006. *The Dark Water*. London: Arrow.

—— 2004. *The Night Calls*. London: Arrow.

—— 2001. *The Patient's Eyes*. London: Arrow.

Pittard, C., 2007. Cheap, Healthful Literature: *The Strand Magazine*, Fictions of Crime, and Purified Reading Communities. *Victorian Periodicals Review*, 40 (1), 1–24.

Plain, G., 2001. *Twentieth-century Crime Fiction: Gender, Sexuality and the Body*. Edinburgh: Edinburgh University Press.

Poe, E. A., 2001 (1972). The Murders in the Rue Morgue. In: *Tales of Mystery and Imagination*. Oxford: World's Classics, 94–138.

Pointer, M., 1976. *The Sherlock Holmes File*. Newton Abbot: David & Charles.
Priestman, M., 2000. Sherlock's Children: The Birth of the Series. In: W. Chernaik, M. Swales and R. Vilain (eds) 2000. *The Art of Detective Fiction*, Basingstoke, England; New York, NY: Macmillan; St. Martin's, with Institute of English Studies, School of Advanced Study, University of London, 50–9.
Prince, S., 2000. *A New Pot of Gold: Hollywood under the Electronic Rainbow 1980–1989*. New York: Charles Scribner's Sons.
Pringle, H., 2004. *Celebrity Sells*. Chichester: John Wiley.
Pugh, S., 2005. *The Democratic Genre: Fan Fiction in a Literary Context*. Bridgend: Seren.
Queen, E. (ed.) 1944. *The Misadventures of Sherlock Holmes*. Boston: Little, Brown & Co.
Ratcliffe, P., 2007. *At Holmes with Doyle*. [online] Available at: http://atholmes-withdoyle.co.uk/joseph_bell.aspx [Accessed 4 April 2010].
Reaves, M. and Pelan, J. (eds) 2003. *Shadows over Baker Street*, 1st edn. New York: Ballantine Books.
Redmond, C., 2009. *A Sherlock Holmes Handbook*. 2nd edn. Ontario and Tonawanda: Dundurn Press.
Reiner, R., 2000. *The Politics of the Police*, 3rd edn.Oxford: Oxford University Press.
Rennison, N., 2005. *Sherlock Holmes: The Unauthorized Biography*. London: Atlantic.
Risinger, D. M., 2007. Boxes in Boxes: Julian Barnes, Conan Doyle, Sherlock Holmes and the Edalji Case. [online] Available at: http://www.bepress.com/ice/vol4/iss2/art3 [Accessed 3 November 2010].
Roberts, S. C., 1984. A Biographical Sketch of Sherlock Holmes. In: P. Shreffler (ed.) *The Baker Street Reader: Cornerstone Writings about Sherlock Holmes*. London: Greenwood Press.
Rogow, R., 2002. *The Problem of the Surly Servant*. London: Hale.
—— 2001. *The Problem of the Evil Editor*. London: Hale.
—— 1999. *The Problem of the Spiteful Spiritualist*. London: Hale.
—— 1998. *The Problem of the Missing Hoyden*. London: Hale.
Roman, K., 2004. David Ogilvy: The Most Famous Advertising Man in the World. Speech to University Club, New York 17 November 2004. [online] Available at: web.mclink.it/MC8216/m/ogilvy2.htm [Accessed September 2010].
Rosenberg, S., 1974. *Naked is the Best Disguise; The Death and Resurrection of Sherlock Holmes*. Indianapolis: Bobbs-Merrill.
Roudiez, L. S. (ed.) 1980. *Desire in Language: A Semiotic Approach to Literature and Art by Julia Kristeva*. Oxford: Basil Blackwell.
Rubin, M., 1999. *Thrillers*. Cambridge: Cambridge University Press.
Rumbelow, D., 1987. *The Complete Jack the Ripper*. Revised edn. London and New York: Penguin.
Saler, M., 2003. 'Clap if You Believe in Sherlock Holmes': Mass Culture and the Re-enchantment of Modernity c. 1890–c.1940. *The Historical Journal*, 46 (3), 599–622.
Samuel, R., 1992. Mrs. Thatcher's Return to Victorian Values. In: T. C. Smout (ed.) *Victorian Values: A Joint Symposium of the Royal Society of Edinburgh and the British Academy December 1990*. Oxford: Oxford University Press.
Satterthwait, W., 1995. *Escapade*. New York: St Martin's Press.

Save Undershaw. [Online at] http://www.saveundershaw.com/ (Accessed 15 December 2012).

Sebeok, T., 1997. Give me Another Horse. In: R. Capozzi (ed.) *Reading Eco: An Anthology*. Bloomington and Indianapolis, Ind.: Indiana University Press, 276–83.

Sebeok, T. A. and Margolis, H., 1982. Captain Nemo's Porthole: Semiotics of Windows in Sherlock Holmes. *Poetics Today*, 3 (1), 111–39.

Sesto, B., 2001. *Language, History and Metanarrative in the Fiction of Julian Barnes*. New York: Peter Lang.

Shankardass, R. D., 1989. Ten Years of Thatcherism in Historical Perspective: Conservatism in Britain. *Economic and Political Weekly*, 23–30 December, 24 (51/52), 2849–58.

Sherard, R., 1916. *The Real Oscar Wilde*. London: T.W. Laurie.

—— 1906. *The Life of Oscar Wilde*. London: T.W. Laurie.

—— 1902. *Oscar Wilde: The Story of an Unhappy Friendship*. London: The Hermes Press.

Sidney Paget: Iconic Illustrator of Sherlock Holmes. [Online at] http://ve.torontopubliclibrary.ca/sidney_paget/holmes.html. Accessed 15 November 2011.

Singer, B., 1995. Modernity, Hyperstimulus, and the Rise of Popular Sensationalism. In: L. Charney and Vanessa R. Schwartz (eds) *Cinema and the Invention of Modern Life*. Berkeley, Los Angeles, and London: University of California Press.

Smee, S., 2005. The Curious Case of the Slashed Horse. *The Spectator*, 9 July, p. 34.

Smiles, S., 1866 (1859). *Self-help; With Illustrations of Character, Conduct, and Perseverance*. London: John Murray.

Solito, E. and Salvatori, G. (eds) 2010. Italy and Sherlock Holmes. (The Baker Street Irregulars International Series) *Baker Street Journal*. [online] Available at: http://www.bakerstreetjournal.com.

Starrett, V., 1974. Introduction to William Gillette's Play, *Sherlock Holmes*. Santa Barbara: Helan Halbach.

Stashower, D., 1999. *Teller of Tales: The Life of Arthur Conan Doyle*. London: Penguin.

Stasi, M., 2006. The Toy Soldiers from Leeds: The Slash Palimpsest. In: K. Hellekson and K. Busse (eds) 2006. *Fan Fiction and Fan Communities in the Age of the Internet: New Essays*. Jefferson, NC and London: McFarland & Company, Kindle edition.

Stephenson, A., 1989. Regarding Postmodernism: A Conversation with Frederic Jameson. In: A. Ross (ed.) *Universal Abandon?: The Politics of Postmodernism*. Minneapolis: University of Minnesota Press, 3–30.

Stoker, B., 2009 (1907). Sir Arthur Conan Doyle tells of his Career and Work. In: C. Wynne (ed.) *The Parasite* and *The Watter's Mou'*. Kansas: Valancourt, 153–61.

Sullivan, W.S., 1962. *Savoy Operas, Vol. 2*. Oxford: Oxford University Press.

Taylor, A., 2003. *The American Boy*. London: Flamingo/HarperCollins.

Thatcher, M., 1984. TV interview for Channel 4, 15 October 1984. [online] Available at: http://www.margaretthatcher.org/speeches/displaydocument. asp?docid=105764 (*Margaret Thatcher Foundation*) [Accessed 4 March 2010].

—— 1983. TV Interview for London Weekend Television *Weekend World*, 16 January 1983. [online]. Available at: http://www.margaretthatcher.org/

speeches/displaydocument.asp? docid=105087 (*Margaret Thatcher Foundation*). [Accessed 10 September 2009].

—— 1979. Speech to the Conservative Political Centre Summer School ('The Renewal of Britain'), 16 July 1979. [online] Available at: http://www.margaret-thatcher.org/speeches/displaydocument.asp?docid=104107 (*Margaret Thatcher Foundation*). [Accessed 10 September 2009].

—— 1977. The Healthy Society (Social Services Conference, Liverpool: 2 December 1976). In: *Let Our Children Grow Tall: Selected Speeches 1975–1977*. London: Centre for Policy Studies.

The Broadcasting Act 1990. Available at: http://www.opsi.gov.uk/acts/acts1990/Ukpga_19900042_en_1 [Accessed 17 July 2009].

The Daily Telegraph, 2008. 'Jude Law to star in Sherlock Holmes remake'. *The Daily Telegraph*, [online] 19 September. Available at: http://www.telegraph.co.uk/news/celebritynews/2989033/Jude-Law-to-star-in-Sherlock-Holmes-remake.html [Accessed 7 February 2012].

The Sherlock Holmes Museum. [Online] Available at: www.sherlock-holmes.co.uk [Accessed 1 November 2011].

Thomas, R. R., 2004. *Detective fiction and the Rise of Forensic Science*. Cambridge: Cambridge University Press.

—— 1999. *Detective Fiction and the Rise of Forensic Science*. Cambridge: Cambridge University Press.

Thorpe, V., 2010. Biographers fear that publishers have lost their appetite for serious subjects. *Observer* [Online] 14 November. Available at: http://www.guardian.co.uk/books/2010/nov/14/victoria-glendinning-biographies-publishers [Accessed 1 November 2011].

Todd, B., 2007. Review of *Sherlock Holmes: The Awakened*, GameSpot.com. [online] Available at: http://uk.gamespot.com/pc/adventure/sherlockholmestheawakened/review.html [Accessed: 29 July 2010].

Todorov, T., 1977 (1966). The Typology of Detective Fiction. *The Poetics of Prose*. London: Jonathan Cape, 42–52.

Trembley, E. A., 1994. Holmes is Where the Heart Is: The Achievement of Granada Television's Sherlock Holmes Films. In: W. Reynolds and E. A. Trembley (eds) 1994. *It's a Print! Detective Fiction from Page to Screen*. Bowling Green, OH: Bowling Green State University Popular Press.

Trow, M. J., 1998. *The Adventures of Inspector Lestrade*. Washington, D.C: Regnery Publishing.

Tulloch, J., 2000. *Watching Television Audiences: Cultural Theories and Methods*. London: Arnold.

Vadillo, A., 2003. Poetics on the Line. In: H. Michie and R. R. Thomas (eds) *The Transformation of Space from the Victorian Age to the American Century*. New Jersey: Rutgers University Press.

Variety, 1 January 1985. http://www.variety.com/review/VE1117796563?-refcatid=31, 31 December 1984, 11:00 pm PT

Violani, C., Zanazzo, G. and Pandolfi, M. (eds) 1997. *La collezione ornitologica di Tommaso Salvadori*. Fermo: Comune di Fermo.

Waagenaar, S., 1964. *The Murder of Mata Hari*. London: Arthur Barker.

Walkowitz, J., 1992. *City of Dreadful Delight: Narratives of Sexual Danger in Late-Victorian London*. London: Virago Press.

Wallace, D., 2008. *The Woman's Historical Novel: British Women Writers, 1900–2000*. London: Palgrave Macmillan.

Ward, D., 1976. The Victorian Slum: An Enduring Myth? *Annals of the Association of American Geographers*, 66 (2), 323–36.

Watt, P. R. and Green, J., 2003. *The Alternative Sherlock Holmes: Pastiches, Parodies and Copies*. Hants, England and Burlington, USA: Ashgate.

Wheeler, T., 2004. *The Arcanum*. New York: Bantam.

Wheelwright, J., 1992. *The Fatal Lover: Mata Hari and the Myth of Women in Espionage*. London: Collins and Brown.

Williamson, J., 2000. *Decoding Advertisements: Ideology and Meaning in Advertising*. London and New York: Marion Boyars.

Willis, C., 2000. Making the Dead Speak: Spiritualism and Detective Fiction. In: W. Chernaik, M. Swales and R. Vilain (eds) 2000. *The Art of Detective Fiction*. Basingstoke: Palgrave Macmillan, 60–74.

Willis, I., 2006. Keeping Promises to Queer Children: Making Space (for Mary Sue) at Hogwarts. In: K. Hellekson and K. Busse (eds) 2006. *Fan Fiction and Fan Communities in the Age of the Internet: New Essays*. Jefferson, NC and London: McFarland & Company, Kindle edition.

Wood, R. , 2003. *Hollywood from Vietnam to Reagan ... and Beyond*. New York: Columbia University Press.

Wynne, C., 2002. *The Colonial Conan Doyle: British Imperialism, Irish Nationalism, and the Gothic*. Westport, CT and London: Greenwood Press.

Young, S., 1992. Last Night's View. *Daily Express*, Friday, 3 January 1992, p. 33.

Žižek, S., 1992. *Looking Awry: An Introduction to Jacques Lacan*. Cambridge, MA. MIT Press.

Index